Malicious Intent

A Detective Liv DeMarco Thriller

G.K. Parks

Copyright © 2023 G.K. Parks

A Modus Operandi imprint

ISBN:
ISBN-13: 978-1-942710-36-3

For my mom and dad

BOOKS IN THE LIV DEMARCO SERIES:

Dangerous Stakes
Operation Stakeout
Unforeseen Danger
Deadly Dealings
High Risk
Fatal Mistake
Imminent Threat
Mistaken Identity
Malicious Intent
Controlled Burn

BOOKS IN THE ALEXIS PARKER SERIES:

Likely Suspects
The Warhol Incident
Mimicry of Banshees
Suspicion of Murder
Racing Through Darkness
Camels and Corpses
Lack of Jurisdiction
Dying for a Fix
Intended Target
Muffled Echoes
Crisis of Conscience
Misplaced Trust
Whitewashed Lies
On Tilt
Purview of Flashbulbs
The Long Game
Burning Embers
Thick Fog
Warning Signs
Past Crimes
Sinister Secret
Zero Sum
Buried Alive
Trouble Brewing

BOOKS IN THE JULIAN MERCER SERIES:

Condemned
Betrayal
Subversion
Reparation
Retaliation
Hunting Grounds

BOOKS IN THE CROSS SECURITY INVESTIGATIONS SERIES:

Fallen Angel
Calculated Risk

ONE

Somewhere in the distance, a phone rang. I wasn't supposed to be on call tonight. And given how dark it was in the room, it wasn't early enough for an overeager dispatcher to forward the call to me. Who was covering tonight? Voletek and Lisco, right? Surely, they could handle whatever was going on.

"Liv, your phone's ringing."

"I know." I curled into a ball, pulling the blankets around me tighter.

"Don't you have to answer it?"

"No."

"Well, in that case." He snuggled against me and placed sloppy, wet kisses along the side of my neck. I cringed, nudging him away with my shoulder. The phone stopped ringing, and I rolled farther away. But he was persistent. "I was thinking since we're both up, maybe we could finish what we started last night."

"We didn't start anything last night."

He laughed, undeterred. "My back's feeling better."

"Great."

"So, what do you say?" His mouth returned to my neck. He kissed a path backward and down.

"Stop." He knew better than to mess with my neck like that. The scar wasn't tender, at least it hadn't been in some time, but now the jagged, raised line stung and itched. I hated it.

"C'mon. Isn't this why you stayed? I thought maybe—" The phone rang again, cutting him off.

Saved by the bell. "Maybe I should answer that," I said.

"I thought you said you didn't have to."

"It's going to keep ringing until I do. That's how these things work."

"Fine." He rolled away from me and left the room to grab my phone. "It's the precinct." He crawled back onto the bed and thrust the phone at me. "Here."

I held out my hand, blindly reaching for it. The second I surfaced from beneath the covers, he brushed my hair to the side and nuzzled a path along my shoulder. Why didn't he get the message?

I let out an unpleasant growl. "I said stop. Leave me alone, Brad."

"Brad?"

Shit. Thankfully, years of undercover work prepared me for this. Plastering on a teasing smile, I turned to face him. "I knew that would get you to stop." I gave him a chaste kiss on the lips to lessen the blow and ignored the confused and hurt look on his face. Desperate for any excuse to get out of here, I answered the call. "This is Detective DeMarco."

"Hey, Liv. We've got a situation. Multiple calls have come in tonight. People are dropping like flies. It must be a full moon or something. Homicide's short-staffed. We could use your help. Can you come in?"

"Sure. What are we looking at?"

"A female vic outside the Stonemore Hotel. We've received several accounts, all contradictory. Someone from homicide needs to check it out."

"Yep." I grabbed my things off the chair and went into the bathroom. "Did you call Fennel?"

"He's on his way."

"Send me the address. I'll be there soon." Disconnecting, I checked my messages, but my partner hadn't called or texted. Since he knew I was on a date, he must not have wanted to interrupt. But I wished he had.

After getting dressed, washing my face, and brushing my teeth, I opened the door to find Sean in the kitchen. "Do you have time for breakfast?" he asked. "I can whip something up."

"Thanks, but I have to get going." I looked at the clock. It was just after two a.m. "Isn't it early for breakfast?"

"We'd eat at all hours at the firehouse. But that was usually after a call, not before." He offered a bashful smile. "Are we okay? Did I do something wrong? I thought we were on the same page. Isn't that why you stayed over?"

"It wasn't, but we're good. I'm sorry if I misled you. We'll talk about this later, okay? I'm just tired, and I have to go."

"I'd say you're exhausted."

"I should have warned you that waking me up is something you should never attempt."

"I'll keep that in mind for future reference." He poured a cup of coffee into a tall paper cup. "Maybe we can try this again another time?"

"We'll see."

"My name's Sean, by the way, not Brad."

"I know. I was just screwing with you."

"Were you? I must have missed that part."

I rolled my eyes. "I gotta go."

He stopped me from leaving. "Hey, I'm sorry. Really. If I've offended you or been too pushy, I'll back off."

"It's me, not you." I ran a finger down my neck, which felt sore, even though I was positive it was in my head. "I'm not used to this." I gestured around his kitchenette. "I'm rusty on dating and sleepover etiquette."

"Are you sure that's all it is? Is there something I should know? Are you seeing someone else?"

I shook my head.

"Who's Brad? An ex?"

"No." This wasn't exactly our first date. Emma had set me up with the injured firefighter a couple of weeks ago, but we were still feeling each other out. We'd only gone out twice before. I was sure I mentioned my partner to him at some point, but Sean didn't remember his name.

"Uh-huh." He held the teasing grin, but his eyes didn't look quite convinced. He took out a pen and wrote something on the side of the cup. Then he snaked his arm around my waist, kissed me goodbye, and handed me the coffee. "Stay safe out there, Detective."

"That's the plan."

"I'll call you later," he said as I pulled the door closed behind me.

Once I was inside my car, I checked to see what he had written. *Made especially for you by Sean.* I laughed. Maybe he'd spent too many hours working in the hospital cafeteria while he waited for medical clearance to return to the firehouse, or he was trying to be cute. I still didn't know what to think of him. He could be so sweet and funny sometimes, and I'd been comfortable enough to fall asleep at his place. But I didn't like his persistence. Truthfully, I barely knew the guy, which would probably explain why I didn't want to sleep with him, but those might have just been my issues and hang-ups from being around so many sleazebags on the job.

I didn't know why Brad's name rolled off my tongue. It was probably because we'd just finished an undercover assignment, posing as a married couple. But I couldn't let that happen again. Sean didn't deserve that. No one did. I double-checked the address and drove to the crime scene.

When I arrived, I found the circus had come to town. The lights from three patrol cars illuminated the area. Patrol had set up a perimeter around the scene, keeping anyone from coming or going. Hotel management, several members of the cleaning staff, and hotel security hung around the lobby. They peered out the windows as the area was secured.

"What's going on?" I asked the nearest cop, holding out my badge for his inspection.

"We got reports of a flying lady." He gestured to a parked car near the building. "That's where she landed."

"Did she jump?" I looked up. This was an exclusive, boutique hotel. It only had six floors. From here, I could see strobing neon lights set up on the roof.

"We're not sure."

"What about witnesses? Did anyone see what happened?"

"Plenty of people were around. Most of them didn't see anything. The few who did can't agree on what they saw."

"Who called it in?"

"The night manager, a member of hotel security, two members of the cleaning crew, and a few anonymous callers. Like I said, we received contradictory reports. No one could agree on where she fell from or even if she fell. Someone thought she jumped. Another thought she was pushed or thrown from the building. One caller said she was an angel who hurtled to Earth."

"Angel?"

"Yeah, but her wings burned up in the atmosphere."

"Gotta love the crazies," I said. "Where's the body?"

"Hospital morgue."

"Already? That was quick."

"Not really. When we arrived, she was still alive. Barely. EMTs loaded her into the ambulance and rushed her to the hospital. They pronounced her in the ER."

"Did she say anything?"

He shook his head and rubbed a hand over his mouth. "She was too far gone. It was pretty gruesome."

"Did you notice anything about her or the scene?"

"Besides a lot of blood, she was dressed to party."

"Party?"

"Yeah, cocktail dress, jewelry, strappy heels."

"It looks like someone's throwing quite the rager on the roof. Why haven't you shut that down yet?"

"Two officers tried. I'm not sure exactly what they walked in on, but the guests are far from cooperative. That's why the music hasn't stopped. We radioed it in and were told to keep everyone from leaving, contain the scene, and wait for orders from whoever takes command. Right now, that looks like you."

"How many guests are up there?"

"Two dozen, plus nearly as many caterers and staff."

"Have you locked down the rest of the hotel?"

"Yep. We haven't been able to conduct a search, but

guests have been encouraged to remain in their rooms. Everyone's complied except the party on the roof."

"Let's keep them happy and entertained for now until more backup arrives. We can't afford a riot. Just make sure no one leaves." I jerked my chin toward the roof. "Have we IDed the vic yet?"

The patrol officer shook his head. "She didn't have her purse with her. No ID. No phone."

My mind came up with a million things that needed to be done. But I had to focus on one at a time. "Where's Detective Fennel?" It'd be best to coordinate with him.

"I haven't seen him."

I checked my watch. Brad lived across town. It'd take him longer to get here, especially if he'd been as unprepared for the call as I was. So much for our night off. "All right, point me toward whoever's in charge of the hotel."

The officer gestured toward the lobby. "The night manager is probably your best bet. His story makes the most sense."

I marched into the lobby and introduced myself. Edmundo Lopez continued to stare out the window at the parked car. The roof had caved in, breaking the windows and leaving shards of glass around the vehicle. All the flashing lights reflected off the pieces, mesmerizing him with the dancing patterns.

"Sir, are you okay?" I asked.

He shook himself, focusing on me. "Yes, sorry. I've never seen anything like that. At least, not in person. In movies, it always looks different. Maybe it's the dramatic music. I'm not really sure."

"Would you like to sit down?"

He dropped onto the nearest plush chair. I sat across from him, glancing at the rest of the staff who whispered amongst themselves while another officer monitored the situation.

"What did you see?" I asked.

"A woman falling. She flew right off the side of the building, arms spread. I only saw her for a moment. I thought I was seeing things, but the crash proved I wasn't.

It was loud. Bang. Like a car t-boning another one. I ran outside, saw her on top of the car, and called 9-1-1."

"Did you try to help her?"

He glanced down at his hands. "I went over to the car. The alarm was going off. She wasn't moving. I saw the blood, and that was it. The 9-1-1 operator asked me a ton of questions, but I couldn't really get to her, not with her crushed into the roof like that. I took her pulse." He rubbed his fingers together. "Her hand was hanging down on that one side." He pointed at the car. "That was about it."

"Do you know who she is?" I asked.

He shook his head. "She's not a guest."

"How can you be sure?"

"All the guests are accounted for. Security checked. The police checked. She isn't registered. Shouldn't you be able to ID her?"

"We're working on it." I narrowed my eyes at him. "Did you say her wings burned up in the atmosphere?"

He looked at me like I was crazy. "What?"

"Someone reported an angel fell from heaven, and her wings burned up in the atmosphere. Was that you?"

"No, of course not. She's not an angel. She might be now, if you believe in such things, I guess. But she kind of looked like one when she fell. Arms spread, facing the sky."

"She fell backward?"

"Yes."

"That might be important. We can work with that."

"Work with what?" a voice asked from behind.

I let out a sigh of relief. "Nice of you to show up."

Detective Brad Fennel smiled at me before flashing his badge and introducing himself to the hotel manager. My partner remained quiet while I asked the rest of my questions.

"Are you sure she came from the roof?" I asked.

The hotel manager looked confused. "She must have. The windows inside the guest rooms don't open."

"What about the balconies?" Brad asked.

"Only the top level has balconies. The entire floor's rented out for the party. I'm guessing all those guests were on the roof when she fell. They must have seen what happened to her."

Brad craned his neck to look out the lobby windows. "Forensics should be able to determine her trajectory based on where she landed."

"What can you tell us about the party on the roof?" I asked.

"It's a three-day affair. It started this afternoon and is supposed to run through Sunday."

"What is it? A wedding?" Brad asked.

"More like a bachelor party, but I'm not even sure of that. I didn't get a lot of details. We booked a dozen room reservations and coordinated with vendors for everything else. Whatever this is, the person running it went all out. Top shelf liquor, bartenders, caterers, entertainment, lighting, sound systems, everything."

"Who made the reservations?" I asked.

"Remington Chambers."

That name sounded so familiar, but I wasn't sure why. "We need to see the security tapes," I said.

"Our system's been on the fritz for the last few days. But I'll give you whatever footage we have."

"Get that together," I said. "In the meantime, we're going to speak to the host with the most."

TWO

Brad pulled the plug, turning off the light show and sound system. The sudden quiet sounded louder than the music. A police officer and two members of hotel security had been covering the door. The lone cop had tried to take statements and question the guests, but the partiers had ignored him. Without backup, he'd decided to wait for help to arrive.

"That's better." Brad held up his shield. "I'm Detective Fennel. I have a few questions. Everyone take a seat."

"Is this about the noise?" a guy in a tailored suit asked. He smoothed down his lapels, but the sweat on his brow wasn't from the heaters. He'd had a lot to drink, so he focused on keeping his speech crisp. No slurring. "I'm a lawyer. Under city ordinance—"

"This is about a dead woman." Brad pointed to the chair. "Sit down, sir."

"Dead woman?" The question reverberated throughout the crowd.

Brad eyed me. We needed an ID. At the very least, we needed a photo. While my partner worked crowd control, I pulled the officer aside. After some back and forth on the radio and a few calls to the hospital administrator, I got a name. Margaret Tenzin. Her fingerprints had been in the system. She'd been picked up twice. Once for solicitation and once for public intoxication. The first was a catch and release, without any charges being filed. The second came with a fine and a few hours of community service.

As soon as I received a copy of her ID photo, I passed it off to Brad. He looked at it and the name. "All right," he said. "What do you want to do?"

"Divide and conquer?"

He looked at the annoyed and expectant faces staring at us. Half of them were already on the phone with their lawyers. "Who's in charge of this shindig?" Brad asked. His question was met with more unhelpful stares. "Let's try this another way. Which one of you is Remington Chambers?"

"He's not here," the DJ said. "He left two hours ago."

"Where did he go?"

The DJ shrugged, but his expression said he wanted to say something else, just not in front of the crowd.

"Anybody?" Brad asked, but all he got was crickets. "We can do this all night. So you might as well settle in, folks."

"He went back to his room," a man said, "which is what I'd like to do. You can't hold us here."

"We can for now. This is a murder investigation. You're all suspects," Brad said.

"The hell we are," another man shouted. "Don't you know who I am?"

I was about to say something, but Brad put his hand on my wrist before I could move forward. "Are we all set?" he asked one of the hotel security guards.

"We've set up a room for you to use. We've also cleared out a conference space if you'd like to move everyone inside." The guard held up his radio. "Do you need more assistance?"

"No," Brad said, "but I thought all the guests were accounted for. Where's Chambers? Is he in his room?"

"He wasn't when we knocked, but we found him in the gym. We told him to return to his room. He said he would after he finished his workout."

"At this time of night?" I asked.

The security guard shrugged. "The gym's open twenty-four hours."

"And the rest of the guests?" Brad eyed the crowd whose grumbling had reached a dull roar.

"Every one of them has been identified. The entire party, except Chambers, is here."

"So you can identify each of them," I said.

"Only the registered guests," the guard said. "The rest are hired to be here." He pointed to some cater-waiters and a bartender.

"Any party crashers or plus ones?" I asked.

The hotel security guard shook his head. "Everyone here is staying at the hotel or hired to work the party. There are no outsiders."

"And you're sure Margaret Tenzin wasn't a guest?" Brad asked.

"No, sir. She wasn't."

"Did she crash the party or was she hired to work the party?" I wondered, but the security guard didn't have an answer.

Brad turned back to the group. "Does anyone know Margaret Tenzin?"

"Is that the dead lady?" the same loudmouth from before asked.

"Do you know her?" Brad repeated.

"No. None of us do." No one else spoke up to indicate otherwise, but the DJ turned away, busying himself with packing up some of his equipment.

"Liv, do you want to see if Chambers is still in the gym?" Brad asked.

"The hotel is secured. No one's been allowed to leave," the officer piped up. "He has to be there."

"Is anyone watching the lobby?" I asked.

"The officer outside."

I read the cop's name tag. *Stanhope.* Given the lack of stripes on his sleeve, he was just a rookie. Excusing myself, I went back downstairs and found the gym. It required a hotel keycard to access it, so Mr. Lopez helped me get inside. The gym was empty. No dirty towels. No sweat stains on any of the benches.

"Dammit." On my way back upstairs, I knocked on every door on the top floor. No one answered. Remington Chambers was in the wind.

When I returned to the roof, I updated my partner and

the other cop as to the situation. Brad and I exchanged a look. Someone screwed up. But we had no way of knowing who.

"Why don't you lead the group into the conference room, Officer Stanhope? I'd like you to make sure no one leaves without my say so," Brad said.

"Yes, sir."

Brad looked at me, but the loudmouth partier mumbled something under his breath. Brad turned back around to face him. "Sir, how about you and I have a chat in private?"

"Where are you taking me?"

"Just inside. We'll get you warmed up, ask you some questions, and get you back to your room for the night. The same's true for the rest of you. The sooner you answer our questions, the sooner you can all return to your rooms. This officer will escort you to a conference room to await questioning."

"I'd rather wait here. We haven't even run out of salmon puffs yet," another man with a silk shirt and diamond pinky ring said. "And I paid enough to be here."

"Me too," a guy at the next table said.

"Yeah," a woman said. "Why do you get to ruin our night? We aren't criminals. We've done nothing wrong. I should have your badge for this."

"Whoever wants to stay can stay," I whispered. "The last thing we need is an angry mob. I'll keep an eye on them."

Brad nodded. "In the meantime, someone needs to locate Chambers." He held out his hand for Officer Stanhope's radio, requesting officers find Remington Chambers. If he was still on hotel property, they better find him and escort him to the empty conference room. If not, we'd issue a BOLO and see if we could locate him before he left town.

While my partner questioned the party guests, one by one, inside the hotel, I spoke to the hired help who continued to behave as though a police raid during an event was something they dealt with often. The caterers and waiters continued to serve trays of finger foods and drinks. I thought about stopping them, but I wondered if I might learn something from their interactions. All I learned was that the salmon puffs were a real crowd pleaser.

A different patrol officer kept a watchful eye over the dwindling group while I flashed the victim's photo around, took down names and contact information, and tried to establish a timeline. The DJ avoided me, packing up his soundboard and other equipment.

"I know Maggie. She was here tonight to perform," Judi Rae, head caterer, said. "We've worked a lot of the same events, so we've gotten to know each other a little bit. Sometimes, I give her leftovers to take home."

"Perform?"

"Yeah, she booked the gig."

"What gig?"

"She's a dancer, an aerial silk performer. She's really good." Judi stared into the distance. "Are you sure she's dead? She was just here. I saw her a couple of hours ago. It's crazy to think she's gone now. Do you know what happened?"

"I was hoping you could tell me. What time did she perform?"

"She was dancing and twirling since things got started. That was around eight." Judi nodded to the white fabric hanging from the large metal sound bar. Right now, it looked more like a long, wispy valence, but upon closer inspection, I realized it was a specialized fabric. "She set that up before the party started."

"What time did she finish her routine?"

"Around midnight."

"I'm guessing her act required a lot of acrobatic work."

"Yeah, she could really fly."

I thought about the 9-1-1 calls. "Did you notice anything off about her routine? Did something happen during her performance? Was there an accident of some kind?"

"No, it went great."

"Did she ever get near the edge of the roof?" I gestured to the ledge twenty feet from us.

"No, she could only go as far as the fabric stretched. Between you and me, I don't think she liked heights. She seemed nervous to be working out here, but conditions were great. No wind. No rain. She had plenty of room. Everything was secure. I saw her do several safety checks. James helped her."

"James?"

"The DJ. It made sense since she used his rigging to hold her silks." The caterer glanced at the few remaining guests. "I'm not sure most of them even noticed her."

"What's the party for?" I asked.

"I'm not sure. From what little I've overheard, it sounds like some bigwig wanted to throw a rager. But as with most of these things, it's all about getting wasted or making deals. The entertainment is the least important part of the night."

"Did anyone in particular seem interested in Margaret or her skills?"

"A couple of guys kept chatting her up every time she took a break. They brought her drink after drink. I heard one of them talking to one of his buddies afterward, saying he'd love to see her bound to his headboard."

"Which guy?" I asked.

"I'm not sure. Good-looking, dark hair, drunk. Like most of the men here."

"Do you think you could point him out?"

"I wasn't paying that much attention. Honestly, Detective, these rich assholes are all the same to me."

By the time I finished interviewing the rest of the food service members, none of the guests remained on the roof. The hired help sat near the heaters. A few of them had nodded off in the chairs. After checking my notes to make sure I'd gotten to everyone, I dismissed the group. I had their contact information, but all I'd learned was Margaret Tenzin disappeared after her performance. She hadn't jumped or been thrown off the roof. And no one admitted to seeing anything suspicious.

Once the servers and hotel staff vacated the area, I cornered the DJ who'd been hunkered down with his sound equipment. He'd need help to get the sound system and light rigging broken down and carried out.

"Do you want a cup of coffee?" I asked.

He shook his head, looking up at the dark sky.

"I'm Detective Liv DeMarco." I didn't bother showing him my badge. "And you are?"

"James West."

"I know you saw something happen. Do you want to tell me what it was?"

The DJ glanced around the roof to make sure we were alone. "Maggie showed up when I was setting up. We had to run several tests to make sure the bar could support her weight. When she booked the gig, she didn't know it was a rooftop party. She thought it was going to be in the hotel ballroom. If she had known, I bet she wouldn't have taken the gig. I'm not sure why she kept it. I guess the money was too good to turn down."

"Is that what she told you?"

"No, but I know her. Knew her," he corrected. "I should have warned her. Maybe then, she'd still be alive."

"How do you know so much about her?"

"We used to date. We practically lived together over the summer." He shook his head. "I'm guessing that makes me a suspect."

"Right now, we aren't sure exactly what happened or how she died. So everything's on the table." I clicked my pen. "Who broke it off?"

"She did."

"Why?"

"I work gigs with a lot of drunk, thirsty, single women."

"You cheated on her?"

"We never agreed to be exclusive." He appeared confused. "Are you sure she's dead? Are you sure it's Maggie? I want to see her. That's the only way I can be sure."

"I'm sorry. Her fingerprints matched what was in the system."

"Damn." After exhaling a shaky breath, he rocked backward, losing his balance and landing on his butt. He stayed there, wrapping his arms around his knees while he stared at the ground. "I can't fucking believe this. Someone killed her."

"How can you be sure?"

"Maggie hated heights. There's no way in hell she'd kill

herself, and there's even less of a chance she'd jump off a building to do it." He shook his head. "I heard you talking to the others. That's what you think happened, isn't it?"

"Why was she an aerial silk performer if she hated heights?"

"She was big into gymnastics as a kid. She showed me photos. She took some acrobatics training or tried to, but she didn't last long there. It freaked her out too much. That's why she designed her own act. She'd never be able to perform for Cirque du Soleil or anything like that, but she worked parties, clubs, places with ceilings not much higher than twenty feet. And even then, she would never swing more than ten feet off the ground. Her act was focused more on fancy maneuvers than dazzling heights. Hang on, I can show you." He pulled out his phone and played a video he'd taken of her performing.

"Did you record anything tonight?"

"I was too busy. I wish I had," he said. I asked him the same questions I'd asked everyone else. Maggie finished her performance just after midnight. After that, she vanished. "Her job was done. I saw her make her way to the door, but I got distracted. I never actually saw her leave."

"If she'd gone off the roof, do you think anyone would have noticed?"

"There were fifty people out here tonight. Someone would have seen it." He looked uneasy. "I would have seen it and stopped it."

Since the roof didn't have security cameras, we wouldn't be able to figure it out the easy way. "Does Margaret normally leave her props behind?" I gestured to the white fabric.

"She wasn't worried about it. She knew I'd pack up her stuff for her."

"Did you notice anyone paying an inordinate amount of attention to her?"

"At first, a lot of people were intrigued by the performance. Maggie has that effect, but when the drinks and food came around, most people lost interest. Half of them were too busy snorting coke and popping tabs to notice anything else."

"Were all the party guests intoxicated?"

"Almost."

That wasn't going to get me anywhere. "Did anyone flirt with Margaret?"

"One guy kept bringing her drinks whenever she stopped to catch her breath."

"Which guy?" I asked.

"The idiot who gave your partner a hard time. Y'know, the loudmouth lawyer douchebag. He didn't strike me as the type to take no for an answer."

"Did you notice if he ever left the party?"

"I wasn't watching him that closely. But I'm sure he did. Do you think he did something to Maggie?"

"I don't know." I jotted down a few notes. "Do you know if she was seeing anyone?"

"I don't think so. No one serious, anyway."

"When we ran her prints, we found she'd been brought in on solicitation. Anything to that?"

"I don't think so. Was that when she got picked up on amateur night at the strip joint?"

"I'd have to check."

"The cops asked about Remington Chambers. Did he have something to do with Maggie's death?"

"Do you think he did?"

West gave a barely perceptible nod. "He left his own party around the same time Maggie's performance ended, just after midnight. I saw him talking to her when we were setting up. At first, I thought he wanted to know the usual stuff, like how long she'd perform, how much room she'd need, if she could work the crowd, but the way he acted, the way he grabbed her arm, I didn't like it."

"How did he grab her arm?"

"Like a man who wants to be obeyed."

THREE

Remington Chambers wasn't in the gym or his room or anywhere on hotel grounds. Officers and hotel security knocked on every door, but he was gone. Somehow, he slipped away. But I couldn't figure out how. Patrol was on the lookout, and officers were waiting at his house. Once we found him, he'd be taken into custody.

"Any leads?" I asked.

My partner flipped through his notes. "A few. Most people remembered the dancer. A handful recognized Ms. Tenzin from her ID photo, but given that they saw her only a few hours ago, I'd think that percentage would be higher. Y'know, closer to one hundred."

"Eyewitnesses suck, especially when they're blitzed out of their minds."

"You can say that again." He rocked back in the chair and rested his hands behind his head. "This is insane. We don't even know cause of death, but considering how recently it happened, we should know a lot more than we do. These people," he gestured at the guest list, "should have seen what happened. I'm thinking we're looking at an *Orient Express* situation, just without the train."

"Refresh my memory. I think I slept through that movie."

"It was a book."

"I must have skipped that one."

Brad rolled his eyes. "The point I'm making is they could all have played a part in her untimely demise."

"Why?"

"I don't know. But I can't imagine that out of a crowd of twenty-something," he glanced at the list, "twenty-eight guests and twenty staff members and hired help, that no one saw a woman take a swan dive off the roof."

"The DJ doesn't think she jumped off the roof. He's pretty sure she left the party around midnight. That means her whereabouts are unaccounted for prior to her death. And I don't think it was a swan dive. She landed on her back. Most people jump face first."

"The smart ones go backward because they don't want to see it coming," Brad said.

"Fine." But I disagreed.

"For the record, I don't think she jumped either. But we still don't know how she ended up on top of that parked car. We can't rule anything out yet. She could have fallen, jumped, been pushed, or thrown." He slid a copy of her ID toward me. "She was one hundred and twenty pounds. There were at least four guys big enough to pick her up and heave her over the side."

"What about the lawyer douche?"

"You mean Francis Fertrie. I don't think he has the upper body strength to heave a bowling ball the distance required to land on the roof of that car, much less lifting and tossing a full-grown woman. But he may surprise me. He was clearly on something, and I've seen plenty of tweakers pull off superhuman feats."

"That's usually because their pain receptors and adrenaline are doing all sorts of weird things," I said. "Any idea what he took?"

"No clue. He denied it and said we'd need a court order if we want to do a drug test. Right now, we're working on search warrants for the entire hotel. That should point us in the right direction. In the meantime, according to what he and his pals said, he was on the roof from midnight on and never left the party after that until I brought him down here to talk to me."

"What do you think?"

"Plenty of guys vouched for him. Depending on TOD, he might be in the clear. We'll have to check with dispatch to see when the first 9-1-1 call came in and take it from there."

"Any other leads?" I asked.

"I'm not sure I'd call them leads." He rocked forward, scanning the names on the list and putting marks beside four of them. "These guys weren't technically guests. Yes, they were on the list, but only because they were serving as personal security for three of the partiers. They'd all have the strength to toss the vic off the building."

"Personal security?" I examined the names more closely. A few sounded vaguely familiar. "What kind of people hire personal security for a party?"

"The rich and famous."

I scanned the guest list, but I didn't recognize any of the names, even if they weren't entirely foreign to me either. "Are we talking celebrities?"

"No. Bankers, lawyers, CEOs, doctors, hedge fund managers, and two former politicians."

"Anyone I voted for?"

Brad laughed. "They weren't local."

"Good. Do we know why they are holding a party weekend?"

"The guests bid on tickets to this event at a silent auction. It was part of a fundraiser to build a new pediatric wing at the hospital."

"So they dropped a ton of money and this is all they got in return?"

"Not to mention the tax write-offs, the positive publicity, and an entire weekend to party. The winners received hotel accommodations, catered meals, entertainment, and access to other powerful people to make as many back room deals as their hearts desired."

"No good deed?"

"It looks that way."

"Since this was the prize at a charity event, who donated the party weekend?"

"Remington Chambers. He made the reservations, put everything on his corporate card, and hired everyone who worked the party, including Margaret Tenzin." Brad's phone chimed, and he glanced at the displayed message. "CSU's here." The phone chimed again. "And it looks like the hospital wants to have a word with us."

"All right."

"Let's get everyone and everything squared away, and then we'll head out." Brad glanced at me. "Did you bring your car?"

"Yeah. You?"

He nodded. "How did you get here so fast?"

"I was in the area."

Brad held the door for me as we exited the conference room. "You were still out with Sean when the call came in. Wasn't it past your curfew?"

"Ha ha."

"What were you two doing?"

Before I could say a word, my phone rang. "DeMarco," I answered, confused by the lack of information on the caller ID.

"I heard you were working tonight. Are you at the Stonemore Hotel?"

"How did you hear about that?" I spun, wondering if I was being watched.

"I hear things," Axel Kincaid said. "I need to tell you something."

"What is it?"

Brad stopped in his tracks and eyed me. "Who is it?"

"I hear Fennel in the background," Axel said. "Don't tell him it's me."

"Why not?"

"Just don't."

I looked at my partner. "Go get everything set up. I'll only be a minute."

Brad looked concerned, but he didn't question me. Once my partner was gone, I turned my attention back to my phone conversation.

"What do you know about this situation, Mr. Kincaid?"

"Jesus, Liv. This isn't a formal interrogation. If I thought you'd make it one, I never would have called."

"Then hang up."

He exhaled. "Fine, Detective. Have it your way." He

paused for a moment, and I wondered if he changed his mind. Instead, the car thief turned club owner continued. "Remington Chambers had nothing to do with Maggie's death."

"How do you know that?"

"I can't tell you. But trust me. He didn't do it."

"Where is he?"

"That isn't important."

"Is he at your club?"

"No."

"Axel," I growled, "he's a person of interest. The fact that he ran from the scene makes him look guilty. Tell him to turn himself in, or I'll send units to pick him up."

"He's not here. And even if he was, he wouldn't be by the time the police showed up. Warrants take time. And cops aren't welcome in my club, with one obvious exception. I'm under no legal obligation to allow them inside, and I won't."

"We could bring you in for obstruction."

"I didn't call to fight with you, Detective."

"Why did you call? How do you know the vic?"

"I don't know her. Not well. But I know Maggie Tenzin was murdered. I'm not sure how much you've determined yet, but she didn't fall off the roof or jump. She wasn't even on the roof when it happened."

"When what happened? Where was she?"

"Not on the roof." The frustration crept into his voice. "She was stabbed then tossed. Whoever did it attended the party. That's all I know for sure, so I need you to figure out who killed her and why."

"Tell me how you know any of this. Were you at the party?"

"I'm not a killer."

"From the things I've seen you do, I'm not so sure."

"Dammit, Liv. I'm trying to help you. She was young and talented. She worked plenty of these gigs. Perhaps too many. She must have seen or heard something she wasn't supposed to. That's the only thing I can think of, but I don't know what she heard or who would do this. I have to know."

"Why?" I paused. "Shit. This was one of your events." That's why the names sounded so familiar.

"None of that matters."

"Were you at the hotel tonight?" I waited, but he didn't speak. "Answer me."

"I'm at work, Liv."

"How do you know the victim's name or what happened to her? Did someone call you?" Brad had taken care to refer to the woman as Margaret. Her friend, the caterer, and her ex had called her Maggie, but we hadn't. She was Margaret Tenzin, which meant either Axel knew the victim personally or whoever tipped him did.

"Like I said, she worked a lot of similar gigs. Powerful people travel in small circles. And there aren't a lot of aerial performers for hire. She was a hot commodity."

Deciding to let that slide for now, I asked the more important question. "How do you know she was stabbed?"

"The hospital should have informed you. If not, I'd think the medical examiner's office would have. Public services are really going to hell. I should have a talk with the mayor about this."

"You do that. But first, tell me what you know."

"In due time." Someone called to him in the background. "I'll be in touch soon. Good luck, Detective."

Resisting the urge to throw my phone, I tucked it back into my pocket. Axel Kincaid was one of the most frustrating men on this planet. It was bad enough I spent six months undercover at his club without ever getting an ounce of evidence to stick to him. But tonight was worse.

I made my way back to the lobby. "Who owns this place?" I asked the hotel manager.

"We're part of a boutique hotel chain." He rattled off the name, but I didn't care. Axel Kincaid owned a lot of property in the city, but this wasn't one of his. My gut said the party had been his idea and that every guest who attended was also a member of Spark, his exclusive private club, but I didn't have proof yet. But I'd get it.

I was on my way to find my partner when he popped up behind me. "Officers will remain stationed here through evidence collection. We're getting court orders to search every inch of this place and all the guests' belongings. We'll figure out where Tenzin was before she landed on the car. But while we wait for the ink to dry, we should see what the hospital can tell us about the fundraiser and what the doctors can tell us about the victim." Brad eyed me. "Is everything okay, Liv?"

"We're dealing with a murder, so not really." I palmed my keys. We'd be back to search the place soon enough. "Do you want to leave your car here for now?"

"Are you going to tell me who was on the phone?"

"Wait until we're in private." I led him to my car and unlocked the doors. Once he was belted into the seat, I said, "Axel Kincaid."

"Why is he calling you at five a.m.?"

"He said Maggie was murdered and whoever did it tried to cover it up by tossing her off the building. He didn't tell me how he knew any of that. He just wanted me to know, so I can find the person responsible."

"What's his connection to the vic?"

"It sounded like he hired her for a few events, but there could be more to it. He said she was a hot commodity."

"Do you think he was pimping her out?"

"Axel doesn't run girls."

"Not out of his club, but he prides himself on getting his members whatever they want. I'm guessing that includes fulfilling sexual fantasies or providing sex workers who will. Does he know Remington Chambers?"

"Probably."

"Liv," he said in that disapproving tone I loathed, "what aren't you telling me?" He eyed the paper coffee cup. But he didn't comment on that. We had far more important matters to discuss. "Does he know where Chambers is now?"

"He said he doesn't, but there's a good chance he's holed up at Spark."

"We should send officers."

"Axel made it clear he won't let anyone inside without a warrant, except me. And maybe you. But he didn't want me to tell you he called."

"He should know better."

"He's hiding something."

"Clearly, he's covering for Chambers. But why?"

"He said Chambers is innocent."

Brad snorted. "I want to know what their connection is."

"I'm guessing Chambers is a member of Spark or an employee. All our notes from that undercover operation are still with the intelligence unit. Chambers' name must be in one of the files."

"I'll have someone pull them for us." Brad started dialing.

"The entire guest list probably crosses over with Spark's clientele. A lot of those names seemed hauntingly familiar to me, but I couldn't place them. But what little we know about this three-day event fits. These are precisely the types of people who go to Spark to blow off steam, and this would be the kind of thing they'd like to do outside the walls of the exclusive club."

Brad passed along his request and rubbed his cheek. It made a scratching sound since he hadn't taken the time to shave. "Why do you think Axel called to tip you off? He has to have a reason."

"He sounded concerned, almost afraid."

"That's a first. When a psycho wanted him dead, he didn't even bat an eye."

I knew that wasn't true, but Axel Kincaid didn't show weakness to his opponents. Why he'd shared his life story with me was anyone's guess, but for whatever the reason, Axel had decided he could trust me, at least to a point. But I wasn't a fool. He only volunteered to help when it served his needs.

"Do you think Axel was at the Stonemore earlier this evening?" I asked.

"The hotel security footage is spotty, but we pulled whatever we could. There's a decent chance one of the cameras caught him or his fancy ass car on the feeds. I'll make sure the techs keep an eye out."

"If he wasn't at the hotel, how would he know Tenzin was attacked before she landed on the car?"

"I don't know. But we'll see what the doctors have to say."

FOUR

The hospital administrator wasn't available at this early hour. Not that I could blame her. I didn't want to be awake at five a.m. either. But the staff on duty was able to assist us with a broad overview of the fundraising event.

Like universities and other institutions, the private hospital relied a lot on donations. The donor list was comprised of previous donors, members of the Board of Trustees, doctors, and those who'd expressed an interest in providing resources. These were the same types of people who enjoyed private clubs and additional privileges. No wonder most of the names on the guest list had sounded so familiar.

"We'll check back during normal business hours," Brad said, thanking the staff member helping us. He scanned the list one more time and pointed to Remington Chambers' name. "Do you have a record of all his donations?"

"We must, but that can't be divulged. You'd need a court order or Mr. Chambers' permission."

"That's what I figured." Brad smiled and followed me down the hall.

"I had someone run Chambers through the database, but he doesn't have a record. The worst things we could find on him were a few speeding tickets." I peered around the corridor, but it was just before the morning rush began. Most of the doctors hadn't started their rounds yet, so we still had some time. "Maybe you could call Carrie and see if she could fast-track the autopsy. It's been over five hours, and the ME's office hasn't even picked up the body yet."

"Someone should be on the way. Like dispatch said, homicide was overrun with suspicious deaths and potential cases last night." He pointed to the reception desk. "Let's see where our victim ended up."

The receptionist paged the doctor who'd pronounced Margaret dead. He emerged from beyond the doors and headed for us.

"I'm Dr. Wallace." The ER doctor extended his hand. "What can I do for you, Detectives?"

"We're here about Margaret Tenzin. The woman who landed on top of a parked car," I said, not wanting to ask any leading questions until he had a chance to share his insights regarding her injuries and cause of death.

"I'll take you to the body." Wallace led us to the elevator and pressed the button.

"Any idea what killed her?" Brad asked as we stepped inside.

"That's not my place to say. I barely had time to examine her." Doctor Wallace tucked his hands into the pockets of his lab coat. "Her BP bottomed out, and her heart stopped. I'd say she bled out. However, that doesn't eliminate the possibility of organ failure, head trauma, and a million other things. The woman was in bad shape. We did what we could, but she was too far gone." The doors opened, and he stepped out first. "She had a deep puncture on her back. I've worked in the ER for a long time. I've seen a lot of injuries. To me, that looked a lot like a stab wound."

"Stab wound?" I asked.

"When we rolled her, I noticed a lot of blood had pooled beneath her. There was so much blood everywhere, it would have been easy to miss. Let me show you." He slid his card through the scanner and entered a code to access the morgue.

The body had been covered with a sheet. They hadn't even bothered to zip her into a body bag yet. I said a silent prayer and waited for him to put on gloves and pull down the bloody sheet. Beside me, my partner tensed.

The doctor indicated the wound on her back. "As you

can see, the edges look too clean to be from the fall."

I brushed against Brad and moved closer to the table. Dr. Wallace had turned Maggie onto her side. She wore a shimmery dress which was practically see-through except for the strategically placed silver detailing and sequins. A dress like that was out of my price range, and given the things Judi had said, I figured it'd be out of Maggie's price range too.

"It looks like a knife wound." I glanced at Brad who stood silently behind me, observing everything.

"No hesitation marks. Whoever did this shoved the blade in and pulled it straight out. That would take some strength and practice." Brad circled the table. "What about the rest of her injuries?"

"They're probably due to the fall, but like I told you in the elevator, this isn't my area of expertise. You need a second opinion," Dr. Wallace said. "The coroner should be able to provide you with cause of death and a better explanation for these injuries."

I snapped a few photos of the wound on her back. Most post-mortem photos were clinical. They weren't obscured by dried bloodstains. Even the sheet was covered in red. She'd landed hard, and it had taken a toll. The sight made me queasy. I swallowed, forcing myself not to focus on it.

"If she was knifed in the back, would that have been enough to cause her death?" I asked.

"I don't know. We didn't bother with x-rays. We didn't have time. She expired before we could run any scans, but possibly. Several organs could have been compromised, her spleen, liver, lungs, potentially even her aorta." The doctor looked uncomfortable and checked his watch. "I have patients to see."

"Sorry we kept you." Brad shook hands with him. "We'll see ourselves out."

Brad and I were silent as we made our way back to the lobby. Once we made it outside, I shook like a dog throwing off rainwater. My partner watched me as I rubbed my hands down my forearms, brushed my hair with my fingers, and pulled it into a ponytail. Gently, I ran my palm down the side of my neck, which stung more now than it had earlier.

"You good, Liv?"

"Fine."

"You don't look fine."

"Well, I am." I forced my thoughts off my own bad memories and back to the present case. "How did Axel Kincaid know she didn't die from the fall?"

"We should ask him."

I checked the time. It was too early for the warrant to have been signed. The judge wouldn't get to it until eight or nine. That meant we had at least two more hours. "Great idea, but what do we do if he refuses to talk to us?"

"You could charm him," Brad teased.

"I don't think that's going to work."

Brad watched as I absently rubbed my neck. "You should say something, if everything's getting to you. Since blood's one of your triggers, you didn't have to go with me to check out Tenzin's body."

"I'm not triggered. At least, I don't think so. I don't know. Going inside isn't what started it. It just exacerbated it." I shook away my wayward thoughts and pulled out the ponytail holder, letting my hair cover the scar. "I was first on the scene. That makes me primary on this case."

"Dispatch called me first. In fact, I told them not to bother you. I said I'd handle it, and I have seniority."

"Not by much. Are you taking this case from me, Fennel?"

"Maybe."

I laughed. "Fine. It's all yours, except we're a package deal. Everyone knows that, even dispatch. Lt. Winston made some kind of announcement that we have to work in pairs whenever possible, remember? But thanks for trying."

"Seriously, Liv—"

"I'm fine. Voletek owes us for this. He was on call. This should have been his scene."

"Really?" Brad gave me a look. "What did Jake do to piss you off that badly?"

"What are you talking about?"

"You didn't hear?"

"All I heard was Lisco was covering for him. I figured they got stuck at another scene. Dispatch said people were dropping like flies."

"That's one way of putting it. Voletek's dad collapsed. He's in the hospital."

"Shit." I froze in my tracks. "This hospital?"

"No. Mercy General."

"Emma's hospital." I squeezed my eyes closed, wondering if she was working graveyard. "Is he okay?"

"No word yet on what caused it, but Jake's staying close until he finds out."

"Why didn't you say something sooner?"

"I thought you knew."

"How?" I gave him a wide-eyed look. "How do you know everything?"

"People talk to me. They tell me things."

"Is there anything else I should know?" I unlocked the car doors, and we got in.

"I'm sure there's tons of gossip I could share, but that's never been our thing. However," he tapped my coffee cup, "I wouldn't mind a brief distraction." He read Sean's note aloud. "When did your boyfriend become a barista?"

"He's not my boyfriend. We've only gone out a couple of times."

"Three." Brad waited, but I didn't confirm or deny. "Where'd he take you last night?"

"Nowhere. We were supposed to go to that movie theater that serves those fancy dinners."

"The place with the candles and tablecloths?"

"Yeah."

"Okay, so what happened? He picked up a shift at the coffee place instead?"

"Sean had PT yesterday, which aggravated his back. He didn't want to sit at a table for three hours, so I made dinner for us and he picked a movie."

Brad stared at me, but I kept my eyes on the road, feeling the weight of his scrutiny. "What movie did he pick?"

"*Casablanca.*"

"You hate *Casablanca*. Did you tell him that?"

"No."

"Why not?"

"He went on and on about how romantic he thinks it is and how movies were movies when they were black and white, and I thought maybe I should give it another chance. Tons of people love that movie. It's a classic."

"When I jokingly asked if you wanted to watch it, you threatened to throw my TV out the window. You must really like this guy." Brad judged my expression. "Or not."

"I'm giving him a chance. Emma asked me to, so I am."

"Except you fell asleep twenty minutes into the movie."

"Forty, we were still eating at the twenty minute mark." Brad laughed. "Jeez."

"After it ended, Sean told me to stay over since I was clearly too tired to drive."

"He thought he'd get lucky in the morning. Third date."

"Shut up."

"What? It's true, unless he already got lucky. But with his back, probably not."

"Brad," I snapped. It was eerie how many of his assumptions were correct.

He held up his palms. "You wouldn't be this irritated if you'd gotten laid, so he didn't get lucky. Or he was a terrible lay, in which case you should cut your losses and run."

I slapped his arm. "That's none of your business."

"I'm just offering some friendly advice. You can take it or leave it." He picked up my coffee cup for further inspection. "What's the deal with the cup? He could have written something more romantic on it. No wonder women are banging down my door."

"We got into a tiff before I left. I think that's an apology."

"Was he annoyed you wouldn't put out?"

I gave my partner a cross look. "It was a miscommunication."

"Sure, it was." But Brad didn't look convinced. "Are you going to see him again?"

"I don't know."

His tone changed. "What did he do?"

"Nothing."

"Liv, come on. Tell me. You know I'll break his fucking face if he hurt you."

"He didn't. We're good. It was a misunderstanding."

"Uh-huh." Brad put the cup down.

"It was. Really. I'm not used to dating or the things it entails. But he tried to be sweet. He got up when I did. He made coffee and offered to cook me breakfast. That was considerate, right?"

"Yeah. I'm glad you found someone who can make coffee."

"Right?"

He assessed me for a few more moments. "Are you sure everything's okay?"

"I don't know."

"What can I do? The guy's got a bum back. I can give him a couple of bum knees to go with it. All you have to do is ask."

I laughed. "I wasn't talking about Sean. I was talking about this case and Axel."

"If you promise to cover for me, I'd be more than happy to break his kneecaps too."

"That might be the only way to get him to cooperate." I pulled to a stop outside Spark. It was after six. The club had already closed. But Axel kept an apartment upstairs for the nights he didn't go home.

We got out of the car. Brad kept an eye out while I headed for the alley entrance. Since the club was closed, I didn't see any reason to waste time on the front door. Glancing up at the security camera, I knocked and waited. When no one appeared at the door, I took out my phone. I was halfway through dialing Axel's number when the door opened.

"Mr. Kincaid's not here," George, Axel's doorman, said. "He left a little after five."

"What are you still doing here?"

"I'm waiting on a liquor delivery. They're supposed to show around eight. Once that gets here, I'm going home."

"Do you mind if I come inside and look around?"

"He's not here, Liv. I just told you that."

"I have to speak to him."

"He knows. He'll be in touch when he's ready. It's been a long night."

I pulled up a photo of Margaret Tenzin on my phone and showed it to him. "Do you recognize her?"

"I'm not sure. She might have been a dancer or hired for a special performance. It's hard to say. A lot of people come and go. I'm sure you remember that."

"What about Remington Chambers?" I scrolled to his ID photo and showed it to George. "Was he here tonight?"

"Tonight?"

"When did he show up?"

George reached behind him and grabbed a clipboard. "He's not on the list."

"That doesn't mean shit."

"We've been keeping track of who comes and goes after some less than savory characters were allowed inside." George looked over my head. "Your partner can vouch for that. Right, Detective Fennel?"

Brad took a few steps toward us. "Kincaid provided assistance before. Why doesn't he want to talk to us now? He called in the tip. It's the least he can do."

George shrugged. "I can't say, but Spark keeps its member list private."

"So Chambers is a member," I said.

George smiled. "I didn't say that."

"You didn't have to," Brad muttered. "Is there anything else you can tell us?"

"Mr. Kincaid wanted me to let you know he'd be in touch. Also," George took a USB drive out of his pocket and held it out to me, "that's security footage from tonight. The timestamp shows precisely when Mr. Kincaid arrived and when he left. He thought you might want to pin this crime on him and figured it'd be best to provide an alibi. Good day, Detectives."

FIVE

"I don't like that Kincaid had an alibi ready and waiting," Brad said as we lingered outside the Stonemore Hotel, watching CSU collect evidence from the roof and point their laser sights at the crushed car while they calculated trajectories to figure out from where Margaret Tenzin fell. "Only guilty people are prepared with things like that."

"He knew we'd show up at Spark the moment he called in the tip," I said. "Axel likes to be proactive. You heard George."

"I don't trust him."

"Neither do I, but there have been several occasions when we haven't had much of a choice."

"This doesn't feel right. He's trying to control the investigation. More than likely, this is going to bite us in the ass."

"You said it yourself. Axel wouldn't hurt me."

"I'm reconsidering my stance on that." Brad sighed. "But even if that's true, that doesn't mean he wouldn't knife Margaret Tenzin in the back. Frankly, I wouldn't put it past him to do the same to either of us if push came to shove. Kincaid makes his own rules. He has his own agenda, and he will do whatever it takes to come out on top. We watched him shoot a man, and that wasn't even the first time you saw him draw down on someone. He's not to be trusted, Liv. You can't take his tip at face value."

"No shit. I never said Axel was a good guy. I know

better. You know I do. I spent six months undercover, getting close to him. We know the things he's suspected of doing. But he wouldn't have called to tell us Tenzin was stabbed if he had done it. We already checked the hotel footage. Axel Kincaid isn't checked into a room. He's not on the guest list, and the exterior cameras never spotted any of his cars on the footage."

"The footage was spotty. We can't be certain. But you're probably right. Still, I want to know how he knew what happened to Tenzin when he wasn't here to see it."

"The judge granted us warrants to pull every party guest's phone records, along with the hotel lines. If any of these people called Axel to tell him about it, we'll know. But my guess is Remington Chambers fled the scene and went running to Axel for help. He must have told Axel what happened. We need to question him. Do we have any idea where Chambers is?"

"He hasn't gone home. His car's still in the parking lot, so he didn't use that as his means of escape, and officers and hotel security checked every room in this place. We know he's not hiding inside." Brad squinted against the sun's reflection off a neighboring building's window. "Like you suggested, he must have fled to Spark. And Axel stashed him away. For all we know, Chambers is hiding in Axel's loft above the club. That would explain why George wouldn't let us inside."

"Maybe. But Axel wouldn't call to tip us about a murder if he's hiding the murderer. If Chambers told him what happened and Axel is protecting him, he must not be the killer."

"Or Axel doesn't know, which is why he wants you to find out. Then he can deliver his own brand of justice."

"That would be counterintuitive. If anything happens to Chambers, Axel would be our prime suspect."

"Ours, yes. The department's, probably not. They'd assume Margaret's killer eliminated a witness. They wouldn't make the connection." Brad looked pointedly at me. "That could be why Axel called you with the tip."

I thought about our phone conversation. "Axel doesn't know who killed her. He wants us to find out what happened. He practically begged me to figure it out."

"He also swore to you Chambers didn't do it. How could he say that with any level of certainty unless he knew who the killer was?"

"I'm not sure. Assuming he spoke to Chambers, he could have taken him at his word."

"In that case, he should have given us more information and handed over our prime suspect or potential eyewitness. With the way things are going, we're not going to get anywhere until we question Chambers."

The radio squawked. "Fennel, we found what may be the primary crime scene. Room 606."

Brad pressed the button and held the radio close to his mouth. "On our way."

One tech was kneeling down, an evidence marker in his hand, while the other photographed a different portion of the room. The table had been knocked over. The ice bucket had landed sideways, leaving a path of wet in its wake. A few cubes remained, but they were minutes away from turning into slivers.

The melted cubes diluted the edges of the bloodstain, turning it a fainter shade of red. A knife lay on the ground. The bedspread concealed it partially from view, but I could see blood clinging to the shiny blade.

"Whose room is this?" I asked.

"It's registered to Remington Chambers," the tech said, not tearing his focus away from the camera's viewfinder as he took several more photographs.

"Any idea what happened here?" Brad indicated the wet spot on the floor before pointing to the specks on the couch and carpet.

"It looks like someone was stabbed. Based on the spatter, I'd say it was one stab, in and out." The tech placed another marker, indicating additional blood droplets. "Whoever got stabbed didn't stay inside this room for very long afterward."

"How can you be sure?" I asked.

"This isn't a lot of blood."

"Are you sure it's a stabbing? Could someone have cut himself?"

The tech nodded toward the knife, which matched the ones I'd seen on the roof at the carving station the caterers had set up. "I don't know anyone who shaves with a knife. Do you?"

Brad peered into the bathroom, but it looked pristine. "Any idea how long ago this happened?"

"A few hours. The floor's still wet, and the ice hasn't fully melted, at least not the pieces which remained sheltered inside the bucket. Purely guessing, I'd say the attack happened within the last six to eight hours. Ice can last in its solid state for up to eighteen hours, depending on circumstances. And given that the thermostat is set to seventy degrees and that's a significant puddle, the bucket was probably full. The computer will be able to run all the variables and give you a more accurate timeline. But if I'm right, the stabbing occurred around the same time the woman landed on the car. I doubt that's a coincidence. DNA will be able to confirm, but more than likely, she was stabbed and then thrown from there." He pointed to the balcony.

Slipping on the gloves which matched the booties we'd been given upon arriving inside the room, Brad went to the balcony door. The sliding glass opened without protest.

"Was it unlocked?" I asked, and he nodded. I followed my partner onto the balcony, noting the smeared blood droplets on the ground. "We might be able to get shoeprints from that."

"Possibly." Brad leaned over the edge, examining the railing before looking down at the ground below. "I can see the top of the car from here."

I peered down at the crushed roof, noticing the pooled blood in the center. "That's not directly below us. She couldn't have fallen. If she had, she would have gone straight down."

"She went backward." Brad looked at me. "Turn around, Liv."

I did as my partner asked, mindful of my footing. "What are you thinking?"

"He stabbed her inside the room. Given the knocked over table, she may have tried to fight her way to the door, but couldn't get out that way. Instead, she ran for the only other exit, realized she was trapped, turned around, and that's when he grabbed her and tossed her over the side." Brad moved in front of me and put his hands on my hips. "Hold on to my shoulders."

I did as he asked, my stomach flipping as he lifted me off the ground. "Don't you dare drop me, Fennel."

"Relax. You're not that heavy." He lifted me higher, peering around my side to check the height of the railing. "It's possible he ran at her, hoisted her up, and over. The momentum would have helped send her sailing. We should have the ME check to see if there's any bruising or injury to her calves or ankles. She might have banged her leg against the railing on her way down." Carefully, Brad lowered me to the ground. "Unless she was already on her way to the balcony when he got the jump on her. Maybe in his haste, he knocked over the table. Or he picked her up, carried her outside, and tossed her. All we know is he must have moved quickly from the time he ripped the knife out to when he threw her over the railing. If not, there'd be more blood and a much more obvious trail."

"For her to land on top of that car from here," the tech came up behind us, snapping more photographs, "she must not have struggled. If she had, he would have had a much harder time throwing her that far, unless she didn't start her descent from here. Have they checked the roof for blood droplets?"

"Have you checked the hallway outside the room?" I asked.

The tech gave me a look. "We found faint staining. It looked more like transfer than actual droplets." He knelt down, zeroing in on a nearly perfectly round droplet a centimeter from the railing. "Never mind. This proves she was standing here after she was stabbed."

"Maybe she wasn't standing," Brad said. "Could the attacker have carried her out and tossed her?"

"Also possible." The tech finished photographing the scene, nodding to another guy to begin dusting for fingerprints. "We'll need to know the extent of her injuries prior to the fall before we can run simulations on potential scenarios. For all we know, the attack paralyzed her. Whoever did it might have had no choice but to carry her."

"Which would also explain why she didn't struggle or fight back," I said.

While forensics finished collecting and photographing everything, Brad and I searched the hotel room. Suite 606 wasn't nearly as swanky as the hotel manager made it sound. It was considered a mini-suite. The main room had a separate sitting area with a couch, table, and TV. The couch was a pullout, but it didn't look like anyone had used it. Aside from the spatter pattern which painted an almost straight line on the cushions and along the bottom of the couch, the result of the assailant removing the blade from Margaret Tenzin's back, the only obvious sign something was amiss was the knocked over table.

It wasn't particularly heavy, which made me think it was cheaply made. For a boutique, luxury hotel, I expected something nicer. This was nothing more than a tripod banquet table, roughly the same size and shape as the ones set up for the roof party. It was black while the rest of the furniture in the room was dark mahogany.

"The table doesn't match," I said.

"I noticed that." Brad glanced at me from where he stood beside the bed. "Did you find anything else?"

"No. What about you?"

"I found this." He held up a leather-bound notebook. "It looks like this may have belonged to the party planner. It has receipts, orders, a guest list, vendor list, and room reservations."

"That should come in handy."

"Too bad we didn't find this before we questioned the guests." Brad slid it inside an evidence bag and placed it on top of the dresser. "It doesn't look like Chambers planned to sleep here. I'm not even convinced he was staying here." Brad indicated the empty drawers and wardrobe. "You know what else is missing?"

"His luggage."

"Bingo."

"He lives locally. Maybe he used this room to hold private meetings. I'll check the bathroom."

A stack of folded bath towels remained on the shelf above the toilet. The complimentary shampoo and conditioner bottles were sealed. And the mat in front of the tub was bone dry.

"Anything?" Brad called from the other room.

"No toiletry bag or shaving kit." I checked the trash, finding a single wrapper from an individual bar of soap. The bar had been placed beside the sink. It looked like it might have been used once. I checked the toilet paper, finding a fresh roll on the holder. The ends weren't folded, and the sanitized label wasn't beneath the toilet seat. "It looks like he used the bathroom, or someone did." Something shiny caught my eye. I picked up a silver sequin from beside the toilet.

I brought it out to the other room, wondering why the techs hadn't bagged and tagged it. "I found this." I held it up for Brad to inspect.

"That matches our victim's dress."

"Which means she trusted Chambers enough to follow him to his room and use the facilities."

"Unless she ducked in there to call for help," Brad said.

"We won't know unless we find her purse and phone."

"Or until we take a look at her phone records."

"Still," I looked around the room, but nothing jumped out at me, "she finished her gig and left the party. More than likely, Chambers left with her. He must have invited her back here, and she agreed."

"It could have been transactional. He could have said he wanted to pay her for tonight, or he wanted to tip her. She follows him inside. He offers her a drink."

"There aren't any glasses. And I don't see any bottles. Why did he have a full bucket of ice?"

Brad's eyes narrowed. "That's weird. Places like this always have glasses."

"I'm getting the feeling this isn't that swanky of a place."

"It should be. Have you seen the room rate?"

"In that case, we need to take a peek at a similar suite and see what else might be missing." I smiled. "It's a good thing we have access to all the rooms."

SIX

The rest of the suites were set up in a similar fashion to our crime scene, minus the blood spatter. However, the furniture in the other suites all matched. The tables were solid wood, stained to match the dresser and nightstands. Each room had a rolling bar cart, along with a separate area set up on the counter with various assorted glassware. Either Chambers had gotten the cheapest room they had, or he'd done some redecorating. Since most of last night's staff had been sent home following our questioning, the answer would have to wait. In the meantime, my partner and I returned to the precinct.

I grabbed Brad's mug off his desk on my way to the break room. With fresh coffee refills in hand, I returned and eased into my chair. My notepad stared at me, asking the questions I hadn't yet voiced.

"Why do you think Remington Chambers' suite was different from everyone else's?" I asked. "According to the hotel staff we spoke to, they had no idea Chambers had redecorated."

Brad leafed through the messages that had been left during our absence. "It looks like they found the missing hotel room table on the roof beneath a tablecloth. The DJ had been using it. I'm guessing he wanted something larger or sturdier for his set-up than the banquet tables."

"He could have asked. I'm sure the hotel would have complied."

"Here." Brad handed me the message. "You can follow up."

I made the call, spoke to our crime scene techs and someone with the hotel. Brad reached for his mug, tearing his eyes from his computer screen while he took a sip.

Putting down the phone, I jotted a few notes on a blank sheet of paper. "Mr. DJ, James West, said he specifically asked Chambers for a larger, more stable area to work. Chambers asked two of the bellhops to move the table out of his room and to the roof. They complied with his request and covered the table with matching linens."

"God forbid it didn't color coordinate."

I scanned the list of other items missing from Chambers' suite. "The woman manning the desk told me Chambers had the mini-bar and glasses removed from his room prior to checking in. She found a note on his account, making sure the bar would not be restocked and he wouldn't incur any charges for the missing bottles or glassware."

"Which is common practice for recovering alcoholics, except Chambers isn't an alcoholic."

"We can't be certain of that."

Brad reached for the mouse and clicked a few times. "We verified he's a member of Spark, along with eighty-five percent of the party guests. I'm guessing the other four names are recent additions to Spark's clientele. They must have joined after your undercover op was blown. But since Chambers has a membership to a private club, one stocked in plenty of high-end booze, frequenting such a place would challenge his sobriety, meaning he's not a problem drinker."

"Do you find it hard not to drink when you're at Spark?"

"Why are you asking me that? I don't have a problem."

I also knew Brad hadn't had a drink in over two months. "I didn't mean to imply that. But Axel intentionally makes it more difficult. When I was undercover as one of his waitresses/dancers, he went out of his way to figure out what type and brand of liquor I enjoyed the most. Ever since, he's kept a bottle of brandy in his office. Until then, I never drank the stuff, but he decided that was my drink."

"I understand your point. He offers me whatever's on hand that he thinks will get me to imbibe every time he sees me, like it's a challenge he thinks he'll win if he just keeps offering. He doesn't get that we don't drink on the job. He probably does the same to every one of his guests."

"I know he does. At least in terms of catering to their desires, be it alcohol or something else. He likes to brag that he creates the Vegas experience."

"I know you said he makes it a point to keep drugs out of his club, but you can't tell me he doesn't provide his members with whatever they want."

"I'm not sure he provides it, but he has connections. He knows people who can, and he's careful. He keeps the illicit shit off his property. The drugs, the sex workers, and who knows what else. Unfortunately, we never found any proof of it. The gambling he'll risk, knowing the DA won't press the issue."

"Is the district attorney a member of Spark?"

"I don't know, but plenty of city officials are."

"It doesn't matter. What matters is we verified that twenty names on that guest list are also members of Spark. More than likely, this weekend blowout Chambers planned is a Spark event. That would explain why Axel Kincaid called you with the tip and wants you to find the murderer. I'm wondering why Axel didn't host the party himself or show up. If this was his event, shouldn't he have been the one running it? Shouldn't he have donated the event to the hospital in order to get the tax benefit?"

"Axel's always been careful. He likes to keep his name out of sticky situations. It's why we've never been able to build a case against him. But I'd think Fox would have been in charge. He is Axel's general manager."

"Maybe having his GM host the party would still be too close for comfort." Brad sipped his coffee. "Axel may have known Margaret Tenzin was going to be murdered and made sure he and his people kept their distance."

"And now he's hanging the murderer out to dry?"

"I don't know, Liv. We need to figure out if anyone had a motive."

"What do you make of the ice bucket?"

"It's an ice bucket."

"But Chambers didn't have glasses in his room. What was he doing with the ice?"

"Does it matter?"

"Maybe."

I brought up the research we'd compiled on Margaret Tenzin. Her LKA was three years old. She'd been evicted for failing to pay the rent. Following that, her financials suggested she'd rented a room in someone's house for almost a year and a half. Afterward, she fell off the map until this past summer when she and the DJ cohabitated. When that fell through, she'd gotten a monthly rental at the crappy motel near the airport. During all that time, she never changed the address on her license or notified the post office. Her mail went to a P.O. box.

"Margaret's estranged from her parents. They haven't spoken in half a decade, despite living in the same city. The DJ looks like the last steady relationship she had. He can probably tell us more about her," I said.

"Have you run his name?" Brad asked, and I shook my head. He entered James West into the database, along with the man's date of birth. "He has a record for assault and sexual misconduct." Brad spun the monitor for me to see. "He followed a woman into the ladies' room at the club where he worked, demanding to have sex." Brad scanned the details, reading me the highlights. "Judge figured it was a misunderstanding, but since West had been persistent, he let him serve six months and pay a hefty fine."

"What about the assault charges?"

"Two separate instances. The judges in both of those cases stuck him with third degree assault charges."

"So three misdemeanors. Did he serve time for the assaults?"

"No, he was fined and given tons of community service hours."

"I'm surprised clubs continued to hire him."

"They didn't care about the bar fights, but the sexual misconduct was another story. After he was released from jail, his employment history dried up. That's probably when he started working private parties and taking other gigs. No club wanted to hire him and open themselves up to lawsuits if he crossed that line." Brad eyed me. "What are you thinking? You have that look."

"West admitted to cheating on Margaret or Maggie, as he called her. He didn't think they were exclusive. He also asked if that made him a suspect."

"How could it? He would have had an alibi. Wasn't he on the roof all night?"

"He must have taken a break at some point. I just don't know when."

"We better find out. Do you think he withheld any other information because he was afraid how we'd interpret it?"

"Possibly. All I know is he didn't like the way Chambers grabbed the vic's arm earlier in the day, when they were discussing her act."

"Axel said Maggie worked a lot of these parties. If she saw something she wasn't supposed to, Chambers might have tried to buy her silence. That could be why he hired her to work last night and why they had a disagreement about her performance." Brad clicked a few keys. "We haven't gotten his financials yet, but they should be arriving any second. Even without them, this guy looks a million different shades of guilty."

"Except Axel swore Chambers didn't do it."

"That doesn't mean a damn thing. She was stabbed inside his room and tossed from his balcony. On top of that, he's on the run. Don't tell me that doesn't scream guilty."

"Unless he's a witness, fearing for his life."

"That can't be it." Brad rocked in his chair. "Axel wouldn't have called you and been so vague. He must have talked to Chambers. If Chambers had seen the killing happen, Axel would have handled the problem himself or given us a better tip."

"You're right, but based on what you've found out about the vic and what little I've been able to pull from her phone records and social media accounts, she could have had enemies. People she owed. Possibly a pimp. This may have nothing to do with Spark or its members."

"I thought the prostitution charges were dropped."

"That doesn't mean she wasn't hooking on the side. West said she was performing at amateur night at the strip club."

"Dancing or working on her routine?" Brad asked.

"What's the difference?"

"One involves taking off her clothes. The other doesn't."

"Unless you talk to someone who was there that night and remembers what happened, I'm not sure you'll ever know. Why do you think that's significant?"

"If she needed cash, she could have been looking to add skills to her resume, like exotic dancing, which is why we need to know if her routine involved a striptease. She could have benefitted from the additional pay bump that goes with the territory, especially if she started working private events, bachelor parties, things like that."

"You mean the kinds of events Axel sets up."

"Exactly. But if she was only working on her routine, she could have been hoping to get more gigs or generate more legitimate interest. Charity functions and socially acceptable events don't hire strippers," Brad said. "Hang on. Chambers' financials just hit my inbox. According to his bank records, he regularly used the ATM at that same strip joint where Margaret was arrested."

"Was he there that night?" I read the date of her arrest to him while he scanned the column.

"It looks like it. He withdrew $200. That's less than his normal $500, but I'm guessing it's because there weren't any pros working that night, so he could make do with smaller tips."

"We'll have to ask him about that whenever we locate him, but until that happens, Judi Rae, the caterer, and James West, the DJ, appear to be the two closest things Margaret had to friends. Maybe one of them can tell us more about her relationship with Chambers."

"We need to speak to her parents too. But I say we check out the room she was renting and see what we find first. You up for taking a ride?"

"Sure."

SEVEN

Margaret Tenzin wasn't much of a housekeeper, and it didn't look like the motel offered maid service for its long-term guests. A hot plate and pot were set up on the counter outside the bathroom where a double sink stood. To the left was a tower of unopened ramen noodles, piled all the way to the towel rack. Beside it were several containers of pudding cups. Beneath the sink was a twenty-four pack of bottled water, a case of canned drinks, and individual cups of rice, macaroni, and mashed potatoes. Just add water, heat, and serve.

"No wonder the caterer sent Margaret home with leftovers. I can't imagine living like this." For an extended stay unit, I expected to find a kitchenette, but there wasn't one.

Brad used his pen to open the tiny microwave. The inside was splattered with food stains and smelled vaguely of burnt popcorn. He closed the door and checked the fridge. Three plastic containers were crammed inside while bottled drinks lined the door. He opened the tiny attached freezer, finding an ice pack and three individually wrapped ice cream sandwiches.

I searched the dresser and closet while he explored the bedside table and the storage bins wedged between the bed and the wall. Her underwear and casual clothes were stuffed inside the dresser drawers. I didn't spot a single designer label or name brand. But the closet told an entirely different story.

Inside were several expensive pieces of couture. Even the items without labels were fancy and high quality. The coordinating accessories were just as nice. Hidden behind a few shoeboxes was a small, fireproof safe. It wasn't attached to the wall and didn't look like it had come with the room. It looked like something Margaret had purchased.

I announced my findings to Brad. "Any idea what the combination might be?"

He flipped through a spiral notebook he'd found in the bedside table. "Try her birthday."

"Nope."

"Um..." He blinked a few times. "7-2-1-8."

I entered the number, surprised when the lock released. "How did you know that?"

"That's her parents' house number. It's where she grew up."

"And you remembered that?"

"No." He held up an old photograph he'd found tucked inside the notebook. It showed Margaret, probably around eight or nine, hugging a golden retriever in front of the house. "But I can read."

"Glad to hear it."

"What's in the safe?"

I pulled the items out, opening the tiny envelopes and shaking the contents into my palm. "Jewelry."

"Do you think it's stolen?"

I examined the pieces. Several had been resized or the stones reset. A few receipts showed where she'd exchanged gemstones for simulations. "I think they were gifts."

"From male suitors?"

"I don't know."

"It could be payment for services rendered."

I made a note of the jeweler, figuring we'd have to pay him a visit. "We'll look into it." I slid the jewelry back into the envelopes and velvet satchels. "The bling goes nicely with everything else in the closet. These must be her work clothes because they are nothing like what I found in the drawers. It's almost like she's two completely different people."

"They say clothes make the man or, in this case, woman. They also say dress for the job you want."

"She performed for the rich and powerful. They'd expect their entertainment to fit in, or they'd never hire her. But I can't help but wonder if the items inside this closet have anything to do with her current living conditions. These dresses cost more than my rent."

"Answer me this," Brad said. "If I were to go through your things, would I think they belonged to two separate people?"

"I doubt it. You've seen my wardrobe. Sure, there's an array, but the vast majority are all reasonably priced. The most expensive dress I own cost $200. Half the dresses in here are ten times that."

"What about the things you have from your undercover days?"

That ran the gamut, from struggling to get by to high-end escort. "The department provided me with the nice stuff, which I had to return." I sifted through the items hanging in the closet. "What are you thinking?"

"Margaret could be a spy."

"For the CIA?"

Brad snorted. "Given the lack of federal agents swarming our crime scene, I doubt it. But y'never know. I was thinking more in terms of corporate espionage or plain old blackmail. She could be a grifter."

"That would explain why someone killed her. Perhaps stabbing her in the back had been retribution, symbolic of what she'd done."

"Hey, listen to this." Brad cleared his throat and read from the spiral notepad. *"I landed another gig today. It's supposed to be for charity. Surprisingly, the pay's good. I still don't understand how that works, but I'm not complaining. The food will be good too. I glimpsed the vendor sheet. Judi's already been booked. So I'll be eating plenty that night. I can't help but wonder if he'll be there. He's been at a lot of these things. He keeps showing up. I'm not sure I want to see him again. I told him it'll never work. That we can't work. He's married. But when we're alone together, all bets are off. He needs to keep his distance. He has a lot more to lose than I do. I wonder if his wife suspects, or if she'll be at this party. She wasn't at the last two, but this is a weekend event, not a four-hour dinner."*

"When did she write that?" I asked.

"It's dated two weeks ago. But I'm assuming she was talking about last night's party."

"It sounds that way." Standing on my tiptoes, I peered over Brad's shoulder as he flipped the pages. "Is that her diary?"

"It looks like it. She has an entry for every day. Most of it has to do with the routines she worked on or what she ate. She was counting her calories."

"She couldn't afford to gain or lose too much weight or those dresses wouldn't fit." I pointed to an entry dated three days ago. "Read that one."

"*He sent a car for me. I never expected that. Of course, he wasn't in it. Instead, the driver dropped me off at our usual spot. He was waiting there. I hate how seeing him makes me feel. I hate how much I want him when I know I can't have him. This isn't a fairytale. Cinderella doesn't get the prince. That's not how real life works. I know it, but he pretends otherwise, just so he can act like the entitled prick he really is. And I let him. He said he heard I'd be at the party, as if he wasn't the reason I was hired to perform there. I know better, and I told him so. But he denied it. He begged me not to show up, but I can't lose a paying gig. I told him I wouldn't give it up, and I wouldn't let him front me the cash. Regardless of what he may think, I'm not for sale. He can't buy me or buy my silence. That didn't stop him from warning me this time has to be different. She's going to be there, and he doesn't want to upset her. So I'll be on my best behavior. Even though, I'm sure he won't be.*" Brad read the next two entries, but Margaret hadn't brought up the mystery man or his wife again. Instead, she spent an entire page figuring out what she'd wear and what gear she'd need. The last entry in her journal contained only one word, *Showtime*. "It looks like we stumbled upon motive."

"Chambers isn't married," I pointed out. "If he arranged for Margaret to perform in order to please this unsub, then this guy must be someone important."

"Or his wife is, and he's coasting along on her purse strings."

"Also possible."

Brad handed me the notebook to peruse. "Our primary suspect list just got a lot longer." He watched as I flipped through the pages. "We need to figure out all the gigs Margaret's taken since she broke up with the DJ. That should make identifying the mystery man easier."

"We don't know how long she's been seeing him. We can't assume anything."

"Good point."

"Axel said a lot of the same people overlap at these events."

"He'd know best. Tell me again why we can't drag his ass down to the precinct and toss him into an interrogation room."

"We can, but he'll be out in a matter of minutes and he'll make our lives hell for it unless we have material proof of his involvement."

"He called you, which is proof enough. We could do it."

"I'll back your play, but do you want to make him our enemy?"

Brad thought about it for a moment. "Let's exhaust all other leads first. But the second I find out he's hiding Chambers or that he lied or misled us to conceal the truth, I'm slapping the cuffs on him."

"I'll hold the car door open while you toss him in the back."

Brad graced me with a smile, and we went back to searching the rest of the room. But we didn't find anything else of interest. No phone. No purse. And no address book with the mystery man's name or number. As we left, I couldn't help but wonder what became of Margaret's effects. Something told me if we found them, we'd find whoever killed her.

"We should swing by her parents' house. The hospital said they made the notification, but—"

"Yeah, that's a good idea," I said.

"I wouldn't say good." Brad pulled up the address and entered it into the onboard navigation system.

EIGHT

When we arrived, we found the front door open. A woman wailed loudly from inside the house while another woman tried to comfort her by rocking her gently from side to side in a warm embrace. Brad knocked against the storm door. They looked up at the sound, and he held his badge against the glass. As soon as they waved us inside, Brad pulled open the door.

"I'm sorry to intrude," he said. "I'm Detective Fennel. This is my partner, Detective DeMarco. We're looking for Mr. and Mrs. Tenzin."

The woman who'd been wailing, sniffed, another sob escaping her throat. "That's me," she choked out. "Are you here about my ba-ba-baby?" Her voice grew increasingly high-pitched, and she shoved her fist over her mouth to prevent another wail from escaping.

"Yes, ma'am." He looked uneasy. "We're investigating your daughter's murder."

"Murder?" Her eyes grew wide. "Someone did this to Maggie?"

"Yes, ma'am. I'm sorry," I said.

The other woman rubbed Mrs. Tenzin's arms before standing up. "I'll get Dick. He should be here for this." She moved toward the back of the house, and I followed.

"Excuse me," I said. "Who are you?"

"Roselyn Peters. I live next door."

"Did you know Margaret?" I asked.

The gray-haired woman nodded. "I watched that little

girl grow up. She used to play outside all the time as a kid. She loved baton twirling and rolling around on the grass, tumbling, doing flips, cartwheels, all that stuff. She was such a happy kid."

"What happened?"

"What do you mean?"

"You said she was happy. What happened?"

"She turned into a teenager and went through a rebellious phase. It drove her parents crazy. When she dropped out of college her first semester to pursue a career performing, that was the last straw."

"What do you mean?"

"Nothing."

"Tell me."

She looked torn. "Maggie and her parents had a falling out. They gave her an ultimatum. She was cut off until she agreed to go back to school. But she was so stubborn. They fought a lot. Mike and I would hear them screaming at each other. Mike's my husband."

"Go on."

"Eventually, Maggie stopped coming around and her parents stopped trying. But they never stopped loving her. This must be unbearable for them." She shook her head. "I happened to be here when the hospital called. Ruth fell apart the moment she heard the news, and Dick," she gestured to the closed door at the end of the hall, "shut himself in his office. I don't know what he's doing, but I'm sure he'll want to talk to you."

"Before that, can I take down your contact information in case I have any other questions?"

"Sure."

Once I finished that, I asked Roselyn if she wouldn't mind giving us some space to do our jobs. She seemed more than happy to have a valid reason to escape the grief, and I continued down the hall and knocked on the door.

"Come in," a rough voice called.

I eased the door open, one hand resting on my holster, unsure what I'd find. Grief could make people unpredictable. "Dick Tenzin?"

He nodded, eyeing my badge. "Are you here to inform

us about our daughter's passing? The hospital called hours ago. Shouldn't you have gotten to us sooner?"

"I'm sorry, sir. My partner and I have been trying to figure out what happened to Margaret."

"Maggie," he corrected. "She hated being called Margaret. She said Margaret sounded like an old lady, and she never wanted to be an old lady." He swallowed, swatting at a tear before it could fall. "She won't have to worry about that now." He choked on the words, his eyes lost as he stared at me for answers.

"I'm sorry for your loss." I sat in a folding chair beside his desk. "This will be hard to hear, but we believe your daughter was murdered."

"Shit."

"Do you know if she had any enemies? Was she seeing anyone? Who were her friends? Anything you can tell us will be most helpful."

"I don't know. I don't know anything about her. The last time we spoke, I told her she was dead to me." His voice cracked, and he turned away. "I never should have kicked her out. I should have supported her. Helped her. She needed us. Why didn't we listen? Why didn't we do something? How could we let this happen? This is our fault, isn't it?"

"You can't blame yourself. Things happen that are unpredictable and beyond our control." I nudged a tissue box toward him. "When's the last time you saw or spoke to Maggie?"

"We haven't spoken in months. She hasn't even been to the house in nearly six years. The last time was Mother's Day. She and Ruth had a huge fight. I asked her to leave. I told her until she got her life together, we didn't want to have anything to do with her." He bit his lip and stared at the papers on his desk. "But she was my kid, and even though I wanted to forget about all of it, I kept tabs on her. She worked in a lot of bars. Sometimes, she'd perform at outdoor events and festivals. Every once in a while, I'd check them out. She was so talented, but no one makes a living doing rhythmic gymnastics or that rope twirling stuff."

"She was an aerial silk performer," I said.

"Whatever." He blinked rapidly. "Why couldn't she have stuck to the plan? College, maybe graduate school, and finding a stable nine to five. That's all we ever wanted for her. We wanted to know she'd be okay. That she'd have things, resources, skills, to fall back on. That isn't so terrible, is it? I bet your parents wanted the same for you, and you listened. You work for the city and get great benefits, health insurance, retirement, all sorts of things."

I didn't bother pointing out how adamantly opposed my mother had been to my career choice. "It's natural to want the best for your children. But they have to figure things out on their own. Did you keep in touch with anyone else in Maggie's life? A friend or boyfriend?"

"Maggie didn't hold on to a lot of old friends. Most of them moved away. When she dropped out of school, any new relationships she had faded. She tended to hang around her work friends mostly. Maybe she kept in touch with some of them."

"Do you remember anyone's name?"

He shook his head.

"Where did Maggie work? We haven't been able to track down her employment history."

"She bartended at McCrary's or McRory's, one of those. That was the last normal job I know about. But she wasn't there long. A few months, maybe. Before that, she worked at a pizza place. She started there when she was in high school. She hung around her coworkers all the time. She always made friends easily, but they weren't deep, lasting connections. They were just people she could go with to the movies or shopping or whatever teenage girls do."

"What about boys?"

"She was never serious about any of them. As far as I was concerned, none of them were good enough for her, so it didn't matter. She was too young to be thinking about any of that anyway." The wrinkles on his forehead deepened. "But there was one guy hanging around her recently."

"How recently?"

Dick Tenzin ran his finger over several flyers he'd laid

out on his desk. "This was eight months ago. And that one was six weeks ago. But I'm sure it was the same guy."

"Did you go to these events?" I asked.

He nodded. "This was an outdoor art festival that took place at the end of the summer. Maggie performed. She did an incredible job. When she finished, a guy came up to her and they talked at the picnic tables. She looked so happy then. I saw him again at her last gig." He made a choking sound. "Dammit, why didn't I say something to her? I should have told her I missed her and that I loved her."

"You're sure it was the same man?"

"I'm pretty sure."

"Can you describe him?"

"Medium brown hair. He was barely taller than Maggie when she wore heels, so he must have been 5'8, maybe 5'9. He looked like he should have been on the rowing team or a polo player or something."

"What do you mean?"

"It's how he dressed, like he came from money. Old money."

"How old was he?"

"Young, around Maggie's age. I'd say he was in his early thirties. Maybe late twenties."

"Would you recognize him if you saw him again?" I asked.

"Probably. I don't know."

I wanted to show him Remington Chambers' photo, but I wasn't sure how reliable a witness Dick was in his grief-stricken state. "We'll put together an array. Perhaps later today or tomorrow, you could come to the precinct and take a look."

"I can do that."

I asked a few more questions, but Mr. Tenzin didn't know anything else. Leaving him alone with his grief, I returned to the living room to see how my partner was faring. Brad looked relieved to see me.

Ruth Tenzin was sobbing. Brad finished asking his questions, but Maggie's mother didn't have anything helpful to share. She hadn't seen her daughter in six years, and unlike her husband, she hadn't bothered keeping tabs on her kid. Apparently, Maggie and her mother shared the same stubborn streak.

NINE

"They fought all the time," Brad said. "It started when Maggie was old enough to drive. She got a car, part-time job, and some independence, and instead of doing all the things her parents wanted her to do, she carved out her own path."

"Nothing wrong with that."

"Says the legacy detective."

"You carved out your own path, and you turned out okay."

"That's debatable."

"Did Maggie ever get into trouble? Did she hang out with a bad crowd?"

"That's the thing," Brad said. "Ruth Tenzin never took issue with her daughter's friends or even her activities, just that she spent too much time on her hobby and not enough time on practical things. The more Ruth and Dick pushed, the harder Maggie rebelled. After she dropped out of college, she worked in several bars and even took bartending classes. That's how she made ends meet while she focused on her skills as an aerial performer."

"The DJ said she took an acrobatics class."

"One, according to Ruth. Maggie hated heights. That was another reason her parents were adamantly opposed to her career choice, not that they saw it as much of a career. Ruth always thought the only reason Maggie wanted this so badly was because they didn't want her to have it."

"Do you think that's true?"

Brad shrugged.

"You saw how she was living. People will do just about anything in order to pursue their passion. If this was how she intended to prove her parents wrong, she wouldn't have stuck with it for so long. It's been almost eight years since she dropped out of college, and they've been estranged for six," I pointed out.

"Things weren't good before then. Every few months, Maggie would turn up for dinner. Inevitably, they'd ask how she was doing and she'd beg for money, which would set off a huge fight. Maggie didn't have much of a choice. Avoiding her parents was the only way to break the cycle." Brad looked at me. "Do you think they're really this distraught over her death?"

"It's the guilt."

"Are we sure they didn't do something to her?"

"I doubt it." I finished compiling the photo array of party guests who roughly fit the descriptors Dick Tenzin had provided, allowing for a large margin of error. "If what her dad said was true, the affair might have been going on even while Maggie was living with the DJ."

"Put his photo in the mix too," Brad said. "He could have lied about the break-up."

I did as my partner said, tapping my pen against my chin while I read my computer screen. "Has the lab verified that the blood found in Chambers' room matches our victim?"

"Not yet. You know how long this stuff takes. But it must be hers. We would have been informed about a second murder if it wasn't. Plus, without a blood trail out of the room, I don't see how the blood could belong to someone else."

I opened a search tab, hoping to determine what other charities Chambers supported and if he'd organized any other events. "Remington Chambers is a corporate accountant. Thirty-two. Single. Dark hair." I held up the printed copy of his ID photo. "Does he look athletic to you?"

"Hotel security said they located him in the gym, so maybe."

I reread the description Mr. Tenzin had provided. "This could be Maggie's mystery man. But why would Chambers lie to her and say he's married? Don't most men lie and say they aren't?"

Brad's gaze shifted to the double doors which just opened. "I'm not most men. But you could ask that one."

I turned in the direction he had jerked his chin, surprised to see Sean making his way to my desk. Brad waved the officer escorting him away.

"Hey, Liv. I didn't want to intrude, but the desk sergeant sent me up here. She figured since I'm an injured firefighter, I didn't pose a security risk. You might want to speak with someone about that." He grinned.

"I'll do that." I tried to erase the confused look from my face but gave up. "Is everything all right?"

"Everything's fine. I was on my way to pick up a shift at the hospital cafeteria and thought I'd drop this off. I thought you might need it." He placed a hair tie on the edge of my desk.

I looked at the elastic band, knowing damn well it wasn't mine. "Why?"

"Don't you wear your hair up at work? The women at the firehouse always do. Leaving it down poses a risk. I figured it was the same way here."

"Where was it?" I asked.

"It was in the couch cushions."

I wondered how long it had been there. Was Sean seeing someone else? We weren't exclusive, so he could have been seeing any number of other women. He was a seemingly nice guy who saved lives for a living, which is how he got hurt. But that didn't mean he wasn't a dog. "If you were married, would you lie and say you weren't?"

"What?"

"It's for our case. We need an uninvolved third party's opinion."

"I wouldn't do that. I'm a stand-up guy. I'm not a cheater."

The hair tie suggested otherwise. Brad peered at it from

across our joined desks. "You said you found that in the couch cushions?" Brad pointed at it. "That's weird. Liv usually leaves them around the top of the shampoo bottle or on the gearshift in the car. Once I found one holding a bag of chips closed."

"How would you know what she puts on her shampoo bottles?" Sean asked.

Brad glanced at me, noting the *behave* look in my eyes. "You can see them the second you walk into her bathroom. She never pulls the shower curtain closed because she's afraid someone could be hiding behind it and with good reason."

"I wouldn't know." Sean gave me a pointed look. "I haven't been invited over yet."

"That's because Liv's in the middle of moving, again." Brad pretended to stare at his computer screen, but I noticed the furtive glances he cast at the foreign hair tie. "It goes back to the hiding behind the shower curtain thing."

"Brad," I hissed, shaking my head, "not the time."

"Do I want to know?" Sean asked.

"Not unless you want nightmares," I said.

He ran his hands over my shoulders. "I'm sorry I asked."

"It's fine." I picked up the hair tie. "You didn't have to come all the way to the precinct for this."

"It's no problem. I wanted to see where you worked. It looks exactly like I pictured it." Sean focused on my partner's nameplate.

My phone rang, and I held up a finger for him to wait as I picked up the phone. "DeMarco," I said.

"You'll be interested in our latest walk-in."

"Who is it?"

"Remington Chambers," the desk sergeant said. "I stuck him in a room down here with an officer on the door. But Chambers asked to speak to you in private. What do you want to do?"

"I'll be right there." I put the phone down.

"What is it?" Brad asked. "What's wrong?"

"Chambers turned himself in. He wants to speak to me. Alone."

"Why?"

"I'll give you one guess."

"Kincaid."

I pushed away from my desk. "I'm giving him five minutes of my time. Then I'm having him moved to one of our interrogation rooms."

"I'll be waiting."

I glanced at Sean. "I'm sorry. I gotta deal with this."

"Actually, I wanted to ask you something," he said.

"All right," I glanced at Brad, hoping he'd be on his best behavior, "can you give me five minutes?"

"Sure. I can wait. It'll give me some time to get to know your partner better."

That was the last thing I wanted. Brad had more dirt on me than anyone, except for maybe Emma. "Okay, but I'm not going to have a lot of time when I get back either. Maybe we could do this another day."

"No, it's not that big of a deal. But I thought it'd be best to ask in person after the way we left things earlier. I can wait. It's fine. Go do your thing. I'll be right here." He offered a bright smile. "I totally get it. Our jobs aren't that dissimilar. Take all the time you need."

I collected a notepad and a few files off my desk while Brad took it upon himself to keep my guest entertained.

"You really didn't have to worry about bringing that to Liv." Brad's eyes narrowed on the hair tie. "I keep a stash in case she ever runs out." He reached into his top drawer, and I kicked him under the desk.

"B. Fennel," Sean read. "B? What's that stand for?"

"Brad." Brad extended his hand. "Liv's talked a lot about you."

"All good, I hope."

"It could have been better."

Sean glanced at me and shook my partner's hand. "She talks about you all the time too. *All* the time. It's nice to finally put a name to a face." He tilted his head to one side. "Have we met before?"

"Do you play softball?"

"No. Hockey."

Brad nodded. "I knew I recognized you. Police versus

fire, four years ago. You scored that final point in overtime."

"It was a lucky shot."

"Damn straight it was."

Sean smirked. "At least that's what the PD's been telling themselves ever since. After all, we are five-time champs."

Hoping the discussion would stay on sports, I headed for the stairs, straining to hear as I walked away.

"You still get out on the ice?" Brad asked.

"Not lately. Not since the accident."

"Right." Brad held up his palms. "My bad."

"It's cool. The doctors are optimistic. They think things look good. A few more weeks in PT, and then I go for another round of scans. If everything's good, I'll be taking the physical and getting back to it soon enough." Sean cracked a smile. "Since I'll be sitting this game out, the PD might actually have a chance to take back the cup."

"We'll take it back no matter what," Brad said.

"Uh-huh," Sean teased.

As the door swung closed, I could no longer hear their conversation. Who knew what I'd be walking into when I returned. But I had a more important question on my mind. What would I be walking into when I got downstairs?

TEN

Remington Chambers looked exactly like his photo ID. He wore a tailored suit and was freshly shaven. Despite everything that happened last night, he looked rested. His eyes weren't red or puffy. And he smelled of soap and aftershave.

"Are you Liv DeMarco?" he asked before I could introduce myself.

"You asked to speak to me." I glanced back at the officer who pulled the door closed, shutting me into the room with Chambers. "Shouldn't you know what I look like?"

"I'm Remington Chambers." He stood, extending his hand toward me.

I ignored the gesture and took a seat at the other end of the table. "They'll be moving you upstairs in a few minutes. Whatever you want to say to me, I suggest you hurry. Have you been informed of your rights?"

"Why?"

"You're the primary suspect in a homicide investigation. You are currently being held in police custody. You need to be aware of your rights."

"Axel Kincaid said you'd help me. He said he spoke to you last night. I didn't kill Maggie. I wasn't even there when it happened."

"You weren't where?" I asked.

"At the party. I ducked out around midnight, got changed, and headed to the gym to get some use out of their equipment before heading home. I'll answer whatever questions I can later, but I wanted you to hear my side of things first. I know how it must look, but I didn't do it."

"Why did you run?"

"No questions, just listen. One of the guests, Clayton Deek, has been seeing Maggie for a while. When we were discussing the event, he asked me to hire her to perform. So I did. But a few days before the party, he freaked out."

"Why?"

"I don't know."

"Is Deek married?"

Chambers nodded. "He begged me to fire her. The morning of—"

"You mean yesterday?"

"Stop asking questions."

I waved my hand in a go on gesture.

"I pulled Maggie aside when she was making sure everything was set and told her to beg off. She knew Clayton must have spoken to me. She was irate. She couldn't believe he'd do that to her. He knew how important the gig was. She promised me she'd never go public with their relationship. But Clayton couldn't call the shots when it came to her life. If he couldn't contain himself, then he shouldn't be attending the party. It wasn't her fault. She didn't want to be punished for it. I tried to smooth it over, but she was pissed. All night, she practically threw herself at every man at that party."

"That's not what I heard."

"Then you've been misinformed. Between the drinks they were bringing her and the flirting, someone got the wrong idea, got angry, and acted rashly."

"Who?"

"I don't know."

"What about your buddy, Clayton?"

"He doesn't strike me as the type, but maybe. Men like us, with wealth and power, occasionally get it in our heads that we can have whatever we want, whenever we want it. I won't apologize. That's just how it is. But that doesn't mean we would kill someone over it. I can't picture Clayton doing that."

"What about his wife? Could she have done something

to Maggie?"

"I don't think she knew about the affair. He didn't think she did."

"Did anything else happen at the party? Were there any altercations?"

"What did I say about questions? The officer said I only have five minutes. Can't that wait?"

"Then tell me something important. Tell me who did this. Tell me why I shouldn't lock you up right now."

"I didn't do it. I wasn't there. Isn't that enough?"

"Why did you run? Did you see who attacked Maggie?"

"I thought you agreed to listen and stop asking questions."

"I'm a homicide detective. It comes with the territory. Deal with it."

"Fine. Off the record?"

"There is no off the record. Just answer the question. Axel said you could trust me. That means you should tell me what I want to know." But I could tell Chambers was stubborn. "Was this a Spark event?"

Chambers looked torn. "It was," he finally said.

"Who was in charge?"

"Me."

"Do you work for Axel?"

"Officially? No."

"What about unofficially?"

Chambers shrugged.

"You do whatever he wants."

"Occasionally."

Chambers' name had never come to light as one of Axel's known associates. I'd only gotten his name off the member list, not the employee roster. He didn't have a record, which meant any offenses he committed had been taken care of. Given his resources, he could have paid his problems to go away or he'd hired a cleaner to handle the situation. Is that what he tried to do last night? But with all the 9-1-1 calls we received, he wouldn't have had time to handle it quietly. That could be why he went to Axel for help.

"This wasn't nearly as robust as most Spark events I've

seen. Why so tame? What was the point of the weekend getaway?" I asked.

"To blow off steam. Spark throws parties for its members to have fun. This weekend was supposed to be fun."

"What else was going on at the party? Drugs? Sex? Gambling?"

"I'm not at liberty to say."

"As I understand it, the getaway was a prize won at a silent auction. The price of admission was donating to the hospital. How did you ensure everyone on the guest list was a Spark member and not some random philanthropist?"

"Maybe they aren't. Maybe that's why things are," he eyed me curiously, "tame. That's how you put it, right?"

"I said they appeared tame. But a woman being thrown from your balcony is anything but tame. Do you want to tell me what was really going on at that party?"

He shook his head.

"You already told me this was a Spark event. Were any non-members included?"

"You'd have to ask Mr. Kincaid that. All I did was donate the weekend party package and set everything up. The guests knew this would be more low-key. No wild yacht parties or car races. It was a weekend away, out of the public eye. Business could be conducted without drawing any unwanted attention or press."

"What kind of business?"

"Every kind."

"I'm going to need a few examples."

"I don't have specifics. Client confidentiality is a priority."

"Client confidentiality? You're not an attorney. You're an accountant."

"NDAs, baby. But I can tell you Maggie performed at a lot of similar events. She doesn't work inside Spark. She never has. But she's been to several events, mostly unsanctioned ones."

"Unsanctioned?"

"Don't ask me what goes on there. I can't say. I have

nothing to do with that side of Mr. Kincaid's business."

I doubted that very much. "The secrets your guests keep may be the reason she was killed."

"That's what Mr. Kincaid thinks. He's hoping you'll be able to figure out who did it and why."

"Did you see it happen?" I repeated.

"I already told you I was in the gym. Check the security footage. I'm sure I have an alibi for her time of death. I was nowhere near the party when it happened."

"Did anyone else see you?"

"Someone on staff must have." Chambers glanced at the clock on the wall. "Is this the best use of our time?"

"Why did you flee the scene?"

"I didn't flee. I stepped out. I had some things to take care of."

"That's convenient."

"Isn't it?" he asked sardonically. "However, that doesn't make me guilty."

"It doesn't make you look innocent either."

"Why the hell would I turn myself in if I killed Maggie?"

I didn't respond. Instead, I asked, "Where was Axel last night?"

"He was at Spark."

"You're sure?"

"That's where he is most nights."

"But you don't know for sure?"

"I'm not his keeper."

"Why wasn't he running this event? Spark is his baby. He takes his members' happiness seriously."

"He can't be everywhere at once. He has other commitments and wanted nothing to do with whatever went on at the party. It may have been too boring for him."

"Are you sure he wasn't there? He knew specific details regarding Maggie's murder, details that have not been divulged. Details that even you haven't mentioned. How would he have known these things? Was he at the hotel last night? Did he pop in for a few minutes to check on things?"

"No."

"Are you sure?"

"Positive. Mr. Kincaid was at Spark all night. Hasn't he

provided you with an alibi? He said he would."

"You just said you didn't know where he was. Now you're positive he was at Spark all night. Which is it?"

"I'm not sure. You're confusing me."

"Okay, let's slow this down." I wondered how many more lies Chambers would get caught in. "Did you go to Spark last night?"

"No, I spent all day at the hotel."

"And where did you go after you left the hotel?"

"I can't remember. I wandered around for most of the night. I went for a walk and lost track of time."

"How did you hear about Maggie's death?"

"Mr. Kincaid told me what was going on and to reach out to you."

"You didn't notice the police cars or ambulance outside the hotel?"

"I was distracted."

"By what?"

"Work. I'm an accountant with lots of clients. Complex equations are always running through my head."

"When did you finally speak to Axel?"

"He called me about an hour ago. I can show you when I received the call." Slowly, he took his phone out of his pocket, tapped the screen, and held it out, showing me the call log with Axel's phone number.

"Did you know Maggie was picked up on suspicion of prostitution not too long ago?"

"I don't know anything about that."

"Are you sure? Maybe that's why she was hired to work these off-site events."

"Like I said, I wouldn't know anything about that."

Before I could say another word, an officer knocked and opened the door. "We're going to take him to processing."

"Am I under arrest?" Chambers asked, incredulous. "Mr. Kincaid said you could help. Can't you do something?"

"It's out of my hands. Remember when I asked you if you'd been informed of your rights before you started speaking?"

"I thought that was just a technicality."

"That's what we do when we take a suspect into custody."

"In that case, I want to contact my attorney." Chambers produced a business card from Reeves and Almeada. The law firm had a reputation for employing the best criminal defense attorneys. They were the same lawyers Axel used.

I waited for Chambers to be taken away before I returned upstairs. My mind was going in a million different directions. At this rate, Brad would get his wish, and we'd be dragging Axel into the station to answer questions alongside his buddy.

When I emerged from the stairwell, I found Sean still sitting in my chair. Even from here, I could feel the tension between him and Brad. As if today couldn't get any worse.

As soon as Sean saw me coming, he got up and pulled my chair out, waiting for me to sit down. He rested his hand on the back of my chair and stood closer to me. Leaning down, he kissed my cheek.

Brad met my eyes but didn't comment on the public display. "What happened downstairs?" he asked.

"Chambers lawyered up the moment the officer came to take him away."

"He is our prime suspect. What did he think would happen?"

"I'm not sure, but he was willing to talk until that happened, sort of." I looked up at Sean. "What did you want to ask me? I don't mean to rush you off, but we need to get back to work."

"Can we speak privately?"

"Um, sure."

"I should check to see if the lab got our results back." Brad got up. "It was nice meeting you. Remember what I said." He gave Sean a look, which lowered the temperature in the room by a good ten degrees.

"Yeah, you too." Sean waited for Brad to leave the bullpen. "So that's Brad."

"Yes, but it's not like that. We're not like that."

"Oh, I know. He told me as much. Undercover as a married couple, that must have been interesting."

"You could say that. The only thing worse is the ribbing

we've been getting ever since. But it's the job. It comes with the territory." I checked the time.

"You really had me going this morning. I thought I had a reason to be worried. I should have known better."

I resisted the urge to rub the side of my neck. It had started to sting and itch again. "I told you I was just messing with you."

"Emma said you were special and a million different kinds of great." He grabbed a chair and sat down beside me, resting his forearms on his knees while he leaned toward me. "If I made you uncomfortable, I want you to know that wasn't my intention. I thought you knew that's why I asked you to stay over. But it's cool. We can take things slower. I have no problem waiting. Brad said you have trust issues, particularly with men."

"Just the one." I glared in the direction my partner had vanished.

"So we can try this again. I'd like to keep seeing you, if you're still interested."

"Um..." I looked around.

"Dinner, tonight?" Sean asked.

"I don't know what time we'll be finished. I really need to get back to work."

"Right, yeah. But I didn't come all the way here just to bring you a piece of elastic. I want to take you out tonight to make up for not having a proper date night last night. No crappy black and white movies, which you apparently hate. I'm thinking no movie at all. Just drinks and dinner, somewhere nice."

"We're in the middle of a homicide investigation."

"I get that. But you have to call it quits some time tonight. I don't get off work until eight. Reservations are for 9:30. What do you say?"

"Reservations?"

"Dino and Emma had reservations at Pomme de Terre, but her schedule got changed, so Dino offered us their table. I know it's last minute, but you deserve to go somewhere nice, especially with the long day you're having. I can be a gentleman. You'll see."

"Can I meet you there?"

"Sure. But they have a dress code. Is that okay?"

"I can swing it."

"Good." He gave me a kiss. "I'll see you tonight."

I watched him head for the double doors as Brad emerged. They nodded to one another as they passed, and I let out the breath I'd been holding. Seeing Sean made me tense. But I wasn't sure why. And now the scar on my neck hurt again.

Brad took his seat, organizing the stacks of papers beside his keyboard. "Lab said the blood found on top of the crushed car is a match to the blood found on the rug and balcony of Chambers' hotel room. They haven't officially matched it to the vic yet, but we know she landed on top of the car. The blood is hers, even if we don't have the official report."

"Thanks for checking."

"Yep." Brad pointed to the hair tie. "You never wear hair ties with metal fasteners."

I looked down at the object. "I know. It's not mine."

"Who do you think it belongs to?"

"Sean said he found it between his couch cushions. It could have been there for months."

"Right." He gave me a look. "Are you going out with him again?"

"Tonight, I think."

"Are you going to break it off?"

"Should I?"

Brad shrugged. "Not my place to say."

"It seems like you had plenty to say." Emma would give me such shit for breaking up with Sean without giving him a chance to explain. "We aren't exclusive. We've only gone out a couple of times. He can have other girls' hair ties in his couch cushions."

"And you're okay with that?"

"We'll have a chat. Like I said, we've only gone out once or twice."

"Three times."

"We're allowed to see other people."

Brad met my eyes. "Who else are you seeing?"

"I'm surprised he doesn't think I'm seeing you,

especially after the shampoo bottle comment."

"Oh, he definitely thought that, but I set him straight. Liv DeMarco doesn't date cops. End of story. The question on my mind is why she's wasting her time with an injured, two-timing firefighter."

"Brad, enough." Luckily, no one was around to overhear our conversation.

"I don't want you getting hurt."

"Thanks, but I can take care of myself." I thought about the way Sean had reacted when he thought I was involved with someone else. Jealousy wasn't attractive, especially if the guy wasn't monogamous. But we weren't serious. Not yet. I rubbed the side of my neck, cringing at the stinging sensation.

Brad's expression softened. "Are you okay?"

"Yeah." I smoothed my hair back. "Chambers is a pain in my neck." I filled my partner in on everything that he said downstairs.

"I'm surprised he turned himself in, but Axel told him to. I don't like that he made it sound like you're a cop who'll do Axel's bidding, though."

"Regardless of what he thinks, it's not true."

Brad sighed. "I still don't like it. We are not Axel Kincaid's personal police force. We work for the city, not him or his cronies."

"Let's focus on Chambers. Once his lawyer gets here, we'll go at him, but we need to be prepared. You know how this works. Defense counsel will shut us down in a heartbeat for using the wrong phrasing to ask a question."

"This isn't a courtroom. It doesn't matter."

"Still, I'd prefer to get as much information as possible without having to deal with the lawyer's interruptions and comments."

"Agreed."

ELEVEN

"What time did you leave the roof?" I asked. Questioning Chambers again was ridiculous, but since he hadn't said enough downstairs, I hoped the interrogation room would loosen his lips.

Chambers thought for a moment. "I guess it was close to midnight, possibly a little after."

"Were you alone?"

He straightened in his seat. "Yes, Detective, I left the party alone. Like I told you earlier, I got changed and went to the gym."

"Did you eat or drink anything at the party?" Brad asked.

Chambers looked confused. "I don't know."

"You don't know? How can you not know if you consumed anything?"

"I had a few appetizers and something to wash them down with."

"What time do you think that was?" Brad asked.

"My client isn't a clock, Detective. I don't see how it's relevant what he ate or when he ate it," Mr. Almeada said in that bored, snobby tone.

"Do you work out?" Brad asked the attorney, who nodded. "Do you make it a habit to exercise after eating or consuming alcohol?"

"I'm sure some people do." Almeada gave us each a hard stare. "Don't judge my client on his physical habits. They have no bearing on your investigation."

Brad looked like he wanted to argue, so I took over. "Mr. Chambers," I said, "walk us through exactly what you did once you left the party."

"I returned to my room, changed into workout clothes, and went down to the gym."

"Where were these clothes?"

"In my bag in the suite I reserved."

"Where did you put your party outfit after you took it off?"

My questions were making Almeada itchy, but he held his tongue.

"I put them in my bag and went downstairs," Chambers said.

"Did you take your bag with you?" Brad asked.

"Yes."

"Why?" I asked. "You said you reserved that suite for your use for the entire weekend."

"I did, but I have trouble sleeping. My best chance of getting a restful night is at home in my own bed. Sticking to a routine is considered good sleep hygiene. I planned to go home after my workout and figured I'd take my things with me."

"But you never made it home last night." I leaned back in the metal chair, resisting the urge to touch my hair or the side of my neck. Despite the burning sensation, I didn't want the attorney to think I was nervous or fishing.

"No." Chambers didn't offer an explanation. He'd been told not to volunteer any information or answer any implied questions. I waited, but he didn't speak. I should have gotten him to answer these questions earlier, but I'd run out of time.

"Where are your clothes now?" Brad asked.

"I'm wearing them."

"You're wearing the same clothes you wore to the rooftop party?"

"Yes." Chambers appeared genuinely confused. "That was only last night. What's the big deal? I wanted to save on my dry cleaning."

"What about your gym clothes?" Brad asked.

Chambers shrugged.

My partner gave the attorney an exasperated look. "You don't remember where you put them, Mr. Chambers?"

"No, I don't. Maybe they're still inside the hotel gym."

"We need those clothes. When did you change back into this?" Brad waved his hand at Chambers' outfit.

"I'm not sure."

"If you want his clothes, you'll need a warrant," Almeada said.

"We have one to search the entire hotel and the guests' belongings. We didn't find anything in the gym or in your suite, Mr. Chambers. Where did you put your clothes?"

"I don't know. Everything's a blur."

"The hell it is," Brad muttered.

"Fine, we'll get a court order for your apartment, your car, and your office. And when we do, we'll see what turns up." Brad leaned back in the chair, giving Chambers an icy glare. "How did you manage to leave the hotel? The place was locked down. Patrol officers were stationed at the exits."

"I walked right out. No one stopped me. No one told me differently. If they had, I would have stayed."

Almeada expected us to protest, so he spoke up before we could. "Unless you have proof to the contrary, I suggest you move on. Pursuing this will do nothing more than waste time."

"Where did you go after you left the hotel?" I asked.

Chambers' jaw went slack while he considered the question. "I went for a walk. Some nights, that's what I like to do. The weather was nice. I find it peaceful and calming. The music and crowd on the roof overstimulated me. That's another reason I wanted to hit the gym. Physical activity helps clear away all the insanity."

"Your apartment is thirty-two blocks from the hotel. If you intended to return home so you could sleep, like you insist, why didn't you drive home and then go for your walk?"

"I didn't think about it."

I brushed my hair back, frustrated. "Did you take your bag with you on this walk?"

"I don't remember."

"Let's back this up for a second," Brad said. "You went to your room to change. Did anyone come to your room while you were there?"

"No."

"Who else had access to your suite?"

"The hotel staff."

"Anyone else?" Brad asked. "Hotels usually offer their guests two room keys."

"I only asked for one. Check with the hotel. I checked in under single occupancy."

"What about the in-room bar?"

"I asked them to empty it. I don't believe in being price gouged on watered down, sub-par liquor. If I'm going to drink, it should be the good stuff."

"Did you notice any glasses in your room?" I asked.

"Glasses?" Chambers cocked an eyebrow. "I don't recall."

"What about the ice bucket?"

"I don't remember seeing one."

"Did you get ice?" Brad asked.

"No."

"What about room service? I'm guessing a nice place like that wouldn't expect its guests to get their own ice."

"I didn't order any room service. You can check with the hotel," Chambers insisted.

"What about turndown service?" I asked.

"No." Chambers gave Almeada a look, begging him to assist. "Didn't I say I wasn't planning on sleeping there?"

Brad squinted at the attorney, waiting for him to speak, but Almeada shook his head, so Brad continued. "What about asking for extra towels or someone to check the air conditioner?"

"I didn't do any of those things."

"Ask your question, Detective." Almeada was growing impatient, sensing where this was going, even if Chambers appeared clueless.

"To your knowledge, did anyone else ever enter your suite during your stay at the hotel?" Brad asked.

"Only the bellhops when I first got there. No one else."

"Not even Margaret Tenzin?" I asked.

"Of course not."

Brad opened the folder and pulled out a few crime scene photos. He placed them face-up in front of Chambers. "We have every reason to believe Margaret Tenzin was attacked inside your suite and thrown from your balcony. Would you care to revise your previous answer?"

"No, I wouldn't. When I left, the room was empty. None of that was there. This must have happened after I left." Chambers leaned back in his chair, looking relaxed for the first time since we'd met. "Clearly, Maggie and her attacker must have found some way to enter my suite without my knowledge. Again, I suggest you speak to the hotel about that because I can't offer you an explanation for something I know nothing about."

"We'll do that," Brad said. "Just one last thing for now. Where is your room key?"

Chambers stared blankly at us for a few seconds. "It must be in my bag."

"With your gym clothes?"

"Yes."

"The bag that you conveniently misplaced." Brad gave me a look. "I think we're done for now."

I wanted to ask more questions, but it'd be better to let Chambers stew. After exchanging a look with my partner, we stood, said we'd check on a few things, and left the room. The hallway was empty. I circled, furiously rubbing my neck, which only made matters worse.

"He's so damn smug, but his story makes no sense. Clearly, he's lying. Why is he acting like he's got an ace up his sleeve?"

Brad rocked back on his heels while he watched me pace. "He's confident we can't prove his story false."

"He had all night to come up with an explanation, but his excuse sucks."

"Maybe that's on purpose. It could be a distraction or misdirect. Or it could be what he was instructed to say."

"By whom?"

"Axel. I'm sure the bastard promised him something. That's the only reason Chambers turned himself in. A guy who runs doesn't suddenly change his mind."

"He might have if he realized he had nowhere to run."

"He has means. He could have gotten away."

"Chambers wouldn't leave his life behind for something as insignificant as murder." I repeated what Chambers had said about being entitled. "But you're right. Let's bring Axel in for questioning. Since Chambers won't answer our questions, Axel better."

We returned to our desks, and I placed the request while Brad checked to see if anything new had surfaced. Then we scoured the hotel security footage and the statements the staff made. According to everything we had, hotel staff hadn't been inside Chambers' suite since they finished cleaning it prior to his early check-in time. That had been at ten a.m.

"Are you sure?" I asked the day manager. "Isn't check-in at four?"

"Three, but because Mr. Chambers booked an entire floor of rooms and had a special event planned, we offered him an early check-in so he'd have more time to get ready."

"And he didn't ask the front desk for anything to be brought to his room?"

"No. In fact, Mr. Chambers kept a Do Not Disturb on the door and gave us the same orders for any phone messages he might have received," the day manager said. "We abided by his request."

"Was that strange?"

"Not really. Mr. Chambers was too busy running around the rest of the day. Whenever a vendor or anyone needed to confer with him, we'd send them to the roof. That's where he spent his time. I doubt he was even in his room."

"Do you remember if he had any luggage with him when he checked in?"

"He had his dry cleaning and a gym bag. That was it."

"Did you happen to find his gym bag?"

"No, ma'am."

"All right. Thanks." I hung up and checked the footage again.

Even though it was spotty, I froze the feed and printed a still. When Chambers checked in, he was wearing a polo and khakis. But everyone at that party had been in formal wear. Chambers must have changed in his room before the party and again after.

I glanced at my notes. "What if Axel Kincaid's telling the truth?"

"We follow the evidence wherever it leads. Right now, Chambers looks good for the murder, but it's too soon to say. Regardless, he's a suspicious son of a bitch. And shady like all get out," Brad said.

"But if Axel knows what happened or enough of the story to tell us Maggie didn't die from the fall, wouldn't he have had to have gotten that information from Chambers?"

"You still think Axel was at the hotel last night."

"I do, but no one admits to seeing him. I'd think someone on staff or one of the caterers would have let it slip, even if the party guests were under strict orders not to squeal." I clicked through the exterior crime scene photos. "But we would have noticed one of his sports cars in these photos. So I guess I'm mistaken."

"Axel has more cars than I have socks," Brad said. "Maybe he used something less ostentatious. We could run every plate and see what turns up."

"It's not a bad idea, but wouldn't Axel have been more careful? He sent us video footage of him entering and leaving Spark. According to that, he was there all night."

"We both know that isn't the most reliable of alibis. Axel knows how to slip in and out without getting caught on camera."

I studied the guest list. Right now, everyone remained a suspect. Guests, vendors, and hotel staff. "The hotel said no one else was on the premises. We asked everyone from the manager to the maids."

"They also said nobody left after we locked it down, and that wasn't true. I don't know, Liv. I'm not sure who or what to believe. It's all very sketchy."

"For argument's sake, let's say Axel wasn't in the building. That doesn't mean he wasn't close by. The neighboring buildings may have had a decent view of the roof party and whatever happened on the balcony. None of the 9-1-1 calls came from there, but that doesn't mean someone didn't see something. We should expand the canvass. Even if no one saw what happened to Maggie, someone might have noticed Axel. He tends to stick out."

"Or they may have seen whoever drove the getaway car."

"The getaway car?"

Brad chuckled. "Unless you believe Chambers went for a walk and wandered around the city for twelve hours before turning himself in." Brad clicked a few keys. "I'll see if any nearby DOT feeds caught anything useful."

We worked for the next few hours. None of the license plates connected to Axel Kincaid or his LLCs. Traffic cam footage didn't turn up anything useful either.

In the meantime, Chambers was cooling his heels in lockup and Mr. Almeada had returned to his office. Unless we found a smoking gun, we'd wait until the morning before going near Chambers again. That should be enough time to get the self-proclaimed insomniac to be more forthcoming.

I hissed when my scratching turned into a sharp pain at the back of my neck.

Brad narrowed his eyes and came around the side of our joined desks. Gently, he brushed my hair to the side. "That doesn't look good."

"What do you mean?"

"It looks like it might be infected." He squeezed some hand sanitizer into his palm and rubbed his hands together. Once it dried, he pressed a finger against my skin. "It's warm to the touch. Let's get that checked out."

"We're in the middle of something here."

"You're more important." He squirted another dollop of hand sanitizer into his hands and grabbed his jacket. "Plus, I want to check on Jake and see how his dad's doing. He should have shown his face by now. I'm worried."

"Have you heard from him?"

"He's been radio silent. Lisco texted me. She's concerned. Jake hasn't been answering her texts either."

"He might have put his phone on airplane mode if they're doing tests. You know the hospital gets weird about using devices sometimes."

"Possibly," Brad agreed.

"But you're right. We should check on him. Maybe I should call him." I reached for my phone, but Brad stopped me.

"If he's ignoring the rest of us, he won't answer you either. That's why we're gonna pay him a visit. Two birds, one stone. And once you get the all-clear and we know Jake's okay, we'll see where we land and finish up for the night. I'm tired of sitting behind a desk."

"Really? Because I'm just tired."

"Me too."

TWELVE

"Why haven't they brought in Axel yet?" I asked while I filled out the intake sheet for the emergency room. "We made that request three hours ago. By now, patrol should have put him in a box."

Brad chuckled. "It's cute how you think he'd cooperate."

"He called us." Exasperated, I handed the clipboard back to the nurse. She read the form, eyeing the badge hanging from my neck and the one Brad had placed on the desk while I filled out the form.

"That doesn't mean he's willing to play by our rules." Brad smiled at the woman. "Can you do me a favor? Manny Voletek was admitted sometime last night. Where would I find him?"

"One second." She called to someone off to the side to find a room where they could check my neck. "Voletek." She turned her attention back to the keyboard. "Room 234."

"How's he doing?" I asked.

"They've ordered additional tests. But he's stable."

"Do you know what happened?"

The woman shook her head just as the door buzzed open and Emma stepped out.

"Liv, are you all right?" She narrowed her eyes at my partner as she made her way toward me. "What did I tell you about keeping an eye on her, Bradley?"

Brad sighed. "I did, which is why I brought her here. Her scar's been bugging her all day. I'm no doctor, but it doesn't look right."

Emma mumbled to herself as she moved behind me and swept my ponytail out of the way. "I'll get her situated in four. Dr. Krause should have a couple of minutes to take a look." Emma led me back through the door she'd come from, glancing behind her to make sure Brad was with us. "When did Liv first start showing symptoms?"

"Em," I said, "shouldn't you be asking me these things?"

"I would, but I know you never pay attention to stuff like this."

"I do too."

"Okay, smartass. When did it first start bothering you?"

"When I woke up."

"When Sean woke her up," Brad corrected.

Emma turned, her jaw dropping in shock. "Okay. Why exactly did Bradley get all the dirty details and I know nothing about this?"

"There are no dirty details," I said.

She forced me into the room and onto the bed. She looked for the thermometer and blood pressure cuff. After taking my vitals, she stepped back. "Tell me everything. How was he? He looks like he'd be good."

"It never progressed that far, which is probably why he's taking her out again tonight," Brad said.

I glared at my partner. "Weren't you worried about Jake and his dad? Shouldn't you go check on them?"

"Voletek?" Emma asked, and I nodded. "He's had quite the night."

"How's Manny doing?" Brad asked. "We heard he collapsed."

"The doctors have run a million blood panels. They wanted to rule out the usual offenders. But everything came back negative. Jake insisted we look for other causes, which led to drug testing. It looks like someone roofied his father."

"Shit." Brad looked torn.

"Go." I jerked my head toward the door, regretting it. "I'll meet you up there."

Brad nodded and disappeared.

"That's one way to clear a room." Emma crossed her

arms over her chest. "Now tell me about last night. What happened? Did you slide down his pole?"

"Ugh. What is wrong with you?"

"Nothing." She grinned evilly. "I've been saving up the firefighter references. Did you at least see his hose?"

I held up my hands. "Stop, just stop."

"Okay, Liv." Emma turned serious. "I'm sorry. No more jokes. I promise. What happened? Are you okay? Do I need to kick his ass? He's in the cafeteria, so I can totally go do that as soon as you tell me what happened."

"Nothing happened. I fell asleep watching a movie. When the precinct called, Sean woke me up."

"And?"

So I told her exactly what happened while we waited for the doctor to arrive.

Emma had that look, like she was deep in thought. "What about his persistence when he woke you up? Do you think he would have stopped without the outside interruption?"

"Yeah."

"Okay. Good. Because no means no."

I rolled my eyes. "Yes, Em. I know that. But we haven't really connected over anything yet. There's no spark." My thoughts drifted to Axel and his aptly named club.

"That's why you didn't like him pawing at you. I can't believe you called him Brad. At least you weren't in the throes when you did it. That would have been worse."

"I only did it because Brad's usually the one waking me up. But he's never that annoying about it."

"Really?"

"Not like that. You know I was sleeping on his couch for a while, so it made sense, especially after our last undercover assignment."

Emma held up her hands. "Whatever you say. But you should give Sean a chance. Dino said he's a good guy. I have no reason to doubt it."

"Em—"

"It's just something to think about, but I get it. You don't want to sleep with him if he's screwing around with other people, and you don't think you've been dating long enough to have the 'where do we stand' talk."

"I'm not even sure where I stand."

Dr. Krause knocked on the door before entering. Emma filled her in on the situation, and she checked the scar tissue, finding the irritated flesh localized to my neck. She asked me to take off my shirt so she could see the rest of the scar, which ran to my shoulder, but the inflammation was isolated to the exposed side of my neck and everything above my collar. "It's not infected," she said. "It might get that way if you keep scratching, though. You have a bad case of contact dermatitis. Have you changed shampoos or detergents recently?"

"No."

"Liv's seeing someone new," Emma volunteered.

"Well, you're clearly allergic to something." The doctor exhaled. "Stay away from perfumes and dyes. Get some anti-itch cream. If the itching gets too intense, try some oral anti-itch allergy medicine. That should help, along with cool, damp compresses. I'll write you a prescription, but see if the over-the-counter stuff helps first. It usually does. But most importantly, you need to figure out what caused this and avoid it. And stop scratching."

"I know the protocol," Emma volunteered. "It's weird it's so localized. I figured it would have been more widespread if it was a detergent or soap issue."

"That area might be more susceptible than other parts. The faster you figure out what triggered it and remove it, the better off you'll be, Detective."

"Thanks, Doc." I buttoned my shirt and slid off the table. "I'm sorry to have wasted your time. It was my partner's idea."

"Better safe than sorry."

Now that I was free to go, I headed for the elevator. Emma followed beside me. "What are you going to do about tonight?" she asked.

"I guess I'll have the talk with Sean."

"Hey," Emma stopped me before I could push the button, "I say he deserves one more shot, but if you're not into him, then you're not into him. Just be honest with yourself, okay? And let me know how dinner goes."

"I will."

"Good. Pomme de Terre is supposed to be amazing. I hate that I'm going to miss it, but I'm glad you're getting my reservation instead of some fashion model or heiress." She smiled. "Plus, Sean can't be all bad. Dino loves him, and I love Dino."

"Does he know that?"

"I told him this morning. It was so great. He's so great." Her eyes twinkled. "I just want you to have that too. But if you give Sean a fair shake, and he's not the guy, then he's not the guy."

"I don't know. He could be. Maybe. He doesn't mind my hours or my job, which is refreshing. But I barely know him. And we don't agree on movies."

"You need to speak up. He's not a mark you need to work for some undercover assignment. You need to be yourself." She smiled and bumped against me. "You could always give Jake a second look. I'm telling you he's got that sexy, cocky thing going for him. If I didn't have Dino, I would have spent all day flirting with him. In fact, I may have, just don't tell Dino."

"He's a cop, Em."

"So are you."

"His dad's in the hospital."

"But he's going to be okay."

I pressed the elevator button, surprised when the doors opened. A group of people stepped out. I waited at the side for them to vacate before entering. "Have you told Mom the news?"

"That Jake's dad is going to be okay?"

"No. That you love Dino."

"I called her on my break. She's having a big family gathering next Sunday so he can meet everyone."

"She's probably halfway through planning the wedding by now."

Emma smiled. "I'm game if Dino is."

"Em," I said, shocked.

"Kidding. Maybe. It depends on how he pops the question."

Alone in the elevator, I scratched the side of my neck.

Maybe this was psychosomatic. A reaction to stress or crazy people. Today, I'd dealt with more than my share. When the doors opened, I stopped scratching and went in search of Voletek and my partner.

A patrol officer stood in the hallway outside Manny Voletek's room. Brad and Jake spoke to him in hushed tones that weren't nearly as quiet as they should have been.

I approached, offering Jake a bittersweet smile. "Hey, stranger. How's your dad?" I peered into the room, finding the older Voletek sitting on the bed, fully dressed, with his arms crossed over his chest while he watched the news.

"He's pissed. So am I. After shift, he and a few other cops who work for the commissioner went out for drinks. Every drink was laced. Fernandez passed out behind the wheel. Luckily, he never made it out of the parking lot, so the damage was kept to a minimum. The other two lieutenants who got dosed made it home just fine, but they woke up with terrible hangovers. Dad got the worst of it. He was the last to leave. Unlike his pals, he probably ingested more than most. He never stops at one or two."

"But he's okay?"

"Yeah. The doctors were worried there could be complications due to his age, but he's fine. However, Commissioner Cross is not."

"Was he drugged too?"

"No," Jake exhaled, "but he's afraid this could have been a coordinated attack on the top brass. Most likely, it was some pissed off restaurant employee who hates the police. But we have to make sure. The commissioner wants the situation resolved before word gets out. He put me in charge of it. I've been coordinating everything from here, fielding calls, sending out reports, dispatching units to the restaurant to have the employees questioned. I haven't had time for much else." As if to prove his point, Jake's phone buzzed. He pulled it out of his pocket, read the message, and typed a response.

"We're just glad everyone's okay," Brad said.

"Me too." Jake eyed me. "How are you doing, princess? Brad said he left you in the ER to get examined."

I pointed my finger in his face. "I'm letting that slide,

but only this once. And I'm okay. It's an allergic reaction to something."

Brad moved closer, examining the angry red scar. "Do they know to what?"

"It could be anything. I have to pick up some ointment. That should take care of it."

"All right, man." Brad held his hand out to Jake and pulled him into a one-armed hug. "You need anything, call me. You got food and whatever?"

"Yeah, we're good. Emma's been great about taking care of us." Jake smiled at me. "Your friend's the best. I'm glad she was here. She made things easier. She handled Dad while I handled everything else."

"That's Emma."

"In case I don't get a chance, thank her for me. I really appreciate everything she did. My dad did too, even if he's too grouchy to show it."

"Will do." I clapped him on the shoulder. "Seriously, Jake, we're here if you need us."

THIRTEEN

"Do you need me to call with a rescue?" Brad asked from behind the door while I changed in the locker room.

"It should be fine." I stepped into my shoes and sat down to fasten the straps. "I need you to zip me up."

Brad pushed the door open and sat on the bench beside me. He swept my hair to the other side, leaving the red, itchy welts exposed to the air. After zipping my dress, he secured the hook at the top. "He doesn't deserve you."

I turned to look at my partner. "Jealous?"

"Not even a little bit."

"That hurts, Fennel." I slapped a palm over my chest. "You're breaking my heart."

"Shut up." He gave my good shoulder a playful shove.

"What did you say to him while I was downstairs?"

"Nothing Vince wouldn't have said."

"Oh god." I cringed. "That's the last time I leave you alone with anyone I'm seeing." Another horrifying thought popped into my head. There was a good chance Sean would be invited to my parents' house on Sunday. The last thing I wanted was to introduce him to my dad or deal with the fallout if I called things off.

"I wasn't that bad. Mostly, I explained to him how important your job is to you, which also explains how I know you keep hair ties on the shampoo bottle and fall asleep during movies you find boring. We're family, Liv. You have my back, and I have yours. I made that clear. I also made it clear that he better not hurt you. That was it."

"Okay."

Brad watched as I applied my makeup. "Give me an honest answer. Why did you agree to dinner? When we spoke about your date last night, you were ready to kick him to the curb. Then he blindsides you at work, and you agree to give him another chance. Why? Do you actually like this guy?"

"I don't know. We're feeling each other out." I pointed the mascara brush at him. "Don't make a joke. Emma already made enough of them."

"I wouldn't dare, especially since there can't be that much feeling going on with you being allergic to him."

"I am not."

"Your neck says otherwise."

I tucked everything inside my bag, made sure I had the anti-itch cream in case the stress made it flare up, and took a deep breath. "How do you do it?"

"What?"

"Date?"

"It's easy. You go out and have fun. If you're not having fun, you're not doing it right."

"If it's that easy, why are you taking a sabbatical from it?"

My partner laughed. "You know I'm working on myself because I want something a little more serious."

"You don't think I'm looking for something serious?"

"Are you?" His eyes held a knowing look. "Because it seems like you're not looking for much of anything with Sean."

I hadn't given it much thought. Most days, I was too focused on work, which made putting everything else on the backburner a lot easier. My mother and Emma had been the driving forces, convincing me I needed to get out there, that I was missing out. But I liked the way things were. I didn't want to be accountable to anyone else. "It would take the right person. Sean's not it."

"There you go."

I sighed. "What is wrong with me?"

"Nothing. You're amazing. You deserve amazing." Brad

grabbed my duffel and held the locker room door for me. "Where did we land on the whole fake emergency check-in call?"

"I can manage on my own."

"All right." He walked me to my car. "Text if you change your mind." He gave me a crooked smile. "By the way, you look nice."

"Thanks."

Brad headed for his car. "Hopefully, the next time I see you, you won't look like a red, splotchy puffer fish. But if you do, I'll know why."

Rolling my eyes, I got behind the wheel. The clock on the dash said 8:43. At least I'd arrive on time.

When I got there, the host greeted me in his suit and tails. It's a good thing I'd taken the time to make myself presentable. Since it was too early to be seated, he pointed me to the bar, where Sean was waiting.

"You're early," I said, sliding onto the stool beside him.

He turned, confused to see me. "I thought you'd still be at work."

"We're nearing that twenty-four hour mark. Lt. Winston hates that. Truthfully, he hates anything that involves OT pay, but we've been short-staffed."

Sean grinned, eyeing me. "You look sexy."

I resisted the urge to fidget. "You said this place had a dress code. Thanks for the heads-up."

"No problem." He wore a suit and tie. The outline of his biceps creased the material, reminding me of the bodyguards who accompanied Spark's more affluent and paranoid members. He gestured to the bartender. "Wine?" he asked me.

I eyed the low ball beside his right hand. "What are you drinking?"

"Whiskey. Would you like some?"

"I don't do grains, unless I'm working undercover and have no other choice."

"You're missing out." He took another sip and ordered a white wine for me. "Did you catch a killer today?"

"Not yet. We have a suspect. But we have a long way to go before we close the case." I thanked the bartender and took the offered glass. "How was work?"

"Fine, I guess. But it's not nearly as exciting as the firehouse. We almost had an oven fire today, but one of the cooks noticed the foil was too close to the burner before it ignited. That's a good thing, but I may have been hoping for a tiny bit of action." He eyed the side of my neck. "What happened there?"

"Contact dermatitis." I left out the part about my trip to the ER, so I could avoid him asking why I didn't stop by to say hi. "It popped up this morning. I'm not sure what triggered it." I sipped my wine, feeling the awkwardness between us.

After forty-five seconds of silence, which would have made even the most hardened criminal crack under the pressure, Sean blurted out, "Why didn't you tell me you don't like black and white movies? I shouldn't have to find this stuff out from your partner."

"You were excited for me to watch it, so I thought I'd give it another try."

"Say something next time. I'm sure we could have found something else we would have agreed on." He gave me a challenging look. "What's your favorite genre? Rom-com? Drama? Horror?"

"It depends. Em always records the rom-coms on TV and makes me watch them with her." I stopped before I mentioned how Brad and I mocked them. "Most of the time, if I'm picking, I do fun action movies or comedies. Life's too hard for a lot of serious films."

"What about superhero flicks?"

"That's what I mean by fun action or things like *Die Hard* or *Lethal Weapon*."

"In other words, cop movies."

"Fun cop movies. Nothing too serious. I also watch more animated movies than any adult should ever admit."

"Me too." He smiled. "See, we have things in common."

I took another sip of wine and glanced at the time. It'd be best to get this over with before we were seated at our table. "Are you seeing anyone else?"

His brow furrowed. "Why would you ask me that?"

"Answer the question."

He frowned. "No."

"When's the last time you had a romantic guest at your place?"

"Romantic guest?" He snorted. "I'd think for a detective you'd be better with the interrogation questions."

"I'm out of practice. I haven't done a lot of dating in recent years. Prior to this year, I'd been working undercover assignments. The only people I was involved with were necessary aspects of the case."

"I haven't seen anyone since the accident. That was almost a year ago. It's taken time to get everything functioning again. I didn't want to add insult to injury or end up with a Nightingale who'd drop me once I was healed."

"Then whose hair tie did you bring me this afternoon?" I placed it on the bar.

"Are you saying that isn't yours?"

"It's not."

"How can you tell?"

"Mine don't have these little metal pieces." I fished one of mine out of my bag. "See?"

Sean picked up the hair tie. "Good to know." He put it back on the bar and gestured to the bartender for another round. "It must belong to the physical therapist."

"You do PT at your apartment?"

"Sometimes. The fire department provided a therapist to help at home."

"And you had PT yesterday," I said.

"Yeah."

"That would explain it." I wondered how much therapy she'd given him, and to think, I'd fallen asleep on that couch.

Sean eyed me. "Why don't you look like you believe me?"

"I'm a cop. We don't believe anyone. But I have no reason to doubt you." Despite my words, I didn't trust him. His behavior had thrown up a lot of red flags, but I was overly sensitive to such things. I saw the worst humanity had to offer, which meant I often assumed the worst too. "Now the only mystery left to solve is what caused this damn rash."

A hostess came by to tell us our table wasn't ready yet.

While Sean and I ran through his list of personal care items, soaps, and detergents, I spotted a familiar face heading toward the bar. *Of all the gin joints,* I thought.

Axel Kincaid smirked as he sidled up to the bar, his eyes on me. Once he was close enough, he let his gaze travel, taking in my slinky dress. The smirk turned into a smile, and he squeezed between Sean and the person on the stool beside him.

"Mr. Kincaid," the bartender said, snapping to attention the moment he spotted Axel, "what can I get for you, sir?"

"A martini, ice cold and very dirty." He eyed my wine glass. "And pour the lady some of our best champagne."

"We only sell it by the bottle."

"Don't you think I know that?" Axel asked.

"Yes. Right away, sir."

"I don't want it," I said before the bartender could grab it off the shelf. "Do you think I'd let you buy me a drink after today? I have half a mind to drag your ass in right now. Officers were supposed to bring you in. Why didn't they?"

Sean turned to see who I was talking to.

"I wasn't buying you a drink, Liv. I was buying you the bottle." Kincaid picked up his martini. "I'll have them gift wrap it if you prefer." He noticed Sean. "The two of you could share." He cocked his head to the side, studying my dining companion. "Excuse my manners." He put his drink down and held out his hand. "Axel Kincaid."

"Sean Grammar, her date."

"Date?" Axel looked shocked. His piercing blue eyes stared into mine. "I didn't know you were seeing someone. Why didn't you tell me, Liv?"

"It's none of your business." It was bad enough Sean volunteered his name. "Why have you been avoiding my calls?" I asked. "We need to talk."

"About this? I agree. We should talk about this." Axel was enjoying himself. "Is she this demanding with you?" he asked Sean before looking back at me.

"I don't know who you are—" Sean began, but Axel cut

him off.

"Why do you think I came here, Liv? I'm here for you. You know I prefer to do these things in person instead of over the phone. And I sure as hell don't need some errand boys with badges pestering me at home or at the club."

"When I came to see you, you weren't there. You didn't leave me much choice."

"It was six a.m. Of course, I wasn't there."

"You had all damn day to drop by. Where have you been hiding?"

"Hiding's not my style. But you know that." Axel held my gaze. "I had to call a few friends to get them to call off the dogs you sent. Threatening harassment lawsuits usually work, but you might end up taking some flak for that tomorrow. For that, I do apologize. But you should have known better. I told you I'd be in touch."

I narrowed my eyes. "How did you know I'd be here?"

"A little bird."

"Stalking's a crime," I retorted.

"Then I'll let you put me in handcuffs. You always enjoy doing that." Axel turned his attention back to Sean. "Has she used her cuffs on you yet? You wouldn't know it by looking at her, but those metal bracelets get her so hot and bothered. Just mentioning them makes her blush."

"You just want to give me a reason," I said.

Axel smiled. "I'll give you every reason."

Sean's fists clenched, like he wanted to knock out Axel's teeth. Instead, he turned toward me. "Who is this guy?"

"Club owner, entrepreneur, very special friend to law enforcement," Axel murmured, swirling the olive around his martini glass.

"He's a car thief," I said.

"Reformed," Axel corrected.

"So you arrested him." Sean looked from me to Axel and back again.

"Yes."

"But it didn't stick." Axel leaned over the bar and grabbed a bowl of mixed nuts.

Sean focused on me. "We should go."

"Unfortunately, I can't." I ignored Axel, who leaned

against the bar with a Cheshire cat grin, enjoying every second like a bored housewife would a particularly trashy reality show. "Mr. Kincaid possesses information relevant to one of my cases. We sent officers to bring him in for questioning, but that didn't pan out like it was supposed to."

"I was far too busy today. I had several pressing business matters to attend to," Axel said. "George was supposed to provide you with proof of my alibi when you decided to drop by to see me. Didn't you receive it?"

"Shut up." I shot a sharp look in Axel's direction before focusing on my date. "I'm sorry, Sean. Can we try this again another night?"

He glanced at Axel before turning back to me. "Maybe you should wait to call me until this case is resolved. I'm not sure what this is, but it doesn't seem over." Before I could say anything else, Sean tossed some cash on top of the bar. "Take care of yourself, Liv."

I watched him walk away, unsure if I was relieved or hurt.

Axel scooted closer. "I would have offered to let him keep the table and comp his dinner, but this felt like a first date to me. If he was really someone important to you, he should have decked me."

"Find me a back alley with no surveillance, and I'd be happy to punch you in the face." I turned to see a glass of champagne waiting beside the bowl of mixed nuts.

"Peace offering." Axel grabbed a halved walnut. "The waitstaff is setting up a private dining area for us. Once we're settled, you can ask your questions."

"How did you know I was here?"

"Anxious, aren't we?"

"Axel," I growled.

"Your reservation."

"It was in a friend's name. Try again."

"Reservation got changed. Whoever did so, put it in your name."

"How would you even know that?"

"You know I own property all over the city, including this restaurant. Let me treat you to dinner, and we'll talk privately."

FOURTEEN

Axel pointed to the grilled salmon sitting atop a bed of greens on my plate. "It's better hot." He sliced through his filet mignon and held the fork toward me. "Unless you changed your mind. Do you want to trade?"

"No."

He popped the steak into his mouth and chewed. After he swallowed, he wiped his mouth. "It's not poisoned. But I can have the server bring you something else. Anything else. Do you want takeout from another restaurant? I'll send someone to pick it up."

"Why won't you answer my questions?"

He sighed and put his fork down. "It's dinner, Liv. It's not a bribe. Neither is the champagne."

"Didn't you call me early this morning and ask for a favor?" I wanted to get him back to the matter at hand. Ever since he appeared, I'd lost my appetite, even if my stomach hadn't quite gotten on board with my brain and instincts. "You told me Margaret Tenzin was murdered. How did you know that?"

He picked up his fork again. "Tit for tat?"

"I'm not in the mood for games."

"In that case, it's a good thing I scared off your date. He looked like a player."

I glared at him again and reached for my phone. "I could charge you with obstruction. Brad was there when you called. Even your pal, Remington Chambers, mentioned your name a few times. I have grounds, which is why officers came to pay you a visit."

"I told you I'd be in touch." He stared daggers at me. "Why do you always resort to empty threats? Is that what they teach at the academy?"

"You said you'd answer my questions."

"I said we'd have a discussion over dinner. You aren't eating. Unless you do, this doesn't count as dinner."

"You called me about this. You wanted answers, which I can't give you until I know what happened last night. Why aren't you helping me figure this out?"

He glanced at the closed door. No one was entering the small banquet hall. Besides the square table, chairs, and a separate stand which held the champagne and a water pitcher, the rest of the room was empty. "I don't know what happened, Liv. All I know is Maggie was stabbed and thrown from the balcony. I have no idea who did it or why, but I'm sure the perpetrator was a guest. And I'm convinced it wasn't Remington Chambers."

"Were you at the hotel?"

"No."

"Do you own the building or have surveillance devices inside the hotel?"

"No."

"Were you monitoring the party?"

He sliced another piece of steak and took a bite, nudging his chin toward my plate.

I picked up my fork and stabbed at the salad, popping a bite into my mouth without thinking. My mind was on work and nothing else. Axel smiled, pleased, which made me realize my mistake. But he'd been right. The food was exceptional. And my stomach insisted on another piece. "What about," I held my hand in front of my mouth while I spoke, ignoring my mother's nagging in the back of my head reminding me of proper dining etiquette, "neighboring buildings?"

"What about them?" Axel reached for his glass.

Bingo. "Property information is public record. Save us both some time."

"I don't own any of the real estate on that block."

"Then answer the damn question. How do you know what happened to Maggie?"

"I can't tell you."

"You damn well can. And you better."

"It won't help your investigation."

"I think Chambers told you." I watched Axel, who focused on slicing another piece of steak. "Why do you believe him? He's a liar."

"He's telling the truth. He didn't kill her."

"How do you know?" A million different scenarios ran through my mind, all illegal, all incriminating for Chambers or Axel. "You'd be implicated in something. That's why you won't talk." I blinked, thinking. "What if I promise to keep it between us? I've kept your other secret."

"You're a detective, Liv. First and foremost. Every time we see each other, you remind me of it." He nodded toward my purse. "And you resort to empty threats and promises of tightened handcuffs, so forgive me if I don't believe you, especially after you spent six months lying to me."

"Why did you call me?" I shoveled more salmon into my mouth. "Wait a minute. How did you know I was working this case? And for that matter, I still don't buy that you knew I was at this restaurant because of the reservation." I stopped eating, hoping he hadn't lied about the poison. "Are you keeping tabs on me?" I pushed away from the table, unsure if I should fight or flee.

Axel tossed his napkin beside his plate and stood, possibly to bar my escape. "It's not like that."

"A psycho stalked me. He broke into my apartment and hid under my bed. And now I'm wondering if you're doing the same thing." I reached into my purse and pressed the speed dial to call Brad.

Axel held up his palms. "Don't flatter yourself. I don't have the time or energy to do something like that. Are you sure I'd even fit under your bed? Maybe you should invite me over, and we can find out."

I stepped backward, glad for the empty space. "How do you know the things you do?"

He looked torn. We'd just spent the last fifteen minutes arguing over this point, and he'd refused to budge. But now, with me halfway to the door, it looked like the unflappable club owner might finally give me an answer. "Fox was in the area. He saw Maggie get stabbed and tossed over the railing. He also saw you arrive at the hotel. That's how I knew."

"Did he see who stabbed her?"

"He was too far away."

"Where exactly was he?"

"I don't know."

I didn't believe that, but pushing wouldn't make him answer. "In that case, I have to speak to Fox."

"You can't."

"Why not?"

Axel retook his seat and placed the napkin back on his lap. "He's currently out of the country on business. He left early this morning."

"That's convenient." Fox was just as dangerous and deadly as his boss. He handled the stickier situations so Axel wouldn't get his hands dirty. And now that he fled the country, I'd have to add his name to the suspect list.

"He didn't do it either, Liv."

"According to you, no one did."

"Someone did," he hissed. "But it's not my job to figure out who. That's your job. And once you have an answer, I'd like to hear it."

"Why? What does any of this have to do with you?"

"Chambers arranged this weekend getaway on my behalf. He's one of my accountants. He handles these things for me. That makes this my responsibility. I paid the people who worked the party. It's like I hired them, indirectly. I should have been able to keep them safe. But a guest broke the rules. And you know I don't tolerate that."

Axel knew a lot more than he let on. He'd also spent a great deal of time pushing my buttons to distract me from the obvious. And it had worked. Those six months I spent working for him had given him more insight into me than I had into him. And I didn't like it.

I returned to my seat and rubbed my neck. "On the phone, you said Maggie worked a lot of these types of events. That it was the same crowd, over and over. You thought she saw or heard something that put a target on her back. What could that be?"

"Anything really." He finished his steak and sipped his drink. "Everyone has skeletons in the closet."

"Did you ever meet Maggie?"

He nodded. "She's like a lot of the dancers who work for me. They love the art, the physicality, being seen. I'm guessing there's a darker psychology to it, but I don't exploit them. You can attest to that."

"Putting scantily clad women in cages for hours at a time screams exploitation."

"Don't twist it. They wanted that job. They could have said no at any time." His ice blue eyes sent a shiver through me. "You could have said no. It's not a condition of the server employee contract."

"But Maggie wasn't a Spark employee. She wasn't allowed inside your club."

"She didn't pass the background checks," Axel said. "She had an arrest record. Minor things. I'm sure you've already pulled her jacket. You know my standards. So I used her for outside events instead."

"How many events?"

"At least six in the same number of months. It might be more. I lose track. But she never reported a problem. She never said anything. She did her job and collected her paycheck."

"Why was this time different?"

"Was it?"

"Chambers spoke to her hours before, when they were setting up. He upset her. I have witnesses. Do you know what their disagreement was about? I heard rumors he might have asked her not to show up last night."

"That's the first I'm hearing of it." Axel held my gaze. He didn't blink. He didn't fidget. But he knew. I knew he did.

"Who was she seeing?" I asked.

"Seeing?"

"As in dating."

"I don't know. What does that have to do with this? Do you think her boyfriend got jealous, crashed the party, and killed her?"

"Her boyfriend asked Chambers to hire Maggie for this party, except he changed his mind once he realized his wife planned to go with him."

"I wasn't expecting that." He picked up his phone and tapped on the screen a few times. I thought he was going to bring up a guest list or provide a name. Instead, he tapped a few more times and put the phone face down on the table. "It looks like I may have been mistaken about everything."

"Mistaken?"

"I figured this had something to do with...other things."

"What things?"

"No need to concern yourself with it at this point, Detective." He looked relieved. "Another bottle of champagne?"

"No."

He looked at my barely touched glass. "Dessert, then?"

"What things?"

"Only if you say yes to dessert."

"Dammit. Tell me first."

"Fine, but I'm choosing the dessert."

"Axel," I warned.

He looked up from the menu. "This is the second time a female entertainer has been attacked at one of my events. I feared there could be a connection, but your theory suggests I'm wrong."

FIFTEEN

I thought getting Axel Kincaid to answer questions earlier in the evening was hard enough. Now it was damn near impossible. He sipped brandy and carefully sliced into a dark chocolate cherry galette.

"It's an almond flour crust. No grains. No dairy. I had the chef make this especially for you. So you have to try a piece." He slid it onto one of the dessert plates and pushed it across the table toward me.

"Tell me what happened, Axel." I nodded toward the plate. "If you do, I'll have a piece."

He laughed. "You don't understand how tit for tat works, do you? Getting to eat dessert benefits you. The answer to that question also benefits you. I'm not getting anything out of this deal."

"You're getting the joy of watching me eat the dessert you forced your chef to make."

"I know you better than that. You aren't that full of yourself. In fact, from what I know about you, Olive DeMarco, you don't think that highly of yourself at all. If you did, you wouldn't be in the business of putting the public's safety or others' safety ahead of your own." He tapped the side of his own neck before pointing at me. "Case in point."

I stopped scratching. "Fine. What do you propose?"

"For every question I answer, you answer a question. This combative interrogation thing we've been doing all night has become rather repetitive. Wouldn't you agree?"

I shrugged. "I can't talk about an open investigation. I've already said more than I should have."

"I won't ask about that." His eyes held a disconcerting look. "Ladies first."

"Why do you think Maggie was murdered?"

He glanced at the dessert, waiting for me to try it before he answered. At least I knew if I ended up roofied like Manny Voletek, my partner would find a way to make sure Axel went down for it. But I didn't think the food was tainted. Axel had already devoured half of his piece.

Once I popped the first delicious bite into my mouth, he answered. "Not long ago, another performer was attacked. She never reported it, and no matter how hard I tried, I never figured out who did it."

"Was she paid off?"

"No. It's my turn." He glanced at his phone. "How long have you been dating the firefighter?"

"How do you know he's a firefighter?"

"I googled him. And that means I get two more questions, as soon as you answer mine."

"A few weeks."

"Does Fennel know?"

"Yes. Now answer my question."

"I didn't pay her to keep silent. But she was afraid, so I gave her enough money to disappear."

"That makes you look guilty."

"I'm not." He offered me another piece of the galette, but I shook my head. "Why would you waste your time with someone who doesn't excite you?" he asked.

"What?"

"You heard me. You don't find your firefighter exciting. Why waste your time with him?"

"I'm not wasting my time. We were getting to know one another."

"He's a pussy."

"He runs into burning buildings. You need to rethink that."

"Ask your partner what he would have done if he'd been in Sean's shoes tonight." Axel snorted. "You deserve someone worthy. Someone who'll challenge you, respect you, and be willing to defend you. I'm not being chauvinistic. You're highly capable. That isn't up for debate. But walking away, that's what a pussy does. And that's what a fucking idiot does when you're dressed like that."

"I appreciate that he minded his own business."

"That's not it. You appreciated that he left you alone and backed off because you don't want to deal with him or his nonsense."

"Are you sure? I've put up with your shit all night." I paused. "And there you go pushing my buttons and distracting me again."

"I know where every button is, Liv." He smiled. "Every button."

I narrowed my eyes. "It's my turn. What's her name?"

"It isn't relevant."

"Unless it is."

"She left town. I don't know where she is or how to find her."

"The same man who attacked her may have killed Maggie, which means he'll do it again."

"I can't help you, even if I wanted to. She changed her name. She got a new identity and a new life. There's no way to track her down. I spent most of today trying."

"You're not a cop. I have resources you don't."

"That's doubtful, but even if you do, you won't be able to find her," Axel insisted.

"The only way would be if she was in WitSec."

"Or if she hired a good paper guy to take care of everything."

"What guy?"

"I don't know. But she had the means to hire the best. Whoever that would be."

"Give me her name."

"It was Isabel Vansan."

"Was that so hard?"

"You tell me. Is that why you were seeing the firefighter or why you were calling it off?"

I ignored that question. "Why are you convinced the

murderer's a party guest? Maggie wasn't attacked or killed at the party. So how do you know another hotel guest, staff member, or caterer didn't kill her?" My mind went back to the knife. It matched the ones from the party, which made me reconsider the staff. But that wouldn't explain how Maggie got access to Chambers' suite if he was gone.

"You make an excellent point." Axel cut another sliver of dessert and put it on my plate.

"That's not an answer."

"It's a waste of a question since you already know the answer."

"You thought Maggie's murder was part of a pattern. Do you still think that?"

"Let's just say I'm open to other possibilities now that you informed me of Maggie's complicated love life."

If I asked about Clayton Deek or his wife, Axel would know that was the man we suspected was carrying out the affair. I'd have to be clever about this. "How many guests are married?"

"Roughly a third, maybe more. Marriage isn't something that sticks, so the percentages are always in a state of flux."

"Will you give me the guest list from the night Isabel Vansan was attacked?"

"It'll be waiting for you when you get to work tomorrow."

"Axel." I hesitated, and he looked up.

"Hmm?"

"Do you personally know everyone who attended the rooftop party last night?"

"I'm familiar."

"Even the staff?"

"Not necessarily. We hire companies who contract out the work. Due to NDAs and other privacy issues, anyone who works one of my events has to be vetted, not always by me."

I described the man Maggie's father had seen speaking to his daughter on two separate occasions. Axel's expression gave nothing away. He might have been considering stock market fluctuations for all I knew. "Any idea who that could be?" I asked.

"You just described half of Spark's male membership." He sat back in his chair and sipped the last of the brandy. "How did you and the firefighter meet?"

"Blind date."

"Who set that up?"

"I already answered your question. You don't get another."

"No," he shook his head, "you asked five questions and got five answers. It's my turn now."

"A friend."

"Anyone I know?"

"No." While he considered his next question, I asked, "Why do you care so much?"

He looked perplexed for the first time tonight. "I'm not answering that. It's still my turn."

"Just answer one thing for me," I said, "and I'll tell you whatever you want."

"What?" He looked suspicious.

"How do you know Remington Chambers is innocent?"

"He wasn't in his room when Maggie was attacked."

"How do you know?"

He shook his head. "One thing. That's what you said." He considered how to phrase his next question. "Would you have preferred eating dinner with your firefighter?" I didn't answer, and Axel smiled. "That's what I thought."

SIXTEEN

Brad slid into the booth opposite me and eyed the carafe and three coffee mugs. "Should I ask? Is Sean still in the picture? Is he joining us?"

"No. Our dinner got canceled."

Brad picked up the menu and opened it. "Oh?" He peered at me over the top. "I guess that would explain why you don't look like an itchy lobster."

"I am not allergic to him."

Brad put the menu down and held up his palms. "Okay. Jeez. It was a joke." He poured a cup of coffee and topped mine off before reaching for the sugar packets and grabbing two raw sugars. "Why did he bail? Did he pick up another shift at the coffee shop?"

"I ran into Axel."

"No one notified me. Why aren't we at the precinct questioning him?" An evil grin came onto his face. "Tell me he's been in lockup all night."

"Not exactly. We had dinner and a conversation." I filled my partner in on everything Axel had said and promised the night before.

"Did he ever tell you how he knew you'd be at that restaurant?"

"He's sticking to the flimsy reservation story. I don't believe him, but I can't disprove it. It isn't relevant to the case anyway, so it doesn't matter."

The waitress appeared a few minutes later, putting

down three sets of plates. Brad eyed the steak and eggs. He winked at me and picked up his fork. "You knew we'd be in a rush this morning. Do you know if Axel ever sent over that other guest list for comparison?"

"The desk sergeant called to tell me I had an envelope waiting. That has to be it."

"He could have e-mailed you." Brad scooped some eggs into his mouth while I divided my fruit salad in half before taking two of the four pancakes off the third plate.

"Axel doesn't believe in unnecessary electronic trails." I intercepted Brad's fork with mine as he reached for a cube of cantaloupe off the other plate. "That's Emma's."

Brad redirected his fork to my plate and snagged a ball of honeydew. "Do we have time for her drama this morning?"

"No, but she didn't give me a choice. She wanted to see if the ointment helped and how things went with Sean last night." I pulled out the list I'd scribbled of all his personal care products and soaps. "Which reminds me, do you use any of these?" I slid the list over to him and cut off a portion of his steak while he crossed off the few products he and Sean had in common.

"Here." He handed it back, eyeing the pancakes on Emma's plate. "Are you sure she's meeting us for breakfast? Her food is getting cold."

"If she's not here in five minutes, you can have hers," I promised, leaving the list beside the unattended plate. "After Axel and I parted ways, I did some checking on Isabel Vansan. Background check came out clean. Up until a year ago, she held down a job and apartment. Nothing out of the ordinary, until the day she quit. A week later, she moved and didn't leave a forwarding address. We can't track her after that. I put in a call to our contacts at the Bureau, thinking they might be able to help, but I'm not counting on it."

"Did she work at Spark?"

"No. She worked for a party entertainment company."

"Escort service?" Brad grinned when the waitress returned with a plate of hashbrowns she'd forgotten.

"Here you go, sweetie," she said to him. "Anything else I

can get you?"

Brad pointed to the pancakes. "Can I trouble you for a short stack?"

"Those are paleo. Did you want regular buttermilk pancakes instead?"

"No, I'll have those."

The waitress nodded and disappeared.

"Pancakes and hashbrowns?" I raised an eyebrow. "I didn't think you'd want both."

"But they look so good."

"Well, in that case." I slid my plate closer and helped myself to some of his hashbrowns. "What were we saying?"

"You were about to tell me if Vansan worked for an escort service."

"No, it's a party entertainment company."

"What's the difference?"

"They don't provide dates, just party entertainment."

"Strippers?"

"Among other things."

"Like?"

"Clowns, magicians, acrobats, and animal trainers."

"Aerial silk performers?"

"Possibly, but the two didn't work at the same company. I didn't find any connection between Isabel Vansan and Maggie Tenzin, at least not when it comes to work history. According to Axel, Vansan was long gone before Maggie ever got hired to work one of his gigs."

"But the guest list remained the same."

"We don't know yet, but probably. Axel thought it was the same attacker. He says all the same people go to these events." I filled half my fork with eggs before adding hashbrowns to the end of the tines.

Brad glanced behind me. "You might want to hurry and eat those before you get lectured about the evils of fried foods."

I turned to see Emma rushing toward us. She smiled brightly, flushed and practically glowing. Whether that was from morning yoga or her night with Dino was anyone's guess. She slid into the booth and brushed her hair out of her face. "I didn't think I'd make it. Sorry I'm late." She checked the time. "We still have fifteen minutes."

"Maybe more. Brad just ordered pancakes," I said to distract her from the hashbrowns I had yet to consume.

"Well, they make them really good here." She grabbed her fork and took a bite. "So good." She placed a layer of fruit on top and picked up the list I'd left for her. "I see you and Sean talked. Any idea what caused that reaction?" She peered at my exposed neck.

"Brad and I ruled a few things out, but it could be anything."

"You had on short sleeves, so I don't think it's the detergent. Your arms would have gotten itchy. You kissed him, so it shouldn't be his lip balm." Her eyes narrowed as she scanned the rest of the list. "Is he a nuzzler?"

"He used Gunnie's technique to wake me up, so yeah."

Brad snorted, choking in the process.

Emma glanced at him, making sure he was able to breathe before turning her focus back to me. "It doesn't look like 'stache rash. The only times I've seen Sean, he's been clean-shaven. But he could have had some stubble which scratched the surface and let whatever irritant into your skin."

"I don't think so. I would have felt that."

"True." Emma's thoughts went somewhere I didn't want to follow, and she blushed. "Dino's growing a beard."

"Good for him."

She rolled her eyes and inhaled the rest of her breakfast. By the time she was done, Brad had stopped choking and his pancakes had arrived. She read the list again. "It must be this. It's one of those men's facial moisturizers." She read the name to Brad. "Have you ever used it?"

"No."

"Do you moisturize?" she asked.

He patted his cheeks. "Why? Do you think my skin looks dry or ashy?"

"Ugh."

"Am I getting wrinkles?" Annoying Emma was one of his favorite pastimes, and he smirked. "Actually, I've never used that. I always went with oil, but that's when I was in Afghanistan. It was so dry there, my skin would crack and bleed."

I cringed, giving him a sympathetic look. But he ducked his head and focused on his food. Even when he brought it up, he never wanted to discuss his time in the service.

Emma searched for the product on her phone. She read the label information. "I'd say that's probably the culprit. To be sure, you could schedule some patch testing to see if that's what caused the reaction. They could probably narrow it down to the offending ingredient or ingredients, but there are several common ones in here. Until you know for sure, ask Sean not to use that moisturizer. And wash up afterward."

"I don't think that'll be a problem."

"Why?" Emma asked. "Did last night's conversation not go well? You didn't call. I figured you'd call if—"

"We had to postpone. We're taking a break until work calms down," I said.

"Your decision?" Emma asked.

Brad finished eating and looked at me, waiting for my answer.

"I'm not sure who decided," I said.

Emma glanced at my partner and back at me. "We're going to talk about this later. But I'm gonna be late, and so are you." She gave me a hug. "Stay safe. You need me, you know where to find me."

"Ditto." After she left, I finished my breakfast with Brad's help. "Do you think Axel's right?" I asked. "Do you think whoever attacked Vansan killed Maggie Tenzin?"

"You said you were hoping for overlap." Brad gestured to the server for the check and pointed to our coffee cups. "Doesn't that mean you buy into his theory?"

"It's a possibility, but he's leaving a lot out."

"Like where Fox was or what he was doing in the area. And let's not forget how he knows Chambers is innocent but refuses to say, or how he helped our suspect evade us."

"Among other things."

While I paid the check, Brad popped the top on one of the to-go cups and added more sugar. Once the lid was secure, he fished out a tip. "I would have gotten breakfast. You didn't have to be so quick on the draw."

"No reason. It was my turn."

"Regardless, someone should be buying you breakfast this morning." He picked up the two cups while I put on my jacket. "Do you think Sean's a dog?"

"Because of my Gunnie comment?"

He gave me that annoying look of his. "I was referencing the hair tie."

"He said he's not seeing anyone else."

"You don't believe that. I sure as shit don't believe that. Did you call things off?"

"No, he did."

"I'm sorry, Liv."

"It's fine."

My partner grumbled but otherwise kept his thoughts to himself. Once we were outside, he handed me my cup. "I'll follow you."

"Why?"

"It wouldn't hurt to make sure you don't have a tail."

"Do you think Axel's stalking me?"

"For shits and giggles, absolutely."

As usual, I couldn't argue with my partner's logic, not when Axel showed up just in time to crash my dinner reservation, which had been delayed, now that I was thinking about it. I'd never been paranoid. It didn't help when working undercover. It'd make me unnecessarily jumpy, which could blow the entire operation and put my life at risk. So I was more of a go with the flow kind of girl, but now I wasn't so sure. Brad was always more cautious and less trusting. So I kept an eye on my mirrors, spotting his car every once in a while a good distance behind me. But I didn't see anyone else following me. But maybe he would.

SEVENTEEN

Most of the same guests who attended the weekend blowout at the Stonemore Hotel also attended the party the night Isabel Vansan was attacked. Only eight names were different, but I couldn't rule anyone out. I didn't know if the same person was responsible for both attacks. Even Axel wasn't sure. And since Vansan never filed a police report and Axel had been vague on the details, I had nothing to go on except the word of a supposedly reformed car thief.

"We need DNA evidence," I said.

"The autopsy report would be nice too." Brad looked up at me. "Are we making our Christmas list for Santa?"

"I wish." I passed him the records Axel had left. "Besides having most of the same guests, Axel hired the same caterers. I'll see if I can find anything that links James West to Isabel Vansan."

"You think Maggie's ex-boyfriend killed her?"

"I don't know. He's been violent and predatory before. It could be a pattern. His DNA must be on file. That's why we need DNA evidence from the crime scene. It'd be an easy comparison."

"Assuming there's anything to compare to," Brad said.

"The killer stabbed Maggie, picked her up, and tossed her off that balcony. He must have left some evidence behind. Fingerprints, hair, fibers, something that will link back to him."

"Most of the guests haven't checked out of the hotel yet. I'll head over there and ask a few more questions. Now that they've had some time, the situation should have sunk in. It'll be easier to establish alibis and whereabouts now that they fear becoming suspects. Can you stay on top of things here?"

"Yep. Go."

It was just after eight a.m. on Sunday. The vast majority of guests hadn't left the hotel. They didn't want to let a little thing like murder ruin their weekend plans, and we hadn't wanted to clear them out. It was better to keep them in one place and observe them.

Officers had been monitoring the situation, paying attention to everyone and everything. The hotel cameras were back to functioning normally. The management had been cooperating to help us find the killer. But we were only thirty-six hours into this mess with weeks of work ahead of us. Everything took time.

Since the ME hadn't finished evaluating the body yet, I couldn't read Maggie's autopsy report. Instead, I called the crime lab and asked if they'd received her personal effects or any samples that needed to be run. They had, which meant the ME hadn't knocked our case to the bottom.

"Did they find any prints on her body?" I asked.

"Several sets, mostly partials and smudges. She wore a shimmery body lotion, which made it more likely that anyone who touched her left a mark. The killer's prints should be more pronounced given the nature of the assault, but if he wore gloves, we won't get anything usable."

"What about prints found in the suite or on the knife?"

"No prints on the knife. We found several sets of prints in the room. The hotel staff provided their prints, and we've matched four different sets to members of the cleaning staff. We still have two unidentified sets to match."

"I'll need the staff's names." Hotel staff would have had a much easier time gaining access to Chambers' room, which meant any one of them could have killed Maggie. "What about Remington Chambers' prints?"

"His prints were also in the room, but that's to be

expected. We found them everywhere. On the doorknobs, the balcony, the bathroom, the remote, the dresser, the table, and the chairs."

"What about on the ice bucket?" I asked.

"The only prints on it matched the vic."

"No one else?"

"No, ma'am."

"What about the blood?"

"We're running the samples we collected now, but some of them aren't human. They're bovine."

"Someone slaughtered a cow in that suite?"

"More like a roast. The knife used to stab Margaret Tenzin in the back came from the caterer's carving station. That's probably how the bovine samples ended up in the mix."

"Thanks." I already knew where the knife originated, but the ice bucket was a surprise. More than likely, the killer had been at the party, pocketed the knife, and used it to stab Maggie in the back. I wondered why he stabbed her and threw her off the balcony. Wouldn't one or the other have sufficed? I scribbled down the note, figuring I'd ask the ME that question whenever he sent over the report.

Going downstairs to holding, I found Remington Chambers stretched out on a bench. Unlike the last time we'd spoken, he looked tired. He had his jacket folded beneath his head and appeared absolutely miserable.

"Are you here to let me out?" Chambers asked. "Your evidence is flimsy. You don't have enough on me. My lawyer says you have to let me go."

"Not yet. I have more questions."

"Notify him. I'm not talking to you until he gets here." He remained on the bench. "And I'd like some coffee. A sugar-free vanilla latte with two shots of espresso and eggs Benedict with Canadian bacon."

"I don't think that's on the menu over at central. But I can have you transferred, so you can find out."

"You can't starve me."

"Do you have any food allergies?"

"No."

I sighed, hoping giving in would get me what I wanted.

"You good with an English muffin, or would you prefer a freshly made biscuit instead?"

"A biscuit?"

"The breakfast place we use has fresh biscuits, if you prefer."

"Eggs Benedict has to be on an English muffin. If not, it's not eggs Benedict. But I'd settle for a fried egg sandwich with cheese on a biscuit, if they have sausage patties."

"Are you gonna answer my questions when we move you to a private room?" I asked.

"It depends."

"Sausage depends too."

"Are you sure you're a cop? You would have been great at the negotiating table. You'd make a killing with contracts."

Resisting the urge to ask him any questions relevant to the case for fear that it would bite me in the ass, I headed back the way I came. After notifying Almeada that his client was to be questioned again, I sent an officer to pick up breakfast. The wait gave me some time to review what little we knew.

"Detective DeMarco?"

I turned, finding an unfamiliar rookie standing across the bullpen. I raised my hand, like a child during attendance, and spotted Dick Tenzin just beyond the double doors. "Is someone here to see me?"

"Yes, ma'am. Is that okay? He said his name is Richard Tenzin."

"Send him in."

The rookie nodded, opened one of the doors, and held it for Maggie's father. After pointing the bereaved man toward my desk, the rookie vanished down the stairs. Mr. Tenzin peered around the bullpen, glancing at the various boards and photos as he made his way to me.

I grabbed Brad's chair and rolled it to the side of my desk. "Have a seat, sir."

"Thanks." He seemed anxious. "I wasn't sure if it was too early to show up. Ruth went to church. She said that's what we needed to do today, but I told her this is what I needed to do." He stared at the mess on my desk. "You look busy. Should I have called first? I can come back some other time."

"That won't be necessary. How are you holding up?"

"About as well as can be expected."

"Has anything else come to mind that might be helpful in figuring out who hurt your daughter?"

He scratched his forehead. "No. I'm sorry."

"It's okay." I gave him a tight smile. "Give me one second to grab a photo array for you to look through." Luckily, I'd already put everything together. After picking up the stack of ID photos of potential suspects, I returned to my desk and handed them to Mr. Tenzin. "Take your time. If you don't see him, that's okay too."

He flipped through the first few photos. "Have you made any progress?"

"We're investigating leads."

"Ruth wanted me to ask when we could make funeral arrangements. With it being the weekend, we haven't been able to get a straight answer out of anyone. The hospital said they couldn't release Maggie for burial."

"The ME will call you."

"When?" He tore his eyes from the photos, which he'd been flipping through like trading cards.

"Soon."

He stopped on one, squinting at it. "Ruth won't be happy with that answer."

"I'm sorry. But they have to be thorough. We can't afford mistakes. We want to make sure we can build a solid case against the person responsible."

"I understand. Any screwup could mean the son of a bitch who did this will get away with it."

"Unfortunately, yes."

He sucked in some air. "I think this is the guy she was seeing."

I took the photo of Clayton Deek from his outstretched hand. "Are you sure?"

"I think so."

"Do you recognize anyone else from those photos? You said you saw a few of her performances. Maybe someone else was in the crowd."

"This guy." He pulled out another photo. "Hang on. I'm sure I know him." He put it down on my desk and reached for his phone. After scrolling for ten minutes, he let out a triumphant grunt. "That's one of her friends from that pizza place where she used to work when she was in high school. For the life of me, I can't remember his name though."

"That's okay."

He held out his phone, showing me a group shot he had of Maggie and her coworkers. They were in aprons and covered in dough and flour. "See? There he is. A lot younger with all that baby fat around his jaw, but it's the same guy. Same eyes. Same nose. Same sloppy haircut."

"Can you send me a copy of that?"

"Sure." Mr. Tenzin forwarded it to my phone without hesitation. "Do you think he had something to do with this?"

"I don't know. Do you know if he and Maggie ever dated?"

"Not that I know of. They were just friends." Mr. Tenzin looked down at James West's more recent photo. "I didn't recognize him at the time, but he was at the bar the night she performed."

"Did they appear to be romantically involved?"

"No, she was drooling all over this guy." He tapped the photo of Clayton Deek. "My daughter wasn't one of those who falls in love every two seconds, but when she was interested in a guy, she broadcast it to the entire world."

"How so?"

"She'd look at him like he was the only person alive. She'd have to hold his hand or hang on his arm or whatever."

"And she wasn't like that with Mr. West?" I tapped the DJ's photo.

"No. They were friends. They'd tease each other, but she never looked at him with the same intensity."

"Did Mr. West seem jealous of Maggie's crush?" I pointed to the photo of Deek.

"I didn't notice."

"Did the three hang out together?"

"No. After her performance, her friend," he pointed to West's photo, "brought her some water. They talked for a few minutes, but it was just a passing thing. I thought he worked there. I didn't actually give it much thought. As soon as this guy," he pointed to Deek's photo, "appeared, Maggie ran off to see him. And it was just the two of them after that. I hung around for a little while, but there was no reason for me to stay." He swallowed, the vein at his temple jumping. "I should have stayed. I should have said something."

"Would you happen to have any of Maggie's old yearbooks or photo albums from when she was in high school?" Since she had worked at the same pizza joint with West, I wondered just how far back their history went.

"I can look around the house. I'm sure we have a yearbook somewhere. Ruth tossed a lot of Maggie's things after their last blowout fight, but a few things survived. Photos might be one of them." He flipped through the rest of the glossies before straightening the stack and putting them down on my desk. "May I ask why you think one of her high school friends is involved or what good a yearbook will do?"

"I can't say much at this time, but anyone who's seen your daughter or has spoken to her lately may be able to shed some light on who wanted to harm her."

Satisfied with the answer, Mr. Tenzin shook my hand. "I'll go home and look. I'll call you if I find something."

"Thank you." I waved an officer over and asked him to walk Mr. Tenzin out.

After he was gone, I found the copy of the flyer from Maggie's gig. *Amateur night – all acts welcome.* I pulled up West's employment history and checked the dates. He wasn't working at the club when Maggie performed. By then, he'd been blacklisted from most places. He had no reason to be there, unless he was performing or wanted to see Maggie. Could her murder be the result of a love triangle or quadrangle?

Picking up the phone, I called Brad and updated him on the situation. "We need to bring Clayton Deek in for questioning. Maggie's father IDed him as her mystery lover."

"Chambers said the same thing. That makes two. But you should know, Clayton and his wife checked out yesterday. They went home."

"Did anyone else leave?"

"Four other guests. I have the list of names. Among them was that loudmouth attorney, Francis Fertrie. I figured he'd stick around just to make a point that we couldn't bully him into complying with our requests."

"Surprise, surprise. All right. I'll call the Deeks and the rest of the guests who thought they should leave and see who's willing to come in to answer some questions."

"Have you made any breaks? Or are these calls just a hunch?" he asked.

"Neither. But we have questions that need answers, and I'm interested in seeing who's willing to play along."

EIGHTEEN

After placing calls to the potential suspects who left the hotel, I still didn't have anything concrete. They all gave noncommittal answers as to when they'd be available for a follow-up interview. Until we had more proof, Lt. Winston didn't want us to drag the city's elite into the precinct. I hated how the head of homicide worried more about politics and public image than solving crimes. But an order was an order, and I'd follow it. At least for now.

Remington Chambers ate the last bite of his breakfast sandwich and washed it down with another sip of his latte. "Are you sure this is sugar-free?"

"It is."

He gave the cup an odd look. "It better be."

I glanced at his attorney, but Mr. Almeada didn't meet my gaze. Something told me he thought his client was a pain in the ass. But I may have been projecting. "Before we move on, I want to ask you again, did you give anyone access to your suite?"

"No."

"You understand Maggie Tenzin was murdered in your hotel room. Evidence proves she was stabbed inside your room and thrown from your balcony," I said. "Unless you can give us an explanation, you look good for the murder."

"I didn't do it, and I can't explain it. I told you exactly what happened."

"Did you take a knife from the party back to your

room?"

"No." Chambers practically laughed. "Is that how she was killed?"

"We found the knife with her blood on the floor of your suite, partially concealed beneath your bed."

"I never slept in that bed. I barely even went inside that room."

"Are you sure?" I showed him a photo the crime scene techs had taken. "We found your fingerprints all over the place."

"My client reserved that room. Of course, his prints were everywhere," Almeada interrupted.

Chambers pointed at him. "Exactly." He reached for the photo, moving it closer to see better. He looked intrigued and a little disgusted after he noticed the bloodstains. He pushed the photo away. "I wasn't there when this happened. When I left for the gym, the room was pristine. Nothing was out of place. I'm guessing someone broke in. I'm being framed."

"That's a bit dramatic," I said.

Almeada gave me a look. "You insist the location makes my client a suspect. Therefore, this could be an attempt by the guilty party to place the blame on him."

"Fine, I'll bite. Mr. Chambers, did anyone know you planned to leave the rooftop party early?"

"No."

"Did you mention that you wanted to work out after the party?"

"I think so. I'm not sure. I exercise regularly. Anyone who knows me knows that."

"How many of the party guests know you that well?"

Chambers exhaled. "All of them."

"Because you've hosted so many charity functions?"

"No."

"Then how?"

"You know how. Mr. Kincaid fucking told you. This was one of Spark's private events. I know everyone from the club, and they know me."

"Are you a member?"

"Yes."

"Not an employee?"

"Mr. Kincaid doesn't issue me W-2s or 1099s. I'm an accountant. I have done work for him before but only in that regard. He does not employ me. If anything, I guess you could say he's my client." Chambers rocked in his chair. "What does this have to do with anything?"

"You hosted the party at Axel's request."

"I volunteer. There's nothing wrong with that. I enjoy my time at the club and want to help make it great."

That was the biggest load of bull I'd ever heard, but I didn't argue. "How long have you been assisting with these private events?"

"A while."

"A ballpark figure would help."

"I don't know. Eighteen months."

"What can you tell me about Isabel Vansan?"

Chambers froze, his gaze dragging across the table and up my body until he met my eyes. "Who?"

"You're a terrible liar. I hope you don't play poker."

"I don't know who that is," Chambers insisted.

"She was a performer, often hired to work these private functions, until something happened."

"That may have been before my time."

"It wasn't."

"I hire a lot of people to work these parties. So many people come and go. I may have met her, but I don't remember her name."

We both knew that wasn't true. "She was attacked at a party after her performance. After that, she quit her job and fled the city. Most of the people who attended that event were also at the hotel Friday night, including you. Does any of this ring a bell?"

"Are you accusing my client of something else?" Almeada asked.

"Do you know who hurt her, Mr. Chambers?" I asked.

"No."

"It'd be in your best interest to tell me what you know." But Chambers wouldn't budge. "Do you have any idea why someone would want to hurt Isabel Vansan?"

"Again, I don't know who that is, so I can't even wager a

guess."

"Fine. Do you know why someone would want to harm Margaret Tenzin inside your hotel suite?"

"How would I know?" Chambers asked.

"That's not what you said when we spoke downstairs."

Chambers glared at me. "That was a guess. I don't know for certain, but more than likely, some intoxicated idiot did something terrible. Maggie was a flirt. Paired with the dress she wore and her performance, I can see why a guy would feel led on. Add to that the late hour, too much liquor, and plenty of recreational substances, and rational thought went out the window."

"Do you think that's funny because her attacker threw her off the balcony?"

"No. I didn't mean it like that. I just meant that things got out of hand. Maggie probably tried to put the brakes on or said no, and that led to poor decisions."

"Since you know the attendees so well, tell me who you think would make such poor decisions."

"I don't know."

"My client can't predict how impaired people will conduct themselves," Almeada said.

"Has anyone from any of these private parties done anything like this before?"

"Not to my knowledge," Chambers said.

I showed him Isabel Vansan's ID photo. "Are you sure about that? Axel thought the same man who attacked her may have escalated when he attacked Maggie."

"You're fishing, Detective." Almeada smugly crossed his arms over his chest. "Unless you have a police report or evidence proving these alleged crimes are connected, you can stop trying to trick my client into answering questions about this other crime."

I narrowed my eyes at Chambers. "You know it's true, but fine. What about Clayton Deek? He and Maggie were having an affair. Could he have done this?"

"He made it a point to stay away from her at the party. I never even saw the two speak. I'm sure he was nowhere near Maggie when she died," Chambers said.

"What about you? Did you find her attractive?"

"My client already said he didn't do this," Almeada reminded me.

"She was pretty in a desperate, trashy sort of way. That's not my cup of tea," Chambers said, despite his attorney's protest. "I wouldn't have wasted my time."

"You spend a lot of time at strip joints for someone who says that doesn't do it for him."

"No, Detective, that's exactly my point. I can get that all the time. I can pay for that whenever I want. I had no reason to approach Maggie when I know how to get in touch with a dozen more just like her."

My neck started to itch. Apparently, Sean's moisturizer wasn't the only irritant in my life. I resisted the urge to scratch and glared at Chambers. "Are you sure you didn't give Margaret Tenzin access to your room?"

"I did no such thing."

"What about Clayton or any of the other party guests? Spark is about fulfilling desires. All desires. A room with a view and an hour with a beautiful woman would be on a lot of wish lists."

"Again, I'll remind you I am not employed at Spark or by Axel Kincaid. That being said, as a member of the club, I can guarantee that sex workers are not part of the deal. Prostitution is prohibited inside the club."

"The party didn't happen inside the club."

"What does this have to do with anything, Detective?" Almeada asked. "You're going down a rabbit hole. Frankly, I have half a mind to file a complaint. I know how much work you personally put in to building a case against Mr. Kincaid, and now, it looks like you're using this murder as a fishing expedition to reopen that."

"I am not. Axel called with a tip concerning this murder. That's why we're here. It all connects. Every damn bit of it."

Almeada looked smug. "You're fishing. Stay on topic."

I glanced at the two-way mirror, wishing Brad was on the other side. I was in charge. I couldn't let them rattle me. "The facts are clear."

"That's right. My client was in the gym when the woman was killed."

"We don't know that. No one's been able to verify his

whereabouts at the exact moment her body crashed into the roof of the parked car. Given the timing, your client could have tossed her and gotten downstairs to the gym before anyone realized what happened. He has no alibi. Following that, he fled the scene and has yet to come up with a viable explanation."

"I didn't do it," Chambers said. "You know I didn't."

"Do you know if any guests have a history of violence?"

"I don't know. I wouldn't doubt it."

"What about the people you hired?"

"I don't remember." Chambers looked worried. "What happens if you can't figure out who really did this?"

"Evidence suggests you did. The DA will decide if it's enough to take it to trial, and that will be it."

Chambers glanced at Almeada, who nodded. "Fuck."

"Help me to help you," I insisted. "Give me something. Anything. Who left the party early?"

"I don't know."

I flipped through the folder again. "Where did you put your room key?"

"I had it in my pocket since I checked in. When I went to the gym, I had to use it to gain access. It must be in my bag."

"Where is your bag?"

Chambers pressed his lips together.

"You have to help yourself here," I said. "Right now, it looks like you're hiding evidence. For all we know, you could be concealing bloody clothing or the victim's personal effects. We need to see inside your bag. If you didn't do it, it could help clear you from suspicion. The sooner we do that, the sooner I'll be able to focus my efforts on catching the killer."

Chambers glanced at the attorney who shrugged.

"Hiding evidence is a crime. Do you want to face other charges?" I asked.

"I must have left my bag in the trunk after I changed," Chambers mumbled.

"Whose trunk?"

Chambers filled his lungs and exhaled slowly. "Fox's."

NINETEEN

Fox was Axel's right-hand man. He didn't move without Axel giving the order. When I'd been undercover, I tried getting close to Fox, but he was a closed book. He never trusted me, but from what I'd seen, he didn't trust anyone, except Axel. The only way Remington Chambers' bag ended up in Fox's trunk was because Axel told him to hold on to it.

Since Fox was supposedly out of the country, I had the cops stationed at the airports check the parking lot for his vehicle. After a bit of searching, they found it. The only catch, it wasn't registered to Fox. The car was in Axel's name.

"What do you want us to do, Detective?" the officer on the other end of the line asked.

"Let me see what kinds of legal hoops we have to jump through. Just keep an eye on it until I get there."

"What happens if the owner returns?"

"He won't."

"How can you be sure?" the officer asked.

"I can't." More than likely, Axel or Fox removed anything damning that had been inside. While a smoking gun would have been nice, at this point, I'd settle for Chambers' room key or some sort of proof that he hadn't killed Margaret Tenzin.

After contacting the district attorney's office, I made sure the paperwork was in order. I brought everything into

Lt. Winston's office and filled him in on the situation.

"Have you contacted the owner?" Winston asked.

"Not yet."

"Call him. We don't want to make enemies. See if he'll give you permission." Winston stared down at the files on his desk. "My phone's been ringing off the hook. Every top law firm in the city is anxiously hoping to file harassment charges against the department for some perceived mistreatment of their clients."

"That's bullshit. They're persons of interest."

"You're not telling me anything I don't know, but you and your partner need to tread lightly. Feather-soft. Got it?"

"Yes, sir."

"Are you any closer to making an arrest?"

"We're exploring several different avenues. Until we get the coroner's report or forensics turns something up, we're relying on eyewitness accounts and shoddy surveillance footage."

"I'll put more techs on that."

"Mac could do it in her sleep," I said.

"When she gets back from vacation, I'll make it her priority." He looked up at me. "Dismissed."

After taking care of a few final details, I headed for the airport. The parking lot was crowded, as usual. The hustle and bustle never stopped. People were always traveling. Coming, going, it didn't matter. But in their haste, no one paid a bit of attention to the police car or the two government vehicles parked nearby. The only thing that got any attention was the shiny, neon orange sports car, and even that was met with nothing more than a few curious glances.

I stood beside Logan Winters, the assistant district attorney, while officers opened the trunk of the shiny luxury sedan. They found a black duffel bag inside. The rest of the trunk was empty. In fact, it looked like it may have recently been steam cleaned.

"Is this it, Detective?" Officer Jackson asked. He read the tag. "Says it belongs to R. Chambers."

"I'd say so. That's just how Remington Chambers

described it."

The officer looked at ADA Winters who gave a curt nod. The officer closed the trunk, made sure it locked, and handed me the bag. We filled out the forms under the ADA's watchful eye, making sure we followed proper procedures.

"Happy?" I eyed the man leaning against the neon orange car.

Axel Kincaid wore a light blue silk button-down dress shirt over black dress pants. The first two buttons of the wrinkled silk shirt were open, making it appear as if Axel had pulled it on in a hurry from where it had been left in a heap on the floor.

He rubbed one of his eyes and yawned. "Not particularly. I'm nocturnal. This is interfering with my Circadian rhythms."

"You didn't have to oversee the retrieval," Logan said. "The bag's owner gave us permission, and so did the alleged car owner, except that's where we caught a hitch. If it hadn't been for the ownership discrepancy, we wouldn't have contacted you. Still, you didn't have to come down here. We could have handled it."

"Someone has to keep an eye on you." Axel turned his attention to me. "Who knows what sorts of things the detective may try to plant inside the car or the bag. She always acts like I'm public enemy number one."

"Get real," I mumbled.

Axel smirked, his eyes teasing me. He was feeling playful. Maybe.

"You should be careful about making accusations," Logan warned.

Axel shrugged. "Must be the lack of sleep talking. I know Detective DeMarco's a good cop. It's just the cop part that worries me. The rest, not so much."

"Why was Fox driving your car?" I asked.

"It's not my car." Axel pointed to the neon orange thing parked beside it. "That's my car. This is his. We haven't had time to transfer the title yet." Axel stared, daring me to say something to the contrary.

"Is that why you have a spare key in your possession?"

Logan asked.

Axel glanced at him before returning his focus to me. "Don't you keep your spare keys with trusted friends?"

Logan tucked his copy of the paperwork into his attaché case. "We appreciate your cooperation. Sorry for the inconvenience, Mr. Kincaid."

"It's not like I had a choice. If I hadn't been here, you would have broken the lock. Getting that fixed would have been costly and time-consuming. The way I see it, the city owes me a favor. And I will collect." He winked at me.

Logan nudged me. "You good, Liv?"

"Uh-huh." I kept my eyes on Axel. "Unless you want to fill out an arrest warrant and get a judge to sign it. Since Mr. Kincaid's sure I have it out for him, we should see about meeting his expectations."

Axel grinned. "You couldn't resist. You always have to mention your handcuffs."

"It's what you were waiting for," I said. "I didn't want to disappoint."

"You never disappoint."

The ADA appeared utterly confused. "Are you sure you're okay here, Liv?" He looked back at the officers who had returned to their car and were chatting to one another over the roof about where to go for lunch.

I tore my eyes away from Axel, hoping he wouldn't disappear into thin air. "I'm good, Logan. In fact, Mr. Kincaid is about to make me feel even better by volunteering to come to the precinct to have a chat. No arrest warrant necessary. Right, Axel?"

"I agreed to no such thing. If you try to press the point, I'll have no choice but to use that favor right now," he said.

Logan looked at me like I was crazy. "All right. I'll leave you to deal with this." He adjusted his grip on the bag. "Call me when you get back. We have that other matter to discuss."

"Sure." But there was no other matter. Logan didn't trust Axel either and wanted me to check in.

Axel waited for the assistant district attorney to walk away before he said, "I'm not coming to the precinct. I called you with a tip so we could keep this quiet. That's why

I met you for dinner. This stays between us. Going public isn't in the cards. Not this time. Not on this."

"I have questions. I need a statement. Something official. Everything about Maggie Tenzin's murder links back to you."

"I'm not a suspect. I was nowhere near the hotel when it happened. George gave you security footage. I have an airtight alibi."

"That doesn't mean you aren't a material witness. You need to answer some more questions."

"Dinner wasn't enough for you?"

"No."

"No wonder the firefighter left you unsatisfied."

"Axel."

"What happens if I refuse? What are you going to do? We both know you can't arrest me, not without serious ramifications to your career and the department. So what?"

"Don't threaten me," I said.

"If you don't like it, don't dish it out."

"You wouldn't."

"Try me."

"You can't refuse to answer questions. We have grounds. Remington Chambers already mentioned you and Spark. Now with this car situation and Fox's involvement, a follow-up is necessary. You connect to the party, the victim, and the suspect we have in custody."

His eyes sparkled. "I can do anything I want, Detective. You of all people should know that by now."

"You wouldn't be here if you didn't want to help. You could have kept us away from the bag if you wanted, but you didn't. So why are you jerking me around when it comes to answering questions? Is this fun for you?"

"You always entertain me, Liv. But we can't talk about this. Not here." He gave the waiting officers a two fingered salute. "Goodbye, gentlemen," he said loudly, waiting for them to get inside their car and close the doors. "Did you get the list this morning?"

"Yes."

"And that wasn't enough?"

"Not even close."

"So you want more?" Fire burned behind those icy irises. "Fine. Meet me at Spark tonight. You want intel, but I require anonymity. Nothing on the record. If you need something official, file the proper paperwork. I've worked as a CI before. I know the protocol. But in case you forgot, no flashing badges. No nothing. George will let you in. Try to dress appropriately. And if you bring Fennel, tell him the same. I don't want to make any of my club members nervous." Axel didn't wait for me to respond before he unlocked his sports car and drove away in a blur of orange.

TWENTY

Frustrated, I returned to the precinct with my newly acquired evidence. At least, I hoped we'd find some evidence inside. But something told me anything damning that may have been concealed inside the bag had been removed before we got there. After all, Remington Chambers had taken his sweet time to disclose its location, and since Axel had a key to the car, he could have done anything to the bag before we arrived.

The voice in the back of my head questioned Axel's helpfulness. Was he manipulating the situation to benefit his associates? I wouldn't doubt it, but there was a desperation to him concerning the murder that made me think otherwise. Unless that was an act too.

Brad was waiting for me when I returned. "Did you get it?"

"Yes."

"Well?"

"I didn't find anything inside. No room key. No bloody clothing. No gloves. And none of Maggie's missing items."

"CSU should go over it again."

"They're doing that now. Afterward, we'll let Chambers take a look and ask if anything's missing. He claimed he had his room key to get into the gym, so it should have been in his bag. But it wasn't. I'm wondering what kind of wild goose chase he'll send us on next or what insane explanation he'll come up with this time."

"Did you find his gym clothes?" Brad asked.

"Yep. They were a little crunchy and slightly damp in the middle, which makes me think he wore them for something."

"Probably running from the scene." Brad slid a folder toward me. "I made a stop before I returned. I thought we could use this."

It was the ME's preliminary report. "I guess I shouldn't have worried Carrie would make sure our cases went to the bottom of the pile since you didn't want to rekindle that flame."

"She's not vindictive."

I gave him a look. "Really?"

"We're friends."

"She owed you for helping her resolve that issue with her ex-boyfriend, the guy she replaced you with."

"Ouch. Low blow, Liv."

"Sorry. I didn't mean it like that. All I meant to say was I don't see why or how she thought she could find someone better than you. Then to ask you to give her another chance after all that, well, it's no wonder you said no, but she's probably kicking herself and feeling like a fool, which would explain why she'd want to avoid us by sending our cases to the bottom of the stack."

"You always ramble when you're nervous." He grinned. "But in this instance, I can forgive you, since you think I'm the best." He glanced around the bullpen, but luckily, not many people were around. If they had been, he would have made some kind of stupid announcement about it just to bust my chops.

I leafed through the report. "Did you see this? The stab wound could have caused paralysis to Maggie's lower extremities."

"That would explain why she didn't run for help."

"But to stab her in the back like that," I narrowed my eyes at the diagram, "at just the right angle to strike between her vertebrae, that's all kinds of messed up."

"The assailant could have gotten lucky." Brad pulled out the guest list. "Or he had medical training. There are two surgeons on the list."

"Great." I scanned the rest of the report. "We need everyone's alibi." The preliminary exam showed blunt force trauma to be the cause of death, but that was only because those injuries were more widespread. If the killer hadn't thrown her from the balcony, she could have died from the stab wound. "Could we be looking at more than one attacker?"

"That was my original thought, remember?"

"You thought everyone on the roof was involved."

"I still think that." Brad grabbed a marker and wheeled the nearest whiteboard closer to our desks. "Let's start at the beginning."

"Again?"

He ignored my quip. "Margaret Tenzin left the party after she concluded her performance, roughly around midnight. Somehow, she ends up in Remington Chambers' room where she is attacked with one of the caterer's knives. Everyone at the party had access, but the waitstaff and caterers had the most opportunity to grab the knife."

"Agreed, but they were too busy serving the guests to follow Maggie downstairs and kill her."

"Not necessarily. They took breaks. They covered for one another. None of the guests recall seeing every single server at any given time."

"They weren't paying attention."

"True, but we haven't focused on them. Until we know what's going on, we have to focus on everyone."

"Is this because the same catering staff worked the party where Vansan was attacked?"

"Maybe." Brad wrote them down under our list of suspects. "That brings us back to James West." He pointed to the notes I made, which were sitting atop my desk. "He didn't tell us he and Maggie had such an extensive history."

"We need to have another chat with him."

"We will." Brad continued reading his notes. "I already mentioned the surgeons from the party. They'd have the skills and training necessary to inflict such a wound, if it was intentional. But getting stabbed in the back may have been more of a symbolic statement than an actual attack plan."

"You think Maggie betrayed someone?"

"Possibly. Clayton Deek and his wife, Nancy, are at the top of my list when it comes to motive. And since they checked out of the hotel as fast as they could, I can't help but think there's a reason for it."

"What about those two surgeons? Did they stay at the hotel?"

"One left." He read the name. "Raj Chopra. The other, Dennis Linson, stuck around."

"Unfortunately, leaving doesn't prove guilt. We need evidence, an eyewitness, or motive."

"While I was questioning everyone who remained and asking for their whereabouts and coming up with this nifty timeline," Brad opened his notebook, laying the two pages flat so I could see where he sketched a line with times, "I realized the one thing we never found during our search. Drugs. The only things we found were some prescription pill bottles. But officers searched every guest's belongings and their rooms. Given that several of them were high when I questioned them, I wonder where it all went."

"They could have flushed it."

"As soon as officers arrived, they kept watch on everyone. There wouldn't have been time."

"Bathroom breaks."

"I don't know." Brad studied the board. "Given the way the party guests acted, I don't think they'd worry about us finding a dime bag of coke or a handful of X. They act like they are untouchable. And in many ways, they are."

"What are you thinking?"

"Chambers was running the event. The party was his responsibility. If things went south, they could have left him holding the bag. Literally."

"You think he got rid of the contraband." I chewed on my bottom lip while I considered the implications. "That would go along with Spark's policy. And it would explain why Chambers fled the scene. But that probably means he didn't kill Maggie. Is that what you think?"

"I don't know. But we haven't been able to connect him to the vic in any aspect that doesn't directly relate to his duties as host. Even his interaction with her at the strip joint could have been related to auditioning and hiring her."

"We have no way of knowing that."

"Okay, so maybe I made two stops on my way back and flashed Chambers' photo around. He's a regular, which we've established, but he only ever watches the main stage. He never gets a lap dance or splurges on a private room or private dance. He always tips the performers and waitresses well and never causes any problems for the management. He doesn't get drunk or loud or handsy. And he always leaves before closing and always alone."

"Okay." I wasn't following.

"Men who act like that usually don't frequent strip clubs unless that's how he starts his engine and has someone waiting to take him for a ride."

"Chambers is single and has never been picked up with a hooker."

"Exactly."

"Exactly what?"

"I'm thinking he's scouting girls for these Spark events, whatever that may entail."

"I wouldn't doubt it."

"We could ask," Brad suggested.

"Do you think he'd tell us? He's been lying to us this entire time."

"We just don't know what he's lying about." As usual, my partner made a great point, but it didn't help us pinpoint a suspect.

I rubbed a hand over my face and closed the ME's report. "Based on everything we know, I'd say Chambers isn't our killer."

"Agreed, but he may know who is. My money's on the boyfriend."

"Which one? As far as romantic entanglements, we know of two potentials."

"What about Mrs. Deek? She could have figured out her husband was screwing Maggie and eliminated the competition."

I brought up Nancy Deek's driver's license. "I'm not sure

she'd have the strength needed to lift Maggie over the railing, let alone hurl her far enough to land on top of the parked car."

"No, but she could have stabbed her in the back and had her husband clean it up. After all, they took a vow for better or worse."

"I didn't realize that included murder."

"Married people can't be forced to testify against one another, so it's implied."

"I'm glad you explained that to me."

"Hey, for what it's worth, I'd help you hide a body. And I know you'd do the same for me."

"They didn't hide the body. No one hid the body." I stretched back in my chair, feeling the familiar kink return to my neck, but I couldn't rub it or I'd irritate my rash. "The only way we figure this out is by determining who had access to Chambers' room."

"The hotel staff."

"And no one else, according to Chambers. But since we haven't found his room key, I'm wondering if someone took it."

"Would he tell us if he gave it to someone?"

"He should. It's the only surefire way to avoid murder charges."

"What would the Spark employee handbook say on such things?" Brad asked.

"He's not technically an employee, so I bet Chambers will squeal if it comes down to it."

"Not if he fears Kincaid's wrath more than the possibility of jail time or the real killer silencing him."

"Either way, with our lack of evidence, he must know his chances are pretty good that he'll walk. That's probably why he's done nothing but jerk us around."

An evil glint entered Brad's eyes. "I think it's time we bluff."

TWENTY-ONE

"We recovered your bag, Mr. Chambers. It's no wonder you didn't want us to find it." My partner whistled.

Chambers looked uneasy. "What about the room key? Did you find that?"

"That's the only thing we didn't find." Brad shut the empty folder he had brought into the room with him, a prop to aid the bluff.

"Any idea where it could be?" I asked.

"I had it at the gym," Chambers insisted. "It's the only way to get inside."

Mr. Almeada stared daggers at my partner. "Shouldn't the hotel have records of who used their access card and when?"

"The place isn't that high-tech," Brad said. "Feel free to double-check. But that's the response I got. If you get a different one, I'd love to hear it."

Deciding a little good cop could go a long way, I settled into the chair opposite Chambers. "We found your sweaty gym clothes in the bag. I'd like to believe that means you're telling the truth, but my partner's jaded. He figures you were wearing those clothes when you fled the scene and that's how they got sweaty."

"You have no proof of that," Almeada reminded us.

I ignored the attorney and kept my eyes on Chambers. "How did your bag get inside Fox's car?"

"He gave me a ride." Chambers glanced at the attorney. "He picked me up a few blocks from the hotel and gave me a ride back to his place. With all the craziness that happened, I forgot all about it."

"You forgot where you spent the night?" Brad asked. "Just like what you ate and drank at the party. But earlier you told us you went for a walk. Which is it?"

"I did go for a walk. I left the hotel and went for a walk. When I got tired, I called a friend for a ride."

"Why Fox?" I asked.

"Excuse me?"

"We checked your phone records. You never called him. You called Spark's main line."

"Same difference." Chambers shrugged. "Why does it matter?"

"Everything matters, Mr. Chambers," Brad said. "The more you withhold, the worse you're making things for yourself. With the contraband we recovered in your bag, you'll be lucky if we don't add a ton more charges against you."

"Contraband?" Chambers practically squeaked.

"What exactly did you find?" Almeada asked.

"Ask your client," Brad said. "He knows what he had in there. I'm guessing those were party favors."

Almeada glanced at Chambers, warning him to keep his mouth shut. The attorney wasn't stupid. He suspected this was a trick, but he knew his client and the inner workings of these illicit events. "Let's say you have something on my client. Given that it was found in an unattended bag inside a parked vehicle registered to another individual and driven by a third individual, those aren't the ideal conditions for getting charges to stick. What do you want from my client in order to make this go away?"

"Well," Brad leafed through the blank pages in the folder again, "it'd have to be something meaningful. Since he can't recall where he put his room key and denies anyone else had access, I'm not sure there's much we can do, unless he knows who wanted to harm Margaret Tenzin."

"I don't—" Chambers began, but I interrupted him.

"Did Nancy Deek know her husband was having an affair?"

"No."

"What about Clayton?" Brad asked. "Where was he around midnight?"

"He and his wife were busy engaging with another couple in the private tent." Chambers blushed then paled, realizing he had said more than he should.

"What kinds of activities happened at this party?" I asked.

"I'm not sure. We had a few private areas set up on the roof, like the tent the Deeks were in, but most sensitive exchanges took place in the rooms below. The party was nothing more than a chance to blow off steam and have fun."

"Were you hosting a sex party?" Brad asked.

Chambers looked increasingly uneasy. "I never said that."

"But you had plenty of recreational substances to go around," Brad said.

Chambers nodded. "The rooftop party had the usual kinds of things you'd expect. Keep in mind, these are the elite. Their jobs are stressful and confining. Their positions place stringent expectations upon them. Sometimes, people like that need to break loose. That's why these events are so popular. It's why the people at the party belong to private clubs. Keeping their activities secret is important to protect their reputations, their jobs, and their privacy. I can't go into details."

I wanted to bang my head against the table or knock some sense into Chambers. "You're potentially facing multiple felony charges, one of which is murder. Do you understand that?"

"Nothing I tell you will help. I don't know who killed Maggie. I don't know why anyone would. The only thing I can think of, which I've mentioned, is that someone got the wrong idea and made a bad decision when she rejected him."

"Who?"

"I don't know."

Brad slammed his palms on the table. "This is ridiculous."

Despite all the lies, I believed Chambers didn't know who killed Maggie. But he was far from innocent. Fortunately for him, his buddies had covered up the rest of his crimes. "Tell us what happened after you left the party."

Chambers went over it again.

"Wait," I said. "When you left your room, did you lock the door?"

"It locks automatically. I didn't check, but I heard the door close."

"Did you run into anyone after you left your room?"

Almeada nudged him. "Tell them."

"Maggie." Chambers licked his lips. "Maybe. She had an ice bucket and was headed down the hall."

"To your room?" I asked.

"No, away from me. That's why I'm not sure it was her. I don't know where she was going. I didn't stick around to find out."

"Why didn't you tell us this earlier?" Brad asked.

"And admit I was the last person who saw her alive and she had an ice bucket. What do you think I am? Stupid?"

Brad stared at him. "Yes."

"I didn't do anything to her," Chambers insisted.

"You had an argument the morning of the party," I said. "You didn't want her there. Did you know what was going to happen to her? Did you threaten her?"

"No and no. I had no idea. Do you think I'd choose to spend my time with a killer?"

"You work for Axel Kincaid," Brad muttered.

Chambers didn't understand the reference or chose to ignore it. Not that we had proof Axel was a killer, but we did see him shoot an unarmed man and threaten to shoot another one. "First, I don't work for him. Second, what does that have to do with anything?"

"Mr. Kincaid is the reason you turned yourself in. He knows we have your bag." My partner let the threat hang in the air.

"I can't tell you what I don't know," Chambers said.

"Until your story changes again or you happen to remember something else," I said. "I'm tired of this. You asked to speak to me, but you've done nothing but complicate this investigation. I can't help you if you won't help yourself. Whose room was Maggie going to? Did you see anyone else in the hall? Did you speak to her before you went to the gym?"

"She was heading away from me. Check with the hotel and find out who had been assigned the rooms at the other end of the hallway. As far as other people, a group had just left the party. Dennis, Nate, Barbie, and two more. I can't remember who."

"Dr. Dennis Linson?" Brad asked.

"Yes."

"Go on," I said, figuring we'd get their full names from our master list.

"They were on their way to one of the suites."

"When we arrived, all the guests were on the roof," Brad said. "Everyone was accounted for."

"People came and went since the party began. I already mentioned that. These events are like frat parties. Each room has something different going on. But everyone congregated on the roof before breaking off into separate groups. When they finished whatever, they'd rejoin the rest of the group before breaking off and disappearing again."

"What are we looking at?" Brad asked. "Lines of coke? Sex? Poker games?"

Chambers didn't say anything but his eyes did.

"All of the above," I said. "Was Maggie the only entertainment?"

"Officially."

I checked the list we'd gotten from the ledger, but all it had were the names of the caterers and serving staff. We'd run backgrounds on them, but they were clean. "Who else was at the party?"

"No one, unless a guest brought his own entertainment. We never prohibit plus ones, but the names would be on the list."

"Maggie could have gotten mixed up in something," Brad whispered to me.

"Did you run into anyone else on your way to the gym?" I asked Chambers.

"Frank."

"Frank?" I asked. "I don't remember a Frank being on the guest list."

"Fertrie," Chambers said. "He was coming out of his room. We bumped into one another."

"His room was next to yours?" Brad asked.

"Between mine and the elevator, yeah."

"Do you know where he was going?" I asked.

"Back to the party, I assume." Chambers frowned, a thought obvious on his face.

"What is it?"

Chambers shrugged, which made me want to smack him with a phonebook. But police didn't do that anymore. For one thing, it was illegal. For another, it was damn near impossible to find a phonebook nowadays. And lastly, I wasn't that kind of cop. But with a man like Chambers, I found myself starting to understand the urge.

"I think we're done here," Brad said. "You haven't told us a single thing that will help us. If anything, you've dragged us around in a complete circle."

"What are you planning to charge my client with?" Almeada asked.

"I'll let you know." Brad got up and went to the door.

"DeMarco," Chambers called, "can I have a word in private?"

Almeada nudged his shoulder. "I wouldn't advise it."

"It's your right," I said, hesitating in the doorway.

"I'll be fine." Chambers dismissed Almeada, who followed my partner out of the room.

I folded my arms over my chest. "What is it?"

"Fertrie left the party to take care of some business."

"What business?"

"I don't know."

"Why does that matter?"

"Frank had been drooling over Maggie since the moment he spotted her. He may have left his room to go after her. Like I said, she was in the hallway. Maybe he heard her or saw her."

"Did you see him go after her?"

"He went in that direction, but I don't know if they interacted."

"Let's say they did. How does that explain Maggie getting murdered inside your suite?"

"They could have gone inside for some privacy. Frank was itching to get laid, and his room was otherwise occupied with a few associates."

"What associates?"

"I don't know."

"How would he and Maggie have gotten into your room?"

"I've been thinking about it, and when we bumped into each other, we literally bumped into each other. I dropped my key. Maybe he switched them."

Chambers was giving me a headache, but I played along. "Okay, let's say that he did. The only problem with that theory is Fertrie checked out of the hotel, and when he did, he returned his room key. How did it come to be back in his possession?"

Chambers glanced uneasily at me. "Off the record?"

"No."

"Fertrie stopped by the gym while I was there. He could have taken back his key then."

"Why didn't you say something sooner?"

"It never occurred to me. But now that I'm thinking about it, Frank had been looking for an empty suite most of the night. He made it clear he wanted to play. He would have known I didn't plan on sleeping in my room, so it'd be the perfect place for him to get some."

I swore, pointing a finger at him. "How long have you been sitting on this theory?"

"It just came to me."

"Liar. Withhold important information again and I will make sure the DA prosecutes you for every single possible offense you've ever committed. I don't care if we start with jaywalking and littering and go all the way to first degree murder. Do I make myself clear?"

He nodded.

"Do you think Fertrie took back his key and kept yours? Do you remember leaving the gym with a room key?"

"I don't know. He showed up at the gym a few minutes into my workout and said a woman was hurt. That's all I could think about. I can't be sure what he did. I had to get things together and run damage control."

"What do you mean?"

"Isn't it obvious? I had to make sure the party wasn't raided and everyone arrested."

"Did you go back to your room or the roof?"

"No."

"Do you think it's odd Fertrie came downstairs to warn you?"

"No, if he hadn't come down to tell me, someone else would have."

"Do you remember if he had changed clothes or if he looked nervous?"

"I don't know."

"Did you notice any blood on him?"

"What?" Chambers looked at me like I was crazy. "I don't think so. I don't know. I really can't remember."

"Why can't you remember anything?"

"The entire night's a blur. As you can probably guess, it's from a mix of what was in that bag."

"Will you submit to a drug test?"

"Absolutely not." He looked me in the eye. "You're already gunning for me. I'm not going to make it easier for you."

TWENTY-TWO

Francis Fertrie, esquire, could use his position and the law to conceal a lot of key facts. Since he was allegedly conducting business during the party, he could argue privilege. That would prevent him from having to disclose his client list or any information related to whatever business was going on inside his suite. Forcing him to comply with our requests would require a sympathetic judge and jumping through more hoops than trained circus animals. That made ascertaining his exact whereabouts at the approximate time of Maggie Tenzin's murder damn near impossible. We couldn't force him to answer those questions. But we could ask him several others.

"I want to kill Chambers," Brad said. "Out of all the suspects we've questioned, he takes the cake."

"We've seen worse."

"Actual killers aren't this bad. They keep their mouths shut, or they blab incoherently. This guy makes it up as he goes along, then backtracks, changes the story, and finally, maybe, gets around to telling us the truth. Maybe. But by then, he's cried wolf too many times for us to believe anything he says."

I drew a large rectangle around Francis Fertrie's name. "That doesn't mean he hasn't finally given us a lead." I stepped back. "It looks like Axel was right. Chambers isn't the killer."

"No, but I kind of wish he was. Honestly, Liv, even if he

did it, I don't think he'd remember doing it. We've searched his bag and his clothes. There's no blood. The hotel staff and guests verified what he's wearing now are the same clothes he wore to the party, and the ones in his bag match what he had when he went to the gym. We would have found blood or hair on him if he attacked her. Forensics didn't show any trace of blood on the bag or the items inside."

"Which means he didn't do it, or he owns at least two matching suits and sets of workout clothes."

"Which is also possible. Kincaid could have switched everything out."

"What about drug residue?"

"They're still testing, but so far we found trace amounts of cocaine, MDMA, and LSD."

"I'm not surprised. After all, it was a party."

"I must not hang out with the right crowd," Brad teased.

"That's a good thing." I dropped into my chair, hoping answers would magically appear on our whiteboard. "We don't have enough evidence. A conviction would be far from a slam dunk. Have we gotten any DNA results yet?"

"No."

"Was Fertrie at the event where Vansan was attacked?"

"Yes."

"All right. Let's bring him in."

Brad grabbed my hand before I could pick up the phone. "Not yet."

"Why not?"

He pointed to the files on our desks. "We're in a mess. We need to take a breath, flesh some things out, make some educated guesses, and go from there. For all we know, Chambers is nothing more than a plant. He could be here to distract us and lead us away from what really happened."

"Which is?"

"I don't know." Brad pointed to the various theories he'd written on the board. "Take your pick. We have a love triangle. We have a jealous ex-boyfriend with a history of violence. We have the possibility that Maggie witnessed some shady thing she wasn't supposed to and died because of it."

"That was Axel's theory."

"True, but we can't rule it out. It could go along with what Chambers said."

"Chambers also said Fertrie could have taken his room key."

"Maybe. It's not like he remembers it happening for sure. Since Chambers was that impaired, anyone could have lifted it. Until he decides to recant or change the story entirely, we should take his theory with a grain of salt. You heard Lt. Winston. We aren't supposed to piss people off. And Fertrie's chomping at the bit to accuse us of harassment. Going after him is going to cause a lot of waves. Are you ready to rock the boat?"

"That could be his way of keeping us at bay. Maybe he's doing it because he's guilty. If Fertrie switched keys, he could have lured Maggie into Chambers' room right after they bumped into one another. Chambers said she had the ice bucket with her when he passed her in the hall. That would fit with the timing."

"Or Fertrie gave Chambers' room key to someone else and went back to his own room or back to the party. Chambers also said he saw one of the surgeons in the hallway around the same time. Given the stab wound to Maggie's back, Dr. Linson would have had means and opportunity."

"What's the motive?"

"The pretty girl wouldn't sleep with him."

"Why was every guy at that party so enamored with our victim? Sure, she's pretty, but there has to be more to it."

"Maybe it was her dance routine," Brad suggested. "Or," he flipped through his notes again, "she was the only female outsider there except for the catering staff. That meant she was the only viable option for those looking to mingle."

"We don't know that."

"No, but Dennis Linson is single. His hotel bill included several charges for adult films, along with a room service order for three cans of whipped cream."

"So?"

"What was he doing with all that whipped cream?"

"I don't know. Maybe he likes whipped cream."

Brad rolled his eyes. "You need to date more. I bet Sean could have explained the whipped cream thing to you. He seems the type. Hell, if you really don't know, you could ask Emma."

I slapped his arm. "I get your point, but that doesn't prove anything. We didn't find whipped cream on our vic or in Chambers' room. In fact, the ME didn't find any signs of recent sexual activity."

"You're missing my point. Linson sounds like a desperate horndog. Witnesses said he spent most of the night flirting with Maggie and bringing her drinks. If Chambers is to be believed, which is a big if, Linson may have left the party after she did, hoping to seal the deal. He followed her down the hall, got Chambers' room key from somewhere, and attempted to impress himself upon her. He stabs her in the back to immobilize her, freaks out when he realizes what he's done, and tosses her over the balcony."

I sunk into my chair. "The ME didn't find any signs of attempted rape either."

"A knife in the back could have put a damper on that."

"Or made it easier for the killer."

"Unless he was interrupted. A lot of people were in the hallway around that time, according to Chambers."

"We could question them again and see who remembers seeing Maggie."

"Except we already did, and not a single person admitted to seeing her in the hallway except Chambers." Brad sighed. "Maybe she wasn't there. Maybe she was already inside his room, and he killed her."

"Ugh, now you're making us go in circles."

"I wish those damn cameras worked and these witnesses had actually witnessed something."

"All right. Like you said, we have a mess. Where do we begin?" I asked.

"Maggie's high school friend turned ex-lover, James West."

"We've already run his background. I was trying to

connect him to Isabel Vansan when Mr. Tenzin showed up." I brought up the search I'd been conducting. "James West wasn't hired to DJ the party where Vansan was allegedly attacked, and he isn't on the guest list either."

"Vansan worked for a party entertainment company. She and West could have overlapped at some other gig." Brad pulled up West's employment history. "Okay, maybe not. The DJ never worked for that party entertainment company, and given Vansan's work history, I can't find any other connections."

"We'll have to get a court order for their phone records, but I don't see any ties on social media either. Isabel Vansan's accounts are shut down. There's nothing on West's pages. I don't think they knew one another. And since West wasn't there the night she was attacked, assuming the same person who killed Maggie attacked Vansan, it can't be West."

"You don't believe the same person attacked both women, do you?" Brad asked.

"Not really. Axel suggested it, but I don't see a clear connection. Maggie and Isabel were nothing alike. Maybe if we knew more about what happened to Isabel Vansan, I'd think differently, but with what little we have, it looks like two unrelated incidents at two similar parties."

"Still, it doesn't hurt to check. Do you know what Vansan looks like?" Brad asked.

"Yes. Nothing like Maggie. So if it is the same offender, he doesn't have a type."

"Okay. At least you got that reference. I wanted to make sure this wasn't a whipped cream situation."

I kicked him under the desk.

"Ow. Stop doing that." He rubbed his leg. "At this rate, I'm going to have to wear shin guards to work."

"You should wear a cup, too," Jake Voletek said, interrupting us.

"Hey, you're back." I offered him a smile. It looked like our fellow detective hadn't slept in days. "How's your dad?"

"He's back at work. The hospital gave him a clean bill of health."

"What about you?" Brad asked.

"Better than you. By now, I figured you'd know better than to piss Liv off."

Brad ignored the redirect. "Are you still leading the investigation into how a group of cops got roofied?"

Jake nodded. "The commissioner wants me to keep on it, but until forensics finishes going over every inch of the restaurant where it happened and officers finish conducting background checks and interviewing the staff from that night, there's not much for me to do. And if I spent another minute in my dad's office, he would have used his service piece to shoot me and claimed it was a cleaning accident. So I thought I'd see how things were going around here without me." He scanned the board. "It looks like you could use some help. Where do you want me to start?"

"Are you sure?" I asked.

"Yeah. It'll be good to think about something else for a little while."

"Great. Take Isabel Vansan and the party entertainment company." I passed him my notes. "She vanished months ago after an alleged attack at this event. I haven't been able to find her."

"Did you check with missing persons?" Jake asked.

"No one ever reported her. Her disappearance doesn't appear to be due to foul play. She emptied her bank account, quit her job, and moved away."

"That's pretty damn suspicious."

"According to a source, she left after the attack and got a new identity. She must have been scared."

"Have you contacted the Marshal Service? She could be one of theirs."

"Our search should have pinged in their system if that was true," Brad said. "But feel free to investigate however you like."

Jake snickered. "Thanks a lot, guys."

"You asked if you could help." I turned to my partner. "I still say questioning Fertrie makes the most sense."

Brad gestured to my phone. "Have at it." But his tone told me he didn't expect things to go well.

I dialed Fertrie's number. He answered on the fourth

ring. "Hello, Mr. Fertrie. This is Detective DeMarco with homicide. I have a few questions."

"I already answered your questions," he said.

"Sir, this is a follow-up. New details have come to light."

"I don't care. I know my rights. I don't have to cooperate."

I eyed my partner, who'd failed to emphasize what a pain in the ass Fertrie was. "Sir, everyone who attended the rooftop party is currently a person of interest. Answering a few simple questions could clear this up and have you removed from that list."

"Regardless, I don't have to talk to you." And he hung up.

"Told you." Brad pushed West's information toward me. "You already built a rapport with the DJ. Call him while I see if I can get any of the named party guests from the hallway to revise their previous statements and verify Chambers' story."

Thankfully, West was much more compliant. He agreed to come to the station to answer more questions first thing in the morning. After scheduling that interview, I called Mr. Tenzin back and asked if he had any luck finding his daughter's high school yearbook. He had, so I sent officers to pick it up.

Shifting gears, I ran backgrounds on everyone who worked at that pizza place. The only name that surfaced in relation to the party circuit was James West. The other high school kids who worked there had moved on.

I looked up their current whereabouts. Most didn't live in the city. One didn't even live in the country. However, the manager and a few of the older employees remained.

"I'm going to see what they can tell me about our vic," I said.

Brad nodded, the phone pressed to his ear while he listened to Barbie Lefevre's account of what happened in the hotel hallway. "Careful," he mouthed.

TWENTY-THREE

The pizza place wasn't far from work. And since it wasn't peak dinner hours yet, only a handful of customers were inside. Most were kids, hanging out with their friends.

"What can I get'cha?" the man behind the counter asked, wiping his hands on a dish towel. He wore a white t-shirt with a white apron over it. A faded tomato sauce stain ran across the apron, and a fresh sprinkling of flour coated the underside of his beefy forearms.

I flashed my badge. "How long have you worked here?"

"Twenty-two years. Why?"

"Do you know Margaret Tenzin? She used to work here."

"That was about ten years ago, wasn't it?" He wiped his forehead with the back of his arm. "What's this about?"

"When's the last time you spoke to her?"

"It's been a minute." He leaned against the counter. "She drops in every once in a while. Not that often. Maybe every six months or so. Usually, she says she just stopped by to say hello, but if I'm around, I give her the employee discount."

"Do you know what she was up to?"

"Like where she works? Yeah, she's a dancer. Like a twirler or something." He shrugged. "I don't know. I don't keep up with the trends."

"What about her personal life?"

"We aren't that close. It's one of those 'hi, how are ya,'

kind of situations." He pointed at my badge. "Is she in trouble? Is that why you're here asking about her?"

"Unfortunately. Do you know if she stayed close with anyone she used to work with?"

"Nah, not really. We hire a bunch of kids every few years. They age out, move on, go to college, graduate, whatever. I can't keep up with who's friends with who or who's on the social media or the instachat stuff. They keep me out of most of that, which is probably a good thing. An old guy like me paling around with a bunch of kids, that would lead to you asking a whole other set of questions."

"Do you remember James West?"

"I swear his parents must have known he was going to be a ladies' man when they named him, just like the character from that show." He looked at me. "*The Wild Wild West*, you ever see it?"

"I saw the movie version."

"Same difference, which means you get the reference. Guy was always getting into trouble, usually for dating too many women at once. They'd always find out he was two-timing them. I can't tell you how many times a group would come in here, and he'd hide in the back. At least, it made assigning someone to do inventory easier."

"Did he and Maggie ever date?"

"I don't know if I'd say date. But they had something going. I don't know what the term was. Hooking up or friends with benefits. Something like that. They'd get bored and mess around. I caught them a few times during break in the back. Things would cool off between them, and he'd have a new girl fawning over him a day or two later. And the cycle would start over."

"What about Maggie? Did she have a lot of boyfriends?"

"Not that I remember," he said. "Do you mind if I ask what happened? What did she do?"

"Do?"

"Yeah, you said she was in trouble. Did she rob a place or something?"

"Why would you think that?"

"Money's always tight for her. Whenever she stops by, she seems like she's struggling. But she's too proud to ask for help. That's why I give her a discount, along with free sodas and a piece of whatever cake has gone stale." He pointed to the selection of boxes in the fridge behind the register.

"I'm sorry to say Maggie Tenzin was murdered Friday night."

His eyes grew wider as the words sank in. "Shit. I never would have guessed that. What happened?"

"That's what I'm trying to figure out."

"Why would you come here? It's been a long time since she worked here and several months since I've seen her. I never would have known if you hadn't told me." He slumped against the back counter and rubbed his mouth with the back of his hand. "Wow. Poor girl." He thought for a moment. "Do you think she was targeted because of her connection to this place? Is that why you asked about James West?"

"No. When's the last time you saw him?"

"Not since he quit. That was like eight years ago, I guess. He came by maybe once or twice since then, always with a group. Usually, it'd be during a rush, so we never got a chance to talk. Maybe that was on purpose. I don't know." He inhaled. "Did he do something to her?"

"I don't know. But they were working the same party when it happened."

"Party?"

"West became a DJ."

"That tracks," he said after a time. "I'm guessing he's still a ladies' man, unless they were together."

"We're still figuring that out. But I thought it'd be best to start at the beginning."

"I doubt you could go much farther back than this. Unfortunately, I haven't seen either of them in quite some time. Maggie more recently, but it wasn't that recent. I'm sorry."

A group entered, so I stepped away from the counter while he took their order. After they were seated and he had gotten to work rolling out the dough, I returned to my spot and held out my phone with the photo Mr. Tenzin had forwarded to me. "Has anyone else been in recently?

Maybe someone asked about Maggie? Or maybe she mentioned one of them?"

He narrowed his eyes at the screen. "No. The rest are long gone. I haven't seen any of them in years, except for those guys." He pointed to the back row. "I see them several times a week. They still work here. I can give you their numbers. But I don't think they know anything I don't." He shook his head as he ladled the tomato sauce onto the crust and added the toppings. "It's such a shame. Maggie was always so hopeful, so determined. This is so senseless. She deserved to have her dreams come true."

TWENTY-FOUR

I returned to the precinct with a few pizzas for the rest of our unit. On the drive back, I called the other current pizza employees. They remembered Maggie, but they hadn't seen her either and had no idea what she'd been up to or who would want to harm her. The only thing I'd learned was Maggie had kept a lot of things to herself. She lied to her dad about dating James West, not that I blamed her. She was in high school at the time, and given how her parents reacted to her career choice, telling them she was screwing around with some lothario would not have gone over well. But given their history, James West must have known more about Maggie than anyone else. If he wasn't the killer, he had to know why someone wanted her dead.

Brad looked up when I returned to my desk. He pointed to the open yearbook. "Looks like West has been carrying a torch for our victim for some time."

I read the sloppily scrawled message the teenage West had written. *Maggie, you're my one and only. Forever and always. Never forget that.*

"Thanks, DeMarco," Detective Lisco called from across the bullpen, as she helped herself to a couple of slices.

"No problem." I exhaled and slumped into my chair. "The guy at the pizza shop said West and Maggie had a friends with benefits thing going. That is, whenever West wasn't banging another one of his friends."

"If the guy could never keep it in his pants, Maggie must

have expected him to screw around on her. It sounds like they had a history of that."

"Maybe he promised to change, or maybe this was the first time they were serious. They were living together. That typically implies some level of commitment."

"It sounds more like she would have had a motive to kill him instead." Brad looked conflicted. "However, that doesn't mean he wasn't jealous of her potential suitors or upset that she wouldn't take him back. Watching men flirt with her all night could have pushed him over the edge."

"But as far as we know, he never left the roof."

"That isn't true," Brad said. "The techs have been stitching together the spotty hotel security footage. They recovered forty seconds from the camera covering the roof exit." He scooted his chair over for me to stand. Once I came around the desk, he hit play. "There's Chambers leaving the party." He wore the same suit he currently had on. His eyes looked glassy and his steps a little uneven. He didn't wait near the door. He moved at a fast clip for someone under the influence and headed toward the stairs. "Maggie leaves the party seven seconds later." Brad redirected my attention to the exit door.

Her hair was damp, and her limbs shaky. "She's spent." I thought about all those hours dancing in a cage. By the time the music stopped, my legs always felt like gelatin. "Running or fighting off an attacker would have been difficult."

A second later, the door opened again. Maggie turned. Francis Fertrie stepped out. He called to her, holding out a bottle of water. She took it and smiled at him. He reached for her arm, but she stepped out of reach. Before he could say or do anything else, the door opened again. James West came through the door. He looked just as sweaty as Maggie, but he was pumped. He looked ready for anything.

Without sound, I could only guess that West asked if she was okay. Fertrie slunk away, sliding past Maggie, his hand tracing a trail along her low back as he went toward the stairs. I waited, wondering how the exchange between West and Maggie would go, but the footage cut out just as West took another step toward her.

"That's it?" I asked.

"So far. But it proves West left the roof. It also places two of our other suspects in the vicinity of the murder."

"What did you get from the calls you made?" I asked.

"Not much. The group Chambers said he saw in the hallway said they only left the party temporarily and returned to the roof before midnight. They didn't see Maggie wandering the halls. But Barbie thinks she glimpsed Chambers getting into the elevator."

"That would give him an alibi for time of death," I said.

"It would. But I don't see any reason to cut him loose yet, not when we have so many unanswered questions remaining and uncooperative witnesses."

"What about the surgeon, Dennis Linson?" I asked.

"Linson claims the last time he saw Maggie was on the roof. He didn't see her in the hallway when he went into one of the suites with the others, but he wished he had. He had planned to invite her back to his room for a nightcap after her performance, but she took off without waiting for tips. He regrets that missed opportunity. Frankly, I don't think he grasps that the woman is dead and he's a suspect."

"Do you think that's denial?"

"I think it's idiocy."

I laughed. "What did he mean by tips? Like a critique?"

"He meant monetary compensation for the performance." Brad handed me his notepad. "That got me to thinking, so I called the caterer. They had a tip jar set up at the bar and another at the carving station. The entertainment had placed a jar at the DJ stand. I'm guessing West would have split the money with Maggie. But I doubt keeping the full share would have been motive enough to kill her."

"I agree." I rewound the footage a few seconds. "It's hard to interpret what this is. West could have been checking to make sure she was okay and no one bothered her. He could have also gone out there to mark his territory and scare Fertrie off. She told West to go to hell and things took a turn from there, or she thanked him and went downstairs to get some water and relax in one of the other party rooms."

"Chambers or Fertrie could have offered her the empty suite to relax in while she waited for the rooftop party to end. I asked the hotel staff, but Maggie hadn't requested a cab. She didn't drive, and no rideshares or taxis ever showed up to pick her up. So it doesn't look like she planned to leave."

"Have you looked at her phone records yet?"

"Yes, but they weren't helpful. All the calls looked like they were business related. The only person she'd spoken to from the party was Chambers."

"That can't be right. What about Clayton Deek or James West? She would have had to have spoken to West at some point."

"She hasn't spoken to West in the last thirty days." Brad passed the printout to me. "But since she had zero texts, I'm guessing she used one of those encrypted texting apps."

"That's going to make our life harder."

"I have the techs looking into it, but we won't be able to find her texts unless we find her phone."

"Are you sure she never spoke to Clayton Deek? What about his work phone?"

"I checked, but it doesn't look like it."

"Most people who have affairs keep a second phone." I scanned the list again, but every number linked to a business. "She must have been texting Deek."

"Her diary said they met in person, that he sent the car for her. Maybe that's what he always did. No phone logs or electronic trail that way."

"True." Another thought hit me. "Do we know if she had her phone with her? She didn't have anywhere to put it, and I don't remember seeing her carrying a purse when she left the roof."

"Maybe she had her stuff somewhere else, in some other room."

"Do we have any other footage?"

"Not yet, but I'm hopeful the techs will be able to reconstruct something from the top floor. Since we know the killer didn't jump off the balcony, he would have had to leave Chambers' room after tossing Maggie over. If we get that, it's case closed."

"We can't count on that happening," I said. "Mac should be working on this. She's the best tech we have."

"She's backpacking through the rainforest or climbing a mountain. She was vague on the details other than her vacation would be an outdoor adventure. Wherever she is, she's disconnected from the tech." He glanced back at our colleagues, who circled the pizza boxes like vultures around a rotting carcass. "Did you forget to bring us dinner?"

"I thought I'd let you take me somewhere a little nicer than this. But you're going to have to lose the badge. Maybe get rid of the tie and do that thing you do with your collar." I gestured with my hands. "You know where you poof it up and out."

Brad looked confused, but he smiled anyway. "Yeah?"

"Yeah."

"Okay, but I don't poof." He glanced toward Lt. Winston's office. But our supervisor had left for the day. With everything going on, it was a blessing we didn't have to deal with his micromanaging or insistence not to work too many overtime hours. "Are you hungry now? We're already three hours past shift change. We could call it quits for the night and hit the ground running tomorrow morning, starting with interviewing West. Depending on what he says, we might have grounds to take Fertrie into custody. Once he's here, maybe we can get him to talk."

"Do you really think so?"

"No," Brad said, "but Chambers looks innocent. We're going to have to cut him loose, so we might as well bring in someone else to question. Fertrie may have had access to Chambers' suite. If not, my money's on West. He has a record which includes violent offenses and sexual misconduct." Brad scratched his cheek. "Since you questioned him, what's your take? Do you think West loved Maggie?"

"He definitely cared about her. But he didn't show much emotion. I thought he might have been in shock or still processing what happened."

"Could he have been playing it cool, hoping we wouldn't put him under a microscope?"

"I'm not sure."

"Do you think he killed her? Stabbing in the back is personal, like maybe he felt she betrayed him."

"I didn't see any blood on him, but he could have cleaned up, I guess."

Voletek held a napkin beneath his folded slice as he made his way back to the desk. The grease had already started to soak through, but he didn't notice as he set the napkin and slice down. "Before I update you on what I found, I have to ask, did you watch the pizza get prepared?"

"It's safe, Jake."

"That's all I needed to hear." He took a bite, swallowing a third of the slice in a single mouthful. "I didn't realize I was starving until I smelled the pepperoni." He finished the slice, glancing back to make sure at least one pizza box hadn't been opened yet before giving me his full attention. "The Marshal Service denied knowing anything about Isabel Vansan. They could be lying. You know how serious they are about WitSec, but I'm guessing they've never heard of her. I put out a few feelers to some of my underground contacts, figuring one of them may have hooked her up with a new ID. I'll let you know if I get any bites, but it's a crapshoot."

"Thanks, anyway."

"Anything for you, princess."

I glared at him. "If you were closer, I would kick you."

"I'd wear a cup tomorrow," Brad said to him.

Jake glanced at my partner. "Liv loves me. It's why she brought me pizza. She knows I'm only yanking her chain." He picked up a computer printout and held it out to me. "Also, you have to be nice since I did all this work for you."

I took the pages from his hand. "This is everything on Isabel Vansan and the company where she worked."

"Yep. No discernible connection between her and James West or Margaret Tenzin. Unless they happened to be in the same subway car one day, I don't think they ever crossed paths."

I checked the information on the party entertainment company. It was a subsidiary of a larger entertainment corporation with its headquarters in Las Vegas. The DJ worked freelance, and so did Maggie. And neither of them had ever worked any of the same events Vansan had.

"I appreciate this, Jake."

"No problem." He tossed the soppy napkin into the trash and headed toward the stack of pizza boxes. Two of them had already been emptied. The third was opened and picked through, but the fourth box remained closed. Jake slid it out from beneath the pile and returned to his desk with it. "If you want some, speak now before it disappears."

"We have other plans," Brad said.

"Oh?" Jake waggled his eyebrows. "A hot date, huh?"

"Oh yeah." Brad shut down his computer and tidied his desk. Once I was finished putting everything away, I met him at the stairs. He followed me out to the parking lot. "What do you have in mind for tonight?" His expression was unreadable. "I'm up for anything."

"I have to stop by my place so I can change first. If you don't want to follow me home, you can meet me there."

"Where, Liv?" He moved closer, glancing around, but no one was outside. "I'll take you wherever you want to go. Anything you want to do, we'll do, but Sean isn't worth it. I don't want him to get to you. He never deserved you."

"Sean? What does he have to do with anything?"

"I don't know." Brad shook his head, as if trying to shake the cobwebs loose. "Let's start again. Where are we going tonight?"

"Spark. Axel agreed to answer questions, but he'll only do it if we can protect him."

"Protect him?" Brad scoffed. "That's a good one."

"I filled out the paperwork, making him a confidential informant. It's done. If he wants to play games, I'm willing to bite, just as long as it gets us closer to finding Maggie's murderer."

"He doesn't know who that is. If he did, he never would have called and asked you to figure it out. The reason he did is so he can keep tabs on the investigation. Maybe he had something to do with Maggie's death, and he wants to stay one step ahead of us."

"I don't know what he knows, but he's done a lot of talking. More than he ever does. We should hear him out and see what else he has to say." I watched Brad fidget. "If you don't want to be a part of this, I can go by myself. I just thought you'd want to come."

"I said we'd do whatever you want. I just thought you had something else in mind."

"Like what?"

"Nothing." He shook his head again. "I go where you go. That's the deal. And the last thing I want to do is leave you alone with Kincaid. That bastard loves to taunt you and mess with your head. Mine too. But it's harder for him to do it when he's outnumbered."

"Great."

"Yeah, great."

TWENTY-FIVE

Brad draped his arm over my shoulders as we headed toward the main club entrance. Axel Kincaid wanted us to blend in, so that's what we were doing. But I could tell my partner would have preferred having vice raid the place. Knocking on the side door and flashing a badge at the security camera was more our speed, but tonight, we were going in the front, like the rest of the club's members.

"How's your neck?" Brad asked before we made it inside. "I haven't seen you scratch it today."

"The ointment helped. It's still red and a little puffy, but it hasn't bothered me much. I only notice it when I get aggravated."

"Is that why you chose a halter? To keep from scratching it when Axel pisses you off?"

"Something like that."

"You didn't have to get all fancy, not for this."

"In case you haven't noticed, Axel's all about presentation and flash." I looked up at Brad, adjusting the edge of his opened collar. "Not all of us can pull it off so seamlessly."

He hid his grin, pulling me a little tighter against his side. "Are you sure covering the rest of your scar in makeup was a good idea when you're already having a reaction to something?"

"You sound like Emma."

"Shit." Brad laughed, that familiar, comforting, velvety

sound. "I'm sorry. I'm in a weird headspace. Maybe my blood sugar's low. Have you given any thought to what you want for dinner after we finish here?"

"You can pick."

"I'm thinking Italian, which is next to impossible to find without dairy or grains. But I have half a tray of baked ziti in my fridge. It's not as good as your mom's, but it is her recipe."

"When did she teach you to make that?"

"The same day she taught me the lasagna recipe." In response to Brad's answer, my stomach growled. "It sounds like we should have stopped for dinner first." He stared at the looming club entrance. "It's not too late. We can always come back later."

"Why are you so opposed to this?"

"It's that whole weird headspace thing. Plus, we're both starving."

I stopped and forced him to turn and look at me. "What's going on? Is everything okay?"

"Yeah. Fine. It's cool. I'm good."

"Are you sure?"

"Yeah."

I narrowed my eyes, but he didn't seem to be harboring some deep, dark secret. "You better be."

I took his hand, and we walked past the few small groups clustered near the doors. Despite the club having just opened, one group appeared to have been overserved and the other seemed to be debating if they wanted to be bothered going in or doing something else instead.

George glanced up from his tablet, looking bored as always. "He's in the office."

"Thanks."

George scrutinized my partner for another five seconds before allowing us inside.

The lights were dimmed. Neon streaks bounced off the shiny dance floor and across the polished tables and reflected off the glassware. The speakers boomed pulsing rhythms. The bar was surrounded by men in suits and women barely over the legal age. The six cages were filled with Spark's latest and greatest hires. I recognized three of the women. They gyrated and bounced to the beat.

Brad watched everything as we made our way around the side of the dance floor, past the high-top tables and bar, and down the short hallway. The doors to the private room where Spark held illegal poker games were shut tight. The only open door was Axel's office, and it was barely cracked open.

I knocked, pushing the door open wider, while Brad kept an eye on what was going on behind us. But we weren't followed. As far as I could tell, no one had shown any interest in us. We didn't attract any unwanted attention.

Axel's eyes lit up when he saw me, and he smiled. "I had my doubts. Honestly, I'm surprised you dressed up."

"I told you you shouldn't have bothered," Brad mumbled, pulling the door closed behind us.

"You too, Fennel." Axel shoved something into a drawer, locked it, and pocketed the key. Getting up, he crossed to the bar cart. "Pick your poison. I pulled that tequila you like." Axel held up a bottle, waiting for my partner to acknowledge it.

"We're here on business, Mr. Kincaid." Brad smoothed the back of his hair and studied the rest of the room.

Axel gave a generous pour, grabbed a second glass, and did the same. Then he capped the bottle. "Liv?"

"Axel, please."

His ice blue eyes danced. "Ooh, begging already."

A low growl emanated from Brad's throat, but he held his tongue.

"You're a busy man," I reminded him. "The sooner you answer some questions, the sooner you can get back to work."

"You're no fun." Axel carried the two glasses to his desk and sat down. Once we joined him, he put one of the glasses in front of Brad. "In case you change your mind. You'll find this is much smoother and less peppery than most other tequilas. The flavor profile has far greater depth. You can taste vanilla and grapefruit. It's very good."

Brad worked his jaw, eyeing the glass, but he didn't touch it even though he wanted it. Instead, he pulled out his notepad and clicked his pen. "Start by telling me where you were Friday night."

"Here. I'm sure you've seen the footage." Axel picked up the glass and took a dainty sip. Leaning back in his chair, he closed his eyes, savoring it before swallowing.

"What about your associates? Where were they?"

"I have so many, it's hard to keep track. Do you have a specific person in mind?"

I glared at Axel, hoping he'd stop torturing Brad. When Axel was done with the theatrics and disappointed that his techniques hadn't worked to break my partner's resolve, he rocked forward in his chair and steepled his fingers together on the desk.

"What was Fox doing near the luxury hotel?" I asked.

"We've been over this ad nauseum. Like I said countless times, he was taking care of business. That's all you need to know. He never stepped foot on hotel property and didn't see who hurt Maggie, so the rest is inconsequential to your investigation."

"Where was he?" I asked.

Axel shook his head and sipped more tequila. "I'm not entirely sure."

"That's bullshit." Brad clicked the pen once more and tucked it and his notepad into his pocket. "There are limited vantage points that have a view of the balcony and inside that particular hotel room. Did you know what was going to happen? Is that why Fox was there? Did he have to verify the kill?"

"No." Axel had one of the best poker faces I'd ever seen. I had no way of knowing if that was a lie. "Fox's presence had nothing to do with that event."

"But it was a Spark event," Brad said.

Axel gave him an exasperated look before turning his full attention to me. "I didn't realize you kept secrets from your partner. I'm delighted you obeyed my instructions." He glanced down at my attire. "Not once, but twice."

"Sorry to disappoint, but I told Brad everything. He's just giving you the chance to clear up some discrepancies."

"Answering your questions will only confuse matters. Fox had nothing to do with the murder. I'd like to go on record and say neither did I." Axel looked from me to Brad. "Did that answer all your questions?"

"Hardly." Brad rubbed a hand down his face. "What are we doing here?"

"Ask Liv. She wanted this meeting. She practically begged for it."

"Has anyone ever punched you in the mouth?" my partner asked. "I think it might help."

"Why did you call me about the murder, Mr. Kincaid?" I asked.

"There you go with that again." Axel drank the rest of his tequila. "You were there. It made sense."

"Why?"

"I told you. I've been cleaning house. I don't want a killer as a member of my club. It would hurt my reputation."

"That ship has sailed." Brad eyed the untouched glass.

"But you contradicted yourself," I said. "First, you thought Maggie had seen or heard something so sensitive or damning that a man would kill her because of it. Then you turned it around and said you think the same person who attacked Isabel Vansan could be behind Maggie's murder. Which is it?"

"Can't it be both?" Axel pushed the tequila a centimeter closer to my partner. "Taste it."

"Which is it?" I repeated.

Axel dropped back in his chair. "If you're making me choose, I'll say it's the first one. However, it could be the second. Or Isabel fled because she'd been threatened with what would happen if she said a word to anyone about what she saw."

"Which was?" Brad asked.

"I don't know." Axel picked up the second glass and swallowed it in one gulp. "Power and money go hand in hand. While plenty of members of my club have respectable jobs, that isn't true of everyone."

"We know. Drug dealers. Car thieves. Arms dealers. Killers. The list goes on and on." Brad glanced at the closed office door. "Despite what you say, you will continue to profit off those people by providing them with whatever they want or establishing whatever connections they need. We're not buying this cleaning house bullshit. You have your fingers in everything."

"Not everything." Axel's cold eyes bore into Brad. "If that were true, if I were that omnipotent, I would have been able to help when you came to me about Liv, but I couldn't."

"Then help us now," I said. "It's how you can make up for it."

Axel looked at me. "Fox was in the building across the street. He happened to be looking out a window at the rooftop party when he saw what happened. But he was too far away to identify the killer."

"Why did you tell Fox to pick up Chambers that night? It makes him look guilty."

"It was Chambers' suite. That automatically made him your prime suspect. Nothing I did could make him look any guiltier. Instead, I addressed other issues that needed attention to prevent him from facing additional charges that would have complicated your investigation. You should thank me." Axel got up and refilled one of the glasses.

Brad leaned closer to me and whispered, "If Chambers left the hotel with a bag of illicit substances, wouldn't he have had to return to the party to get them after the murder took place?"

"They weren't passing out drugs at the party. It'd be too open. Too public. There would be too much exposure, particularly on that roof. That's why people kept leaving and returning," Axel said, reading the label on a jar a maraschino cherries.

I cleared my throat, causing him to look at me. "I filled out the paperwork, so answer my question truthfully, Mr. Kincaid. Where were the drugs kept? Were they inside Chambers' suite?"

He struggled with the lid for a moment before it popped open. "Don't be like that, unless you want me to start calling you Detective. This is supposed to be anything but official. So ditch the formalities." He took a cherry out and dropped it into a glass which he'd filled with something besides tequila. "Manhattan?"

Brad met my eyes, silently communicating that he'd been right all along. This was a bad idea. "We don't care about that. All we care about is who had access to the room in order to stab Maggie. If people were popping in and out all night, the door could have been propped open or the room key was passed around. We need to know the situation in order to properly assess our suspect pool."

"How would I know the situation? I wasn't there. However, if there were illegal substances on the premises, they would have been kept in a guest's room." Axel took a sip before stabbing the cherry with a toothpick and swirling it around inside the glass. "I don't want anything like that connected to Spark or a representative of the club. Chambers would never be so careless. Ideally, illegal substances would be housed by a member of the court. Someone who could argue they needed to be afforded additional privacy protections."

"They were in Fertrie's room, weren't they? That was the business he was conducting," I said.

Kincaid shrugged. "That would make sense. His alleged clients were going there to get wasted before returning to the party. And since he's claiming he was conducting business, you can't question him about it."

"Wanna bet?"

"Wouldn't they have seen Maggie?" Brad asked.

"They'd never admit it, not when they were getting stoned," Axel said. "It's Vegas rules. Whatever happened inside that hotel, stays at that hotel."

"Do you think that's what Maggie saw and that's why she was killed?" I asked.

Axel shook his head. "She worked in bars and clubs. What do you think goes on there? She'd be used to that. MDMA, LSD, coke, heroin, it's hard to find a club that doesn't have that on the menu. Spark is the exception, not the rule. No one would have bothered to threaten or kill her over any of that. More than likely, they asked her if she wanted a bump or a hit or whatever they were circulating."

"You know damn well what it was." Brad stared at Axel, but the club owner wouldn't budge. "What would they kill her over?"

"That's what I want to know." Axel pointed the skewered cherry at us. "You're the detectives. Figure it out."

TWENTY-SIX

Axel Kincaid affirmed what we already suspected but didn't offer much beyond that. He refused to say when Fox would return or what business he was conducting overseas. But since Fox was in the area the night of the murder, he had been given the thankless job of picking up Remington Chambers and removing the illegal substances from the hotel premises before the police arrived.

Axel refused to admit Fox brought Chambers to Spark. Instead, he said they must have gone out for a late night burger or early morning breakfast. After that, the two parted ways and Fox headed for the airport, forgetting Chambers' bag was in his trunk.

Nothing Axel said made much sense. Perhaps it would have if he wasn't so concerned with concealing other illegal acts from us, but no matter how many times we told him we didn't care about those things, he didn't believe us.

I wouldn't have believed us either. It was no secret the PD had been gunning for him for a while. Brad and I were the latest recruits in the war against one of the city's wealthiest men. It wasn't Axel's money so much as the blackmail he possessed on key government officials that made him powerful, almost to the point of being untouchable. Except, if he went down, he could take down all the crooked government players too. But that never happened. And more than likely, it never would. Instead, our energy was now focused on finding Maggie's killer.

Brad took the casserole dish out of the oven and put it on the table. "The pasta always gets crumbly when I reheat it."

"It doesn't matter. With all the sauce and vegan cheese, it's hard to notice."

He spooned a large portion onto my plate before helping himself. "At least we learned one thing tonight."

"What's that?" I picked up my fork, excited to dig into dinner.

Brad laughed, his eyes twinkling. "I told you we should have eaten first."

"Is that what we learned?" I blew on the steam rising from my plate.

"Okay, so we learned two things. But I was talking about Axel verifying where Fox was at the time of the murder. I figured he must have been in one of the neighboring buildings."

"Is that why you called in a request for security footage and access to that building?"

"Yes. And now we know precisely which building he was in."

"We do?"

"I asked Axel for the address on our way out."

"And he gave it to you? He started the night by telling us he didn't know."

"It surprised me too." After filling his plate, Brad looked around the table. "Do you want salad?"

"I don't want you to go to any trouble."

He went into the kitchen and came back with a bowl he'd taken out of the fridge. "It was already made." He put a bottle of homemade dressing down beside it. "I've been on a romaine kick lately. I hope Caesar's okay. It's Emma's recipe."

"When did Emma give you her recipe?"

"It was a while ago. I refused to believe her dressing didn't have real cheese and eggs in it. She was so determined to prove it that she dragged me into the kitchen and made me watch her make it."

"I don't remember that."

"You might have been asleep or under the influence of a

heavy dose of painkillers at the time." He tapped the side of his neck.

"Oh."

He shoveled some food into his mouth, chewed, and swallowed. "I'm hoping we might find a security camera or something on that other building that caught sight of what happened inside Chambers' suite."

"That would help a lot."

"Yeah."

We ate in silence. Too focused on filling our empty bellies to pause long enough to engage in conversation. But my mind continued to turn over the facts. When we finished the tray of ziti and bowl of salad, I helped Brad clear the table.

"Let's say Axel told us the truth. The party favors were kept in Fertrie's room. Most of the guests who disappeared from the party stopped by that suite, which means they had to pass Chambers' room," Brad said.

"Even if they saw something, they won't tell us the truth."

"But the footage showed people going into other rooms."

"For sex. For private conversations. For all sorts of things. It was a party with a bunch of people looking to blow off steam and enjoy a lost weekend," I said.

"Okay, but Chambers was in the gym when the murder occurred. We've checked his phone records. No one called or texted him after it happened. We're still waiting to get phone records for the rest of the guests, but Chambers said Fertrie went down to the gym to tell him something happened and the police were coming. How did Fertrie know what happened?" Brad asked.

"Maybe he killed her. That's what it looks like." I mulled it over. "No one saw Chambers go back upstairs. How could he have packed up the contraband and fled the scene before officers arrived and had a chance to search him?"

"Search him?" Brad scoffed. "They didn't even stop him."

"Still."

"The hotel staff didn't see him leave the gym, but that

doesn't mean he didn't. Maybe he snuck back upstairs and then went back down."

"I doubt it. By then, the manager was on the phone with 9-1-1, patrol units were arriving, and hotel security was buzzing. Someone would have noticed."

"Do you think, before Chambers went to work out, he shut down the fun?" Brad asked.

"That doesn't make any sense. Given the amount of food left and the reluctance of the guests to vacate the roof, the party should have continued until three or four in the morning. I doubt they had a mandatory sobering up period. No one was planning to leave the hotel or drive home."

"Except Chambers, which might explain why he went to the gym." Brad led me into the living room and turned on his computer. He brought up the hotel's website and showed me the photos of the gym. It had several fancy machines, large TVs, free weights, and several fridges with all sorts of electrolyte focused energy drinks. "When I was in the military, we'd go out on benders. On a few occasions, we needed to sober up quickly. Banana bags help, but we didn't always have access, so we'd sweat out as much alcohol as we could and guzzle sports drinks. Emma could tell you if there's any science behind that, but it seemed to work. Or we convinced ourselves it did."

"Just because Chambers wanted to flush his system, I doubt anyone else at the party had the same goal in mind. They wouldn't have wanted him to stop them from having fun."

"Whoever killed Maggie ruined their fun."

"Fertrie makes the most sense. He had the chance to take the room key and he went down to the gym to warn Chambers what happened. He has to be our guy."

Brad nodded, but his mind was elsewhere. "Let's say we present this to the DA's office. What is he going to say?"

"That it's circumstantial. We can't put Chambers' room key in Fertrie's hand or connect Fertrie to the knife used to stab Maggie." I thought about the crime scene. "What about shoeprints?"

"We might be able to get a court order for Fertrie's

shoes, but again, we're going to need something solid. Chambers' statements are too flimsy for that."

"Too bad Fox didn't see what happened."

Brad thought about it. "When we made the announcement on the roof, most people seemed genuinely surprised. Some may have been faking it, but I don't think everyone was. Fertrie became petulant. He was the drunk loudmouth. I don't know if he was surprised. He was too busy being a pain in our asses."

"That could have been intentional."

"That's one working theory. But we got no way to prove it." Brad glanced at the clock. "We could head back to the hotel, talk to the staff, walk through the place, and see what we can figure out now that the guests are gone and the rooms are empty. Whatever staff members that are at work now should be the same people who worked Friday night. Maybe someone will remember seeing Chambers, Fertrie, or West lurking in the halls or wandering around with a bloody shirt."

"It's worth a shot. Let's do it."

We left the kitchen a mess and got into the car. It didn't take long to arrive at the hotel. The roof and top floor remained empty. Everything had already been searched, but now that the guests had been forced to vacate, it wouldn't hurt to search again.

Edmundo Lopez, the night manager, gave us a wary look. "Any progress?"

"We have more questions," I said.

"Sure." He gestured to the empty chairs and couches in the lobby. "We might as well make ourselves comfortable." He dropped into a plush armchair and rested his feet on the edge of the coffee table. "Ask away. The sooner we can put this behind us, the better."

I went over the situation again, focusing on the gym and Chambers. But the manager didn't remember seeing Chambers return to the elevators.

"We thought he was still in the gym," he insisted.

"Do you mind showing us?" Brad asked.

The manager got up and led us down the hallway. The first room on the right was the gym. Beside it was another room marked sauna. On the other side was a full-service spa, which closed every night at nine, and farther down the hallway was the door that led to the indoor pool. "As you can see, the hallway's a dead end. Anyone who uses the gym or any of these facilities has to pass through the lobby. Mr. Chambers had to pass the front desk to get here, but I never saw him leave."

"But we know he left," Brad pointed out.

"That must have been after the woman flew past the windows. It was chaos after that."

"How do you know Chambers didn't go back upstairs during the commotion?" I asked.

"I guess I don't, but the elevator takes time. And it dings. Even if I missed him going back up, I'm sure someone else on staff would have seen him when he came back down."

"We'll want to talk to all of your employees again," Brad said.

"Sure. Absolutely."

"What about other exits?" Brad asked. "Could he have gone up to his room and left through another exit, possibly on another floor?"

The manager thought about it. "All the exits are on the bottom floor."

"What about the stairs?" I asked.

The manager pointed to the door labeled with the stairs symbol. "It's right here. But it's louder than the elevator ding. Someone on staff would have heard it and seen who it was. Plus, after the incident, security guards split up, covering both the elevator and stairwell while we tried to determine what happened, who had been hurt, and where it occurred."

Brad went to the door and pushed it open. It let out an ear-splitting shriek, which drew the attention of the housekeeper who'd been vacuuming on the other side of the lobby. "Guess you're right." Brad let the door go. "Did anyone else come down to use the gym after the woman impacted with the car roof?"

"I ran outside when that happened."

"So you don't know any of this," Brad said.

"I feel like I do. We've been questioned so many times, by so many officers, I know what my people saw or didn't see."

"Fine," I said, shaking my head at Brad, urging him not to press the issue. "Did anyone else want to use the gym?"

"One guy came down. He wasn't dressed for it, but he had his gym bag with him."

"Which member of your staff saw him?"

"Lucy. She's in charge of guest relations."

"Like a concierge?" I asked.

"Sort of," Edmundo said.

"Is she here?" Brad asked. "We'd like to speak to her again."

Lucy told us the same things the night manager did and repeated what she'd told the officers who questioned her. Until now, no one had bothered to ask if anyone else had gone to the gym. It hadn't been relevant. Chambers was the only missing guest, which is where our concern had been, but had he not vanished from the gym, we may have never worried about a random amenity on the first floor since it didn't have a clear connection to the crime that occurred on the sixth floor. That was our mistake.

"Mr. Deek came to use the gym that night. I saw him get out of the elevator," she said.

"Was this after the woman was thrown from the balcony?" I asked.

"Um..." She blinked a few times and blew air through her pursed lips. "It must have been. He came down with his gym bag, saw or heard what was going on, and changed his mind."

"What do you mean?" Brad asked.

"He let himself into the gym, realized how crazy that was, and went back upstairs. I didn't see him again until the following morning when he and his wife were checking out."

"Clayton Deek?" Brad pulled up his ID photo and showed it to the woman. "This man?"

"Yes. That's him. It's my business to remember faces."

I exchanged a look with my partner. "Do you remember seeing Margaret Tenzin prior to her death?" I asked.

"She came early that day to set up, left, and came back much later. She had an amazing dress. I don't think she was with anyone. She left alone and arrived alone."

"Did any of the other guests ask you about her or seem infatuated with her?"

"I stayed down here all night. A few guests asked for things. Most called in their requests. Only one or two stopped by my office upon their arrivals. No one said a word about her."

"What kinds of things did they want?" I asked.

"Scheduling spa treatments, asking for special accommodations for their pets, one couple wanted lunch reservations, another dinner reservations. Things like that."

"Did you see Mr. Fertrie at all that night?"

Lucy thought for a moment. "I can't say for certain. But if he came down to the lobby or went to the gym, he couldn't have stayed more than a few seconds. We were rushing around, trying to help that poor woman. So if he came down, he must have immediately turned around and went back up."

"One last thing," I said. "When you saw Mr. Deek heading back upstairs, had he changed clothes?"

"No. He wasn't in the gym long enough to have used the locker room to change. He still had on his suit."

"What about his gym bag?" Brad asked.

Lucy frowned, crow's feet forming around her eyes. "I don't remember seeing it on his return trip."

"But you remember seeing him?"

"Yes. We were waiting for the ambulance and police to arrive. Edmundo wanted us to make sure the guests remained calm and inside the hotel. So when the elevator dinged, we kept a careful eye on Mr. Deek."

"Why not Mr. Fertrie?"

"I don't remember seeing him. If he came down, it must have been when we were in the thick of it, before we received our instructions, when we were still figuring out what happened, who to call, and what to do."

TWENTY-SEVEN

We searched every inch of the property, but we never found Deek's missing gym bag. But I didn't expect to. We'd already gone through all the rooms, even the ones labeled authorized personnel only, searched every guest's belongings, and found nothing damning.

Since the knife used to stab Maggie had been left in Chambers' suite and Maggie had been tossed over the balcony, we didn't have to concern ourselves with the murder weapon. But we never found Maggie's phone, wallet, or any of her things, except for the few items she'd left on the roof which had been part of her show. Until we spoke to Chambers and Kincaid, we didn't have proof illegal substances had been on the premises, but now we knew they'd walked off before we commenced our search. I just wondered if more evidence had walked away with them.

"Clayton Deek brought the bag down to Chambers after Maggie was attacked. I wasn't expecting that." Brad slid the master key through the slot and pushed open the door.

"Neither was I. That's something new we'll have to explore."

Brad surveyed Chambers' room before stepping inside. "We need to take a closer look at Clayton Deek. Hotel surveillance never showed him leaving the roof, but Lucy told us otherwise."

"He could have been occupied while Chambers was still

on the roof, but after Maggie left, Clayton Deek made an excuse to follow her." I moved deeper into the room, unsure where to begin.

My partner studied the sideways table. "Based on what we've been told, Maggie had the ice bucket in her possession. She must have come inside the suite and placed it on top of the table." Brad pantomimed putting the bucket down. "You found a sequin from her dress in the bathroom, so she went in there." He froze in the doorway. "Do you think we're looking at this all wrong?"

"What do you mean?"

"We can't find her phone or purse, but would she have brought them with her?"

"She'd need money to get home."

"Not if she planned on getting a ride with someone else." Brad entered the bathroom and searched the stack of towels and lifted the lid on the toilet tank.

"I'll ask West about that in the morning. We could also check with the caterer. They weren't that close, but they seemed friendly enough that I'm sure Judi would have given Maggie a ride home."

"That would eliminate the need for cash or credit cards."

"Still, Maggie may have needed her ID for something else. What if she got stopped or the hotel wouldn't let her go up to the roof without proving she was here for the party?"

"The ME didn't find it tucked into her stockings or bra, and none of the crime scene techs or clean-up crew found it outside, so maybe she didn't have it with her."

"Nowadays, it's rare for someone to be without a phone. We know Maggie has one. But when we searched her home, it wasn't there either. I had the techs ping it, but we got nothing. They believe it's turned off."

Brad nodded as he listened, but he continued to search the bathroom. When he was satisfied we hadn't missed anything, he returned to the main room. "That night, she came in, put the ice bucket down, went into the bathroom, did her business, and came out. Someone else was here, waiting for her. He couldn't have been on the bed. It was perfectly made and unrumpled when we found it."

"He could have been standing here or sitting on the couch." I pointed.

"She turns her back to him to pour herself a drink. That means she knew him and trusted him."

"Or she didn't notice him. He could have snuck up on her."

"From where? I don't see any hiding places."

"True. Do you think he entered the room before her?"

"Probably not. Either they came in together or she let him in. If he was already inside, he would have brought the ice bucket and had drinks waiting."

"You're forgetting something. There are no glasses," I said.

"She could have taken a plastic cup out of the bathroom."

"I doubt it. We saw Fertrie hand her a bottle of water. She would have drunk that."

"Maybe she was still thirsty. Since the bottle wasn't found in the room, she could have finished it on her way down the stairs and discarded it in one of the trash bins in the hallway. CSU found several discarded water bottles in the recycling container."

"Did they dust them?" I asked.

"They checked them for blood residue. That was it."

I took a step back, picturing the scene. "She didn't get the ice for her drink. She got it because she was sore." I went into the bathroom and checked the folded towels. "I only see three wash clothes. Shouldn't there be four?"

"CSU checked. The hotel doesn't worry about how many the maid leaves when it's only a single occupant. The maid just grabs a stack and goes. They always leave at least two, but sometimes three or four."

"That doesn't help us."

"You think she was making herself a cold compress?"

"That's what I would do."

Brad scrutinized me. "What's that look?"

"Nothing."

"Bullshit, Liv. What's that look?"

"After Axel would let me out of the cage, he'd always make sure I rehydrated, and on occasion, he'd massage the cramps out of my legs."

"You never mentioned that in any of our debriefs."

"It wasn't relevant, but he made it a point to take care of his performers. Fertrie gave Maggie water. He could have told her to use this suite to relax and recover."

"Shouldn't Chambers have been in charge of that?"

"Not if he was too overwhelmed with everything else."

"Or too inebriated."

I returned to the fallen table. "Maggie grabs a wash cloth and fills it with ice. Her killer comes up behind her and stabs her in the back. Her legs give out, she grabs for the table to keep from falling, and knocks it over."

"He rips the knife back out and slings her over his shoulder, allowing him a free hand to open the balcony door. That would put her at the perfect height for him to toss her off the balcony without the railing getting in the way. It'd also decrease the blood trail." Brad stepped around the stained patch of carpet and moved to the balcony door. "Fox was over there when it happened." Brad pointed to a building diagonally across the street. "He would have had to been directly across from this room or on the floor above. Any higher or lower and he wouldn't have seen her get stabbed."

"That's a pretty good distance." I squinted across the dark street. "All I can see is shadows. Axel wasn't lying when he said Fox didn't see who did it."

"But they knew it wasn't Chambers." Brad glanced at me. "How could they assume that?"

"They knew he was in the gym when it happened. The bigger question is why was Fox keeping an eye on this particular suite."

"Do you think Axel wanted him to keep an eye on Maggie? Clearly, he has a thing for his performers."

"That wasn't my primary role at Spark."

Brad snorted. "But you admit he has a thing for you."

"Ugh, not this again."

My partner didn't argue. Instead, he studied the balcony and the street below. When he was done looking at the nothingness, he slid open the door. "Let's go across the street and see what we can find."

The building across the street was under construction. Just what the city needed, more luxury condominiums that most people couldn't afford. We flashed our badges at the night watchman and asked if we could look around. After we explained the situation, he let us inside.

"Did you see the men who were here Friday night?" Brad asked.

"Men? You mean the realtor lady and her potential buyer. Yeah, they were here."

"What time was that?" Brad asked.

"Eleven." The watchman shook his head. "I've never seen someone trying to sell a condo that late. She took him upstairs to check out the model unit. You might want to get one of those black lights like they have on TV because I'm guessing they were doing more than examining floor plans."

"Like what?" I asked.

Brad gave me an exasperated look. "Whipped cream," he mumbled.

The night watchman cocked an eyebrow at me. "Are you serious?"

"Did they have anything with them? Bags? Briefcases? Anything like that?"

"Come to think of it, she had a briefcase, and the guy had a backpack."

I gave my partner a look. "You know better than to jump to conclusions."

Brad held up his palms. "I stand corrected."

"I figured they were knocking boots. Were they doing something illegal?" the night watchman asked.

"We don't know. But we'd like to look around the building." I glanced at the elevator. Dry wall surrounded the metal doors. We'd already made the request. The paperwork should be waiting for us, so a quick peek wouldn't hurt.

"You can walk around, but if the room's locked, I can't help you. You'd have to contact the owner."

"I didn't think there was an owner," I said. "Aren't the units for sale?"

"They are, but this entire building and the construction

inside is being paid for by Wire Bros. Construction. Technically, they shelled out, so I guess that makes them the owners for now. I'm not really sure how that works for you, but if you want to look around, I say have at it."

Brad scribbled the name of the construction company into his notepad. "All right. If we run into any locked doors, we'll give them a call. But we're more concerned with the view than anything else." My partner hesitated. "Did you see what happened across the street Friday night?"

"I heard the sirens and saw the police cars, but I'm not sure what that was about. Some cops came by that night, but they just wanted a copy of our security footage."

"What about the two people who'd been inside the building? Were they here when it happened?"

"Yeah, they were upstairs."

"Did the police question them?"

"Nope."

"Did you mention they were inside the building?" Brad asked.

The night watchman rocked in his chair. "It must have slipped my mind."

I didn't like that response. "Do you remember when they left?"

"I'm not really sure."

"Did they say anything to you?"

He shook his head.

"Did they leave together?" Brad asked.

"Come to think of it, she left first. He was going to walk her out, but he stopped right over there to take a call." The guard pointed to an alcove where a plastic sheet covered a fake plant. "By then, things were crazy outside, so I wasn't paying that much attention to them. She was parked right over there." He pointed to a space half a block away. "I watched her get into her car, but she couldn't get it started. I went out to help, and when I got back, the guy had left."

"Are you sure he left?" I asked.

"Where else would he have gone? The police were all over the place, checking out the smashed car. I'm sure they told him to move it along."

"Smashed car?" I wondered if the night watchman was

playing clueless on purpose to avoid being asked more questions. Was he in on whatever business Fox was conducting inside the building?

"Yeah, it was parked across the street." He pointed to the spot where Maggie had landed. "That's where all the ambulances and cops gathered. I didn't see what banged up the car, so it must have been a hit and run. Anyway, after that, I came back inside and waited for morning so I could go home and get some sleep. Being up all night with nothing to do and no one to talk to gets boring fast, even with all the flashing lights."

Brad made a few notes. "Did officers ask to search this building on Friday night?"

"No, sir. They just wanted to know what I'd seen and if I could give them a copy of the security cam footage, which I did."

My partner nodded. "We appreciate that." He took a step toward the elevator. "What floor are the model units on?"

"Seven."

"Thanks." Brad pushed the button for the elevator, which made a weird metallic shriek before the doors opened. "On second thought, we could use the exercise."

The watchman pointed to the stairs. "I don't blame you. Until they complete construction, I wouldn't trust anything in this building. When I was using the john, the hand dryer fell off the wall." He gave us another look. "Maybe you should be wearing hardhats. It is a construction site."

"Thanks, but we'll take our chances." I glanced back at the night watchman who'd settled into a chair near the door. As soon as we were safely in the stairwell, I grabbed Brad's arm. "Fox must have posed as a buyer to get the realtor to let him inside. Or she's part of it. I'm thinking whatever business they were up to, the guard is in on it."

Brad gave the lobby a wary look. "What do you think they were doing upstairs?"

"I don't know." I ran through the night watchman's story again. "The call Fox took must have been Axel or someone else from Spark telling him Chambers needed someone to bail him out."

"That was what I was thinking too. We'll call the realtor in the morning and ask her some questions, but I agree with the guard. Looking at condos this late at night doesn't make a lot of sense. At least, he admitted that much."

"I'm sure that's not what Fox was doing here." I peered through the tiny window into the lobby. "Something's not right." The night watchman took out his phone and played with the screen. From this distance, I couldn't tell what he was doing. "Do you think he's calling someone?"

"Who knows?" Brad shrugged it off. "Let's check out upstairs. Once we determine if a clear view of the hotel room is possible, we'll come back down and grill the guy for more information on what was going on inside this building Friday night."

We took the stairs up, pausing on every floor to make sure it was empty. I opened the door each time and peered out. Plastic sheeting hung from the exposed ceiling beams and tiles. Sawhorses, dry wall, and various tools covered the makeshift tables. The building was nothing but a skeleton. The separate units hadn't been built. Most of the walls weren't even up yet.

At first glance, the seventh floor didn't look that much different than the others. Brad exited, pointing at the small dome lights. At least it had emergency lighting. Pulling out my flashlight, I shined it in all directions. But the beam of light didn't penetrate the clear plastic sheets. The place was quiet.

"It's a little eerie," I said as we followed the painted arrows on the floor down what would eventually become a hallway. I aimed my light higher up on the ceiling but didn't spot any security cameras. "Isn't it weird to have a night watchman guarding a building that's still under construction?"

"That's what I was thinking." We stopped when the arrows abruptly ended. An unfinished wooden door blocked our path. Brad tucked his hand into his sleeve, using that to tug on the doorknob, but it didn't budge. "Locked."

"Hang on." I shone my light around the edges of the door. "There." I pointed to a hide-a-key box.

Brad slid the cover off and removed the key. After inserting it into the lock and twisting, the door opened. "Seems stupid to hide a key in plain sight." He removed the key and placed it back where he found it.

I stepped inside and flipped the switch. The condo looked like it belonged in a different building. Two table lamps came on at opposite ends of the living room. I tucked my flashlight away and looked around. "Damn."

"Don't get any fanciful ideas," Brad warned. "You can't afford this place."

"I wish I could." Nice furniture and expensive fixtures filled the model unit. The large windows faced the hotel. Even from the couch, one could still see the glowing sign and individual room lights. "That's Chambers' balcony." I moved closer to get a better look. "I can't quite see inside the room."

"Let me see something." Brad took out his phone, selected the camera, and zoomed in. He snapped a few shots and handed me the device. "It's blurry, but Fox must have been able to see figures moving around inside. That could be why he didn't make a positive identification. Fertrie and Deek are built differently than Chambers. Maybe that's how they knew Chambers was innocent." Brad took his phone back and tucked it into his pocket. "He must have had a camera or binoculars. We don't know what he was looking for, but I don't think he was bird watching, and I don't think he came here because he's in the market for a new house."

"If he was here to spy on the rooftop party, he could have had a telescopic lens." I spun, carefully scanning the entire apartment, but there was no telescope. "Do you think that's why he was here?"

"I doubt it was the only reason. Let's hope we can persuade the guard or realtor to tell us since Axel hasn't been forthcoming."

I stepped away from the window and moved toward the kitchen. The refrigerator wasn't plugged in. But I opened the doors anyway. It was empty. Next, I checked the cabinets. They were also empty. Since I was here, I checked the oven.

"Anything?" Brad asked.

"No."

"I'll check the bedroom." He disappeared through a doorway. "The night watchman was mistaken. I don't think a black light is going to show much of anything. The room is pristine. This bed doesn't even look like it's been sat on."

"How can you tell?"

"It has that dirt protector cover thing that they have at mattress stores. The thing is spotless."

"That doesn't mean anything." I checked the bathroom which was devoid of everything except a few decorative towels. The closets were also empty. Returning to the main room, I lifted the cushions off the couch. "They could have replaced the mattress protector after they were done canoodling."

"I highly doubt it." He leaned against the doorjamb, watching me take the couch apart. "Are you looking for more hair ties?"

I glared at him.

"Too soon?" he asked.

I ignored his teasing, replaced the cushions, and sat down. The glass coffee table had faint smudge marks. Kneeling on the floor, I gave them a closer look.

"Did you find something?" Brad crouched down beside me. "What is that?" Putting on a glove, he ran his finger over the smudge and carefully examined the white residue left on the latex.

"Cocaine?" I asked.

Before Brad could answer, something crashed outside the room.

TWENTY-EIGHT

I exchanged a look with my partner. "Sounds like we aren't alone." I edged closer to the door. Brad took up a position on the other side, and I reached across to open it. The knob turned, but the door didn't budge. "It's stuck." More banging and crashing sounded from the other side of the door, followed by power tools turning on. "You don't think they're doing construction at this time of night, do you?"

"They shouldn't be. When we heard that first crash, it sounded like something fell over. I'm guessing it's wedged up against the door."

"And the chainsaw noise?"

Brad looked uneasy. "Let me try."

I took a step back, resting one hand on the butt of my gun. Brad twisted the knob and rammed his shoulder against the door, but it barely moved. He tried again, cracking it open. The saw sounded close, like it was right outside the door.

"What the hell?" Brad tried to see what was going on, but he couldn't with the limited view.

"On three." I took up a position beside Brad.

After counting down, we ran at the door, bursting through it. Several sawhorses fell over, as if they'd been propped against the door like a barrier to keep us inside. The clanging echoed and reverberated through the drafty building as we came face to face with a crazed man holding a buzzing circular saw.

"Stay back," the man lifted the spinning blade higher, pointing it in our direction. "The police are on the way. I called to report the intrusion." He glanced into the model apartment. "What were you doing in there?"

"Sir, turn that off and put it down," I said.

"The hell I will." He took a step closer to me. The whirring of the blade made me a little nervous.

"I'm glad you called the cops," Brad said. "But we're already here." He shifted his jacket to the side and tapped his badge before moving his hand closer to his holstered weapon. "Turn off the saw and put it on the ground. We don't need any accidents."

The guy looked at Brad's badge. "Bullshit. You're not real cops. Real cops don't dress like that. What cereal box did you get that badge out of?"

"It's real," I said, moving slowly to show him mine.

The man looked determined. "Prove it. Tell me what you were doing in there."

"Checking out the view." I held my hands up at chest height. "I'm Detective DeMarco. That's Fennel. Sir, we need you to turn the saw off and put it down. Now."

"I don't think so." The man looked scared. He wore a knit cap and fingerless gloves. He had on an orange safety vest over a worn black denim jacket.

"Sir, please," I repeated in that calm, forceful voice.

Brad reached for his weapon, and the guy shoved the heavy, spinning blade closer to my chest. "Drop it," Brad said, pulling his piece. "That's an order."

"Why should I? Because you say you're cops? I know you're not. You're just like the people who were here the other night. They said they were looking to buy a condo, but that was bullshit too. No house hunter does that at such a late hour, and they don't carry around large duffel bags either. I don't know what this is, but I don't want to get involved in it. So you're going to stay there until the police come, and then you can tell them your bullshit story."

"We are the police," I said. "But even if you refuse to believe that, put the saw down, so we can talk. Okay?" He looked uncertain, so I pushed on. "You said you saw people the other night with bags. I have questions about that. Obviously, you must have seen something. Do you know what they had inside those bags? Was it the same night the woman across the street was killed?"

"Liv," Brad warned. It was best to discuss such matters when a spinning blade wasn't being held a foot from my chest.

"Why don't you put your guns on the ground instead," the man suggested. "Then we'll talk."

"We can't do that," Brad said. "Not when you're threatening our lives."

"Isn't that getting heavy?" I asked. "Even if you won't put it down, just turn it off."

The man had locked his arms, pinning his elbows at his sides while he supported the saw, keeping it turned at an angle to protect himself while still threatening me with the tool turned short-range weapon.

"Turn it off," I repeated.

The man glanced from me to Brad, over and over, like we were in the middle of a tennis match. "Are you really cops?"

"Yes, sir. And if you don't stop threatening my partner with that weapon, I'm going to have to shoot you," Brad said.

The man stared uneasily at the gun before giving us a slight nod. "Okay."

Just as he reached for the switch to turn it off, a bullet ripped through his right shoulder. He lost hold of the power tool and fell to the ground. The blade cut into the side of his leg, chewing into it, just beneath his pelvis. He screamed as blood sprayed from the wound.

I jumped backward, getting out of the saw's path while drawing my own weapon. My partner didn't fire. The shot had come from behind the plastic sheets hanging at the other end of the building. Brad spun, shifting his stance and aim.

While keeping one eye on the spot where the shot had originated, I maneuvered around the screaming man and the spinning blade. As soon as I was clear, I yanked the cord out of the wall, glad it hadn't been battery powered.

Blood clung to my clothes and skin. It hung in the air, making everything appear tinged red and taste coppery.

"Are you okay?" the night watchman asked, stepping out from behind the sheet. "I heard the noise all the way downstairs. I saw him lunging at you. I had to do something."

"Drop your weapon." Brad continued to draw down on the night watchman.

"He was turning it off." I waited for the night watchman to holster his gun before kneeling down beside the injured man. "Shit." I grabbed my phone, put it on speaker, and called 9-1-1.

Brad crossed the expanse, removed the watchman's gun, and spun him around. After a pat down, he cuffed the man and returned to my side. The 9-1-1 operator was giving me instructions on what to do since the blade of the saw appeared to be lodged in the guy's leg. I removed his orange vest and used that to secure the blade and apply pressure to the sides of the wound to slow the bleeding while Brad found a roll of electrical tape and wrapped it around everything to hold it in place.

"Hey," I checked the man's shoulder, seeing a large red stain rapidly blossoming across his right pec, "stay with me."

The man had stopped screaming. Instead, he let out silent hisses. His face contorted in anguish. He had gotten significantly paler in the last few seconds. His eyelids fluttered and closed.

Brad checked his pulse. "He's going to bleed out if we don't get that under control." My partner climbed off the floor, frantically searching the nearby work stations for any towels. "You," he barked at the night watchman, "help me find something to stop that bleeding."

"But he was going to kill you," the night watchman protested.

"Just help me."

"Where's that ambulance?" I asked the operator.

"Two minutes out."

"Tell them to hurry." I pressed against the bullet wound and glanced down at his leg. Neither looked good. "Brad, the model unit."

"Right." He raced to the door, sliding on the slippery pool of blood as he went past me and into the condo. But he kept his feet beneath him. A moment later, he returned with the decorative bathroom towels. After we packed the bullet wound as best we could on both sides and secured everything in place with tape, Brad checked the man's pulse again. "He's still with us, but barely."

I hadn't taken my eyes off the night watchman. "Did you know he was up here?"

"No." He shook his head, moving a little closer but maintaining a safe distance. "I would have told you."

"Do you know who he is or how he got inside the building?" I looked down at the man who'd fallen unconscious.

"I don't know. No one's supposed to be working this late, but he's dressed like one of the construction crew."

"Is he one of the crew?" Brad asked.

The night watchman came closer, his arms bound behind his back. He bent over to get a better look at the guy's face. "Shit. That's Bud. I don't know how many times I've caught him in the building after hours. He never knows when to quit. He shouldn't have been here. He should have gone home. He knew better." The watchman looked at us. "Am I in trouble? I saw him attacking you. I only shot him because he was going to hurt you."

"We had it under control," I said.

"It didn't look like it. In fact," he was spinning out, "I only acted in order to save you. I saw two detectives in mortal danger and did the only thing I could." He tugged against his handcuffs. "And this is the thanks I get? I'm a hero. You can't do this to me."

"It's called attempted murder." I hadn't taken my hands off the towels, which were now soaked through. "Depending on how much longer the ambulance takes, maybe just plain old murder."

Brad gave me a hard look before focusing on the watchman. "Turn around."

I gawked at my partner. But he ignored me as he uncuffed the night watchman.

The man rubbed his wrists. "That's better."

"Try to see it from our perspective," Brad said. "It was already a tense situation. A bullet flew in our direction."

After thinking about it, the watchman nodded. "Yeah, no, you're right. You did what you had to. Same as me."

The wail of sirens sounded on the street below.

"Are the doors unlocked?" Brad asked.

The watchman shook his head. "I made sure to lock them after you arrived."

"Go downstairs. Let the EMTs in, and bring them up here. Can you do that?" Brad asked.

"Yes, sir." The watchman dashed down the hall.

"Fennel," I started, once we were alone, "he tried to kill this guy, and you're letting him walk?"

"It'll be for the incident commander to determine." Brad searched the injured man's pockets, finding his wallet, cell phone, and a rusted, well-worn pocket knife. "Bud Rapshaw. Forty-four." He leafed through the wallet, frowning.

"What's wrong?"

"No credit cards. No debit cards. He's got a transit pass, a library card, and this." Brad held out a crinkled old photo. Based on the clothes and hairstyles, I'd guess those must have been Bud's parents. Brad tucked everything back into the man's wallet and checked his pulse again. "Hang in there, man. Help's almost here."

The elevator made that same metallic crunching sound, and the doors opened. Two EMTs emerged with the night watchman a step behind them. He pointed them toward us. At least he hadn't made a break for it after shooting one of the construction crew.

The EMTs took over, inserting IVs, and making sure they had the saw securely in place so it couldn't move or cause more damage before sliding Bud onto a board and getting him onto a gurney.

"We have some O neg in the rig. Hopefully, that'll be enough to keep him going until we get to the hospital. He's at least two pints short, maybe more." The paramedic in charge glanced at the pool of blood and spray that covered the walls, the tools, and me. "We'll radio ahead and have a trauma team waiting." The PIC wheeled the gurney into the elevator.

"This is why you should never play with power tools, boys and girls," the other paramedic said.

"No shit." Brad glanced at the night watchman, who held the elevator doors open.

Once we were all inside, the paramedics asked for more details on what happened. As soon as we hit the lobby, they rolled Bud into the waiting ambulance, just as a patrol car pulled up.

A moment later, another vehicle arrived. Two patrol officers rushed out of the car, watching the ambulance speed off with lights and sirens.

"Damn, if this isn't a busy neighborhood," Officer Roberts said.

"Are you okay, DeMarco?" the other cop asked.

I looked down. Suddenly, it was too hot, and I felt sick. Swallowing the bile that burned the back of my throat, I took a few deep breaths, hoping to get the wave of dizziness in check. "I'm fine. But we need to figure out exactly what just happened and why."

TWENTY-NINE

Lt. Winston paced in front of his desk, giving us the evil eye. He hadn't said a word in the last two minutes, but it was clear he didn't want us to speak or leave. Beside me, Brad seemed resigned to whatever was about to happen. No matter how I twisted things, I couldn't fathom how this was our fault. But blame was the name of the game, and the optics on this were less than ideal.

Finally, Winston stopped pacing and rested his hips against the edge of his desk. Crossing his arms in front of him, he exhaled slowly and loudly. "Tell me again why two of my off-duty detectives were snooping around a construction site after dark."

"We received a tip immediately following Margaret Tenzin's murder that she was stabbed," I said.

"That was days ago, and that tip was hearsay. That doesn't explain what you were doing there last night."

"The same tipster told us he'd received his information from someone inside that building. When we asked the night watchman about it, he sent us to the seventh floor. Fennel and I wanted to make sure it was possible to see across the street and into Chambers' hotel suite before calling for backup and CSU to sweep the place. If we couldn't see across the street and into Chambers' hotel room, we'd know the tip was bogus.

"But since we could, we now know there's a witness to the murder," Brad said.

"Where is this alleged witness?" Winston asked.

"He's out of the country," Brad said. "But the night watchman told us he wasn't alone. A realtor, Helen Matthews, was also inside the building that night. And given the few things Bud Rapshaw said before he was shot, he must have been there too. He had to have seen something."

"Like what?" Winston asked.

"I don't know. We didn't get a chance to question him before he was shot," I said. "Has the night watchman been questioned? He could be involved in—"

Winston turned to me. "In what? You don't have proof of anything."

"Check the model unit. Brad found white powder on the table. There could be other evidence inside that we missed."

"That's unlikely. I've seen the photos. As far as the white powder residue you found on the table, it wasn't drugs. It was chalk and dust from all the construction going on beyond the door."

"When we arrived, there was no construction nearby. The night watchman told us the building was empty and offered to let us look around," Brad said. "We gave each floor we passed a cursory look. We didn't see anyone. Even after the incident—"

"Incident?" Winston snorted. "You call a security guard shooting a civilian who is threatening two detectives with a jigsaw—"

"Circular saw," I piped up.

Winston glared at me. "I don't give a shit what it was. A guard shot a man because you two were incapable of defending yourselves."

"That's not what happened," Brad said. "Bud Rapshaw was distraught. His confusion and anxiety made him hesitant to comply with our commands. Before he could turn off the saw, which he was about to do, the guard shot him."

"Which caused the blade to fall and the seventh floor of a prestigious future housing complex to turn into something out of a grindhouse flick. Didn't the two of you get enough of that with your last case?" Winston rubbed a hand over his eyes and took a seat behind his desk. "What I want to know is why you were even in that building during off hours. You called in your request. Why didn't you wait until the morning to follow up? That is not how things are done here. You of all people," he turned to me, "should know better."

"Yes, sir," I mumbled.

Letting out another exaggerated breath, Winston rocked back in his chair. "We can't keep doing this dance. I'd suspend you both, but it'll make it look like the department is to blame, which we aren't. On top of that, we're short-staffed, especially now with Voletek pulling double-duty for the commissioner. But this has to be the last time, or I'm demoting both of you and kicking you over to traffic. Is that clear?"

"Yes, sir." Brad stared straight ahead. "For what it's worth, this was my idea. Liv thought we should wait."

"I don't care. The two of you have some bad habits you need to break. I've told you this before. Too many times, in fact. Either do it, or I'll break you up. Got it?"

"Yes, sir," we both said.

Winston leafed through the folder, skimming our incident reports for the third time. "You're sure this is exactly how it played out?"

"Positive," I said.

"Yes," Brad agreed.

Winston closed the folder and grabbed a pen. "Do you think the night watchman set you up?"

"It looks like it. He told us the building was empty." I filled our unit commander in on everything else we'd been told about the night of the murder. "He's guilty of something. He withheld information from officers the night Margaret Tenzin was murdered. He didn't want them looking around the building. Since he shot Rapshaw, I'm thinking he's afraid the construction worker saw something and wanted to shut him up before he could say anything. I just don't know what Rapshaw wanted to tell us."

"I ran Rapshaw through the database. He doesn't have a

record, but he's newly divorced. The address on his license is his ex's place. A few of his construction crew buddies let it slip that Rapshaw sometimes stays on site after the crew leaves for the day. He doesn't have a place to live. He's got another week until he can move into the apartment he just rented," Brad said.

"Do you think he was sleeping in the model unit?" I asked.

"It had electricity but no running water. Also, the place was practically spotless. If he came in after working all day, we would have known," Brad said.

"He wasn't staying in the apartment," Winston agreed. "But he was staying inside the building or close to it. The construction crew works certain areas at certain times. Officers found some takeout containers and a sleeping bag hidden away in a secluded alcove, walled off by all that plastic sheeting. According to his financials, Rapshaw just signed up for a monthly gym membership. He probably showers at the gym since it's only a few blocks away. He's been sticking around that area since his divorce."

"He must have seen something," I repeated. "It was weird he thought we were fake cops."

"That makes you wonder what kinds of things were going on inside that building, doesn't it?" Winston rubbed an eyebrow. "You should know, Rapshaw's car had been parked across the street the night of Tenzin's murder. She landed on top of it, so Rapshaw must have been close by."

"Whatever freaked him out about our presence must have had something to do with whatever went down Friday night," Brad said.

"Maggie crashed into Rapshaw's car?" I asked, wondering how we missed this.

"Yep. It had been his ex's, but he got it in the divorce. The change in registration hasn't been processed yet. But I did some checking. It looks like Rapshaw might be the witness you should be questioning, assuming he survives," the lieutenant said.

I turned to Brad. "Do you think Rapshaw saw what happened to Maggie?"

"I don't know." My partner squinted, scratching a

thumbnail against his cheek. "He didn't say much, but he didn't trust us. He might have more to say now that he knows we're the good guys, but that makes me wonder why he didn't come forward sooner."

"Didn't he say he called the police on us?" I asked.

"He did, about five minutes before you called for an ambulance. The patrol car was already on the way when an ambulance was directed to the same location." Winston clicked a few keys. "The call he placed tonight was from the same number as one of the anonymous callers from Friday. Maybe he tried to come forward and changed his mind, or he didn't see anything."

Brad shifted in his chair. "Or someone warned him to keep his mouth shut."

Winston cocked an eyebrow, as if to say *who knows.* "Is this Rapshaw's voice?"

The lieutenant played the recording of the Friday night 9-1-1 call. "*A woman fell from the sky. Shit. She crashed into a car. Oh, fuck. It's my car. She crashed into my car.*"

"Is that all he said?" I asked.

Winston pulled up the rest of the transcript. "Dispatch asked for his name and location, but he hung up."

"Maybe he knows more about what happened to Maggie or why Fox and the fake realtor, as he called her, were hanging out in the building across from the hotel with duffel bags." I glanced at my watch. "Is Rapshaw out of surgery yet?"

The lieutenant shook his head. "The hospital hasn't informed us of anything."

"He might not make it," Brad said quietly. "You saw the damage. That was a lot of blood."

"What do we know about the night watchman?" I asked.

Winston glanced at Brad before looking back at me. "He doesn't have a record. His background check came out clean, and he has no known ties to Helen Matthews, the real estate agent who allegedly showed the apartment Friday night, Fox, Tenzin, or anyone associated with the rooftop party, the hotel, or Spark."

"That doesn't mean shit."

"Fine." The lieutenant was willing to bite. "What proof

do you have the shooting wasn't as innocent as it appears?"

"None, but—"

"But nothing." Winston held up his hand before I could protest. "You have no basis for thinking that. Your partner made the right decision to cut the night watchman loose, and the watch commander who assessed the scene said the same thing. The watchman acted within his duties. His actions, while extreme, could be considered justified. I don't doubt that he had ulterior motives for shooting Bud Rapshaw, but until you find an irrefutable link between the night watchman, Rapshaw, and whatever transpired Friday night, it'd be best if you two stay the hell away from him. In fact, consider it an order."

I wanted to argue, but it would have been a waste of breath.

Winston jerked his chin toward the door. "Go home for a few hours and come back refreshed. No more working off the books. I don't know what kind of ship Captain Grayson was running, but this is homicide. Remember that."

"With all due respect, we can't go home," I said. "We have that interview with James West in twenty minutes."

Winston considered his options. "Fine. But this is why you do not work during your off hours. Do it again without permission, and you are out of my unit, DeMarco. Dismissed."

My partner and I returned to our desks. "I'm sorry, Liv."

"It's not your fault. I'm the one who dragged you to Spark so we could speak to Axel. So stop trying to throw yourself under the bus to protect me. We both thought checking things out was a good idea."

Brad pulled some files out of his drawers and adjusted the items on top of his desk, lining them up neatly. "How many times has the LT threatened to kick us out of this unit?"

"You mean today or since we started working here?"

"Either."

"A lot." I scanned the papers scattered across my keyboard, making sure they weren't important before moving them out of my way. "But he sounded serious this time."

My partner didn't say anything, but he didn't like the threats. We'd gotten used to playing by a different set of rules, mostly since undercover work didn't run on a clock. Things were different now. But the LT was right. We had caused a lot of trouble in the last few months. Between my partner getting roped into an in-house sting and almost dying and me getting jumped in a liquor store, Lt. Winston had every reason to berate our actions, especially now that an innocent man was fighting for his life.

"It'll blow over," Brad said. "We do the work and solve the murder, and everything will be fine."

"That's funny. I was going to say joining homicide was the biggest mistake I ever made, and I'm sorry for dragging you into this."

He grinned at me. "Nice of you to say. Now can we get back to work?"

"Sure."

"For the record, I came pretty close to shooting Rapshaw last night. If he lunged at you again, I would have. So I see how the night watchman could make that argument, but I agree. He fired because he didn't want Rapshaw talking to us. The man was surrendering. Even from behind, I think it would have been obvious."

"See, that's what I don't understand." I leaned forward, glancing at the LT's office to make sure he didn't surprise us. "The building only has one security guard on duty at a time. Basically, he makes sure people don't wander in off the street and steal the construction equipment and the copper piping. That means he watches everyone who comes and goes. How did he not know Rapshaw was in the building last night?"

"He probably saw most of the construction crew leave and didn't bother with a headcount. I don't know any guard who actually has a sign-out sheet for a building."

"Okay, but Rapshaw was also in the building on Friday night. And the night watchman admitted he's found him inside the building on occasion. Wouldn't it have made sense to keep us out of the building instead of sending us upstairs to find Rapshaw?"

"He probably didn't think fast enough, or he figured

Rapshaw would stay hidden."

"Do you think he stayed hidden on Friday night?"

Brad mulled it over for a moment, tilting his head to the side. "I'll do some digging and see what turns up. Also, I'll follow up with Helen Matthews and question her concerning her whereabouts Friday night. Hopefully, she'll be more apt to speak to us. Can you handle the DJ on your own?"

"Yeah, no problem." I watched my partner's fingers fly over his keyboard. "Divide and conquer is a good plan, but is this because of what Winston said?"

"No, it's because this is the second time we've been up all night in the last three days. After everything that happened last night, I'd like to duck out early, if possible. We could both use a break."

"Sure." But I knew my partner. He was worried Rapshaw wouldn't make it and wasn't in the right headspace to deal with it today, not when we played such a large role in the man's potential demise.

We worked silently for the next thirty minutes. When my phone rang, I answered, not surprised when the desk sergeant informed me James West was waiting for me in one of the interrogation rooms. I collected my notes and pulled the yearbook Mr. Tenzin had lent us out of my drawer.

"I'm going to see what West has to say," I told Brad.

He pushed away from his desk and grabbed his keys. "I'm heading out. Call if there's a break in the case. If not, I'll meet you at that jewelry store around lunchtime. Hopefully, someone can tell us something today."

THIRTY

James West caressed the pages of the yearbook, a bittersweet smile on his face. "Maggie was so vibrant, so full of life. God, I miss her. I've thought about texting her a few times, and then I remember she's gone." He drew his eyes away from the book. "You're sure she's—" He swallowed. "You're sure she's the one you found?"

"I'm sure."

He flipped to the back of the book where he read a few of the notes Maggie's friends had written. "Do you have any idea who killed her?"

"That's why you're here." I'd already gone over the basics with him, but West hadn't given me anything but a bunch of excuses about why he hadn't disclosed the extent of their relationship. "When we spoke Friday night, you said you never saw Maggie leave the roof, but that wasn't true."

"It wasn't?"

"No, sir." I eyed him, unsure if he was lying or suffering from the same forgetfulness that afflicted Chambers. "We found some security footage. It showed Maggie leaving the roof. You followed her."

"No." He shook his head emphatically. "I didn't follow her. It wasn't like that. I just wanted to make sure she was okay. One of those creeps went out after her."

"Which means you saw her leave the roof," I pointed out.

"Yes, but she came back to the party with me. Didn't you see that on the feed?"

I didn't want to tell him we only had a few seconds of footage. Instead, I said, "Why don't you tell me what happened?"

"Maggie took a break. She'd been twirling most of the night. People don't realize how physically taxing that is. It requires a lot of strength and a lot of energy. She needed to recharge. But one of those guys who'd been drooling all over her went after her. At least he brought her some water, but I know Maggie. The last thing she wanted was to deal with some drunk idiot in her face, so I took five and went out the door. I asked her a few questions about her equipment. The loser took the hint and went on his way. Maggie came back to the party with me. The last time I saw her, she was near the bar. I didn't see her leave the party a second time."

I couldn't verify it yet, but West appeared to be telling the truth. "What was she doing at the bar? Toxicology didn't show any alcohol in her system."

"She wasn't drinking. She wanted to get some ice for her hands and wrists. The stress from swinging on the silks all night always made her achy. That was her routine. But the rooftop bar didn't have any plastic bags, like the clubs where she normally performs. They gave her one of the ice buckets."

"Ice bucket?" My ears perked up.

"Yeah. They had a stack of them. They used them to keep the champagne bottles cold."

I flipped through the file and pulled out a photo from the crime scene. "Is this the bucket?"

West took the photo and leaned closer to it. "Looks like it. It's got the Stonemore insignia. But they all looked like that. There were a dozen on the roof that night."

I returned the photo to the folder. "You said you've thought about calling or texting her. Do you know if she had her phone with her on Friday night?"

"Of course. Why wouldn't she?"

"Do you have any idea where she kept it during her performance?"

"She had it in her bag. When she showed up that night to work, she left her bag with the front desk. She always brought a backup outfit in case of a wardrobe malfunction." He raised an eyebrow. "You haven't found her bag either?"

Even though West had originally misled me, he was doing a fantastic job making me feel incompetent now. "She didn't have it with her when she died. We didn't find it in the suite where she had been. I thought she may have left her belongings with you since the two of you had to meet up later."

"Maggie never trusted me around her phone. She thought I'd check her messages or look at her social media pages."

"Why didn't she trust you?"

He wet his lips and glanced at the yearbook. "We have a history. We were friends. We had fun together. Sometimes, I'd tease her. Call it payback for her giving me shit about whoever I was dating. But she didn't like me poking fun at her boyfriends or getting in her business."

"Why?"

"I may have scared off one or two of them. To be fair, they weren't good enough for her."

"But you were?"

He sobered, his gaze dropping to the table. "No, but I never pretended to be. I made that clear from the beginning. We were always on the same page about that, or so I thought. I guess you'd say she was my best friend. After I offered to let her stay with me, we fell into our usual pattern. We were both unattached. And for a while, things were good. We were good together."

"She wasn't seeing anyone else?"

"Maggie wasn't like that. She didn't juggle guys. Before we got together, she had hooked up with some douche she met while working. After they spent the night together, she found out he was married. The asshole even had the gall to try to pay her."

"I have to ask, are you sure Maggie was never paid for sex."

"She wasn't a whore. She was a dancer. Not a stripper or anything like that. She was an aerial performer, a dancer, and a gymnast."

"Unfortunately, those things don't always pay the bills."

"Which is why she worked her ass off. She was a waitress, a bartender, a dog walker, a personal shopper, and whatever other gig she could get in order to make ends meet. She wanted to live her dream, Detective." He bit his lip and blinked a few times. "I'm guessing that's what killed her."

"No, some asshole at the party did."

"Yeah, but if she'd gotten her head out of the clouds, if she'd done what her parents wanted, if she'd given up, she'd be alive right now. I shouldn't have encouraged her." He took a few steadying breaths.

"Let's go back for a minute. You said she slept with someone before she moved in with you. Do you know who that was?"

"She always referred to him as the rich prick or the married asshole."

"Did she talk about him a lot? Did she give you any details about their night together?"

"We talked about our conquests, but not in graphic detail. Mostly, we'd just share funny stories. He took her somewhere nice after the performance, some swanky hotel. She bitched about how she forgot to steal the little shampoos because she'd been so upset about the way he treated her."

"But you don't remember where they spent the night or when this happened?"

"It was springtime. Maybe the end of spring. April, May, somewhere around there."

"Did she ever see him again?"

"I doubt it. She was pissed. We pretended none of that happened. We were kind of in our own little summer fling bubble after that."

"Until you cheated."

"We were never exclusive. I didn't realize that had changed."

"Maggie didn't ask for a committed relationship?"

West looked uncomfortable. "She'd bring it up from time to time, but I always blew it off. Things were good the way they were. We didn't need to rock the boat."

I pointed at the yearbook again. "Why didn't you tell me you knew Maggie since high school?"

"You didn't ask."

That was fair. "Do you know anyone who would want to harm her?"

"No."

"Did she owe anyone money?"

"Besides the credit card companies, her landlord, and the utility people, no." He held up his hands before I could ask. "Maggie never borrowed money from any creeps or skeezy folks. No one she owed would have hurt her unless the banks are operating under a new set of rules."

"What about her parents?"

"She couldn't stand them." West opened his mouth to speak and rubbed his lip, as if reconsidering. "I...um...saw her dad a few times. He'd show up at some of her gigs. He never talked to her though. And I don't think she ever noticed him."

"Do you have any reason to think he'd hurt her?"

"Emotionally? Sure. Physically? Nah."

"Are you positive?"

"Uh-huh. He had a terrible way of showing it, but he loved her. He fought with her and ordered her around because he wanted what was best for her. She never saw it that way. Her mom, on the other hand," West whistled, "is a crazy, controlling bitch." He realized how that must have sounded. "She wouldn't physically hurt Maggie either. At least, I don't think so. I mean, if she were going to, she would have done it already. Maggie told me about the screaming matches they'd have and their fights. If the woman didn't do something in the heat of all that, I don't see why she'd do that now."

"Do you know if she ever reached out to Maggie?"

"She didn't. She wanted Maggie to go home, begging and apologizing." He snorted. "The stubbornness is one thing they had in common."

"It sounds like you know Maggie's parents pretty well."

"We met a few times. They used to stop by the pizza place where we worked every Friday. I'd talk to them then. They were pleasant to me. But I mostly know them from the things Maggie has said over the years."

West had cleared up a few inconsistencies, but he hadn't told me much that I didn't already know. "You've been a DJ for a while."

"Years."

"That must be difficult since you got into some trouble. Did you disclose your record when you were hired to work this party?"

"I never did anything wrong. Those charges were bogus."

"You didn't answer my question."

He crossed his arms over his chest and slumped back in the chair, allowing me to imagine what he must have been like as a sullen teenager. "Yeah."

"Who interviewed you for the job?"

"Mr. Chambers."

"And he didn't care?"

"He judged me on my skills and nothing else. In fact, he never even asked me about any of that. I'm guessing he's gotten himself into quite a few scrapes." West scowled. "I never really liked the guy. He wanted things done precisely, and he bossed everyone around. I didn't like the way he spoke to Maggie. Have you looked into him? I can picture him hurting someone because his iced tea wasn't cold enough."

"Do you remember what he said to Maggie?"

"I only heard bits and pieces. It sounded like he changed his mind, but they had a contract. She reminded him of that, and he let her stay. I don't know why he wanted to axe her act. It's not like he had any other entertainment lined up. But I guess he figured it'd be easier to just have a DJ and the dance floor."

"Was anyone dancing?"

"Several people. Maggie would coast into the crowd and swing back. They left a path for her."

I showed him a few photos of the guests. "Do you remember seeing these people?"

"I guess. I'm a DJ. My attention was on my soundboard."

"Do you remember this guy leaving the party?" I showed

him the photo of Clayton Deek.

"No."

"What about her?" I showed him the photo of Nancy Deek, Clayton's wife, but I got the same answer. "Any of them?" I showed him the group who may have bumped into Maggie in the hallway.

"I don't know, Detective DeMarco. I was too busy to pay attention. In fact, I didn't even realize anything was wrong until your partner pulled the plug on the music. That's why I'm having such a hard time believing any of this is real."

"Did you ever wonder where Maggie went?"

"Not really. I didn't notice she was gone, but thinking about it now, I must have figured she was lounging in one of the little tent things or had gone to hang out inside the hotel. I really have no idea why anyone would do this to her."

"Do you think that rich prick who treated her like a prostitute would do something like this?"

"Are you telling me he was at the party?"

"We believe so. We found Maggie's journal. She mentioned some things which indicated that was the case."

"You need to find out who he is. I wouldn't put it past him. Not after the way he treated her that first night."

"Did he physically harm her?" I asked.

"I don't know. She never said. Maggie wasn't into the rough stuff, so I doubt it. The married guy had been great until he wasn't. That's why it came as such a surprise. If he'd been violent or abusive, she would have gotten out of there before he could have treated her like a hooker."

I showed him the photos again, spreading a few out but making sure Clayton Deek's picture was in the mix. "Have you ever seen any of these men at any of Maggie's gigs?"

"No. Do you think he was stalking her? She never mentioned any of that to me."

"Is it possible she was still seeing him?" I asked. "Maybe he reached out again after you two broke up, and she gave him a second chance."

"No way. Maggie didn't like juggling. She especially didn't like her guys juggling. I would know. There's no way she'd knowingly get involved with a married man."

"What if he said he'd leave his wife? Would that have changed anything?"

"I don't know. You sound like you already know the answer to that question. But I don't see why Maggie would do that. She hated the guy."

"Hate's a strong emotion. It's not that different from love."

"You think she loved him?" Something flickered behind his eyes.

"Do you think it's possible?"

West thought for a moment. "I don't know, but I've never seen her that hurt before." He bit his lip, shaking his head at a memory. "One night, she told me she'd thought he was the prince, rescuing her from the tower. Y'know, like in the fairytales. That's why his behavior the next morning was so abhorrent."

THIRTY-ONE

After my conversation with Mr. West, I called every bartender who worked the party. One of them told me he gave Maggie a bucket of ice. When she left the party the second time, he didn't remember anyone else going after her. And every single witness I spoke to vouched for West. He took that one brief break around midnight and didn't leave the roof or his DJ booth until Brad turned off the music. West couldn't have killed her, so I marked his name off the list. Two down, way too many to go.

But my conversation with West led to another question. If Maggie left her bag at the front desk, who claimed it? Brad and I had spoken to every member of the staff. No one ever mentioned anything about it. Could West be wrong or had we focused too much energy on the party guests and not enough on the staff?

The thought of dragging Chambers back inside an interview room held no appeal. As it was, we ran out of time and had to cut him loose. Calling him back now would not go over well with anyone, including Lt. Winston. And since Brad and I were already on thin ice, we had to tread carefully.

I phoned the Stonemore Hotel. As I expected, no one admitted to handing Maggie's bag over to a third party. But a bellhop said he had agreed to stow it behind the counter for her. Since that had been an unauthorized favor, the management stuck to their guns about not knowing anything about it.

"Great, thanks." I put the receiver down. The bellhop hadn't locked it in a safe or secured it. Anyone could have gone behind the counter and grabbed it, especially when most of the staff had been distracted by the dying woman outside. But how many people knew she left her bag at the front desk?

I checked to see if any more security cam footage from that night had been recovered, but the techs were still working on it. As far as I knew, three men had gone to the lobby and stopped by the gym around midnight. Remington Chambers, Francis Fertrie, and Clayton Deek. Any one of them could have detoured to the front desk and grabbed Maggie's bag. But the only person who could have walked it out of the building was Chambers.

Why would he do that? I wondered. Chambers had an obligation to protect Spark, the club's clientele, and the management. Did that duty extend to protecting a murderer? That flew in the face of Axel's latest proclamation.

However, Chambers tried to stop Maggie from performing at Deek's request. They must have been friends. After all, Chambers knew Deek was having an affair. Depending on how deep their friendship went, Chambers would want to protect Deek. But how far would he go?

I jotted a note down and stuck it to the board. Given what little we knew, it was a toss-up. Either Francis Fertrie or Clayton Deek could have killed Maggie. We knew Fertrie had left the roof prior to Maggie's death. He may have had access to Chambers' suite, and he had informed Chambers of Maggie's death. That gave him means and opportunity, but what motive did he have? Was he so desperate to get laid that he'd kill the woman because she refused his advances? Shit like that happened all the time, but without any hard evidence, I couldn't place Fertrie in the suite, let alone prove that he murdered Maggie. Without a history or existing criminal record, I didn't have a strong enough basis for these claims to compel Fertrie to speak to me.

On the other hand, Clayton Deek was having an affair

with Maggie. He had wanted her at the party and then changed his mind. Even though none of his fellow party guests remembered him leaving the roof, a member of the hotel staff saw him go to the gym with a duffel and leave without it. Since he and Maggie had been intimate, he could have been privy to her routines and where she kept her bag. It would have been easy enough for him to pass it off to Chambers. But since we didn't find Maggie's bag in Fox's trunk, I wondered what became of it. Did Chambers ditch it somewhere else, or did someone else do something with it? Again, I lacked proof. And I had no reason to think Clayton Deek had been inside Chambers' suite. So that was another bust.

The only other explanation would be Maggie was in possession of something sensitive and intended to harm someone with that information. That person killed her and absconded with her bag in order to destroy whatever intel she possessed. This reinforced Axel's initial theory, but nothing about Maggie screamed blackmailer. If she had been blackmailing people, she should have started with Clayton Deek. Given the squalor she lived in and her stubborn and bitter journal entries, she made it clear she didn't want anything from him. Maybe this had nothing to do with him. After all, she had a safe full of expensive jewelry, which she had been selling off in bits and pieces.

Again, I replayed the conversation I had with West. He didn't know anyone who wanted to harm Maggie, but he remained suspicious of Chambers and Deek. However, Brad and I no longer liked Chambers for her murder. Sure, he covered things up, but if he knew who the killer was, he would have told Axel. And that person would be facing something far worse than the criminal justice system. At least, that's what I assumed. Unless Chambers had a greater allegiance to his pal, Clayton Deek. But if Axel found out, Chambers would be in a world of hurt.

Shaking out my shoulders, I tackled this from another angle, except I'd gotten enough conflicting stories to only confuse me further. Why did the cameras have to be on the fritz that night?

Since I wasn't any closer to a lead, I spoke to Judi Rae.

She didn't know Maggie that well. They only hung out at work. They'd covered several of the same gigs. But Judi wasn't able to tell me anything I didn't already know, and she had paid even less attention to the men who'd been flirting with Maggie than West had.

I ran background checks on every hotel employee. Nothing turned up. Hitting dead end after dead end was getting old. Once I ran out of leads and paperwork, I grabbed my keys. Hopefully, Brad was having better luck.

I was a block and a half from the precinct when I spotted an aqua convertible behind me. He flashed his lights at me. *This ought to be good.*

Pulling into the nearest garage, I stopped my car near one of the security cameras and got out. Axel revved his engine, but I wasn't moving. "What do you want?" I asked.

He wedged in closer to my rear bumper, glancing behind him. "Are you going to write me a ticket for parking illegally?"

"What do you want?" I repeated.

"You're bitchy this morning." He killed the engine and climbed out of the car. Again, he glanced behind him, but traffic wasn't backed up. In fact, the only other car that entered the garage had already found a place to park. "Is that because of last night?"

"Last night?"

"Me, you, Fennel, and a bottle of tequila. Your partner was practically salivating over it. I wonder if he would have had a drink if you weren't there."

"I don't control Brad," I said. "He can do whatever he wants. But you should know, he's a damn good cop. He follows the rules. He's by the book. He won't drink on the job."

"You weren't on the job when you showed up last night." Axel snorted. "Why are you so mad? I was trying to be nice."

"No, you weren't. You wanted to tempt him. Why do you do that?"

"It's fun."

I exhaled. That wasn't important now. "What do you want, Mr. Kincaid?"

"Well, Detective DeMarco, you seem to have gotten off-track on the investigation."

"What are you talking about?"

"You haven't seen the papers?"

"No one reads newspapers anymore."

"It's a figure of speech. The story broke online. *Two police detectives involved in construction worker maiming.*" His eyes searched mine. "I didn't think you had that in you."

Thoughts of all the blood came to mind. I leaned against my car door as I fought to keep my mind from wandering further. All I had to do was stay focused on the task at hand. "Bud Rapshaw was in the area the night Maggie was murdered. He saw Fox and his female companion. He didn't buy the line of bullshit about the two checking out available real estate. Don't you think it's time you tell me what Fox was doing in that building and who else was there?"

"Your partner already took care of that."

"The realtor called you?"

"Are you surprised?"

"Why are you in the middle of this damn investigation?"

"Liv—"

"No," I spat. "You can stop doing that. Stop feeding me shit and calling it chocolate cake. You dragged yourself into this. I didn't do it. Not this time. Maybe I would have once I realized it was a Spark event, but that would have taken time. You could have used that time to cover things up or hide the evidence. Unless you already have. Did you make Maggie's bag and phone disappear? I know you made the drugs go poof. Did you tap a wand over them and say voila?"

He bristled. "It was abracadabra."

"Great." I exhaled loudly, like they taught us in yoga class, but it didn't make me feel any better. I still wanted to punch Axel in his smug face. "Is that how you made Fox disappear? Did he take Maggie Tenzin's bag with him? Is that why we can't find it?"

"What are you talking about?" But I saw it on his face. He knew.

"I need her fucking phone, Axel. The records aren't enough. She never made or received any suspicious calls or texts. I assume it's because she used an encrypted texting app, but I don't know because I don't have the phone."

"Are you finished yelling at me?"

"No." I found the lines of his tailored shirt and dress pants were almost as crisp and provocative as the lines of his sports car. "This is the third time you've known exactly where I'd be. You've established a pattern and crossed the line into stalking. Why are you following me?"

Aggravated, he turned and grabbed something out of the back seat. My hand moved to my gun, which he snorted at when he turned back around to face me. "You have no reason to fear me, Liv. I won't hurt you. I promise."

"I know who you are and the kinds of things you are capable of."

"Right, so why are you afraid of me?" He raised both of his hands to shoulder height. A woman's wallet was in his right hand. Slowly, he spun, lifting his jacket and shirt and showing me he wasn't carrying a weapon. "I'm not a threat. Not to you."

Shifting my stance, I let my hand fall away from my holster.

"May I?" He held the wallet toward me. "You said you wanted this."

"Is it Maggie's?"

"Yes."

"Where was it?"

"I can't tell you."

"Because you tampered with evidence."

He smiled. "You can't force me to incriminate myself."

I took the wallet, hearing the DA's warnings about how defense could argue against its admissibility in court. But I doubted it would matter, unless the killer wrote and signed a confession and tucked it inside. "How did you get it?" I said each word slowly and forcefully.

But he wouldn't answer.

It contained roughly fifty dollars in cash, a bank card, a metro pass, her driver's license, an old student ID wedged beneath the license, and another three dollars in change.

"Was there anything else in it?" I asked.

"I wouldn't steal from the dead."

"Where's her phone?"

"There was no phone."

"Dammit. I can't keep doing this. You're in possession of a dead woman's property. That makes you a suspect. And I am so tired of cutting you slack or looking the other way or doing this because your damn attorney will make my life a living hell over it. As it is, Lt. Winston's ready to give me the axe, so I might as well go out on my terms." I reached for my cuffs. "Axel Kincaid, you're—"

"It was in a ballet bag. Black and light pink. It was canvas and satin. Odd mix, if you ask me."

"Where is the bag?" I peered into his car, but I didn't see it.

"Maggie had another dress, a pair of ballet flats, two sets of tights, and her wallet, which I've given to you, inside the bag. There was nothing else."

"How did you get her bag?"

"Chambers had it."

"How did he get it?"

"Someone gave it to him."

"Who?"

Axel shrugged. "I don't know."

"Where's the rest of her things? I need to see the bag."

"Self-incrimination, remember?"

"Why didn't you give me her bag last night or mention it before now?"

"I can't. I don't have it. It met with an unfortunate accident."

"It could have contained evidence, proof as to who her killer is. At the very least, it would have given me grounds to bring my two suspects in for questioning."

"Two? Give me their names."

"Give me the bag."

"Liv," he warned, his voice a growl.

"You tampered with evidence. You interfered in a police investigation. You don't have grounds to stand on this time. Cooperate or else."

"I didn't notice her wallet. It was zipped into a hidden

compartment."

"What about her phone?"

"There was no phone."

"Bullshit."

"I swear, that's the truth. It wasn't there." For once, I believed him.

He watched a car slowly circle around us. They looked mildly interested, as if wondering if either of us was going to move our vehicles or if we'd been in a fender bender. But they kept going. Axel watched them until they crept up the ramp and disappeared on the floor above.

"I can't give you the bag," he said quietly. "We had a transportation mishap. White powder everywhere. Her bag got covered. If it hadn't, we would have left it in the trunk and you could have searched it. But it implicates Chambers and the party guests and my club. I can't have that."

"You would have left it in Fox's trunk?"

He shrugged which was the closest he'd get to answering in the affirmative. "If you want, search my car. Search me. I don't have her phone or her bag. And you can't prove that I ever did."

"You had her wallet."

"I found it and handed it over."

I hated when he played these games. "I need her phone."

"I don't have it," he hissed. "I never did."

"How did you come into possession of her bag? Who gave it to Chambers?" I could see the protest on Axel's face. "You want me to trust you, so in order for me to do that, you have to trust me."

"I have a hard time doing that."

"I know, which is why I have a hard time trusting you."

He considered my point for a moment. "From what I was told, Chambers left the hotel with three bags. He didn't realize or mention that the third bag belonged to Maggie. I'm not even sure he was aware he had it."

"What three bags?"

"His bag," Axel ticked them off on his fingers, "Maggie's dance bag, and a third bag, a leather duffel. Her bag was inside the last one, along with other private, inconsequential things unrelated to your investigation."

"The mysterious white powder."

Again, he shrugged.

"How did the leather bag and Maggie's bag come to be in Chambers' possession?" I asked.

"Remington Chambers had his bag with him. It's my understanding the others were brought to him."

"How did Maggie's bag end up covered in cocaine?"

"I never said it was cocaine."

"You didn't have to."

"This is not an omission or acknowledgment," Axel said.

"Of course, it isn't."

"Maggie's bag was small. It was stuffed inside the other bag. Chambers never opened the bag. He took it and fled, figuring it'd be best not to know what was inside in case he was stopped or questioned. We've found it's best not to tell him things since he has such a sucky poker face."

"We?"

"The royal we."

"You mean you and Fox?"

Axel grinned. "I'm glad you think we're royalty."

"What did you do with the cocaine?"

He shook his head. "I never admitted to that. It could have been talcum powder. That's common for dancers. I bet it's even more prevalent for aerial silk artists."

"What did you do with it?"

"That's beyond the scope of your investigation, Detective. It's best if you stay on task."

"Based on what you said last night, Francis Fertrie's suite held the illicit materials during the party."

Axel stared at the garage entrance, but he nodded, finally, which meant it was my turn.

"Fertrie was seen entering the gym after the murder happened. He told Chambers what happened."

Axel's gaze snapped to me. "How would he have known? Did he kill her?"

"I don't know. He's on the shortlist."

Something flashed behind the club owner's eyes. "I see. And the other name on the shortlist?"

Two could play at this game. "I can't remember."

Axel smirked, a chuckle escaping. "Careful, Detective. I might think you're having fun."

Ignoring his comment, I said, "No one remembers seeing Fertrie bring a bag to Chambers. However, someone else was spotted going into the gym with a gym bag. Could this leather duffel that you described be confused for or considered a gym bag?"

"It could. Who had it?"

I shook my head. "Bring me both bags, and we'll talk."

THIRTY-TWO

The jeweler examined the pieces with his loop before rereading the receipts. "I have the vaguest recollection of working on these. Give me a few minutes to check my records. My memory's not what it used to be."

"We appreciate it." Brad pointed to the security cameras posted in every corner of the room. Another two covered the exits. "How long do you keep the recorded video?"

"Ninety days." The jeweler stopped halfway through unlocking the door to the office. "Come to think of it, it might be one eighty. We upgraded last year. I don't remember which system we got. The dealer offered a ton of different upgrades. It was like he couldn't give them away fast enough."

"Would you mind giving us whatever you have?" I asked.

He waved a hand at me as he opened the door. "Yeah, yeah. Not a problem. My office manager usually takes care of all this stuff. I just gotta figure out where she put everything."

"Do you think she might remember who originally purchased these pieces or the woman who came in to return the gemstones?" Brad asked.

The jeweler chuckled. "She'll tell you she remembers, but it's a damn lie." He saw the confusion on our faces. "My wife and I run this place together. She's the self-appointed office manager. When we first started, it was just the two of us. Now, we have two other people who work for us. But based on the timestamps and dates on these receipts, I would have been the one who dealt with these customers. You can speak to my employees if you'd like, but I doubt they'll be able to help." He disappeared into the office.

I peered up at the security cameras. "What do you think we'll find on the footage? I'm guessing aside from Maggie making the returns and Clayton Deek making the purchases, there won't be anything else of interest."

"Do you remember Maggie's journal entries? Clayton Deek would send a car to fetch her. He might have had someone else run the errands for him. That would give us someone else we could question about their relationship and affair. Or," he peered into one of the display cases, "Maggie may have stopped in with a friend when she sold the gemstones back."

"James West?" I asked.

Brad leaned closer to the glass, seemingly distracted, but I knew better. "Possibly, but any friend would do. We've been digging into this woman since she was killed and we know next to nothing about her. It'd be nice to find out she had some friends. Real friends."

"Those are hard to come by. I only have two."

"That's not true. You have plenty of friends. We'd have dozens of interviews to conduct."

"Oh, so in this scenario, I'm dead?"

Brad straightened and glanced over his shoulder. "When you were stuck investigating me, how many names came to mind?"

"Several."

"That's the only point I'm making here. We have friends, coworkers, and family. We already tried Maggie's family, but that was a bust. She doesn't exactly have coworkers, unless you count the caterers and DJs, so that's done. But what about her friends? We haven't found any, but there must be someone she confides in."

"Everyone agreed she didn't maintain tight bonds with people. She was probably a loner."

"Even loners have friends, Liv." Brad moved to another display case. "Your birthstone's a blue topaz, right?"

"Sapphire." I went to see what he was looking at, but he

moved to another jewelry counter.

"I knew it was something blue." When he was done browsing, he returned to our original spot and peered into the office. The jeweler was bent over in his chair, searching the middle drawer of a filing cabinet. "It looks like we have a few minutes." Brad lowered his voice. "I'll catch you up on my morning."

"You never texted or called. I didn't think anything turned up."

"It didn't, really. The realtor said she and Fox spent most of the evening scouting up-and-coming neighborhoods and future hotspots. Fox wanted to see all kinds of places, from event venues to luxury condos. According to her, he's a regular customer."

"He is?"

"AK Holdings is."

"That's one of Axel's companies."

"Yeah. Fox's duties as GM must include finding places to host private parties."

"Did she say anything else?"

"She mentioned she only gives her most valuable clients preferential treatment, letting them check out the spaces and use them for practice runs to see if they'd be suitable for future needs."

"What exactly does that mean? Does she let Fox use the listings to hold Spark events?"

"Poker games, usually. She doesn't know what else might be involved, but the places are always professionally cleaned afterward and the owners never know."

"How did you get her to admit that?"

"I didn't." Brad glanced back at the office, but we remained alone. "Axel must have told her to cooperate. Right after I flashed my badge, she said she had to make a quick call. I swear, I heard her say, 'I'll do that, Mr. Kincaid.' But maybe I was dreaming. We haven't exactly slept yet."

"You weren't dreaming." I peered out the barred windows, making sure there were no fancy sports cars or men lurking in the shadows.

"Are you sure you're okay after your latest run-in with

Axel?" Brad moved behind me, brushing my ponytail to the side so he could check my scar. "At least you aren't scratching, so he must not have stressed you out that much."

"Winston stressed me out more." I turned to face my partner. "I don't think Axel found Maggie's phone."

"I know. You mentioned it three times already."

"What do you think?"

"I trust your gut, which is why I called for a search warrant for Clayton's place. Unless we have something solid, we can't touch Francis Fertrie. But since Clayton Deek isn't a lawyer and he was having an affair with the deceased, this is the easier way to go. We should have more than enough to search Deek's home, car, and office."

"Should we give Deek a chance to come clean?" I smiled as the jeweler returned from the office with pink and yellow receipts. "After all, the man didn't want his wife to find out he's a two-timing lowlife. We can offer to save him the embarrassment in exchange for his full cooperation."

"That sounds like a plan."

The jeweler put the paperwork down. "These pieces were originally purchased by Mr. Deek." He scanned the page, pointing out the customer information. "C. Deek."

"Clayton?" I asked.

"Maybe. He never provided his first name. As you can see here, he paid cash." The jeweler spun the copy of the order around. "He bought each of these seven pieces on different occasions. But this one," he reached for the bag containing a glistening pink diamond heart, "he asked us to deliver." He turned the order form around and pointed to the address line.

"That's where Maggie lives," I said.

Brad read the date on the form. "This was last week."

"Yeah."

"Do you remember anything about this particular shopping trip? How did Mr. Deek act? Was he nervous? Hurried?" Brad asked.

The jeweler shook his head. "He took his time, like he had to find the perfect piece. The only time men do that is when they're about to propose or when they majorly screw up."

"Which do you think this was?" I asked.

"Beats me. All I remember is he kept asking if I thought she'd like it. I didn't have the heart to tell him she'd be back in the next week or two to return it or swap the stone out for a cheaper alternative."

Brad showed the jeweler a photo. "Is this Mr. Deek?"

"Yep, that's him."

"And he always came in alone?"

"As far as I can remember. He'd show up in a fancy chauffeured thing. They'd park right out front, and he'd come in to shop. Then he'd get back in the car, and it'd take off."

"Did you ever see the driver?"

"Nope. But I was never very interested in that. The only time I pay plenty of attention to the vehicles outside are when they are far less fancy and I worry about getting robbed."

"Does that happen often?" I asked.

"Not lately. Most thieves are men or women who try to pocket a piece and walk out. That's why we keep a close watch on everyone, and with all the cameras, most of those people are pretty easily deterred. As far as getting knocked over, that hasn't happened in a couple of years. Knock on wood." The jeweler stepped back and banged on the table against the back wall.

"All right. Thank you for your time." Brad picked up the order forms. "Do you mind if we take these?"

"I figured you'd want them. I already made copies." The jeweler tapped a piece of paper he paperclipped to the top. "That'll give you access to the cloud where the security footage is stored."

"Great." Brad made sure it contained all the necessary log-in information we'd need.

"Oh, and in case you're ever in the market for anything special, necklaces, engagement rings, whatever, please keep me in mind," the jeweler called after us.

I read the order forms and receipts carefully, placing each one in the corresponding bag with the jewelry we had seized from Maggie's apartment. After I secured the items in the locked box inside the trunk, I scanned the neighborhood. The jewelry store didn't stick out from the rest of the shops in the upscale shopping district.

"Why do you think Maggie didn't sell back her jewelry instead of just having the stones replaced and accepting cash to make up for the price difference?" I wondered.

"She didn't want Clayton to know. Maybe she was afraid he'd stop buying her nice things, or he wanted her to wear them whenever he snuck away to see her."

I thought about the dresses and accessories in her closet. "Do you think he bought her clothes too?"

"We'll make sure to ask him about it."

I narrowed my eyes at one of the fashion boutiques down the street. But I had no way of knowing if Maggie owned anything from that store. "Clayton Deek works eight blocks from here." I pointed to one of the skyscrapers. "This jewelry store is on his way to work. It makes sense why he'd stop here."

"What are you thinking?" Brad asked.

"I don't know. The jeweler didn't find any other receipts, so I don't think Clayton had other mistresses. He must have bought the pink diamond as an apology. Maggie was pissed at him in her last few journal entries. According to West, she'd been pissed off since the first night they spent together."

"But she kept going back for more." Brad nodded toward the jewelry store. "The vic wasn't a sex worker, but she needed the money. The jewelry could have been Clayton's way of helping her out without offering her cash. Maybe he knew she was returning the gemstones. Maybe that's why he always used this particular jeweler. Most places don't offer exchanges or replacements. But this one does. Clayton Deek would have known Maggie would make more getting the retail value than trying her luck at a pawn shop and getting back a fraction of the jewelry's value."

"Do you think Deek thought he was acting out some kind of *Pretty Woman* fantasy?"

"I doubt any of the guests who attended that rooftop party are that generous. Clayton Deek was in it for the sex and whatever else he got out of their interactions. Who

knows? Maybe he even loved her."
"Enough to kill her?"
"I guess we'll find out."

THIRTY-THREE

The search of Clayton Deek's office and car didn't result in any evidence. We didn't find Maggie's phone or any of her personal possessions. Deek was too smart to leave remnants of his affair where his wife might find them. But we searched his house anyway.

Clayton stood in his foyer while an officer kept watch on the man. His wife, Nancy, was at the salon for her weekly appointment. She and several of her friends had a standing appointment where they'd have all sorts of cosmetic treatments performed, followed by lunch, a shopping trip, and drinks. Usually, Nancy would return home by seven, which may have been why Clayton was rushing us to finish.

"You could save us all some time," Brad said. "Point us in the direction of Margaret Tenzin's phone."

"Who?" Clayton asked.

Brad glanced around the house, not spotting any interior cameras as part of the home security system. "The woman who was murdered at the hotel Friday night."

"Oh." Clayton didn't bat an eye.

"We know you were having an affair with her, Mr. Deek." Brad had taken point on the questions while I helped conduct the search. Right now, I was looking through the luggage, jackets, and storage bins in the hall closet. So far, I hadn't found Maggie's cell phone, but I remained hopeful.

"You've been misinformed. I didn't know the woman

who died." Clayton coughed and crossed his arms over his chest. "It's a shame, but like I told you the other night, I was on the roof when it happened. You can ask Nancy about it."

"Stop lying. I've already spoken to the jeweler. He's identified you. We have copies of the orders you placed and the receipts. You paid cash, but your name is on the forms and Maggie's address was on the receipt for the heart pendant you purchased last week."

"That doesn't prove I was having an affair."

"Other witnesses have seen you two together. Don't bother denying it, unless you'd prefer to get your wife involved in this discussion."

"No," Deek said quickly. "You don't need to do that."

"How about we start over?" Brad gestured to the dining room table.

"Fine, but we need to wrap this up before seven."

"That depends entirely on you, Mr. Deek. The more you lie, the more time you waste."

"I'm sorry. I don't want Nancy to know. I never wanted anyone to know."

"Really? Didn't you ask Mr. Chambers to hire Maggie to provide entertainment for the party?"

Despite the situation, I grinned. Brad enjoyed conducting interviews, particularly when he got to announce ah-ha things like that. I could almost picture the satisfied look on his face.

"Yeah, I guess, but that wasn't so we could see each other. Maggie was really talented. I always loved watching her perform. She made an otherwise stuffy event fun. And she needed the gig."

Brad clicked his pen a few times. "Clear something up for me. What went on at this stuffy party?"

"It was appetizers and drinks on the rooftop. The DJ had a light show, and Maggie twirled for hours. Everyone else was chit-chatting, talking business, politics, and sports. Like I said, boring."

"Then why did you attend?"

"It was for charity," Deek insisted, "and Nancy wanted to go."

"What did the two of you do all night?"

"We mostly stayed under one of the canopies with the heaters and chatted with another couple. I watched Maggie most of the night. She was the only thing that kept me sane." His voice cracked. "It's a shame what happened to her."

"Did you speak to her at all that night?"

"Um...I don't think so. No, maybe I did. Maybe I offered her a bottle of water or something. I'm not really sure. I tried to keep my distance because of Nancy."

"And Maggie respected that?"

"She didn't want to blow up my marriage, if that's what you're asking. She understood her place."

Her place? Bolting upright, I bumped my head on the shelf. I wanted to give Deek a piece of my mind, but something sparkly caught my eye. Bending over again, I picked it up in my gloved hand. It was a sequin, just like the one I found in the hotel bathroom. I documented where it was found and placed it inside an evidence bag.

"Fennel," I called.

"Just a sec, DeMarco." Brad wasn't done with his questions yet. "What do you mean, Mr. Deek?"

"She knew where we stood. We were just having fun. Our interactions were casual. It was our secret. No strings."

"The expensive gifts you bought suggest otherwise."

"I wanted to incentivize her to continue to see me. She knew this couldn't go anywhere. Giving her nice things kept her on the hook."

"Despicable," I muttered from my position in the other room.

"Huh." Brad scribbled furiously in his notebook. "Did Maggie want to end things?"

"She tried, but she always came back for more." Deek snickered. "You could say she always came when I called."

"Brad," I tried again, a little more forcefully.

My partner knew that tone. "Excuse me for a moment." He got up from the dining room table and joined me at the hall closet. "What?" Despite his annoyance, he knew I wouldn't interrupt him unless it was important.

"I found this." I glanced into the room where Deek was

waiting. He drummed his hands on the table slowly, looking around like a kid hoping to get released from detention. "This looks like a match to the sequin we found in suite 606."

Brad examined it before peering into the closet. "I don't see anything else with sequins in here."

"Neither do I. CSU should be able to tell us if it came from Maggie's dress. Unfortunately, I haven't found anything else."

"Hey," Brad called to one of the techs with the Luminol, "make sure you check for blood. Liv will show you where to look."

"Go get 'em, tiger," I said.

Brad took the evidence bag and returned to the kitchen. "I'm sorry about that. You said you couldn't remember if you had any interactions with Maggie at the party. Are you sure you didn't come into physical contact with her?"

I took a step back, keeping one eye on the interview while I pointed to the bottom corner of the closet, so the tech could check for trace amounts of blood. I wanted to see how Deek would react to the sequin. But the man barely glanced at it.

"I don't know," he said. "We weren't in close quarters, exactly, but the dance floor wasn't that large. I'm sure we bumped into plenty of people."

"We?" Brad asked.

"Me and Nancy."

"Right, but you just said the two of you stayed near the heaters in one of those little private tents."

"It was more a canopy," Deek corrected, "but we stepped out a few times to get refills and snacks. The caterers didn't understand we wanted table service. Instead, they only circulated around the other groups. They were told to avoid private areas and conversations. That's a pretty standard rule at these events."

"Rule?" Brad asked.

"Yeah. Like, knock before entering."

"Uh-huh." Brad tapped the evidence bag. "Any idea how this got in the bottom of your hall closet?"

"What is that?"

"It's a sequin."

"So?" Deek's brow furrowed and his eyes widened, giving him a comedic caricature look. "Why does that matter?"

"Since you watched Maggie's performance, didn't you notice what her dress looked like?"

Deek chuckled. "I was picturing her without it. She was taut and trim with curves in all the right places. I can't believe she's gone. I'm really going to miss her."

"Uh-huh." Brad tapped the sequin again. "So you don't know how a sparkle from her dress ended up in your hall closet? Has she ever been to your house?"

"No. Never. Are you sure that's from Maggie's dress? Nancy has all sorts of glittery things. Handbags, clutches, sweaters. It could have come from anywhere. Why would you think that's Maggie's?"

"Witnesses saw you leave the roof. You took a bag and went to the gym where Mr. Chambers was waiting. When you stepped into the elevator to return to your party, you didn't have the bag with you. Care to explain what you were doing and what was inside the bag?"

"I don't know. Someone at the party asked me to run it downstairs. They said it belonged to Remy. That's Remington Chambers," Deek clarified. "He needed it."

"Who asked you to bring him the bag?"

"I don't remember."

"Why did you agree? Had Maggie left the party by then?"

Deek appeared to be running through computations in his head. "She had, which was why I volunteered to bring the bag down. As far as what was in it, I didn't think that was any of my business. Chambers forgot it when he ducked out. And yes, I left the party in the hopes of catching up to Maggie. We hadn't spoken that night, and the last time we did speak, it didn't end on the best of terms. I wanted to make sure there were no hard feelings. I wanted to make sure she was still open to seeing me."

"Was she?"

"I don't know. I never found her."

Brad eyed him. "Am I understanding this correctly? You

and Maggie had a fight?"

"It was more of a tiff. I told her Nancy wanted to go with me to the party, so I thought it'd be best if Maggie called in sick. But she wanted the gig. When I told her I was the reason she even got it in the first place, she stormed off. I wanted to make it up to her, but she was stubborn and angry."

"Angry enough to blow up your marriage?"

"No, she wasn't like that. She'd give me the silent treatment or make out with some guy in front of me to show me how it felt. That would have been the extent of it."

"Are you saying Maggie was making out with some guy at the party?"

"Not making out, but she was all over plenty of guys, and they were all over her."

"I bet that made you mad."

"I didn't enjoy it, but she was free to see whoever she wanted. I'm sure she had plenty of guys she rotated through. A hot piece of ass like that had to learn those tricks somewhere."

"And that didn't bother you? You didn't want her all to yourself?"

"I did, but," Deek shrugged, "I was in no position to make demands like that."

"It doesn't mean you didn't try. You bought her nice jewelry. I even heard you tried to pay her for sex."

"That happened a long time ago, when we first hooked up. That was a misunderstanding. And I already explained to you why I gave her jewelry. There were no conditions or terms that came with the gifts I gave her, but I hoped she'd stick around since there was always the promise of more."

"DeMarco," the tech drew my attention away from the dining room, "we found blood." He blotted the recently sprayed carpet and held up the sheet. The chemicals had interacted with whatever invisible substances had been on the carpet, turning it a faint purple. "It's not much. Looks like transfer."

I went into the dining room and interrupted the interview. "Where are your clothes from the night of the party?"

Clayton Deek looked confused, like he'd never seen me before. "They're at the cleaners."

"Any particular reason why?"

"What are you talking about?" Deek asked. "They were dirty and sweaty from me wearing them all night."

I thought quickly, figuring he destroyed the evidence. "Where are your shoes from that night?"

"I'm wearing them."

"Right now?" I asked.

Deek nodded.

"Check them," I said to the crime scene technician, who joined us with a few swabs and solution. It only took a few seconds for the blood to register.

"What is that?" Deek asked, unsure of the expression on our faces. "What are you doing to my shoes? These are designer."

"Is that why you held onto them?" I asked.

"Excuse me?"

Brad took over. "You said you left the party to return Mr. Chambers' bag. Where were you when you were given the bag?"

"I was on the roof."

"Who gave you the bag?"

"I don't remember. It could have been anyone. Frank, Evan, Josh. I really can't say."

"Would anyone else remember this happening?" Brad asked.

"Nancy, Tim, and Becky were with me. They were in a debate over healthcare, and I interrupted to excuse myself." Deek's brow crinkled. "They weren't paying much attention to me, so I doubt they'd remember who gave me the bag. But you could ask them."

"We will." Brad made a note. "Walk me through what happened after that."

"I took the bag and went down the stairs to the floor below, knocked on Chambers' door, but no one answered. Since he has this compulsive gym routine, I took the elevator to the first floor and went to the gym."

"Did you find Chambers?"

"He was wiping off the weights, like he'd finished his

workout, which didn't make a lot of sense since he hadn't been gone that long."

"Was he sweaty?" I asked.

"A little, his lip and forehead, but his shirt didn't have any sweat stains or anything like that. Why does it matter?"

"It doesn't," Brad said. "Was Chambers alone in the gym?"

"Uh-huh." Deek peered down at the tech who had removed his shoes and was examining the treads more carefully. "I gave him the bag."

"That was it? You didn't make any other detours?"

"No."

"What about Maggie? Did you find her?" Brad nodded to the tech who put the shoes into another evidence bag.

"Hey, what are you doing with those?" Deek asked.

"Did you see Maggie?" Brad repeated.

Deek looked up at him. "No. I figured she left. She and the DJ were close. I'd seen them together at several of her performances. I figured he was going to pack up for her since she wanted to get the hell away from there. Like I said, she was mad at me. Maybe she found someone else to screw. We all had suites. That was the only fun part of the party, to get absolutely blitzed and stumble down to our rooms to sleep it off. Whoever she snuck off with must have killed her. That's the only thing I can figure."

"And you're sure that wasn't you?" I asked.

Deek turned to look at me again. "What is your problem?"

"You have blood on your shoes, Mr. Deek. The lab will verify that it's Maggie's blood. Why don't you tell us the truth?"

Deek stared, open-mouthed, at us. "You've got to be fucking kidding me."

"Is that all you have to say?" I asked.

Brad gave me a look, but Deek didn't say another word. "Fine, you've left us with no other choice. Clayton Deek, you're under arrest for the murder of Margaret Tenzin." Brad cuffed him and read him his rights.

THIRTY-FOUR

"I didn't kill her," Clayton Deek insisted. "Maggie was very special to me. I'd never hurt her."

The lab hadn't yet verified the trace amounts of blood on Deek's shoes belonged to Maggie, but coupled with the stray sequin we found, the matching shoeprint in Chambers' suite, and Deek's history with the vic, the blood had to be Maggie's. It was the obvious conclusion.

Prior to this, Clayton Deek had never been arrested. His prints weren't in the database and his DNA wasn't in the system. We'd gotten court orders for everything. No reason to leave any stones unturned. A part of me wondered if he'd committed any other crimes. Once everything was processed, we'd find out.

"You said she was mad at you," I pointed out. "You lavished her with expensive gifts. Make this easier on yourself. What other things did you do to incentivize her to continue seeing you? Did you threaten her?"

"No. That was it. Maggie was proud. I offered her the world, and she turned it down."

"What did you offer her exactly?" Brad asked.

"Whatever she wanted. I told her to say the word. If she needed money or opportunities for more gigs, introductions to agents or talent scouts, or whatever, I'd be more than happy to make it happen. I know club owners, people who work on Broadway and in other parts of the entertainment industry. I also know influencers and online marketers. I wanted to help her succeed."

"In exchange for what?" Brad asked.

"Nothing. I didn't want anything from her."

"You didn't offer her these things in exchange for sex?"

"That wasn't a condition." Deek looked exasperated. "Yes, I liked being with her, but it was more than that. I liked her. She knew that."

"Did you ever buy her clothes?" I asked.

"No."

"She had several high-end pieces, including the dress she wore Friday night. Given the money in her bank account and the state of her credit cards, I'm curious how she afforded them."

Deek didn't answer. Instead, he checked his reflection in the mirror. "Is anyone watching this?"

"Maybe," Brad said.

"Nancy?" Deek asked.

"No, she hasn't returned home yet. Once she does, an officer will inform her that you've been arrested."

"I don't want her to know about Maggie."

"She's a witness, possibly an accomplice. It's out of our hands." Brad flipped through the thick folder. "I'm sorry."

"Maggie sold some of the jewelry I bought her. The first piece I gave her was an expensive pair of diamond earrings. But I never saw her wear them. She said they were too heavy, so I called the store and was told they'd been returned," Deek admitted. "I didn't care. In fact, I was glad. She didn't have much. The earrings gave her a leg up. They probably covered her rent for the year."

"So you kept buying her jewelry so she could return it?" I asked.

"She wouldn't take my money," Deek hissed. "But she needed it, so she could focus on perfecting her act."

"So you weren't paying her for services rendered?" I arched an eyebrow, waiting for an answer, but he didn't give me one. "She wasn't stupid. She knew what you were doing. She didn't like the way you treated her. She told you no. She said enough was enough. You made it clear your relationship couldn't go anywhere. You had no intention of leaving your wife, but you wanted to keep your mistress.

Except Maggie wasn't having any of that. She wouldn't let you control her. That must have made you mad."

Deek huffed. "Irritated, not mad."

"You gave her too much," Brad said. "If the earrings covered her rent. The rest must have covered her living expenses and then some. That must be how she could afford the equipment and pretty dresses she wore for her performances. You overpaid her, so she didn't need you anymore."

"Stop it. You're twisting things. That's not what this was."

I folded my arms over my chest. "Why don't you tell us how it was between you two?"

"You're not wrong, but you're perverting the facts. We had fun. Both of us. She said I made her feel like Cinderella. She got to dress up and be the princess for one night. She enjoyed that. That's why she kept coming back. She got more out of our relationship than I did, but the circumstances weren't fair to her, which is why I made sure she was compensated."

"The fairytale had to end at some point."

"She didn't want to call it off permanently. She was just mad. We had disagreements before. She'd ignore me for a few weeks or a couple of months, but eventually, she'd come back around. She always did."

"How did you communicate?" I asked.

"Text, video chat, things like that."

"We have no record of it," I said. "Your phone records are clean."

"I have a second phone. Prepaid. It's not registered under my name."

"Did you use any encrypted apps?"

Deek nodded. "I couldn't risk Nancy finding out."

"We'll need the names of those and your log-in information," Brad said. "If you don't have Maggie's phone, you should consider that someone else does. I hope you don't have any embarrassing videos or photos floating around."

But Deek wasn't taking the bait.

"If you were so enamored with Maggie, why didn't you

consider leaving your wife?" I asked.

Deek looked at me like I was insane. "You don't bet on a donkey to win the Kentucky derby."

Brad stopped me before I could say anything else. "Was your wife suspicious? Is that why you brought her to the party?"

"Nancy's crashed a few of Maggie's performances. The last time it happened, Maggie and I managed to sneak away. It was so fucking hot. It was the added risk that heightened everything. But Maggie hated every second. She'd been freaked out the entire time. She was terrified we'd get caught. She was afraid it'd destroy her reputation and budding career. She made me promise it'd never be like that again. So when Nancy changed her plans to come with me this past weekend, I told Maggie I'd keep my distance, but she didn't believe me. She knew how I got, what turned me on, and exactly how to get under my skin." Deek let out a derisive snort. "That's why we fought."

"That's when she broke up with you for good," I said.

"I don't believe that. She was just angry."

"So were you. And then to see her flaunt herself in front of those other men, to flirt with them, to entertain the possibility of spending the night with them, that must have driven you crazy."

Deek didn't say anything, but his cheek twitched. I'd hit a nerve.

"Is that why you went looking for her when she left the roof? You wanted to make sure she knew it wasn't over?"

"I didn't..." Deek licked his lips.

"You didn't what?" I asked.

"I never found her after she left the roof."

"Then how did her blood get on your shoes?" Brad asked.

"I don't know," Deek spat, his volume increasing. "I have no fucking clue. I never saw her."

"But you went looking," Brad said.

Deek nodded.

"Where did you look?"

"In all the open suites. Most of the doors were unlocked. I figured she wanted me to find her sucking someone off.

She was juvenile and petty like that. But I didn't see her anywhere. When I got to the lobby, the place was crazy busy. I thought maybe she'd gone down there to wait for a rideshare or hang out until the party ended. But I didn't find her curled up on the couch or anything. So I gave Chambers his bag and went back to the party. That was it."

"Maggie always brought a change of clothes with her to performances. Did you know that?" I asked.

"What's your point?" Deek asked.

"Did you go looking for her bag?"

Deek looked guilty.

"You found it," Brad said, "so you knew she hadn't left the hotel."

"Did you find her bag first or did you find her first?" I asked.

"I didn't hurt her," he screamed.

"But you found her?" I waited, but he shook his head. This was getting us nowhere. I leaned against the wall and glared at him. "You said you searched the other suites. Maggie was stabbed and killed inside a suite. We matched the tread of your shoe to a print left near the scene. Explain that."

"I can't."

"Did you take off your shoes or change clothes at any point Friday night?"

Deek glared at me. "This is crazy. Why would I?"

"Did you look for Maggie in suite 606?"

"I checked all the open doors. I don't remember that one being opened."

"Are you sure?"

"Not entirely."

"Maggie was murdered in that room. She was stabbed before she was thrown from the balcony. The killer got her blood on his clothing and his shoes. The carpet in that room was stained. Today, we found blood, her blood, on your shoes. If you never went inside that room or took off your shoes or clothes, I'm having a hard time figuring out how that could have happened."

Deek looked angry and a little queasy. "I don't know."

"Did you let someone else borrow your shoes?" I asked

sarcastically.

"No."

"Then how do you explain the evidence against you?" Brad asked.

"I...I can't. But you saw me that night. You questioned me. I didn't have any blood on me. And I never went inside that room. There must be some way to prove it."

My phone buzzed. I checked the message. It was a text from the lab. The blood found on his shoes was a match. And two prints pulled from the interior door handle of Chambers' suite were a match to Deek's pointer and ring fingers. Brad's phone buzzed a second later with the same message.

"That was the lab. They just placed you inside suite 606. That's Chambers' suite, in case you're curious. Would you care to revise your story?" Brad slid a blank legal pad toward Deek. "A confession will go a long way to lessening your sentence."

"I told you the truth."

"That's not what the evidence says."

Deek shook his head, his nose and chin crinkling in anger. "Fuck you. I'm done talking."

"Fine. We'll ask your wife and colleagues what they remember."

THIRTY-FIVE

Nancy Deek and her two friends, Tim and Becky Pickford recalled Francis Fertrie giving the bag to Clayton to take to Chambers on Friday night, just after midnight. Tim and Becky didn't remember Clayton going anywhere near Maggie, who they simply referred to as *the performer*. However, Nancy had a slightly different story to tell.

She had suspected for a while her husband had been unfaithful. His behavior had caused her to question him on numerous occasions. It's why she had followed him to a few of Maggie's other performances and the club events that he chose to attend. However, she'd never caught him in the act.

"I'm not surprised he's cheating," she said. "But to kill that poor girl, that's unforgivable. He's always had a vindictive streak. He'd never take no for an answer. When we were dating, he was pushy, but I just thought it was because he was always so sure of himself. He knew exactly what he wanted and made sure he got it. That bastard. I hope he rots."

"Do you remember if he changed clothes that night?" I asked.

Nancy tapped her newly manicured fingernails on the table. "He must have. He had on the same suit he'd worn to work when we left the house. But later on, I remember looking at him while we waited to be questioned, and he had on a different shirt. He'd taken off his tie hours ago, which is probably why I didn't notice immediately." She rubbed her eye, stopping a tear from falling. "He despises those things. God, I bet most women in my position tell you how they'd never imagine their husbands doing anything like this, that you must have gotten it wrong, that he was incapable of such violence. But he's not."

"Was he ever violent with you?" Brad asked.

"He wasn't abusive," she said. "I...I don't know. Before we got married, the wedding planning got to be too much. I just kind of snapped. I felt suffocated. I told him I changed my mind and called everything off. My girlfriends took me on a getaway weekend to the Bahamas. When I got home, I found my windshield smashed to bits. I never found out who did it, but I always thought Clayton had gotten drunk and pissed and needed to smash something." She sighed. "That should have been my warning sign."

"Any other incidents since?"

"Not that I can think of, but he's not nearly as passionate about me as he used to be. He hasn't been in over a year. I'm guessing that's why he sought her out."

Unfortunately, Nancy never glimpsed Maggie's phone or discovered her husband's second phone. She hadn't seen any bloody clothing when they unpacked, but Clayton had made sure to unpack his own bag when she wasn't around. She gave us the name of their dry cleaner, which matched what Clayton had told us, but there was no record of him dropping off anything in the last three days. We'd searched their trash, but it had been picked up yesterday. After Nancy answered the rest of our questions, she left the precinct, vowing to start divorce proceedings immediately.

Lt. Winston appeared at our desks a few moments later. "I heard you arrested the man who killed the dancer."

"Aerial silk performer," I corrected.

The lieutenant glowered at me. "That's what I said."

"Yes, sir." I glanced at Maggie's photo, pinned to the center of our board. The distinction had been important to her.

Winston followed my gaze, looking slightly remorseful. "As long as you closed the case, you can call her whatever you want. I take it you have evidence to support all this."

"Yes, sir." Brad put down the phone. "I just finished going over the basics with the prosecutor's office. They want to move forward and get this expedited. Even though Maggie wasn't anyone special, our initial suspect list included a lot of people who'd like their names publicly cleared as soon as possible."

"We've all been getting pressure to deal with this one." Winston rolled his eyes. "I hate these privileged assholes." He shook the thought away. "Of course, last night's incident didn't help matters. The hospital called a few hours ago."

"How is Mr. Rapshaw?" I asked, fearing the worst. "Has anyone spoken to him?"

"He's out of surgery. They're keeping him sedated for the time being. He's not out of the woods, yet. I'm guessing the complaints and lawsuits will be forthcoming, not just from Rapshaw, but from the night watchman, the construction company, and lord knows who else will come out of the woodwork to claim their piece of the pie."

"Damn." Brad bit his lip, fighting to keep from saying anything else. "He should have believed us when we showed him our badges. If he'd just turned off the saw, everything would have been fine."

"Any word from IAD?" I asked. Even if Winston didn't reprimand us, with lawsuits pending, our heads would be on the chopping block.

"Not yet, but I wouldn't expect that to last." Winston examined our board. "You get anything solid on Fertrie?"

"We're still working on it. We can put Clayton Deek in Chambers' suite around the time of the murder. Maggie's blood was on his shoes and possibly his clothing, but we can't prove the latter. However, Chambers never gave his room key to Deek. He thought Fertrie might have gotten a hold of it."

"Do you think Fertrie was Clayton Deek's accomplice?" Winston asked.

"It's possible the two were working together. Various people have claimed Fertrie was looking to get laid and had set his sights on the deceased. Perhaps he provided Maggie with access to the suite. But when she turned him down, he sent her boyfriend in to teach her a lesson. Then he cleaned up things for the rest of the party guests and told Chambers what happened while Clayton changed and removed what he could from the hotel."

"That sounds like Chambers also played a part in the murder," Winston said.

"He may have been an unknowing and unwilling participant." I had no proof. "We don't know what he did and didn't know, and without the other duffel bag he allegedly received, we don't have anything that will stick to him."

"Unless Clayton Deek gives up his accomplices." Winston made a whistling sound as he blew through his pursed lips, lost in thought. "But that will be up to the DA if they want to cut him a deal. What do we know about this alleged second duffel bag?"

"It was a leather gym bag. The only thing we know for certain about it is Fertrie gave the bag to Clayton Deek to give to Chambers. The bag contained a white powder and Maggie's dance bag," I said. "We assumed her phone and belongings were inside, but the only item recovered was her wallet. Supposedly, her phone was not inside the bag."

"But we can't prove Fertrie had knowledge of what was in the bag that he passed off to Deek, and we don't know who retrieved Maggie's bag from behind the check-in desk or who took her phone. We've asked Fertrie to clarify these things for us, but he refuses to answer," Brad said.

The lieutenant nodded. "Not much we can do without evidence or a witness. We need to find the vic's phone. Tomorrow, retrace Clayton Deek's steps from Friday night until you picked him up this afternoon. If he had it, he may have kept it or destroyed it since it held all sorts of incriminating evidence of his affair."

"That's what we figured," Brad said. "But it's not in his house, car, or office. We're running out of places to look."

"Then look harder."

I tried not to glare at our commanding officer. But I was tired and aggravated. Brad kicked me beneath the desk, which probably meant I wasn't doing a great job of keeping my temper in check.

Winston scanned the board, reading our scribbles. "All right. For all we know, Deek acted alone. You found a sequin in his closet and her blood on his shoes. We know they had an affair, and she wanted out. That made him mad. He left the roof to look for her, and the next thing we know, she's dead. That seems pretty open and shut to me. If that's what happened, that's what happened." He examined the photo of the knife used to stab Maggie in the back. "Too bad we don't have Deek's prints on this. That would make this a slam dunk."

"His prints were on the door handle inside the suite," Brad said. "We can place him in the room where she was killed."

"Did the DA say that's enough?"

"They sounded hopeful."

Winston nodded. "All right. If Fertrie's involved, we'll find a way to get Deek to name his accomplice. But right now, we collared the killer. So let's try not to piss off anyone else, okay?"

"Yes, sir," Brad said.

"Great. Now go home." He gave each of us a sharp look. "And I mean home. Do not go anywhere else or do anything else. Do I make myself clear?"

"Yes, sir," we said at the same time.

"Excellent." Nodding, Winston returned to his office.

Brad logged off his computer and locked up his files, pausing when he noticed I wasn't hurrying to leave. "What's wrong?"

"Nothing."

"That's bullshit, Liv. What is it?"

"There's more going on here. With Fox in the building across the street and the shit that went down last night with the night watchman and the construction worker, I... I don't know. I don't like any of this."

"Me neither, but evidence strongly suggests Deek's our killer."

"Is he the only one?"

"I don't know."

"I guess I'm stuck wondering how Deek gained access to Chambers' suite in the first place."

"Maybe he didn't. Maybe Maggie did. He admitted to looking for her. He could have knocked on the door, she answered, and he came inside. He tried to apologize, she refused to accept, she turns her back on him, and that was that."

"If she was mad and didn't want to see him, like he insisted, why would she choose to be alone with him in a room?"

"You read her journal entries. She may have despised him, but she couldn't resist him either."

"That's what you got from her journal entries?"

Brad's eyebrows lifted. "What did you get from them?"

"She wanted out."

"But she couldn't stop. You heard his wife. Clayton didn't take no for an answer. And Maggie hated how much she loved him. That's what I got from the entries and what West said."

"I guess you're right." I thought about Emma and how many times she went back to the wrong guys. "Now I'm wondering how the sequin got in Deek's hall closet when he changed his clothes at the hotel."

"He had to carry her from the center of the suite out to the balcony. The sequin got stuck to his clothing. He takes his bloody jacket and shirt off, along with the sequin, and puts them in a bag, probably a plastic bag or one of the garbage bags from Chambers' room. He returns to his room, stuffs that bag into his suitcase, and puts on new clothes. When he gets home, he waits for his wife to leave and unpacks. That's when the sequin fell out. Or it was stuck to his shoe and survived the trip home. Given the blood transfer we found, he must have kept his shoes in the hall closet."

"And his wife didn't notice any of this?"

"You heard her. She suspected, but she had her own things going on. Clayton made sure he kept it away from her."

"Okay."

He narrowed his eyes at me. "You don't sound convinced."

"I just wish we found Maggie's phone and knew what

Rapshaw was going to tell us."

"He's out of surgery, so I'm choosing to believe his odds are good. He'll be able to tell us whatever it is soon enough. In the meantime, we'll see what surfaces when we retrace Deek's steps tomorrow."

"Do you think he put Maggie's bag inside the leather gym bag? Or do you think Fertrie did that?" I narrowed my eyes at the board. "I think it was Deek. He would have known she had her bag. After killing her, he'd have to hide the evidence and hope we didn't find out about the affair."

"He should have thought about that before he opened his big mouth and asked Chambers for a favor." Brad rubbed his hands down his face, tired and frustrated. "But this is tomorrow's problem."

I collected my things and pushed in my chair. "Where are you headed?"

"You heard Winston. We are going home."

"Are you coming with me? I'm heading over to my parents' place. Mom has book club, so Dad's cooking. He mentioned something about firing up the grill, but I don't know if that's changed."

"Maybe next time."

"Sure." I watched my partner head toward his car. "Hey, Brad, are we okay?"

He turned to look at me. "Yeah, always. At least we caught the killer, right?"

"Right."

He offered a tight smile and winked. "I'll see you tomorrow."

"Good night."

But he wasn't okay. My partner was worried how everything would turn out. I couldn't blame him. I was worried too.

THIRTY-SIX

The drive to my parents' house was quiet and peaceful. No gumball-colored sports cars followed me or flashed their lights.

Gunnie, my parents' puppy, greeted me at the door. He jumped up, practically knocking me over in the process, desperate to lick my face. I scratched behind his ears. "Hey, buddy. You always know exactly what I need." He barked happily, ran around me a few times, and rolled over for a belly rub.

"Liv, is that you?" my dad called from the kitchen.

"It better be, or you need a new guard dog."

Dad stepped out of the kitchen to find me in the foyer. "We definitely need a new guard dog. This one's defective."

"You should have gone with another shepherd instead of a Bernese mountain dog. If you want, I can take him off your hands, so you can start fresh." I gave Gunnie a final pat and got up from the floor. "You want to come live with me, right?"

"This guy will outgrow your apartment in a few weeks. Get a house, and I'll think about letting you share custody."

"Whatever you say, Dad." I stretched, my back popping. "God, I'm tired."

"Are you hungry?"

"Famished."

My dad peered behind me at the closed door. "Is it just the two of us for dinner tonight?"

"Three." I pointed to the puppy.

"What about your partner?"

"He went home."

Dad's eyebrows knit together. "Brad knows he's always welcome here. Did you guys have a fight or something?"

"No, but we had quite the evening last night and our shift today's been something else. It's this case. It's...I don't know." I followed my dad into the kitchen and took a seat at the counter. Gunnie put his front paws on my thighs and laid his head on my lap so I could pet him.

"Want to tell me about it? I may no longer be Captain Vince DeMarco, but I remember a few things. I haven't been retired that long."

I gave my dad the rundown on our case and everything that happened the previous night while he prepared vegetables to grill on the electric griddle. "Maybe we shouldn't have gone to the building last night, but we were told it was empty. We were given the all-clear. We even checked each floor as we went."

"Rapshaw didn't want his presence known. He came at you with a power tool. You had every reason to draw down on him, and you attempted to deescalate the situation. However," Dad squeezed some lemon over the asparagus spears before picking up the pepper grinder, "you need to reach out to your union rep and have some things prepared for when the shit hits the fan."

"You just said we didn't do anything wrong."

"That doesn't always matter. This isn't the first time a suspect has been injured by a third party on your watch. Last time it happened, you and Brad had the suspect in custody when he was shot. This time, you were trying to take him into custody when he was shot. IAD won't like that." Dad put down the cooking utensils and opened the junk drawer. Pulling out a recipe box, which he used to keep business cards for important contacts, he flipped through the cards until he found one. "I can call a few friends and see what's going on and if any lawsuits are in the works."

"I appreciate it, but this is my mess. I'll clean it up."

Dad put the business card on the counter beside me,

figuring I might change my mind. "I'll keep Rapshaw in my prayers. Hopefully, he makes it. If he does, you might be able to talk him out of filing a suit. The city will offer him compensation. If he takes it, that'll help your situation. The arrest you made today will help too."

"I don't even want to think about this. I hate what happened to Rapshaw. I really do. But what irks me is why the guard acted the way he did."

"It sounded pretty damn reasonable to me."

"It wasn't. He's covering something up. Brad said the same thing. We just don't know what it is or if it relates to Maggie's murder."

"What does your CO say?"

"He's less concerned about that and more concerned about why we didn't wait before going inside the building."

"That is his prerogative."

"He's wrong."

"You're not running the unit, honey. Remember that."

"Yeah."

Dad gave me that look I always got whenever I was in trouble. "Yeah." He went back to cooking. "Is that why you and Brad are fighting?"

"We aren't fighting. Brad's worried, which makes him introspective." I feared my partner had a rough night ahead of him, but he had wanted to face those demons alone. And I'd learned that I couldn't save him from himself.

"Is that all it is?" Dad stopped what he was doing and looked at me. "Honey, what's wrong? What's bothering you?"

"The man we arrested had motive and means for killing Maggie Tenzin. But it's the timeline that gets me. It's one of those chicken and egg situations that I just can't explain. The only thing we could come up with is the killer had an accomplice or several, but he denies it. He denies all of it."

Dad took two tuna steaks out of the fridge, patted them dry, covered them in a mix of seasonings, and placed them on the hot griddle. The resounding sizzle made my mouth water. When was the last time I ate? "Run through it with me," Dad said.

"Clayton Deek supposedly left the party after receiving the duffel bag from Francis Fertrie. From what we've gathered, Fertrie collected the illegal substances from the party and put them into that bag because he knew the police were on the way to the hotel to investigate the possible murder. But if Deek didn't leave the roof until Fertrie gave him the bag, and Fertrie only gave him the bag because Maggie was killed, there's no way in hell Deek could be the murderer."

"What about the evidence?"

"If he'd gone into the room afterward, that would explain the blood on his shoes and his prints on the door handle. But it wouldn't explain the sequin."

"Are you sure he didn't leave the party before that, kill the woman, and return to the party? He said he got up a few times to get drinks and appetizers. According to his wife, she didn't even remember exactly when he changed, so it doesn't sound like anyone was paying that much attention, especially if they were tripping on hallucinogens. LSD, MDMA, things like that."

"True."

"Well, there you go. Problem solved."

"Do you really think it's that easy?"

"Nothing about homicide investigations is easy, but you found a piece of her dress at his home. Her blood was on his shoes. And his prints were inside the room where she was murdered. Can you say that about anyone else?"

"No, but there was a lot more going on at that party than we know about."

"You'll figure it out. I know you will." Dad finished cooking the tuna and veggies while I washed my hands and set the table. Once we were seated, he cleared his throat. "New subject?"

"Please."

"Anyone new in your life?"

I paused from cutting the asparagus. "Are you asking if I'm dating?"

"I heard something about a firefighter from your mother and Emma."

"Yeah, that's over." I went back to cutting the asparagus.

"Not that it ever went anywhere to begin with."

Dad's tone got serious. "What did he do?"

"He's a liar."

"Is that it?"

"Isn't that enough?"

"Oh, it's plenty. Maybe I should call a few of my pals who are still on the force. They could make sure his tags aren't expired and his brake lights work."

"Dad, it's fine. Really. It's for the best since I was allergic to him."

"Allergic?"

"That's what Brad said."

Dad busied himself with slicing the cauliflower florets, a slight grin on his face. "I'll have to remember that one." He looked up. "So if you have to see this putz again, will that be a problem?"

"No. Why?"

"You're sure? If he hurt you—"

"We didn't go out long enough for that. Why are you so concerned? This is usually the kind of thing Mom bugs me about."

"He's invited to the house this Sunday."

"Why?"

"Emma's supposed to be bringing Dino by to meet everyone, and Mom's holding a big family dinner."

"Why does Dino have to bring his friend with him? Is he afraid we're going to bury him in the backyard if he doesn't have backup?"

"We might."

"Why would we do that?"

Dad studied me closely. "What do you know about Dino?"

"Not a lot. He works in the hospital. He's divorced. Emma's crazy about him. And that's the end of it."

"Did you run a background check?"

"I didn't have grounds. That would have been an abuse of power and illegal."

"I'll have a skip trace I know look into him."

"Why?"

"You really don't know?"

"Know what?" Lack of sleep must have impaired my deductive skills and logical reasoning. No wonder this case had been driving me crazy. I was incapable of thinking.

"Dino came to see me yesterday. He asked for my blessing." Dad put his fork and knife down, his appetite gone. "He plans to ask Emma to marry him. He's popping the question Sunday in front of all Emma's family and friends. He asked if it'd be okay if he invited a few people to join us."

THIRTY-SEVEN

I couldn't believe Emma was getting engaged. "Does she know?"

"Based on your expression, I doubt it." My dad got up to clear the table. "I'm sure she would have told you the news if she knew."

"I can't believe this. They haven't even been dating that long."

Another thought crossed his mind, and his expression soured. "Is she in trouble? Did he knock her up? I'll kill him."

"Dad!"

He gave me a look. "It's a reasonable question."

"No." I thought about how she'd been glowing lately. "I don't think so. I'm sure if she was pregnant she would have told me."

"You're right. You would have known before he did, so that's not it." He loaded the dishwasher. "What do you think she'll say?"

"Yes." I was unsure what I was feeling.

"But we don't want that to happen?" Dad asked.

"I don't know him well enough. All I know is he makes her happy, but they all make her happy at first. What if it doesn't last? He already has one ex-wife. No kids, but still. He's cut and run before. He could do it again. The only thing I know for certain is he has lousy taste in friends."

"Do you want me to intervene? I'll say we don't have

enough chairs for him to invite anyone. Maybe he'll wait if he doesn't have his posse with him."

"Dino doesn't seem the type to travel with a posse."

"What about the Rat Pack?"

"Wrong Dino. Though, I spent the first few weeks of their relationship thinking he was a dinosaur."

Dad laughed. "Seriously, honey, I can tell him no. It might not keep him from proposing, but it'll keep his crappy friends away from this house."

"It's fine. Really. Sean is the least of the problem. It doesn't matter if he shows up. Dino will do whatever he wants. Honestly, I think Emma wants this too. Maybe that's why she'd been so insistent on me dating Dino's friend."

"How long did that go on, or should I not ask such questions?"

"We went out twice. I got called to work during our third date, and by our fourth, I'd determined he was seeing someone else and lying about it."

"I'll break his legs."

"Dad, we weren't in a relationship. We were getting to know one another. He had no reason not to see other people, but he shouldn't have lied." I shook my head. "What did you think of Dino? I only met him once. They seemed very lovey-dovey, but what if he and Sean are just alike?"

"Emma would have caught on by now," Dad insisted. "Twenty says she breaks his heart before he breaks hers."

"Be nice."

"What? You know how she is. The next time something sexy struts by, she'll forget all about him."

"Oh god, you're right. Like Jake in the hospital. That's even worse, isn't it? Maybe Dino is attracted to all these two-timing types. But Emma wouldn't cheat. She'd call it off first." I blinked. "Ugh. Too much to think about."

Dad laughed. "At least, I got your mind off other things. So say thank you."

I stuck my tongue out at him. "You know, I finally realize now where I get that from. It's all you."

"Face it, kid. You've always been one hundred percent

mine."

"That's why Mom likes Emma better. Did you tell her about the impending engagement?"

"First, you know your mom loves you more than anything. Second, hell no. She'd turn this entire house into a three-ring circus. The cousins from Italy would be on the next plane out if they heard the news. We don't want that."

"No, we don't." I pantomimed zipping my lip. "Mum's the word. And if I pretend not to know anything about this, Emma can't hold it against me for not telling her."

"Great, so I'll be stuck in the doghouse."

"Gunnie will keep you company. Right, boy?"

The dog lifted his head and looked at me, but when he realized I didn't have a treat, he went back to staring at the space beneath the couch, making sure his ball didn't try to escape from where he'd hidden it.

Yawning, I got up and stretched. "I'm going to take a shower and get ready for bed. I've been up for thirty-six hours. After all this excitement, I'm ready to sleep. Don't expect me to wake up before Monday. If I miss the engagement party, Emma can give me the highlights."

"Chicken." Dad picked up the business card and held it out to me. "Do me one favor and hold on to this, just in case."

"Fine." I took the card and headed up the steps, hoping we wouldn't need it.

After showering, I climbed into bed. Mom hadn't gotten home yet, but I was too tired to stay up to see her. The moment my head hit the pillow, I was out.

My ringing phone woke me. 2:02 a.m. The green neon light from the clock stared at me. *Brad?* My first thought was my partner was in trouble. But his name wasn't on the display.

"Hello?" I answered, my voice hoarse.

"I heard you made an arrest."

"Axel?" I squeezed my eyes closed, hoping I was dreaming.

"Why didn't you tell me you caught the killer? I need details. Did you find out why he did it?"

"How did you hear about the arrest? The DA's office

hasn't issued a statement or press release. It's too soon."
They wanted this wrapped up quickly, but they wouldn't do
it at the risk of more evidence turning up or accomplices
being named. "That news is not for public consumption."

"I have friends in high places."

"Good. Call one of them." I hit end call and put the
phone down. A moment later, it buzzed again. I hit ignore,
but Axel Kincaid was persistent. He called again. "It's two
in the morning."

"Were you asleep?" He sounded utterly bewildered by
the prospect.

"Yes. Please, stop calling me. You're adding more
evidence to the stalking case I'm building against you."

"Then stop hanging up on me and ignoring my calls."

"I can't talk about the arrest. This is an ongoing
investigation."

"Fine. I can respect that. For now." But I knew better
than to believe him. "Can you tell me who was arrested?"

"No."

"It's no matter. All I want to know is that you're sure
he's the killer."

I didn't say anything.

"Detective," Axel prodded, "are you confident you
arrested the right man?"

"I can't discuss this with you."

"I'm not convinced Clayton Deek killed her," Axel said.

"How did you—" I stopped, realizing I just verified it.
"Shit."

"Don't worry, it's no secret. His wife posted it all over
social media. He was having an affair with Maggie. That
much is clear. You believed that was the reason she was
murdered. Now you've found evidence, fingerprints and
blood, which back up that theory. But his prints aren't on
the murder weapon, and I'm sure you've already wondered
why they were on the door handle to leave the suite but not
on the door to the balcony. If he wore gloves to commit the
crime, why did he take them off before he left the room?
That makes no sense."

I hadn't even thought of that. "Shit."

"Have you found any bloody clothing? What about

Maggie's phone? You were anxious to get your hands on that when we spoke yesterday."

"That was today."

"As you pointed out, it's two a.m. That makes it yesterday." Axel sighed. "You're avoiding answering my questions. That's called deflection. You need to work on that."

"My job security is already hanging by a thread. You know I can't talk to you about any of this. Why are you asking?"

"You made me an informant. You need to keep me apprised of the happenings so I can assist your investigation. I may possess valuable information."

"Do you?"

"I might." But it was another one of his games. Tit for tat, as he called it.

"You didn't call to assist. You called because you have an agenda." I sat up in bed. "How do you know the things you do? Did Nancy Deek post all of that on social media?"

"Just the basics. I've done some of my own digging."

"Did anything turn up?"

"No."

I hated myself for asking, but if Fox had been across the street watching the rooftop party, he may have seen something and told Axel about it. "Do you know if Clayton Deek left the roof prior to Maggie's murder?"

"I thought you didn't need my help."

"Dammit, Axel."

He laughed. "I love it when you scream my name. Do it again, this time with an *oh god*."

It took a conscious effort not to hang up on him. "It doesn't matter. We'll follow the evidence. Right now, everything points to Clayton. If that changes, the department will reassess."

"Give me a few hours. I'll see what I can find out." He hung up without another word.

Unsure what that might entail, I had trouble going back to sleep. Every time I started to drift, my mind would wander to the possibility of Axel Kincaid dragging members of Spark into a back room and torturing them for information. It'd be bad for business, but murder was also bad for business. And Axel had been hell-bent on flushing out the killer, even if I wasn't sure why.

Eventually, I drifted into an uneasy sleep. When the alarm went off at seven, I reset it for eight. But that was a waste of time. Between my mother making breakfast and Gunnie whining at my bedroom door, I barely managed to squeeze in another ten minutes of sleep. This was why I needed to go back to my place or pull the trigger on a new place. If only I could convince my landlord to let me out of my lease. Maybe I could stay at Emma's if she moved in with Dino.

After getting ready, grunting a few good mornings, and filling two travel cups with very strong coffee, I headed to work. Brad was waiting when I arrived. I put one of the cups down on his desk, beside the one he had brought. He smelled strongly of aftershave and looked about as good as I felt.

"Morning," Brad looked up, concern etching his features. "Rough night?"

"Eventful. You?"

"Don't ask." He waited for me to sit down. "What happened?"

I yawned. "A late night caller woke me up. We need to check Nancy Deek's social media accounts and look for any press releases. Axel Kincaid knew a lot of details about the arrest we made yesterday."

"He called you?"

"Yeah. Over and over again."

"You need to do something about that."

"I'll change my number first chance I get."

"I mean it, Liv."

"I know." I rubbed my forehead, feeling a migraine on the way. "How was your night?"

Brad didn't answer. Instead, he swiveled his screen toward me. "Mrs. Deek posted about her cheating husband's arrest. She never calls him a murderer or elaborates on the evidence we have against him, but a lot of it is implied. It looks like she's trying to gain sympathy. This looks like some kind of smear campaign a publicist would run. Do you think her divorce attorney told her to do that?"

"Who knows? But if she didn't list any hard facts about the case, which it doesn't look like she has, how did Axel hear about it?"

"Did you ask him?" Brad shook his head. "Never mind. Talking to him is like talking to a wall." He adjusted his screen and nodded toward Lt. Winston's office. "Rapshaw's doing better today. The hospital called. They said he's awake. Winston made it clear he doesn't want us to show up and exacerbate the situation."

"I take it Rapshaw's going to pull through."

Brad nodded. "A few detectives will question him later about the incident and ask why he reacted to our presence the way he did. There has to be a reason why he flipped out like that. I'm guessing it had to do with whatever shit Fox was doing inside the building."

"Probably. Or it had to do with Maggie's murder."

"Or both." Brad rocked in his chair. "I've been thinking. The two events have to be related."

"Didn't we establish this yesterday?"

"We did, but I needed to give it time to settle." Brad sipped the coffee I brought for him. "I still can't fathom how they're connected."

"All we know is they are." I thought about Axel's interference in the case. "But I'm guessing we'll never be able to prove it."

THIRTY-EIGHT

Brad and I retraced Deek's steps from the hotel to his house. Thankfully, Nancy was able to fill in the blanks. We knew which roads they took, where Deek stopped for gas, and what time they made it home. After that, figuring out where he went became a tad more complicated.

Checking his cell records gave us a general idea, and traffic cam footage filled in the gaps. Despite what Clayton Deek had told us, he never went to the dry cleaners or laundromat. The garbage trucks had collected refuse from his neighborhood, so if he'd tossed his bloody clothes or Maggie's phone in his personal trash bins, we'd never find them. But that didn't stop us from searching the garbage at his office.

"I'm sure everything is long gone," Brad said after climbing out of the dumpster outside the high rise. "Where's the last place Maggie's phone pinged?"

"The hotel. It was shut off after that."

"Damn." Brad peeled off his gloves and tossed them into the dumpster. "That does not help us."

I checked behind the large rectangular bin, but I didn't see any phones or bloody clothes. "I need a shower."

"Me too." He checked the time. "Should we head back?"

"I guess, unless you have any other ideas."

Brad thought for a moment. "We've looked everywhere."

"What about his chauffeured car? The jeweler said Clayton always showed up with a driver. But when he and his wife went to party the weekend away, they drove themselves. Is that weird?"

"They own two vehicles. It makes sense they would use them on occasion." He plucked a piece of goo off the side of his pant leg. "But we should check with the car service."

"I'll call Mrs. Deek for the information."

Brad crinkled his nose. "Do you want to head over now or shower first?"

"I don't know. Let me see what they have to say."

Instead of stinking up our cruiser, Brad and I stood outside the car while I made the calls. Clayton's normal driver had taken him to work on Monday. But he didn't remember Clayton leaving anything behind.

"Did you make any other stops?" I asked.

"Mr. Deek asked if we could visit the newsstand and pick up coffee on the way."

"Is that unusual?"

"No, ma'am. We don't do it every day, but we do it several times a month."

I copied down the locations and asked if it'd be okay if we stopped by to search the car.

"You can, but it's policy to clean out the vehicle between clients. Many of them leave important or sensitive items behind. Most of our clients value our discretion and appreciate the extra steps we take."

"Did Clayton Deek leave anything behind?" I asked.

"No, ma'am."

"What kinds of things normally get left?"

"Phones, briefcases, computers, and undergarments."

"Oh."

"Like I said, Mr. Deek didn't leave anything in the car. He took his briefcase with him. He's always been very good about that."

"And you haven't found any cell phones in the last few days?"

"No."

"All right, thanks."

After filling my partner in, we headed to the newsstand and coffee shop. Since it looked like we'd be doing more dumpster diving, we might as well get it over with.

The newsstand was a bust. The man running the kiosk said Deek was a regular. He'd stop by every two weeks and pick up the latest copies of the economic and business journals. Deek was one of his only regulars. Not many people still bought print. But Deek didn't leave anything behind.

The coffee shop was our last shot. Entering, I ignored the way several people crinkled their noses. The barista didn't remember Deek, but she pulled out a wicker basket from beneath the counter and shoved it in our direction, desperate to get us to leave.

"This is our lost and found. I didn't find it, but Stacy, that's the girl who works the mornings, noticed a busted phone in the bathroom trash can yesterday. It should be in there somewhere. She picked it out, figuring a customer accidentally dropped it in the can."

Brad sifted through the basket, looking for the aforementioned item.

"Just take the whole thing. Whatever you don't want, you can toss or bring back. Just whatever." She gave us a fake smile. "Have a nice day, Detectives."

"Yeah, okay." Brad pointed to the security camera near the front door. "Could we get a copy of the footage too?"

"I don't know how that works. That's something the manager would have to deal with, and he's not in today. I can get you his number, or you could come back tomorrow."

"Sure, we'll do that." Brad hefted the basket.

"That's one way to get quick cooperation," I said.

"Here," he handed me the basket while he drove us back to the precinct, "see what you can find."

"This phone has a broken screen, so that may be it. And this one," I picked up a cheaper model with push buttons, "could be a burner." I tried to turn the first one on, but the low battery notice flashed at me once before the screen went dark again. "We'll let the techs take a look." I went back to checking inside the basket, but I didn't find anything that remotely resembled what Maggie or Deek would have worn Friday night. "Do you think this phone could be hers?"

Brad gave the phone with the cracked screen a sideways glance. "Let's say that it is. We'll go back, get the security footage, and prove Deek had her phone. That will mean he took her bag from the hotel. It'll be another nail in his coffin. Not to mention, whatever incriminating evidence may be on it."

"Do you think Deek acted alone? Like it was entirely his decision to kill Maggie?"

"I would assume so. Most of these things are crimes of passion. Deek had a clear motive. But we've gotten a lot of conflicting stories." Brad glanced at me. "Do you think Axel intended to confuse us by calling in the tip?"

"That's not his style."

"Are we talking about the same Axel Kincaid? He's refused to help every time we've asked, and when he does help, it blows up in our faces. Case in point, the situation with Rapshaw."

While I mulled that over, we arrived at the precinct. The tech department would analyze the phones we found and determine who they belonged to while Brad and I showered and changed. By the time I secured my wet hair into a bun, word had come back. The phone with the cracked screen was registered to Margaret Tenzin.

"What about the other one?" Brad asked. "Is that Deek's prepaid?"

"No. This one is registered to Tyler Forrest." The tech shrugged. "Does that name mean anything to you?"

"Not off the bat? Can you run a background, just to make sure?"

"No problem." The tech did as we asked, pulling up the information on the sixty-four year old retiree.

I read the details on the screen, but the phone appeared to be legitimately lost. "Let's get an officer to bring it back to Mr. Forrest and while he's there, he can ask a few questions, but it looks like the guy just left it behind."

"Probably." The tech rummaged through the basket. "What do you want me to do with the rest of this stuff?"

"We'll have forensics check for blood, but I doubt any of this relates to our case. Once it's cleared, we'll return it to the coffee shop and pick up the security cam footage." Brad rubbed his eyes. "How long will it take to pull everything off Maggie's phone?"

"We should have everything within the hour."

"Including texts and messages sent via encrypted apps?"

"As long as she didn't delete the messages, they should be here. Either way, we'll get her user information. We should be able to file a request with the company. If they have any data stored, we'll get access to it."

"Do they store data?" I asked.

"It depends. They aren't supposed to, but terms of service vary from place to place." The tech had plugged the phone into his computer. The home page displayed on his screen, and he opened the only encrypted texting app. The loading screen came up, followed by dozens of back and forth messages. He scrolled up, finding no end in sight. "This may be all of it."

"How many people did she speak to?" Brad asked.

"I'm seeing at least four conversation threads."

"So four people?" I asked.

The tech nodded. "At least. I'll get you a printout as soon as I can."

Leaving him to work, Brad and I returned to homicide. It was time to update Lt. Winston on our progress.

"I'm surprised you found her phone. I was sure that was in the crapper." Winston shuffled some papers on his desk. "See what the text messages show and follow up if there's anything to follow up on."

"Yes, sir," Brad said. "Whatever happened with Rapshaw?"

"Voletek went to speak to him. He should be back any minute with an update." Winston glanced at his open office door and lowered his voice. "So far, no complaints have been filed against you or the department, but that could change at any moment. Remember that and tread lightly."

"Will do." Brad turned to leave, hesitating when I didn't follow.

"I'll catch up. Close the door," I said.

My partner nodded and let himself out.

Winston looked less than pleased that he had to speak to me alone. "What is it now, DeMarco?"

"My CI called late last night. He knew about Deek's arrest and the evidence we have against him."

"And you're wondering how he knew these things."

"Yes, sir."

"Did you ask him?"

I resisted the urge to say something insubordinate. "Yes, but as usual, he refused to answer."

"Are you suggesting the department has another leak?"

"I don't know what's going on."

Winston exhaled dramatically. "Find out and get back to me on that."

"Yes, sir."

As I was returning to my desk, Voletek came through the double doors. He headed straight for us, pulling out his notebook on the way. He didn't waste any time. "I'm glad you're back. I just finished up with Bud Rapshaw. That poor guy."

"Do we want to know?" Brad asked.

"He's got a long road to recovery ahead of him, but that's neither here nor there." Voletek grabbed the arm of his chair and dragged it across the expanse so he could sit down beside our desks. Spreading his notebook on top of the first empty space he found, he clicked his pen and smiled. "Rapshaw had been on his way back from getting some takeout when Margaret Tenzin was murdered. He was across the street when she crashed into the roof of his car. That's when he called 9-1-1."

"We figured as much," I said.

Voletek winked at me. "Patience, princess." He flipped to the next page. "When that happened, the security guard," he pointed to the night watchman's name, "went outside to see what caused the noise."

"Did the night watchman know Rapshaw was returning to the building?" Brad asked.

"Yep." Voletek smiled. "Rapshaw paid him two hundred bucks to keep his mouth shut. The night watchman knew Rapshaw was staying in the building. He knew he was there the night you and Liv showed up, and he knew damn well who he fired upon."

I gave Brad's arm a shove. "I told you he did it

intentionally."

"Do we know why?" my partner asked.

"Rapshaw wasn't clear on that or exactly how or what happened that landed him in the hospital. His mind may have blocked out some of the trauma, but Rapshaw said he saw the night watchman let someone else into the building late Friday night. I let him look through photos of our suspects, and he pinpointed Chambers. He said Chambers ran across the street about fifteen minutes after Maggie crashed into the roof of his car. The night watchman ushered him inside, and he saw him get into the elevator where the man with the backpack was waiting."

"Fox," I said.

Voletek nodded. "I didn't have his photo handy, but Rapshaw said it was the man he'd seen with the realtor lady. He said the realtor left, but the two men remained in the model unit until nearly daybreak."

"They must have waited for us to head to the hospital before they slipped away. At that point, officers were too busy keeping people from leaving the hotel to worry about what was going on in the surrounding buildings," Brad said.

"So that's where Chambers spent the night." I glanced at my partner. "He wasn't at Spark."

"But Kincaid said what he did so we'd assume Chambers was there. He wanted to keep us distracted and away from the area so his guys could get out scot-free." Brad shook his head. "I told you not to trust him."

"Regardless," Voletek said before I could respond, "Rapshaw overhead the men talking inside the model unit. Fox sounded concerned that the murder across the street would cause additional scrutiny and keep them from moving in and out. Rapshaw's not positive what they were talking about, but he figured it was something illegal. At first, he thought it might have been sex workers, given the woman he'd shown up with and the dead woman on top of his car, but given the two duffel bags Chambers had and Fox's backpack, he now thinks it could be drugs or weapons."

"We know drugs were in one of those bags," I said. "But

we still don't know what Fox was doing."

"Officers searched the entire building and every inch of the construction site. They didn't find anything else." Voletek scanned the rest of his notes before closing the notebook and tucking it back into his pocket.

"The realtor said Fox usually scouts locations. That doesn't tell us much, but I'm guessing AK Holdings wants to use the construction site for something. I just don't know what." Brad thought for a moment before clicking a few keys. "I have no idea what that could be or how it connects to Maggie's murder."

"Did Rapshaw say anything else?" I asked.

"He heard Chambers talking about the dead girl. He said Chambers sounded distraught and terrified. He had no idea who could have done it or why, but he kept saying he hired her. Something about Frank wanting time alone with her. That Frank sent him to the club to find her." Voletek shrugged. "It didn't make much sense to Rapshaw either. He only heard bits and pieces through the door, but that's what he remembers."

"You're sure he said Frank?" I asked.

"Rapshaw seemed pretty certain of it." Voletek looked at the suspect list on our board. "You got a Frank up there?"

"We do, but we don't have anything solid on him."

Voletek stood. "Maybe now you do."

THIRTY-NINE

An hour later, we received printouts of Maggie's encrypted text messages. She spoke to four different people using the app, James West, Clayton Deek, Remington Chambers, and an unknown fourth party. That was it.

The company that designed the app was dragging its feet to give us the rest of the information, but the tech was confident Maggie had used the app to speak to other people previously. However, none of those communications had taken place within the last thirty days, which was all that her phone had stored.

"She really didn't have many friends," I said. "James West appears to be her best friend. Even after their breakup, they stayed close. They spoke several times a day, every day."

"He loved her," Brad said. "Do you think he was in love with her?"

"I think it was complicated. Now that she's gone, he may have realized just how much she meant to him."

"That happens with dicey situations. He must have thought they'd have time later. That he had time to play and be free before settling down with her, but it was always her he wanted."

"He had a funny way of showing it."

"Didn't you tell me he said he didn't think he was good enough for her? Maybe he wanted to become a better man or get a better job before telling her how he felt."

I looked at my partner. "Are we still talking about Maggie and James?"

"Liv—" My phone rang, and Brad swallowed. "Your phone's ringing."

"Thanks." I picked it up. "Homicide. This is Detective DeMarco."

"The judge denied your warrant," ADA Winters said. "He says you still don't have enough to arrest Francis Fertrie or search his phone. He has only the one device registered in his name and he uses it for business and personal matters, meaning you'd gain access to privileged materials, and since he's been known to take criminal cases on occasion, your request is coming under additional scrutiny."

"It's not fair," I said.

"I know, but there's nothing we can do. Find something else, video footage, a reliable eyewitness, anything irrefutable, and I will march back to his chambers and demand he reconsider our request."

"I'll see what we can dig up. Thanks for trying, Logan." I put the phone down. "That's a no-go on Fertrie."

"No surprise there." Brad held up a sheet of text messages. "Could he be the unknown fourth? According to the records Axel sent over, Maggie performed at another event the night before the fourth texter contacted her. He even starts by saying, 'Hey, it was great watching you last night. When are you going to let me buy you that drink?' It had to have been someone she met that night."

I picked up my copy and read her responses. They were congenial but not particularly flirty. But the unknown texter didn't take the hint. He kept asking her to meet him. She'd come up with excuse after excuse. Finally, he said he couldn't wait to see her at her next performance. He asked if she'd be at the next amateur night at the strip club. He'd caught her last act and made several lewd comments, suggesting she'd be a much more sought after commodity if she performed without her clothes on.

"I'll call Chambers and find out who else was at the strip club the night Maggie was arrested." I reached for my phone while Brad entered information into the computer.

While I waited for Chambers to answer, Brad picked up his phone and dialed.

"Mr. Chambers, this is Detective DeMarco," I said. "New details have come to light, and I could really use your help. Maggie was hired for several other Spark events. In between, you watched her act at the strip club. Do you remember that?"

"Haven't we already gone over this? That was part of your basis for believing I had harmed her."

"Was anyone at the club with you that night?"

"What do you mean?" By his tone, he knew exactly what I meant.

"Were you there with a friend or another representative of Spark?"

"I don't recall. Why would that matter? Nothing happened that night."

"No, but you and Maggie texted several times afterward," I said.

"In a professional sense only. We only ever spoke about her performance and contract details."

"Yes, I can see that." I hoped Chambers wouldn't shut me down. "Did you give her contact information to anyone else?"

"I thought you arrested Clayton Deek for her murder. He was having an affair with her."

"Yes, he was, but I need you to answer the question."

"Liv," Brad held his hand over the receiver while he grabbed a pen, "I got something."

"I really don't remember," Chambers said. "It's entirely possible, I suppose. But I don't recall."

Brad put the phone down, realizing my call wasn't going anywhere. "Hang up."

"Just think about it and get back to me if you remember." I put the receiver back in the cradle. "What is it?"

"The same law firm where Fertrie works sent an attorney to represent Maggie during her hearing."

"Fertrie wasn't the attorney of record, was he?"

"No, but he sat second chair. He could have seen her get arrested and volunteered to help."

I sighed. "That's not enough. We don't even have proof Clayton Deek had an accomplice."

"But you think he did."

"It's the only way I can see Deek gaining access to Chambers' room, and it's the only reason he and Fertrie gathered everything up and did what they could to hide the evidence before the police arrived."

"They should have cleaned the room," Brad said.

"Not if they hoped to frame Chambers."

"True." Brad got up. "I'll talk to Winston and see what he has to say. Until we get more information from the company that designed the encrypted texting app, our best bet is convincing Clayton Deek to cooperate."

While Brad pled our case to the lieutenant, I continued digging through everything we had. Fertrie's involvement was no more than a hunch. Everything we had was circumstantial, and without the man's cooperation or a court order, we had no proof. And something told me we'd never get it.

Brad returned to his desk. "Winston said he'll get someone from the DA's office to join him, and they'll speak to Clayton Deek. Hopefully, they'll be able to convince him to tell us everything he knows."

"Do you think he will?"

"I'm guessing the only reason he hasn't is because there's no way to do it without implicating himself. Depending on what kind of deal they offer him, they might be able to sway him."

"Too bad Rapshaw didn't overhear anything concrete. Even a last name might have gotten us one step closer to a warrant."

Crossing my fingers and hoping the lieutenant could convince Clayton to squeal, I finished going over the information that had been contained on Maggie's phone. The techs had sent digital copies of everything. She had a few photos saved. Mostly fun shots of her and West being silly. She had received several dick pics and provocative images of Clayton. He had even sent a few of the two of them in bed with captions like, *I can't stop thinking about that night. When can I see you again?* But that was the extent of it.

Several times, his messages had gotten possessive and overly aggressive. He never physically threatened her, but he warned her that if she continued to ignore him, she'd regret it. That could be interpreted several different ways, but since she was dead, I only took it to mean one thing.

"Even the texts point to Clayton Deek being the killer, but this unknown fourth wasn't giving up. He was persistent in his text messages, making him sound like a stalker, and we know how most of those situations end." Brad sighed. "Speaking of, what are you going to do about your stalker?"

"Axel's not exactly stalking me. But he's clearly up to something. He's following me for a reason."

"More like monitoring your movements. I don't like it. Have you told Winston or any of the brass about this?"

"I mentioned it to Winston."

"And?"

"He told me to figure out what was going on and let him know."

Brad cursed quietly. "Go to Captain Grayson. He knows the situation."

"Brad—"

"I don't like this, Liv. It worries me."

"Grayson's already left for the day. I'll speak to him tomorrow."

Brad didn't look happy. "Fine."

But by the end of the day, nothing had changed. Clayton Deek refused to cooperate. He wouldn't confess. He insisted he knew nothing about what happened to Maggie and had no idea who had access to Chambers' room besides Chambers. Even when presented with physical evidence that he'd been inside, all Deek was willing to admit was he'd stopped by Chambers' suite when he and Nancy first checked in to say hi. That's how he figured his prints got inside the room, but we weren't buying it since Chambers hadn't been in his room during the day.

"You've built a solid case," Lt. Winston said. "Deek had means, motive, and opportunity. I'd like to get the timeline ironed out a bit more, but we have time to work on that.

Since the forensics is sound, I don't anticipate any surprises, not after you found Maggie's phone and video footage showing Deek disposing of it. He's clearly our guy. Case closed."

"What about the situation in the building across the street and the night watchman intentionally shooting Rapshaw?" Brad asked. "Something is going on in that building that needs looking into."

"Another unit is investigating that. Like I told you before, stay the hell away from it. Are we clear?"

"Crystal," I said.

"Great." Winston dismissed us with a jerk of his chin.

I packed up my things, unsure how I felt. Tossing my bag over my shoulder, I stopped and studied Maggie's ID photo which remained at the center of our board. She wanted to perform but ended up in a bad situation.

Brad came up behind me. "We caught the guy. He was in the room. He tossed her phone, and he ditched the clothing he wore at the event. Her blood must have gotten all over him. We found it on his shoes. Why are we trying so hard to let him share the blame?"

"You're right. This needs to stop. We caught her killer." I turned to look my partner in the eye. "But it's going to drive me crazy not knowing how Deek and Maggie ended up inside that room."

"Deek couldn't have taken her back to his room. His wife could have walked in on them. We know Fertrie's room was headquarters for party central, and it sounds like all sorts of sordid things were going on in the other suites. That was the only unoccupied room on the top floor." Brad led the way to the stairs. "Chambers is a company man. He's all about Spark's mission statement. Let's say Chambers didn't drop his key. Let's say he intentionally switched with Fertrie. Whoever went into Fertrie's room to get wasted may have wanted to go somewhere private afterward. Fertrie could have been passing around the key, and Deek happened to catch him at a great time. Deek stopped Maggie before she could go to the lobby and asked if they could speak in private. He gets the key from Fertrie, takes Maggie to Chambers' room, and they argue. He gets mad and kills her."

"Except," I pushed open the side exit, "Deek stabbed her in the back with a knife he'd taken from the roof. That makes it premeditated."

"That doesn't change anything else. Fertrie and Chambers may have had no knowledge of Deek's intent. In fact, I'm sure Chambers didn't know about any of it. If he had, I think he would have talked in order to avoid a potential murder charge."

"True." I let out a breath. "Are we closing the book on this one?"

"Unless something changes."

"Okay." I peered around the parking lot. It wasn't dark yet.

"Where are you headed?" Brad asked.

"Home, I think, to my apartment."

"Do you want company?" Brad asked, but he looked beat.

"I'll manage. It's time I face these demons alone, unless you wanted to do something else."

He shook his head. "Nah, nothing special."

"Okay. I'll see you tomorrow."

We parted ways and I headed for my car, which was parked on the other side of the lot. Hitting the trunk release, I tossed my bag inside and closed the lid. When I turned, a man was standing beside my door. I screamed in surprise. Brad raced across the parking lot, gun at his thigh.

"Jesus, Liv," Axel rubbed his left ear, "it's only me."

"Freeze," Brad announced.

Axel turned ninety degrees, so he could see both of us and quirked an eyebrow at Fennel. "Impressive response time."

FORTY

"What the hell are you doing here?" I crossed my arms over my chest and stared at Axel, waiting for an answer.

Brad had holstered his weapon, glancing around the parking lot, but no one else had heard my surprised yelp. He shook out his left hand and tucked it into his pocket to hide the nervous twitch.

"We need to talk. I'm glad I caught you before you left." Axel gave Brad a bewildered look. "If you have somewhere else to be, by all means, please."

"Not on your life," Brad muttered.

Axel gave me a look. "See, that's the kind of thing your firefighter should have said."

"I'm losing my patience," I warned.

"How about we take this somewhere private? I thought dinner."

"You thought wrong."

Axel gave Brad an exasperated look. "Tell her you'd like to have dinner."

"Go screw yourself," Brad said.

Axel turned back to me. "Again, an excellent choice of response. Should I take notes and have them delivered to Mr. Grammar? He could stand to learn a thing or two."

"He's out of the picture. Now cut to the chase."

Axel's grin grew larger. "Weren't you supposed to contact him when your case wrapped? For all intents, hasn't that happened?"

"How do you know any of this?" Brad asked.

"I'll tell you once we aren't quite so exposed." Axel sneered at the police cars. "The lights and sirens are going to give me a twitch. Stepping inside that building might just kill me." He nodded down at my partner's hand. "I'd hate to have that happen."

"Brad," I interjected before he said anything else, "let's continue this at my place."

"Are you insane?"

"No." I gave my partner a sharp look. We'd fight about that later. Right now, I wanted to know what brought Axel Kincaid to the precinct. "Meet me there."

"I'll follow you." Brad took another step closer, practically nose to nose with Axel. "Let me make one thing clear. Whatever you have up your sleeve better not hurt Liv."

Axel nodded. "As always, we're in agreement on that."

Brad gave me one final look. "I better not regret this." He headed for his car, glancing back every few seconds to make sure Axel didn't pull a knife and stab me.

"Do you need the address?" I asked Axel.

"You know, I'm not actually stalking you, so it would help if I knew where to meet you."

"Fine." I rattled it off and got into my car. By the time I put the key in the ignition, Axel had vanished. I didn't spot his car or anything worth more than fifty thousand in the parking lot, so I wasn't sure how he arrived at the precinct or how he disappeared so quickly, but I didn't care. All I wanted to know was what new kink he was about to throw into our case.

Brad stayed on my ass the entire drive to my apartment. When I parked, he pulled in behind me and got out before I did. "Why did you tell him where you live?"

"I'm guessing he already knew."

"You can't stay here tonight, possibly never again. If you don't want to go to your parents', you're staying with me."

"We'll work that out later." I nodded to a jet black SUV with chrome hubcaps which pulled in behind Brad's car. It hadn't been parked in the police lot or in any of the visitor spaces, so it must have been on the street, just outside the fence. Axel stepped out of the car, clicking the locks, which made the lights flash. "How many vehicles do you have?"

"I didn't want to be noticed." Axel peered around. "Can we take this inside?"

I led the way up the stairs and unlocked my apartment door. Axel had gone mute, taking in the building as we went. Flipping on the lights, I made sure the place was empty before joining the men in the living room. Axel studied the stained carpet while Brad stared at him.

Upon hearing my approach, Axel looked up. "Last time we spoke, I promised you I'd look into things. I'm not convinced Clayton Deek acted alone. He's a hothead. He doesn't lose gracefully. Poker, car races, it doesn't matter. He likes to win. He likes getting what he wants when he wants it."

"Maggie rejected him," I said.

"Still, killing her means no rematch. That's not Clayton. When he's losing, he doubles down, over and over. He doesn't know when to quit." Axel smirked. "I've made quite the killing in high stakes games with him."

"Deliberate word choice?" Brad asked.

Axel didn't reply. "However, the evidence you've gathered suggests otherwise. It's possible he snapped. I won't deny that. He gets squirrely on coke. Too much pressure, and no release valve. Maggie would have been his release valve. If she said no, he could have exploded."

Brad dropped onto the couch. "You're contradicting yourself."

"That's because, like you, I don't know what happened inside that room. Fox doesn't know either. We've spoken at length."

"When is he returning from his trip? We need to question him," I said.

"He'll be back sometime next week. He'll make himself available. You have my word." Axel looked straight at me. "In the meantime, a makeup event has been planned for

Friday. Aside from Clayton Deek and his wife, the rest of the guests will be in attendance. I'm here to invite you to accompany me. A few libations should loosen their lips. Perhaps you can finally get some answers."

"Why do you think they'd talk?" I asked.

"Gossip is king, particularly when one of their own is charged with murder."

"That doesn't explain why you've suddenly decided Deek didn't act alone," Brad said. "Did someone say something to you? Do you have something concrete you could share with us?"

"A few minutes after Maggie was thrown off the balcony, two men notified Remington Chambers of the tragedy that struck. They came to him separately. Neither had any reason to take it upon himself to do so. They do not work for Spark or act as ambassadors for these unsanctioned galas. Deek would have had no reason to worry. He did not have large quantities of illegal substances on his person or within his room. That leaves me to believe he had physical evidence of his involvement in the murder or feared his proximity to Maggie Tenzin would tip his wife to the affair once the police began asking questions. However, Francis Fertrie had much more to lose. He was in possession of enough illegal substances to be facing a decade long prison sentence."

"Were the drugs yours?" I asked.

Axel fought to keep from scowling. "I do not deal drugs. I do not serve poison to people. You know my policy."

Brad snorted, but he didn't argue. "Do you know where Fertrie got these alleged substances?"

"He has connections. One of the partners at his firm represents a certain crime family. Fertrie may be using Spark to form new connections and assist the crime family in their illegal enterprises."

"We'd need proof," Brad said. "Our investigation into Fertrie never turned up any of that."

"No one would want this known, particularly his boss or the mobster. You need to look harder."

"Fertrie wasn't acting in Spark's interest at the party?" I asked. "It was my understanding he was selected to distribute the illegal substances from his room because of the privilege that comes with his career choice in order to insulate you and the rest of the guests from potential criminal charges in the event of a raid."

"That isn't entirely untrue, but Fertrie's acted beyond the scope of what Spark condones."

"Are you planning to kick him out?" I asked.

Axel almost smiled. "It depends on your investigation."

"What do you think he did that was so bad?" Brad asked.

"I believe he's using my club to further outside interests. Crime family interests. Cartel interests. Outside factors like that could change the entire landscape of my club."

I watched Axel closely. He was always hard to read, but he didn't bother to conceal the anger and betrayal, two of his looks I personally knew very well. "You're afraid someone more powerful could take over and take everything away from you. That's why you wanted information on the investigation. You thought Fertrie had something to do with Maggie's death this entire time."

"I can't be certain. But he took Chambers' room key, and he warned Chambers what was coming. He convinced Chambers to leave the hotel before the police could question him. If Chambers hadn't done that, the contraband would have remained, as would evidence of the murder. You do the math."

"Why didn't you tell us this sooner?" Brad asked.

Axel exhaled slowly. "These facts only came to light after Clayton Deek was arrested."

Brad wasn't buying it. "How did they come to light?"

"Tell us," I insisted.

"I conducted my own interviews."

Brad caught my eye. "Even if any of this is true, and even if you expect us to squash what I'm guessing is a hostile takeover of your precious club, Liv and I can't accompany you to your replacement shindig. We questioned everyone at the party. They know we're cops. They'll clam up the second they see us."

"I agree. You shouldn't be there," Axel said. "That's why I didn't invite you. I asked Liv to go as my date. She's the only cop I know who doesn't exude cop. Her undercover work is beyond reproach. I'd know. She lied to my face for six months, and I believed every word of it." His ice blue eyes grew colder as he faced me. "I've seen you pull off plenty of disguises. With the right clothing and makeup, you'd pass for one of my typical Friday night liaisons. You know how to dress, to act, and what I like. You could have everyone convinced."

"It's too dangerous," Brad said. "They've seen her. If you're right and Fertrie had something to do with Maggie's murder and he's involved with a crime family, Liv will be made the second she walks in."

"I'll make it a masquerade, if that helps."

"No," Brad insisted, but my mind was turning over the possibility.

"Is that why you've been keeping tabs on me?" I asked Axel. "Do you think Fertrie or his associates would make a move against a homicide detective?"

"I don't know anything, but I saw no reason to risk it, particularly after our conversation over dinner. I thought it best to make sure you were safe since I had no idea who we were dealing with." Axel looked around my place. "Is this where that deranged psycho hid?" He pointed to the stain on the floor. "Did he attack you here?"

"No, that's my blood," Brad said. "Someone else showed up. Different occasion."

Axel raised an eyebrow. "You're right, Liv. You need to move to a better neighborhood."

"Tell that to my landlord." I sighed. "Do you really think Fertrie will say something damning regarding his involvement in Maggie's murder?"

"Even if he doesn't, plenty of people were in and out of his room. Someone is bound to say something."

I glanced at Brad. "If we can get recordings, we'll have proof. We can piece everything together. Even if no one else was involved, it'll iron out the timeline. That is what Winston wanted."

"Are you sure about this?" Brad asked.

I shrugged before turning my focus back to Axel. "We have to run this by our CO, but if he approves, I'm in. The department will have stipulations, protocols that have to be followed. You'll have to agree to the terms, or this is a no-go."

Axel nodded. "Got it."

FORTY-ONE

Brad and I spent the entire week looking into Axel Kincaid's claims. We couldn't refute them, but that didn't mean much of anything. Clayton Deek hadn't offered anything in exchange for a reduced sentence. In fact, his silence gave credence to Axel's story. If Fertrie had ties to a crime family or cartel, Deek had every reason to keep his mouth shut. Either that, or he was solely responsible. Regardless, I had no doubt he was guilty.

"Are you sure about this?" Brad asked. "No one will blame you if you changed your mind."

"I want to know what happened to Maggie."

"We know what happened. Deek killed her. The rest is icing. We don't need icing. I'm sure Emma could come up with a million reasons why icing is bad."

"Remind her of that when she's picking out her wedding cake," I said.

Brad gently grasped my arms. "I'm serious. There's no reason to put yourself at risk. Axel came to us with this because he's afraid of rivals encroaching on his territory. That's something he's always worried about. It is not our job to stop that from happening."

"What if it's more than that?" I searched Brad's eyes, finding nothing but concern in the warm brown depths. "What if everything he said is true? Taking down Fertrie could lead to sweeping arrests. This could be huge."

"Which is the only reason the LT signed off on it. He's always in things for the grandeur, but this is a mistake. This isn't something homicide should be working. Hell, I'm not even sure this is something the department should be handling. This seems more like an FBI or DEA issue. Doesn't it?"

"The guys in the suits shouldn't get to have all the fun."

"You really think this is fun?"

I smiled. "You know that's how I keep my head on straight."

"All right. Remember I will be on comms the entire time. Say the word, and we will pull you out."

"I know."

Brad picked up the thin, lace mask. "Do you think this will be enough to convince them you're someone else entirely?"

"Look at me, Fennel. Do I look anything like Detective Liv DeMarco?" I wore a designer cocktail dress and stiletto heels. My hair had been recently highlighted with lots of honey and caramel tones, and with the artful makeup, glistening jewel accents and mask, I looked like I fit in perfectly with the women Axel rotated through on a weekly or monthly basis.

"Fine," he offered a small smile, "you have me convinced."

"Good. Now I just have to convince Fertrie and the rest of them."

"Word of advice, try not to talk too much, and avoid asking questions. That might trigger something in their reptilian brains."

I laughed. "I have done this before. We've done this before, remember?"

"What I remember is how much I hate this."

"Good thing you get to hang out in the surveillance van." I took the mask and held it in place. "Do you mind?"

Brad took the two silky straps and fastened it for me. "Too tight?"

"No, it's perfect."

"Your chariot awaits, princess," Voletek said, gesturing to the limousine. "I'll deliver you to Spark, and an unmarked unit will follow you from there while Brad and the surveillance team set up outside the venue."

"Aren't you guys taking this to extremes? No one has any reason to suspect Axel would assist the police in infiltrating one of these events."

"He's the one who wanted the added precautions," Voletek said.

"He may know something we don't." Brad checked the computer. "Remember, everything is getting recorded, so there's nothing you have to do except gather intel. If everything goes according to plan, we'll meet up after the party."

"I'll see you then." I winked and followed Voletek to the car. He wore a suit and the traditional black cap associated with limo drivers. "Looks like we're not taking any chances on this one."

Voletek eyed me through the rearview. "For all we know, these are dangerous people."

"Speaking of dangerous people, how's your dad doing?"

"His ego has been irreparably harmed, but physically, he's healthy as a horse."

"What ever became of your investigation? Did you find the person responsible for lacing their drinks?"

"I have my suspicions, but it'll be damn near impossible to get evidence. Nothing showed on the security footage, but the bartender's brother is serving a life sentence. My dad arrested him fifteen years ago, when he was heading up the gangs task force."

"And your dad didn't recognize him?"

"To be fair, the guy looks a lot different now than he did when he was a snot-nosed kid sitting in the court room watching his brother stand trial. The commissioner authorized a surveillance team, so we're keeping tabs on him. But I'd say it was a family vendetta."

"Why did he lace all the drinks?"

"The waitress brought them to the table. He had no way of knowing who ordered what, and he probably figured cops travel in packs. We're a bit like wolves when you think about it." Voletek let out a howl.

"Wolves, huh?"

"Our bite is worse than our bark, and you have to keep an eye out for the vicious ones."

"You may need to work on your analogy."

Voletek checked the mirrors, but no one was tailing us. "I'll give it some more thought." He slowed to a stop outside Spark. "Should I circle a few times while you get your head in the game?"

"No, I'm good." I took a deep breath, imagining the excitement of senior prom in order to get the perfect level of giddy anticipation. "Thanks for the ride."

Voletek got out, opened my door, and offered me his gloved hand to assist me in getting out of the vehicle. When I made it to the main entrance of Spark, George asked for my name.

"Melinda Belville."

"Yes, Ms. Belville," he didn't break from character either, "Mr. Kincaid is waiting for you at the bar." He removed the velvet rope and waited for me to pass before clipping it back in place.

Despite the Friday night crowd, I spotted Axel easily. He had on a silver blue silk shirt, unbuttoned halfway down his chest. His sleeves were rolled up, and he was helping the bartender with something.

"Axel," I said, "why are you working? I thought tonight we were going to play."

He turned to me, his lip curling in the corner. "Oh, we are." He dried his hands on a towel and tossed it to the bartender. "If the tap gets stuck again, tell Jerry to replace it. And make sure nothing's leaking. I don't want any accidents tonight." Carefully, he rolled down his sleeves, which were wrinkled beyond belief. "Dammit." He grabbed his jacket from where he'd hung it from one of the shelves. "This will never do. Come upstairs with me."

"I thought you'd never ask."

He came around the bar, leaning in as if for a kiss, but I turned my face away. "Don't start that now or we'll never make it to your party," I said.

"So true." He hooked his arm around my waist and led me to the hidden staircase which led to his loft. Once he closed the door, shutting out the vibrant pulsing music and the drone of chatter, his demeanor changed. "Are we set?"

"Yep."

"You remember the rule. No guns."

Brad hated that stipulation, but the venue had metal detectors. Plus, it'd be next to impossible to conceal a weapon in my tiny purse or anywhere on my body. "I know."

"Okay." He finished unbuttoning his shirt on the way up the stairs. "I'll just be a second."

I waited at the bottom of the steps. Three minutes later, Axel emerged in a silver pinstriped shirt. He adjusted his cufflinks, making sure they didn't snag on his jacket sleeves. His shirt was buttoned almost to the top, but he didn't bother with a tie. He looked anxious.

"Is everything okay?" I asked.

"Uh-huh." He handed me a plain white mask, his disguise for the party. It had an elastic strap. "Hold on to that for me."

We left the club and made it to his car without incident. He unlocked the doors and held the door for me to get in. I'd seen Axel leave Spark with plenty of women, so I knew what to expect. Once we got on the road, he glanced at me. "That dress looks fucking hot on you."

I pointed to the side of my mask. "Remember, we have audio."

Axel smirked. "I know. That's impressive tech for the police department. The only time I see pieces like that are usually with the Feds."

"You work with the Feds a lot?"

"What's a lot?"

I watched him drive, aware of his restraint not to open up the engine and speed through traffic like he normally did. "Do they know about any of this?"

Axel shrugged, but that wasn't an answer. However, before I could ask anything else, he slipped into the valet line. Tonight's party was being held at the indoor botanical gardens. The enclosures were heated, but there were plenty of areas where people could sneak away for some privacy. The valet opened our doors, and Axel tossed him the keys and slid a tip into his shirt pocket.

Coming around to my side of the car, he pulled me against him. His feather light touch traced my cheek. "You're going to love this." He grasped my chin and tilted my head up. His eyes held a slight challenge, but I saw the amusement dancing just behind it. He leaned down, his lips nearly brushed against mine, but before they could, someone cleared his throat.

"Good evening, Mr. Kincaid." It was Chambers.

"Remy," Axel ran his hand down my arm, taking his mask from my hand, "has anyone else arrived yet?" He secured the strap behind his head, but didn't slide the mask into place. Instead, he left it hovering at his hairline.

"Things are just getting underway." Chambers smiled at me. "It's no wonder you picked such a beautiful place. But everything here pales in comparison to this gorgeous creature you brought with you."

"You're not getting an introduction," Axel said. "She's here with me. Make that known."

"Yes, sir."

I smiled at Chambers, but I didn't notice the slightest hint of recognition on his face. Instead, he excused himself and disappeared back inside. "Do you always talk to him like that?"

"After the shit that went down last week, he deserves it." Axel took my hand and led the way inside.

Fancy lights, high ceilings, manmade streams, and waterfalls filled the property. White linens fluttered from the small tents which shielded the couches, tables, and chaises. The place looked like a fancy resort with a tropical rainforest theme. Several of the women wore animal print dresses with coordinating masks. Some had ears. Others had tails. A few of the men wore light-colored suits, possibly in an attempt to appear like explorers, but instead, it gave me Havana vibes.

For the most part, I kept my mouth shut. The same catering staff covered this event, so I made sure to keep my distance since I'd spoken at length with everyone who worked last week's party. If anyone were to recognize me, it'd be Judi or someone on her crew.

However, Axel had little interest in the food. He had his

sights set on something else. We moved from one area to another. Any time Axel sat down, I'd hang on his shoulder or crawl onto his lap. He barely paid me any attention, which is how he behaved with most women. He talked to everyone.

After two hours, I had a pretty good idea of where most of the guests had been around the time of the murder. Several people recalled Clayton Deek getting up to leave the party several times. From what we'd pieced together, he'd been back and forth between the roof and the top floor most of the night. No one knew exactly what he had been doing, but in light of Maggie's murder and the news of his affair, they speculated he'd been looking for somewhere private to off her.

The vast majority of the guests alibied out. They'd been in the company of at least one other person the entire night. Only a few people had wandered off on their own. Aside from Deek, Chambers, and Fertrie, the only other person who'd wandered away from the group for an extended amount of time had been Dennis Linson, the surgeon with the whipped cream fetish.

Once Axel located Linson, he pushed his way into the open tent. Barbie Lefevre and Raj Chopra, along with two other guests, were in the midst of a strip poker game.

"Deal me in," Axel said.

"Are you playing too?" Linson asked me.

I shook my head.

"Melinda's going to watch." Axel left no room for debate.

"Pity." Linson shuffled and dealt.

"What are the side stakes?" Axel asked.

"There aren't any," Barbie said. "These boys are too chicken shit to put their money where their mouths are. They know I have zero interest in seeing their junk, so I've been letting them win." She grinned at Axel. "However, the new player adds an exciting dynamic." She glanced at me. "You should really play. Two are always better than one."

"I have nothing on under this," I said. "It wouldn't be fair."

The men eyed me.

"Really?" Raj asked.

"Keep your eyes in your heads and your tongues in your mouths. That goes for you too, Barb." Axel reached for the cards. "I'd hate to have seen how all of you behaved last week."

The two other guests politely bowed out, finding the tent crowded and a little hostile.

"He didn't," Barbie said, nudging Raj. "But as usual, no one bought his BS except me."

Axel glanced at his cards. When it was his turn, he asked for two more.

"How come there's no outside entertainment tonight?" Dennis Linson asked.

Axel showed his hand. Two pair, jacks high. "The police are still sniffing around. I didn't believe it'd be prudent."

"Why not? They arrested Clayton. He was fucking her, after all." Linson dropped his cards on the table. He had nothing but ace high. The group discarded another article of clothing, adding it to the pile on the empty chair. "You know these things are always a crime of passion."

"I'm not surprised about the affair, but I didn't think he had it in him to kill someone." Barbie shook her head. "Did you see that coming?"

"He could have been on a bad trip," Raj said. "The rest of us were microdosing, but Clayton never knew where the line was. He could have freaked and done something crazy while he was out of his head."

"Who was the supplier?" Axel asked.

Looks were exchanged. "Who do you think?" Linson asked.

Axel nodded. "Was the quality checked?"

"As far as we know." Raj shrugged. "No one else had a problem. But again, Clayton had a problem knowing when enough was enough."

"That's because he couldn't stand being out with Nancy. Half the time, she's queen of the ice queens, and the other half of the time, she's inviting other couples to join them. I'm guessing Clayton didn't like that." Barbie looked at the cards she was dealt, frowning. "Three."

Linson gave her three more. "They spent most of the

party with the Pickfords. I would have figured that would have been enough to keep him satisfied. Becky's a freak."

"You'd know. Weren't you their third at that beach house retreat?" Barbie asked.

Linson chuckled quietly. "When's the club holding another one of those, Axel?"

Axel won again, and Barbie looked down, having to decide between her panties or bra. "Screw this," she said. "I'm getting a drink." She smiled at Axel. "Have fun."

"I'll join you," Raj grabbed his belt and slid it through the loops on his pants while she slipped back into her dress.

"The game's over," Linson said, watching them leave, "unless you want to play, beautiful."

"She doesn't," Axel repeated.

"Right. Sorry." Linson shuffled the cards a few times and put the stack down. "I hate to say it, man, but this party is freaking lame."

Removing his jacket, Axel folded it and tossed it over the end of the chaise lounge the two of us were sharing. He ran his hand up my side, stopping to caress my exposed skin where the back was cutout.

The surgeon hadn't taken his eyes off of me. I kept thinking about the cans of whipped cream, afraid what sorts of devious thoughts were going through his mind this time. But he'd been chatty about Clayton Deek, so I followed Axel's lead and ran my instep slowly up the inside of Axel's leg, appearing bored. Axel grabbed the back of my thigh and pulled my leg higher, running his fingers down to my knee. Linson licked his lips.

"It's a shame we don't have any outside entertainment." Linson peered across the expanse, where a tiki bar was set up. "Next time, there better be women. Plenty of them."

"You could have brought someone," Axel said.

"Who? Some dog from one of those dating apps? I get enough of that in my day-to-day. This is supposed to be a fantasy. Some overweight chick with facial hair and a stretched out downstairs is far from my fantasy."

"Did you ever think it's your bedside manner?"

Linson laughed. "That could be. But I should be able to

get what I want. If Clayton could and he was fucking crazy, why can't I?" Linson smiled at me. "You have lovely legs. Do you dance?"

"I used to," I said.

"Really? What club?"

"She danced for me," Axel said, his tone shutting down whatever ideas were forming in Linson's mind.

"Well, you're lucky. Maybe I should invest in a club. That might work."

Axel tried again to get the conversation back to Maggie, but Linson was too wrapped up in figuring out a way to get laid to stay focused. Instead, we left him and moved to another area.

"We need to talk to Fertrie," I said. He was one of the few people we hadn't found in a tent or touring the gardens.

Axel pinned me against a willow tree of some sort. "He's at the bar. He's been at the bar since we arrived. He's not going anywhere."

I watched the man in the eagle mask drink his scotch. He'd lean over, offering handshakes to his friends. Sometimes, he'd put the baggies inside a napkin, or he'd slip one into the bowl of nuts or pretzels before sliding them over. "He's dealing."

"What else would he be doing?" Axel pressed against me, his hands sliding around the small of my back and pulling me against him. "Did you notice the Pickfords?"

Tim and Becky were seated in the tent nearest the bar. They'd been ogling us since we emerged from the last tent, which was why Axel was putting on a show. At least, I hoped that was the reason. I didn't like the way he'd been taking liberties, but that was how he usually operated. Plus, he knew what they liked, what they were interested in, and another couple to play with was right up their alley.

I opened another button on his shirt and slid my palms against his rock-hard chest, playing with the faint smattering of hair. Axel was all lean, sinewy muscle. He pulled me closer, feasting on my collarbone. The ever-present faint stubble on his jaw sent jolts through me, and I gasped when his lips latched on to the hollow of my neck.

"Oh god, Axel."

"I knew I'd get you to say it," he murmured.

My mind wandered to Brad, listening to this from the surveillance van. But I had to stay present. I was Melinda Belville, former dancer, and Axel's Friday night booty call. He grabbed my hands and lifted them over my head, his chest heaving. He stared at me for a moment, the blue flames of his eyes scorching everything in their path. Then he took a step back.

"Now I need a drink." He headed for the bar, expecting me to follow.

I glanced at the Pickfords, who had turned their attention to the platters of food the nearest waiter carried, and joined Axel at the bar.

He leaned against it, his back to the bartender, a martini already in his hand. His eyes were on Francis Fertrie. The air crackled. Dangerous, unpredictable energy radiated off Axel. "What the fuck do you think you're doing, Frank?"

"What does it look like?"

Axel put his glass down. He acted like he didn't even notice me. I sat down, three seats over, unsure how to proceed. Worst case, I'd call for backup. But for now, I had to let this ride and hope Axel knew what he was doing. However, past experience told me something was about to pop off. He had a violent streak, which worried me.

"Were you passing around the same shit last week? You know my policy."

"Fuck your policy." Fertrie tried not to slur, but his cheeks and nose were red. Again, he'd been overserved. "You say you fulfill desires, cater to everyone's whim. This is what they want." He waved a baggie in Axel's face that contained what appeared to be a small, thin, square of paper.

"There's a reason I keep this shit out of my club."

"Everyone pre-games. You know it. Why not double-down?"

"People end up dead. Case in point, Maggie Tenzin."

Fertrie rolled his eyes, snorting. "She wasn't a guest. She wasn't even using."

"What about Clayton?"

"What about him?"

Axel shoved Frank, almost knocking him off the stool. "You tell me. Did you give him this shit? Is that why he flipped out?"

"He just wanted to talk to her. I don't know what he intended to do."

"But you cleared out everything as soon as she hit the car. How did you know she was dead if you didn't know what happened between her and Clayton?"

Frank snorted, picking up his drink. "How do you think? It's not that complicated. Even a dumbass like you should be able to figure it out."

"Watch yourself, Frank."

"Or what? You'll revoke my membership?" He took another sip of his drink. "I'll do whatever I want. Good luck, stopping me."

"You gave your shit to Remington Chambers to hide. He does not work for you. If he'd been caught—"

"What?" Frank grinned. "You and your precious little party would have been compromised. Boo-hoo."

Axel pulled his arm back. "Don't," I warned. Axel glanced at me. Fire burned in his eyes, but he lowered his fist.

Frank laughed, not realizing how close he'd come to getting his teeth knocked out.

"Tell me how it went down. How were you involved?" Axel asked.

"Jeez, now you sound like the freaking police. This is all because Remy said I took his room key." Frank climbed off his stool, puffing his chest out as he stood up to Axel. "You want to know why I took his room key? It's because you've lost touch. You've gone soft. Ever since you cleaned house, things have been different. You forgot what business you're in. I don't like this change. No one does."

Surprisingly, Axel didn't react to the accusations. "Did you give Remington Chambers' room key to Clayton?"

"Why would I do that when I had every intention of using that room to scratch my own itch?"

FORTY-TWO

Frank had a sick, ugly grin on his face. "Maggie didn't want to be with that asshole anymore. She called things off. But I knew her type. I'd seen it a hundred times before. She was a whore playing dress-up."

"What did you do?" Axel growled.

"Nothing."

Axel grabbed Frank by the lapels and yanked him closer. "Tell me what you did to Maggie."

"I didn't do shit to her. I would have. I planned to, but things didn't work out between us."

"Tell me all of it. Now."

Frank snorted. "You can't talk to me like that. I'm one of your members. I pay your fees. You work for me."

"Is that what your clients say to you all damn day?" Axel leaned in, whispering something in Frank's ear that I couldn't hear. Frank jerked backward, but Axel held on tight, whispering something else to him.

The flush drained away, leaving Frank's skin sickly pale. "Isabel was an accident. She knew what I wanted and where to meet. She stepped out of line. I didn't have a choice."

Axel clenched Frank's jacket so tightly, his knuckles turned white. "Is that what happened to Maggie?" Spit flew from between his clenched teeth as he asked the question.

"Maggie didn't know what I had planned. It was her friend. I got her to help me get Maggie alone. Maggie had been hot and cold with me, but I figured once we were alone, she wouldn't be able to say no."

"What friend?" I asked.

Frank looked at me, attempting to pull free from Axel's grasp. "Who are you?" His expression grew suspicious.

Axel gave his collar another jerk. "Answer her."

"Judi, the caterer."

I glanced back at the woman who remained near the serving trays, chatting with a few of the waiters while refilling the platters.

"What about her?" Axel asked.

"A few months ago, I paid her for Maggie's contact information."

"What does that have to do with my performer being killed last week?"

"Judi told her the host had a room set up for her to use to rest. Maggie didn't know which room, but she wandered the halls, hoping to find it. That's when I found her and unlocked the door for her."

"What did you do?" Axel spat.

"Nothing. She said no. She always said no." Frank sneered. "She wouldn't name a price. She wouldn't do anything. She asked me to leave. When I refused to take no for an answer, she threatened to call the cops. That's when Clayton showed up." Frank pulled free from Axel's grasp. "He told me to leave. That dumb fuck thought she'd think he was her knight in shining armor and drop to her knees for him. But she didn't. She wanted him to go too." Frank smiled evilly. "He just needed a little push, some encouragement, maybe a little goading. But that's all it took to get him to do what needed to be done."

"You fed him this poison, and then you took advantage. How dare you."

"How dare I?" Frank looked incredulous. "How dare she threaten me like that. Who the hell did that bitch think she was. She was nothing more than street trash. Someone like that shouldn't be able to threaten my business." Frank laughed. "You crawled your way up from the streets too.

You act like you're so high and mighty, but you're still garbage. I don't cower to garbage."

"You feared her, just like you fear me."

"It's not fear. It's survival. She knew who I was, what I'd been doing all night. She'd seen inside my room, the bags I had, the ledger. She could have ruined me. She would have taken all of us down. You included. I did you a favor by convincing Clayton to kill her."

"A favor?" Axel lunged forward, grabbed Frank, and heaved him into the bar. "She died because of this shit." He knocked the pretzel bowl away. "Assholes like you are the reason for the rules." He kicked him. "I'm going to give you exactly what you deserve."

"Move in now," I said, hoping a tactical team was nearby. I climbed off my seat, putting myself between the two men. "Axel, stop." Anger radiated off him in waves. I didn't try to touch him, knowing he'd lash out. But I held my ground. "Look at me. Don't do this."

After three interminably long seconds, the animal instinct faded, and I hoped Axel was in control of his baser desires. He swallowed, noticing the group of onlookers gawking at him from a safe distance.

"Clear out," he said. "The party's over. Police are on the way."

Frank crawled out from where he'd landed against the bar. Getting to his feet, he grabbed a knife from the cutting board where the bartender had been slicing lemons. He lunged for me, and Axel shoved me out of the way.

The blade went into Axel's side, just beneath his last rib. Instead of flinching, Axel grabbed Frank's wrist, holding it steady and plunging the blade in deeper to get closer to Frank. "You're gonna regret that." Axel head-butted him before delivering a bone-shattering right cross to his jaw. Ripping the knife out, Axel held the handle tightly as he took a step toward the downed man.

"Police," Brad shouted. "Drop the knife."

I moved to grab my cuffs, but Brad shook his head. He didn't want me to compromise my cover, but I wasn't sure why.

Brad circled. "Put it down, Mr. Kincaid. I won't ask you twice."

Axel tossed the blade to the ground with enough force that it stuck straight up, an inch from Francis Fertrie's groin. Axel staggered backward and clutched his side. "Happy?"

"We need help over here. Someone call an ambulance." I eased Axel onto a stool before he hit the ground. "What the hell were you thinking?" I grabbed one of the bar rags and pressed it against the wound. Blood soaked through almost immediately. I grabbed another rag and pressed harder.

Axel hissed. "I didn't really expect that to hurt this much." He reached for the nearest liquor bottle and pulled the cork out with his teeth and took a long swig while I maintained pressure on his wound.

Brad cuffed Fertrie and passed him off to two plain clothes officers. Four uniforms came in, working crowd control. "Let's clear the area. Get everyone moved out of here. We'll give the paramedics room to work." Brad looked at me. "You okay, miss?"

"Yeah."

"Did you see what happened here?"

"Uh-huh."

"In that case, I need you to stick around to answer some questions."

"Of course, you do."

Brad smiled at me. But he didn't drop the act until the area was secure.

*   *   *

Brad scrubbed a hand down his face, taking in the twinkle lights and roaring fire in the hearth on the back patio. "I'm surprised we got the night off."

"Me too. Lt. Winston wasn't particularly happy when he heard our informant practically beat a confession out of our suspect."

"However, the recording gave us everything we needed to dig deeper into Francis Fertrie. When we left this afternoon, I heard the lieutenant on the phone with someone from the FBI. Axel's tip about the crime family connection seems to have paid off, which is all Winston really cares about."

I shook my head. "Poor Maggie. These freaking assholes—"

"I know, Liv." Brad pulled me into his chest for a quick hug and released me. "It sucks. Homicide sucks."

"Clayton never loved her. He used her. And she knew it. She knew it from the beginning, but she couldn't break free. Do you think it was the money?"

"That was a factor, but I read her diary cover to cover. She wanted to be wanted, to be loved, to be desired. It's what everyone wants."

"She had West."

"Not the way she needed him." Brad exhaled. "Judi feels terrible she ever gave Francis Fertrie Maggie's contact information. She didn't know he wanted to use Maggie the same way Clayton did."

"That's because Fertrie lied and told her he was interested in hiring Maggie to work additional gigs. That's why he offered Judi a finder's fee, insisting she should get a cut since he was lucky enough to find someone who could put him in contact with some new talent." I thought about how distraught the caterer had been after the fight broke out between Axel and Fertrie. "She really had no idea, just like when she told Maggie to chill out in one of the suites."

"Between Clayton Deek and Francis Fertrie, Maggie didn't stand a chance. Fertrie would have killed her if Clayton didn't."

"I know, but given what everyone said, Fertrie pressuring Deek to act makes him an accomplice. If not for his actions, providing the hallucinogens and the encouragement, Deek wouldn't have stabbed her in the back."

"He freaked out," Brad said. "I spoke to him again after you left today. He doesn't remember a lot about that night. He thought most of it was a bad trip. He still won't confess, but he's open to discussing a deal in exchange for sharing details regarding Fertrie's other crimes."

"Drug dealing shouldn't trump murder."

"But organized crime connections sometimes do."

I stared out the kitchen door. "The wire didn't pick up whatever Axel whispered to Fertrie, but whatever it was scared the shit out of the man. That's when he spoke about Isabel."

"Axel didn't say anything to you about it?" Brad asked.

I shook my head. "Fertrie's done despicable things before. Whatever he did to Isabel Vansan made her run for her life."

"Given his connections, I can see why." Brad cleared his throat, looking uncomfortable. "How was it pretending to be Axel's plaything for the evening?"

"You were listening." I shrugged. "That's how it was."

Brad tucked a tendril of hair behind my ear. "I was opposed to the whole thing, but I'd say it was worth it. However, I didn't have to make out with the guy. So what do you think?"

"We didn't make out. And yeah, it was worth it." I spotted my mom, two of my aunts, and three cousins moving through the living room. In another few seconds, they'd spot us. "Shh." I pushed Brad backward into the walk-in pantry and pulled the doors closed behind us. "I'm not ready for this yet."

"What do you think will happen if they find us hiding in here?" he whispered.

I waited until I heard the patio door open and close. Then I cracked the door open and peeked outside. The kitchen was clear. We stepped out of the pantry, and I considered making a break for my bedroom. But the doorbell rang.

"Honey, can you get that?" Dad called on his way up from the basement with more folding chairs.

"I'll get it," Brad offered.

"Thanks." Dad put the chairs down to open the door, and I closed it behind him while Brad went to the front door.

"Why are you answering the door, Bradley?" Emma's voice traveled, and all hope of finding somewhere to hide disappeared.

"Why are you ringing the bell? You have a key," Brad retorted.

I went into the living room before more barbs were exchanged. Emma had dressed up. She clung to Dino's arm as they stood awkwardly in the foyer. She spotted me and smiled.

"Brad's right, y'know," I said. "You never ring the bell."

"Pfft." She stuck out her tongue. "I know how crazy things get around here. I didn't want to just walk in. Last time I did that, Maria had a fit."

"Mom was throwing you a surprise party," I said. "She was mad because you walked in before everyone had a chance to hide. This isn't a surprise party. This is just a dinner so Dino can meet the family." I gave Emma's boyfriend a stern look. "Right?"

"Hey, Liv." He freed himself from Emma's grasp and offered me a hug, which was uncharacteristic since we'd only met once before. When he pulled back, I saw it in his eyes. He knew I knew. "I wanted to apologize to you about Sean. I had no idea he and Sheila had something going on. He never mentioned it to me. He always just said she was his physical therapist. I guess because his sessions were coming to a close, she decided to say something. He should have talked to you first."

"It's not your fault."

Dino gave Brad an uncertain look and held out his hand. "I don't believe we've met. I'm Dino Gallanti."

"Brad Fennel."

"Nice to meet you." He smiled warmly. "Emma's talked a lot about you."

Emma rolled her eyes. "I have not."

"Everyone's out back. You should go introduce Dino." I gestured toward the patio, where Dad had unfolded the awning. "We'll be out in a few minutes."

"Okay." Emma led Dino through the house and out the back door. Even from the foyer, I could hear the delighted squeals.

"Are you okay, Liv?" Brad asked.

"Yeah, but I'm going to need backup."

FORTY-THREE

With thirty guests, dinner was chaotic. Dad served everything buffet style, and as it always goes, every one of Mom's extended family showed up with some sort of dish since they didn't buy into the alternative eating choices Emma had inflicted upon us over a decade ago. For the most part, the family remained focused on my best friend and her new beau. But two of my great aunts cornered me, asking where my date was.

Brad provided the backup I needed and came to the rescue.

"Oh, is this him?" Sylvia smiled. "This must be him."

"He's quite handsome." Blanche winked at me. "How long have you been together?"

"Over two years," Brad said.

I elbowed him in the ribs. He knew better than to fan the flames.

"Really?" Sylvia smiled brighter. "That's a long time. Have you looked for rings yet?"

"Sylvia," Blanche scolded, "you'll scare him off."

"Actually, we were looking last week," Brad said.

"Brad," I growled, finding the amused look on his face. He was feeling playful. He didn't understand this would be the gossip for the next decade. "It wasn't like that," I corrected. "It was for work."

"Work? I thought you were a police detective," Sylvia said.

"We both are. Brad's my partner."

"Partner?" Sylvia looked confused.

"That's the new term they use for boyfriend and girlfriend," Blanche said.

"No, it's not. It's like Dad and Captain Grayson. They used to be partners," I said.

Sylvia looked even more confused. "Does your mother know about that?"

"You started it. You explain it, Brad." I turned, hoping to find something on the dessert table to distract them from the conversation when I spotted Sean standing off to the side with a petite brunette. "You've got to be kidding me."

Brad turned. "Oh, hell no."

"Brad." I tried to stop him, but he took off before I could grab his arm. "Excuse us," I said to my aunts and jogged after my partner. "Brad," I called again, "wait."

My partner stopped halfway to Sean. "This guy has some balls, bringing a date to your parents' house. I'm gonna take care of this, Liv. You have enough on your plate tonight."

"No. Don't. I'll deal with this my way."

"Are you sure?"

"Yes."

"Fine, but I'll be right here if you need me." Brad backed away, and I caught Sean's eye. He excused himself from his date and met me near the hearth.

"I thought you didn't date cops," he said.

"Brad isn't my date. He's part of the family."

"Uh-huh." Sean shook it off and attempted a smile. "I...uh...wanted to apologize for the restaurant. The way I acted, I shouldn't have done that. It wasn't right." He exhaled. "How's the case coming along?"

"We closed it yesterday."

"That's great." He glanced back at his date, who I assumed was Sheila.

"Is that your physical therapist?"

He nodded. "I'm sorry."

"You shouldn't have lied. How long have you been seeing her?"

"We hooked up Friday before you came over. Prior to that, we were just friends. Not even, we were therapist-patient, I guess. I really didn't believe it was going anywhere. I figured it was a one-time thing. That it wasn't worth mentioning."

The thought that he'd slept with someone and hours later tried to sleep with me made my stomach turn. But that was life. That's how people lived. "I'm glad things worked out for you."

"Liv, I am sorry. Truly. You're a great girl. We could have had a lot of fun."

"Yep." I took a step back. "Enjoy the party."

Emma spotted the exchange and made her way over to me, giving Sean's back the evil eye. "Want me to kick his ass?"

"Get in line. Brad's first."

"I'm going to show that asshole the door."

"Em, stop. He's Dino's best friend. You don't want to make enemies with him. It's okay. Live and learn."

"This doesn't mean I have to like him."

"Good, because I don't. But you have to be civil. Maybe he's just a guy who made a mistake."

She narrowed her eyes. "When are you ever this forgiving? You see guys who make mistakes every day. You call them killers and lock their asses in jail."

"Em, he saves people, remember? Firefighter." I saw the nervous expression on Dino's face. "Bygones, just this once. I don't want to cause a department turf war."

"Fine." She hugged me. "But I'm sorry I fixed you up with him."

"Yeah, yeah. Don't do it again."

"I won't."

"Good. Now go rescue your boyfriend. Aunt Miriam looks like she's about to suffocate him."

Emma cringed and ran into the kitchen where Dino was being crushed in a bear hug. A few minutes later, Dino asked everyone to gather outside. I found a place near the back and watched as he got down on one knee, proclaiming his undying love for my best friend. Emma squealed, dropping down beside him to kiss him.

"Twenty says she calls it off before the night's out," Brad joked.

"Seriously, you sound like my dad. Do you think they'll make it down the aisle?"

"Maybe." He shrugged. "Either way, remind me to get Dino a condolence card."

After the announcement, things started to die down. I went inside to check on Gunnie, who'd been locked in the bedroom for most of the night. He needed a treat and a walk. While I was out front, watching the pup search for the perfect spot, a cherry red sports car cruised down the street. I didn't recognize the car, but I knew who it belonged to.

It slowed in front of my parents' house. The tinted windows kept me from seeing the driver, but when the front door opened behind me, the car zoomed away.

I turned, finding Brad on the front step.

"Did you see that?" I asked.

"What?" he caught the taillights as they disappeared at the end of the street.

I handed him Gunnie's leash. "I have to take care of something. Can you cover for me? I'll only be gone a few minutes. An hour tops."

"What's going on?"

"It's just a quick errand. I forgot something at home."

"Do you want me to get it for you?"

"I'd rather not be stuck here with Emma, Dino, and Sean."

Brad nodded. "Okay. Go."

After grabbing my purse, keys, and gun, I got into my car. It was Sunday night. After what transpired Friday at the party, I didn't think Axel would be at Spark. Instead, I sent him a text. *Where are you?*

Home.

I'd been to his place once, but I remembered where it was. Twenty minutes later, I rang his doorbell. The cherry red car was in his driveway, the engine still warm.

Axel checked the monitor and opened the door. He had his shirt off, his jeans slung low on his hips. The white gauzy bandage on his side looked like it'd just been changed. He looked surprised to see me. "Liv?"

"Don't give me that bullshit." I stormed into his house, my heart racing from anger and nerves. "This has to stop. If you come near my family again, I will bury you."

"That's a bit dramatic." He turned his back to me and went into the living room.

"I mean it. You can't threaten them and get away with it."

"I didn't threaten anyone."

"Then what the hell were you doing outside my parents' house?"

"I wanted to talk to you, to make sure you were okay after everything that happened Friday night, but I saw Fennel and changed my mind. You can't blame me. Your partner was ready to put a bullet in me two nights ago." He made his way to the bar and poured two drinks. He left one for me and took a sip from his glass. "The smart move was to leave. Not to mention, it looked like quite the party. I didn't want to crash it."

"You could have called."

"And give you more fodder for your stalking case, I think not." He leaned one arm against the high top. "I like your dress. It fits you better. It's more you."

"What do you want now, Axel?"

He put the glass down and approached me. My stomach flipped, and I backed up. He cocked his head to the side. "That's interesting."

"What is?"

"You saved my life, but now you act like you're afraid of me. Two nights ago, you were all over me. In fact, you kept me from bleeding out. If I make you that nervous or uncomfortable, you should have let me die."

"You wouldn't have died. The hospital said it was a flesh wound."

"Whatever you have to tell yourself. But you saved me."

"You kept me from getting stabbed. Why did you do it?"

He moved a little closer. "You have enough scars."

I searched his blue eyes. "Who are you? One minute, you're this aggressive, scary son of a bitch, and the next you're whatever this is."

He moved closer, backing me against the wall. Gently, he grabbed my hand. "I can be whoever you want me to be." His fingers slid around my wrist. "God, your pulse is racing. Relax, Detective. I won't bite." He smiled. "Much."

"Axel—"

He rolled to the side, keeping a grip on my hand while he switched our positions. "Is this better? I don't want you to feel trapped." He grabbed my other hand, raising them both over our heads and pressing his own against the wall above us. "Do you want to cuff me now?"

"Stop."

"Stop what? I just want to give you what you want."

I tried to pull back, but he held tight, forcing my body to collide against his. He hissed. A flash of pain crossed his face but disappeared immediately. Tilting his head, he captured my lips with his. A jolt went through me, and I pushed away from him. "Let go."

"Fine." He remained against the wall while I stepped back. A devilish smile played across his face. "Admit it. You felt that too."

"What is wrong with you?"

"A lot." He looked down at the fresh red stain on his bandage. "Dammit." He moved past me, going into the kitchen and grabbing another one of the clean bandages off the stack. "I just changed this too."

I followed him, unsure if I should help or leave. "Are you okay?"

"Yeah, fine." He removed the old bandage, revealing a neatly stapled line about two inches wide. Blood dripped from the center, and he used the old bandage to wipe it before putting on a new one.

Legal contracts caught my eye, and I moved closer to the table to see what he had left out in the open. They looked like purchase agreements.

Axel was too busy to remove them from my view. "I am not stalking you, nor do I plan to start, in case you were curious. However, I will be keeping my ear to the ground when it comes to Frank's pals. Their vendetta should be aimed against him, not us, but I'll make sure. I don't want anyone paying me a surprise visit. If I hear something along those lines, I'll let you know."

I kept one eye on him while I scanned the documents on the table. "AK Holdings bought my apartment building? Are you insane?"

"I did you a favor. Your landlord no longer expects you to honor your lease. Feel free to move whenever you want. I'll make sure you get back your security deposit. And no, that isn't a bribe."

"Why would you do this?"

"It's a nice gesture." He straightened, his eyes still on me. "You had a problem. I gave you a solution. It's what you did for me."

I studied him. "Why can't I figure you out?"

"Try giving up your preconceived notions. I'm not the villain, Liv. I never was. But don't confuse me for a good guy because you'll be disappointed."

"So what does that make you?"

"Human."

My phone buzzed, and I checked the display. Emma sent a text, saying we needed to talk. I told her I was on my way back and tucked my phone away.

"Was that Fennel?"

"No."

"The firefighter?"

"No."

"That's over, huh?"

"Can I ask you something? What did you say to Fertrie that freaked him out?"

Axel shook his head. "It's best if we don't get into that."

"Right." I headed for the door. Confused by our entire interaction. "What about Spark? Fertrie said you changed the way things operate."

"Fox and I are working on some things, but again, it's probably best if you don't ask too many questions. You may not like the answers."

"Does it have to do with whatever's going on in that building across from the Stonemore Hotel?"

Axel smirked. "I wonder what you'd do if I ever gave you all the answers."

"I'd arrest you."

He laughed. "You'd try."

"Don't worry, Axel. No one would ever confuse you for a good guy."

He stopped me before I could reach the front door. "Is that what you want, Liv? Do you want a good guy? Do you want me to be a good guy? Because I don't think that's what you want at all. I think you like the danger. That's why you thrive undercover. It's why you became a cop, and it's why you came here alone tonight. It's also how you ended up in some not great situations." He brushed a finger down the back of my neck which made me shiver. "That's why the firefighter didn't work out. You thought he'd be dangerous, but he was dull. Boring. You crave the excitement, the unpredictability."

"You're crazy."

"Am I?" He opened the door. "Just think about it. When you decide you want to finish what we started under that tree, you know where to find me."

DON'T MISS THE NEXT NOVEL IN THE LIV
DEMARCO SERIES.

FIND CONTROLLED BURN (LIV DEMARCO
#9) IN PRINT AND AS AN E-BOOK

ABOUT THE AUTHOR

G.K. Parks is the author of the Alexis Parker series. The first novel, *Likely Suspects,* tells the story of Alexis' first foray into the private sector.

G.K. Parks received a Bachelor of Arts in Political Science and History. After spending some time in law school, G.K. changed paths and earned a Master of Arts in Criminology/Criminal Justice. Now all that education is being put to use creating a fictional world based upon years of study and research.

You can find additional information on G.K. Parks and the Alexis Parker series by visiting our website at
www.alexisparkerseries.com

www.ingramcontent.com/pod-product-compliance
Lightning Source LLC
Chambersburg PA
CBHW020436270626
47155CB00022B/388